Inveigle

Invitati

Enjoy the read

Inveiglement: Invitation by Abrams & Elliott

Published by Australian eBook Publisher

www.AustralianEbookPublisher.com.au

1st Edition 2015, pbk.

ISBN: 978-1-925271-30-0

Typeset in 12 pt. Helvetica Neue

Printed by: IngramSpark

Designer: Australian eBook Publisher in association with Abrams & Elliott

Editor: Angelique Jurd, Small Black Cat Media

National Library of Australia Cataloguing-In-Publication Entry

Creator:	Abrams & Elliott, author.
Title:	Inveiglement : Invitation / Abrams & Elliott.
ISBN:	978-1-925271-30-0 (paperback)
Subjects:	Erotic stories.
	Australian fiction.
Dewey Number:	A823.4

Also available as an ebook from major ebook vendors.

inveiglement.co

abramsandelliott.com

Inveiglement
Invitation

The Inveiglement Series
Book One

Abrams & Elliott

Australian eBook Publisher

Inveiglement Series Reader's Guide

Welcome to the *Inveiglement* Series. Inveiglement is told using two narrators: one male and one female, so in order to help you enjoy the story we have made their voices clearly identifiable as follows:

Bold—when Tom's voice is being used, the text is bold;

Callie—when Callie's voice is being used, the text is normal.

Tom and Callie often communicate via email and to reduce the formalities of structured beginning and endings the infinity symbol ∞ designates the commencement and conclusion of their email threads.

We hope you enjoy *Inveiglement*.

Abrams & Elliott

Prelude

I point to the tap with the stag emblem, "One of those thank you," I say to the barman, digging money from my pocket. I take a long pull of the cold beer and look around. Three women noisily enter the bar laughing and giggling like schoolgirls, shattering the tranquility. Like a mini twister, they whirl through the room and finally settle. Something about the one closest to me grabs my attention—it is the way she flicks her hair and the look in her eyes. I certainly wasn't expecting a charade at this time of the afternoon but I'm intrigued.

The trio exudes the soft ripeness of mature fruit. One of them, though, shows her age more than the others, despite the heavy make-up. The second woman is in the autumn of her life revealing softness in her hazel eyes, but it is the third that captivates me. She seems to wear the evidence of life's challenges with pride and wisdom; she looks like someone who esteems character more than the others. This woman is giving me the eye.

Her floating floral skirt does justice to her curves and her soft brown hair falls past her shoulders. The purple stockings she is wearing are the sexiest I've ever seen.

The rustic little bar has down-lit glass shelving holding knick-knacks, glasses and bottles. I wander over to take a closer look at the mounted red stag on the far wall. The 'Stag and Hunter' sign brings a smile to my face as a reminder of my last hunt. Floorboards deck the entrance and sprawl throughout adding to the weatherworn look, creating a nonchalant flow. Every wall seems to be dotted with open windows. Deer heads from a bygone era mesmerise me and a massive set of buffalo horns overhang the bar as a focal point.

I wander from one deer head to the other, my foot tapping to the beat of music from the jukebox.

I perch myself at one end of the bar and surmise what adventure lies behind each lifelike mask. Enviously, I can only imagine this as my trophy room.

"Shouldn't you be at work?"

Her chuckle catches my attention. Leaning against the bar, she is so close I can smell her scent. She is as cool as ice. My country wide-open space is being invaded and it's intimidating and exciting at the same time. Is she really talking to me?

"Me?" I ask and shoot a nervous look over my shoulder. My gaze darts to the bartender and the clock on the wall.

"Another?" the bartender asks. He's smirking. "Same again?"

I nod.

He wanders over to the beer tap and yanks down the curved lever and brown ale swirls into the frosty glass. He slides the glass along the polished wood bar towards me. As if on purpose, it halts a metre short.

"I guess this is yours?" she says, snatching my glass from the counter. She speaks to the bartender over her shoulder, offering him a wink. "Same for me."

Her hand wraps around my glass, the other strokes it downward flicking the condensation away. A wicked sparkle in her eyes reveals a hint of mischief. This is one smart city bird winding up a simple country boy I fear.

"I've never seen you here before," she says.

"I'm from out of town," I tell her, eyeing those amazing purple stockings. I get the distinct feeling she's getting ready to make a move.

"What's your name?" she asks.

"Thomas," I say, aware I'm about to be interrogated. I feel all the hairs on the back of my neck stand vertical.

"And, what do you do?" she asks, leaning forward.

"I work for an accounting firm out in the country. My boss needed some papers dropped in for a meeting down here. I have to hang around to pick them up in the morning once they've been signed off."

"Sounds important," she says. She leans back on the barstool and flicks her black stilettos off. She twists and flexes her feet as she settles herself more comfortably on the barstool and she turns front-on to face me.

"So what does your job entail?" she asks, raising her eyebrows.

I shrug.

"I'm an accountant," I answer, hoping to make myself sound important. "I do bank reconciliations and stuff like that."

"Where are you staying?" she asks, eyeing me closer.

"At an inn across town. At least I will be if I survive the traffic," I sigh, "I hate driving in the city."

"Crazy isn't it?" she chuckles again and I catch my breath.

"Crazy? How about insane? Where I come from, we don't even have traffic lights."

"You're kidding me?"

"Nope." I shake my head to confirm my statement.

"You like those deer heads?" she asks, tilting her head, her eyes glued to mine.

"I certainly do. I did my first deer hunt not long ago, it was amazing," I say, looking back at the master stag head on the wall. "Saw one just like that, but it was last thing in the afternoon and it was going over the summit of the mountain and there was no way I could get near it."

"Really?" she says, pointing. "A live one of those?"

"Yep," I respond. "It was over in New Zealand. A friend gave me a map and some general pointers. It was an adrenaline rush like I'd never experienced. And now I want to hunt all of these."

"A mountain man," she says. "And besides hunting these deer, do you do any other type of hunting?"

Her statement catches me totally off guard as she places her hand on my knee and her foot on mine.

"So, is this your first time in the city?" she sips her beer, never taking her eyes off me.

"No," I protest. She raises an eyebrow and I feel myself blush. "Second time. First time driving myself."

"Well, you are game aren't you?" She's laughing, but I sense there's nothing mean in it.

"Tell me about it, I pulled over at least half a dozen times to look at the street directory," I admit, trying not to think about returning to the chaos outside.

"What sort of car do you drive?" she says, taking her hand from my knee.

"A hatchback." I gulp my beer to settle my nerves.

"I'll do you a deal," she says. "How about I drive you to where you are staying and you let me seduce you tonight?"

Her comment hits me straight between the eyes.

"What?" I stutter—she can't be serious.

"You heard," she says, and then leans forward to put her hand on my knee again. "I want to nail your country boy arse. I have a fuck plan. You won't get a better offer tonight and trust me you definitely won't be disappointed."

I try to breathe and am unable to drag my eyes off her.

She continues.

"You will love the things I'm going to let you do to me," she says. "It's an open invitation, no strings. You can have your wicked way with me and I will show you things you never dreamed possible."

Her inveiglement strategy is in play.

"Did I hear you right?" I'm still gob smacked.

She leans forward and I get a glimpse of her breast as her blouse gapes a little. Her hand slides up my thigh.

"Unless you are stupid and I don't think you are," she says, "I want someone to fuck me tonight. All night. Are you in?"

I am astonished by her audacity and aroused.

"I'm horny. Finish that drink so we can get out of here, country boy."

I have been hunted.

She grabs my hand in a vice-like grip and hauls me off my stool. Her girlfriends almost fall off their barstools laughing. They are astounded at how quickly their friend has moved in for the kill. She waves back at them cheekily as we leave.

"How old are you, country boy?" she asks. She is manoeuvring my car through the traffic at speed.

"I'm twenty-two, Ma'am."

"Virgin?" she asks with a chuckle. Without taking her eyes from the road she reaches for my hand and places it on her knee.

Music is blaring through the speakers. She glances at me singing to the tune. Pausing in the traffic she waves her hands above her head to the pulsing beat.

Then she leans over and gives me a passionate kiss; her tongue darts into my mouth.

Her hot, horny chatter encourages me and I begin tracing little circles on her thigh. I increase the pressure of my fingers with each circle and when she shivers I take a chance and slide my hand further up. I smile when she shivers again; I'm enjoying this newfound boldness.

"Fuck." Her scream cuts through my haze of lust and I look up. Brakes screech and we narrowly miss slamming into the car in front, almost becoming passengers in their back seat as we practically pepper their tailgate.

"That was close," she says with a laugh. "I totally lost my concentration there for a moment. Keep doing that. I love having an orgasm while driving a complete stranger's car. Now put those fingers back so I can feel them through my stockings."

She wriggles in the seat while spreading her legs wider. I slide my hand back under her skirt and my fingers feel clumsy as they plough into her wet patch. She slaps her hand with force over mine.

"Press harder and follow that lump. Do you know what that lump is?"

She double shifts the gears.

"Ah, not really," I say, aware I'm way out of my league.

"That's my clitoris, my clit, and you are going to love it."

The traffic stops just as she cums and her hands clench the steering wheel, her head falls back onto the headrest and her eyes close.

"It has been twelve hours since I had my last one. God, that was good. Don't take the pressure off there."

Timing it to perfection, as the traffic slows I increase my finger pressure, quickly mastering the technique. I feel her sex energy. I'm timing her orgasms with the traffic flow using my fingertip, it's insane and I love it. I'm hooked. It seems so natural and the pulse between my legs hardens my cock. The smell of her orgasm hangs thick in the air and she oozes stickiness on to my car seat. My cock is so hard it hurts.

We reach our destination. She smiles and leans over to kiss me, darting her tongue deep into my mouth while fondling my crotch. I'm as embarrassed as hell as we cross the lobby, the head of my cock is oozing pre-cum and I have my own wet patch. I'm sure everyone can see it.

We are finally in the elevator and as soon as the door closes her hand wraps around my growing hardness.

"I like what I feel," she whispers in my ear. Her voice is husky with lust. "Every time you drive your car, your balls will be resting on my wet patch. That should make you smile."

She smiles as I rediscover my boldness from the car.

"I could smell it as we left the car. I've known you for less than an hour and you got me to make you cum just with my fingertip. How did you do that?"

I'm caught in her spell.

"Might tell you later, now shut-up and kiss me," she says and grabs my head. Her tongue darts into my mouth like a viper.

The sparse room is as warm as an oven and I have the feeling I'm about to be basted, baked and served up. I am so aroused. I am scared I'll cum in my pants if she touches me again.

There is a high backed chair in one corner, a small sofa scattered with cushions fitted against the wall and a king sized bed. Tones of ruby red tie everything together and give the room a sensual feel.

She pushes me onto the sofa spreading my legs wide. Before I can do anything she is kissing me. Her tongue feels as though it's prodding my tonsils. Her fingers are tugging at the zipper of my trousers, exposing my throbbing cock. In a single swift movement she is on her knees flicking her tongue around the rim. She drags it across the tip, licking up the oozing pre-cum. Not once does her intense gaze leave mine; finally she speaks.

"That's your reward for doing such a good job with your agile finger."

That's it? I'm about to explode in her hand and all she does is lick over the tip?

She stands and saunters over to take a seat in the high backed chair in the corner of the room; she spreads her legs, slips her fingers inside her stockings and begins to rub her clit.

"Undress," she instructs.

Swallowing, I loosen my tie and toss it on the floor. I unlace my shoes kicking them aside. Unbuttoning my shirt, I let it slither off my back. My belt is unhooked and as my pants fall to the floor, she climaxes.

Just watching her, my cock hardens—'how is this possible?' a voice deep in the back of my brain asks. I have never seen a woman so openly display her desire, let alone her orgasm and it arouses me even more. What have I let myself in for? Despite what she thinks, I'm not a virgin but I'm not very experienced and I'm eager to learn.

I stand totally naked, waiting. Finally she cocks her wet finger at me.

"Come and get me, country boy."

When I get to her she runs her finger across my lips.

"Taste that. Like it? That's me," she says and pulls me closer, one hand gripping my arse cheek.

Her finger tastes sweet, like liquid candy and I am immediately hooked. It's like a bull lure, a scent that has served nature's purpose since the beginning of time and she's using it to entice me in.

Kneeling between her legs my chest presses against her breasts as we kiss. Driven by an intense urgency I am unable to resist thrusting toward her wetness. She pushes me away.

"Do you know why you're here?" she asks. "You are here to satisfy my needs. I have plans for you. Trust me, you'll love them."

I have no doubt about that. Rising out of the chair she stands in front of me, undresses and tosses her clothes to the far reaches of the room. I gaze mesmerised.

Lowering my head, I inhale her heavenly musk, and then plant my tongue firmly into wet heat. She grips the back of my head with both hands and moans.

"Lick it harder."

As soon as I obey, a squirt of hot cum hits the back of my throat. I gasp, taking the shot straight down my throat, spinning like a wounded duck.

I can't take my eyes off her. She pushes me back onto the bed and mounts me; my cock surges to its full length. She pushes down in one long, deliberate movement, and then stops. Leaning forward she rests her hands on my chest and glares at me.

"We have to have a talk, a serious talk."

She pauses and I struggle for control.

"I have rules," she says, "and the first rule is you will not cum under any circumstances unless I tell you to. If you do I'll be out of here instantly and you will never get to fuck me ever again, and since I'm your best chance tonight, you'll miss out. And one you miss, is one you'll never get."

I nod. I want to taste all she has to offer.

"Rule number two," she continues, "this is only between you and me, and will remain a total secret."

I'm not married and I'm not seriously involved with anyone, so that causes me no confusion.

"Rule number three: You can never call me. I will call you. And when I do, you will make yourself available to satisfy my needs and I will certainly make it worth your while."

For a moment she is silent, watching me.

"This brings me to the reason I have you here on your back," she says, "I am a Sex Savant and my purpose is to educate a promising student. I'm currently looking for one. It might be you. By morning I'll know and I'll tell you."

She pauses and looks me over.

"If I want you."

She continues.

"And if you are successful, you will refer to me as Teacher."

She lifts herself up the length of my cock. I bite my lip and listen.

"Rule number four: I might, just might, make you my student and if I do, you are under no circumstances to use what I teach you till I'm satisfied you are ready. When I think you're ready, I'll tell you."

She teases my cock with her pussy muscles, making me groan.

"Rule number five: If either of us wants out, out means out, no questions asked."

I feel her pressing her clit against my pubis.

"Push up, now," she orders and begins to slide up and down on my cock.

With each stroke she grinds her clit harder against me.

"Don't you fucking cum," she mutters and her body convulses, juice gushes down the full length of my cock, over my balls and onto the sheets. Her fingernails rake across my chest—I hiss in pain but never take my eyes from her face.

"Fuck," she screams in frenzied delirium.

Motionless, I use every ounce of self-control to stop myself from ejaculating. My cock twitches once, twice, and then I relax. It takes an indomitable mindset to overcome.

"Good boy," she says as she opens her eyes and plants her lips on mine. "Shall we try it again?"

"Hell yeah."

She begins to move again. Her movements are slow and rhythmic. After a moment her movements increase until she hits her sweet spot and her body begins to jerk.

"Don't you cum," she reminds me. "If you do, I'll leave."

Her head thrashes from side to side, her satisfaction growing with each pulse darting through her body. The urge, the need to cum is building again, increasing with each of her strokes. Opening her eyes she smiles down at me.

"That was good," she says. "God I needed that. Ready for more?"

Her rhythm begins to pick up again.

"You know the rules, don't you do it," she mutters with a force to match her thrusts. I manage to hold on and push up harder. I can't believe how turned on I am. Making this woman cum is unbelievably exciting. My girl might climax once, maybe twice, and after twenty minutes it's all over for both of us. I didn't know something like this could happen. I'm savouring it. I need to see her get off again.

She's peering down at me again.

"Cocky young bastard aren't you? Don't get too smart and shoot your load or I'll go and find myself someone else," she says. "I don't teach cocky men."

I desperately want to be her student, and I want to learn.

I place my hands around her hips and pull her down a little harder. She grinds into me, her pussy gripping me tightly, her clit rubbing back and forth against me. Ready for her, I feel the shudder begin to roll through her. Focusing all my reserves, I climb over the hill and soak up every ounce of energy she transmits. My hips and belly are covered in her honey. The pounding increases again and as each stroke becomes longer, I pull down firmly enough to ensure I don't slide out.

I thrust up to meet her and get the reward I'm hoping for. Orgasms begin to string together in a constant stream. Willing myself to retain control, I revel in her pleasure.

"Don't you cum," she mutters through gritted teeth.

She drops onto my chest, changing the angle of her thrust and the change of sensation catches me off guard. I wrap my arms around her body, her mouth grabs my shoulder, and she sinks her teeth in deep and hard, biting and suckling a love-bite into my flesh.

I can't believe it. I am still full. Without even thinking I begin to caress her back.

"Unreal," I murmur.

She rises off me and my cock slithers out. Her juice pours freely over me.

"Time for a little reward for being such a good boy," she says with a smirk.

Placing a pillow under my head, she fusses over my position. The anticipation is killing me. Turning around she places one leg either side of my head lowering her vulva to within an inch of my lips.

"Stick your tongue out," she instructs, and lowers herself to my mouth. "Suck, lick and explore. Pay attention to my responses."

I do as I'm told as she grips the base of my cock ready to swallow my entire length. Her tongue flicks across my tip licking up my pre-cum. Her hands clench my thighs and she grinds against my face. All I want is for her to tell me I am the one, I am *the* student. My focus is purely on her pleasure.

Darting my tongue deep inside her pussy gets a completely different reaction to the one I get when I use a long, flat licking motion.

I can feel her clit protruding and draw it between my lips. Within seconds there's an instant release, her hips push down and for a second I almost suffocate as I try to manoeuvre and gasp for air. My hands are placed firmly around her arse cheeks to help me control the action while my tongue wickedly tangos. The intensity of her responses drives my desire to impress even more.

Rolling off me, she lies on her back gasping for air. I watch and wait in awe.

At last she inhales, coming around.

"That was incredible," she says. "Now it's your turn."

She spreads her legs wide and I push into her as deeply as I can.

"Now," she commands, "I want to feel you cum."

As I begin to surge in and out, I realise I've gone beyond the point of climaxing several times and it's not so easy to obey. The more I ride her, the more she shakes beneath me, with her legs wrapped around my waist. Her tongue deeply penetrates my ear and there's a tease of hot talk, building and manipulating my flow of thoughts.

"You know you're not my first today don't you?" she pants against my neck. "I had a man early this morning. I've been wet from it all day."

That is enough to tip me over the edge. Everything tightens and I cum in hot spurts.

"Fuck," I yell.

I collapse on top of her, savouring my first real sex lesson. I know she has much more in mind and pray she will select me. I'm being imprinted and totally captivated by her manipulation. Her sex is like a drug that has infiltrated my being and I've only had a taste.

Rolling onto my back, I look at her closely for the first time. In her mid-fifties, carrying a few extra kilos, she has large breasts and a smooth mound. I ask the obvious question.

"Is being shaven better for fucking?"

"Yes, by a country mile," she answers with a girlish giggle.

"Rest for a bit," she continues. "I have plans for you. You're a long way from finished, I want more and soon."

She is spread out on the bed as if she's been nailed to a cross.

"Would you like a drink?" I ask.

"Champagne should be on the list," she says, probably guessing I don't know much about room service, "and see if they have any strawberries."

There is thick tang of sex in the air and when the waiter knocks on the door, I realise he is going to be able to smell us. I poke my head around the door and snatch the tray of champagne and strawberries away as fast as possible.

I look at the glass dish of strawberries and wonder what they are for. They're round and plump and for some reason make me think of her pussy. Still wondering, I begin to fill a glass with champagne.

"That's enough," she says, "two thirds of a glass will be plenty. Then bring me the strawberries."

I obey and notice she is grinning at me as she plucks one from the dish and drops it in her glass. A frenzy of bubbles fizz up the glass as the strawberry drops to the bottom. By now she is lying back on the pillows, her legs spread wide, holding the slender flute in her hand. I take a strawberry, but as I am about to drop it in my glass, she stops me.

"Stop, don't do that yet," she says.

She guides my hand, the strawberry still between my fingertips, and dips the red fruit in her pussy. She swirls it in her juices, then raises it to my mouth. Now, that is kinky, I think to myself. I get another strawberry and this time after a double coating of her sex juice, I drop it into my drink.

Before long we are ready for the next round.

"Under no circumstances are you to use that tool of yours unless I tell you to," she whispers in my ear. "I'm going to teach you cock control. It's your main lesson for tonight and it's a critical lesson since it's impossible to keep it hard all night. I want you to give it a rest this time around."

This time when we finish she lays back with tears flowing down her cheeks. In the half-light she looks spaced out and I watch her in awe. It's more powerful than anything I can imagine. I am spellbound.

I lean back and refill my glass as I watch and wait for her to return to earth. The strawberry flirts with the bubbles in my flute and champagne spills over the top. Smiling to myself, I realise that's just what has happened to this woman—she has overflowed.

Her recovery is slow and she comes out of her haze blinking like a dazed owl. Finally she pulls me toward her by the neck and kisses me.

"You're a quick learner," she says. "God help women once I've finished with you. I'm looking forward to teaching you."

"Does that mean that I'll be your student?"

Her glass touches mine with a clink.

Yes. I'm in. I can't wait.

"Men are generally poor performers you know," she says. "They just don't have it worked out. Women are built more for sexual pleasure than they can possibly comprehend and once the door has been opened, there's no turning back. So if you're going to do it, then do it properly. My purpose as Sex Savant is to make sure these skills are not lost. Your job is to continue the tradition."

She raises her glass and we clink again. The agenda is set.

1

"G'day Brad, how are you?" I say. I'm excited to be here, after thirty hours of travel, it is great to see his familiar face. We clutch hands firmly.

"Howdy, Tom. How was your flight?" Brad asks. I smile at his drawn out Canadian accent. A strapping forty-year-old man, he appears clean cut with brown curly hair. He is working hard to carry on the family tradition and proud to be a mountain man. I immediately feel as if I'm amongst friends.

"I love this place, Brad. It's really beautiful," I comment. "It smells so fresh and clean and those mountains look spectacular in autumn. We don't get fall down-under you know."

The ambiance of the distant mountains is surreal. My eyes adjust to the fading light as I take in the shadows thrown over the mountain peaks to reveal an amazing spectacle. I drink in the grandeur. Amber leaves are beginning to appear as the season turns; a slight breeze makes them shiver revealing their magnificent auburn tones. The mountain spruce along the airport perimeter shows the first signs of change. I take in the northern hemisphere's impact. Foliage of varying shades of red and purple peep through the fading greenery. Trees disappear as the majestic Rockies reach skyward, and the smell of fresh pine is overwhelming. I inhale freshness.

"I can't imagine that, we live for the fall," he replies with a surprised look.

"I have to go to New Zealand to get my hit," I answer with a chuckle. "It's my secret hideaway. And you know what's so good about it? It's only a couple of hour's flight across the ditch and I can disappear."

"Every man should have a hideaway," he says with a laugh. "That sounds pretty good."

He helps me with my bags.

Tossing my backpack into the tray of Brad's RV, my natural inclination is to attempt to get into the wrong side of the vehicle.

"I hate how you guys drive on the wrong side of the road," I utter. I'm in remote control and the door even confuses me. I shake my head, Brad laughs and as he pulls out of the car park I look the wrong way for oncoming traffic. We would be dead if I was driving.

"So, how's the hunting been this season?" I ask. I'm keen to find out some specifics. Hunting is my passion; I have been hunting since my early teens. Trips to Canada are a pure self-indulgence; my normal playgrounds are the slopes of the New Zealand mountains. I long to escape at every opportunity just to be out there on the mountain. I'm always planning my next hunt.

"Been excellent. The survival rate from last winter has been exceptional," Brad says. A mule deer buck wanders out to cross the road in front of us bringing the traffic to a halt. I smile, winding down my window to take pictures.

The aroma of brewing coffee, sizzling bacon and eggs, and the sound of muffled conversation in the next room wakes me. I find my crumpled clothes and my first attempt results in me putting my T-shirt on inside out. My body is trying to come to terms with the time zone differences.

"Good morning, gentlemen," I say as I stagger around like a drunk, rubbing my eyes and grab a chair for support.

"Good morning, Tom, how did you sleep?"

Brad's beaming face is cheery.

"Like a log."

"Tom, I'd like you to meet Ed Flannery," Brad says.

"Thomas Banham," I say, "pleased to meet you."

"Likewise, Tom," Ed replies. His handshake is firm.

"Ed is your guide for the next fifteen days. I have your hunting tags and licenses here," Brad says as he spreads the mandatory paperwork on the table. "So, we have mountain goat, mule deer and elk."

"Okay, sounds good to me," I agree. "So, what's the plan for today then?"

My brain is in need of direction; these time zone changes really mess me up.

"We'll head into the main cabin today, then you, Ed and Haley will ride out tomorrow to spike camp," Brad updates. He looks over at Haley and she smiles as if she is coming on an adventure of a lifetime.

"Hi Haley, I'm Tom," I say. She puts down the coffee pot to shake my hand.

"Haley is our camp cook," Ed says with a grin.

The guys leave to wrangle the horses. Haley looks like a real country girl. I'll bet she's a bit of a live wire, sporting a red-checked shirt, long blonde hair, tight jeans and well-worn cowgirl boots. I devour two helpings of her bacon and eggs; they taste even better than they smell.

I grab a tea towel.

“Excited about coming up the trail?” I ask, helping to dry the dishes.

“You bet I am, it’s my second time,” Haley says. Her excitement is infectious.

“Awesome, it’s my favourite type of hunting, being on the tops and staying up there. I love it. Living with the animals, it’s the only way to hunt as far as I’m concerned,” I say, wiping up the last implement.

There are no roads where we are heading. Outside, I watch on in total amusement, perched on a pew out of harm’s way. It’s organised chaos. I witness the traditional roundup of the horses and loading the pack train with our supplies. There are three other hunters starting out today, each provided with an experienced local guide and a cabin cook.

The track into the main cabin climbs along the bush-clad valley as we head up river. Above the bush line the open rocky bluffs and mountain meadows look as if they ascend into the clouds, I absorb the picture postcard views. Stunning hues of mountain greys change with every glimpse of sunlight that kisses the peaks, highlighting the rugged cracks and crevasses. Fluffy clouds saunter overhead throwing shadows in the distance, dancing over the trail ahead.

Next morning we saddle up, climbing the steep narrow mountain track across precarious sections; one slip could result in disaster with vertical overhangs that would spin anyone scared of heights into oblivion. Finally we ride up to the head of Stony Creek.

Our camp is on a plateau two thousand feet from the tops. We are at seven thousand feet; the views are panoramic and simply breathtaking. Majestic in all forms, the searing beauty remains even after the sun sets in the distance. It's a glorious location, I feel honoured to have the opportunity to be out here. I waddle around bow legged like I've had my balls in a sling all day and head to a stream to fill the containers with clear mountain water.

A shot of whiskey mixed with pure mountain water is the perfect relaxant for tired, sore muscles. Back slapping each other for luck, we toast the safe day of travel and the adventure ahead. Mountain peaks are crisp against the sunset. I'm surrounded by serenity. The air is fresh and pure, there's not a cloud in the sky — it's a spectacular sunset as I swirl the amber liquid in my cup. I am beginning to feel warm and relaxed, out here living my dream.

Leaving the horses hobbled to graze on the high mountain meadow, we load up our daypacks and hike our way over towards the Narrows Valley for our days hunt. The fresh mounds of dirt tell us mountain grizzlies have visited. Gopher holes have been destroyed in their quest to find a tasty treat. Everywhere I look there's sign of bear, adding a thrill of danger to being out here.

I adjust the focus of my binoculars. Slowly, I methodically view the mountain faces as my brain's software calibrates my deciphering skills. It takes time to master the identification process of what's living and what's not. The vision through the lens is crisp and clear, I breathe deeply to control my breath as I scan the vast mountainside. Shutting out the sounds around me for clear concentration until I can only hear the beat of my heart pulsing in my chest wall.

This is my playground and what I live for. Just like working out if there's a potential student out there amongst the crowd. The image of my next student is like a haze in the background, you get a sniff and your senses tell you, you have to check it out further. That haze has become clearer. It has been several years since my last, but my sights have been set on one to aim for, yes, it's time I closed the distance. I'm deep in thought. I'm selective, quantity does not interest me; I want quality.

The campfire flickers under Haley's favourite cooking implement: the steel grill. A large helping of sausages, potatoes and onions drowned in smoky BBQ sauce hits the spot.

"So what do you do back in Aussie-land, Tom?" Ed sits with his back perched against a mountain spruce.

"I started out as a trainee accountant for one of those big number crunching firms. I had to do all my university studies part-time. Mum and dad were poor. I was the eldest of six kids," I say.

Haley rustles into her sleeping mat under the stars and snuggles in, resting her head on her elbow.

"That took almost eight years. I was one of the dumb ones," I continue and take another sip of whiskey.

"I can't believe you are an accountant," Ed says with a chuckle. He's right and it's one of the few things that eat at me. Boxed and counted, I hate it.

"That's what everyone says," I reply. "I seemed to get all the tough jobs, like when people's businesses were in trouble. My job was to get them back on track, to refocus and make sure they stayed that way."

I offer a top up of whiskey.

"Sort of like a business consultant?" Ed suggests.

"Yeah, you could say that. Then an opportunity came along to buy into a small recruitment business that needed a mathematical brain. So, I took it. My business partner and I turned that business into a two hundred-person operation. We were eventually bought out by a public company because we had some really choice contracts they could leverage. It was amazing, ninety-five percent of our staff were female, including my business partner," I say, staring up into the northern sky. "I loved dealing with that many women."

This brings a smile to Haley's face and I continue.

"I've always loved working with females. They challenge, inspire and bring out the best in me."

I am beginning to feel mellow as the whiskey takes hold. That time in my life was like being on the biggest hunting reserve, but my rules of play prevented me from pursuing, I simply observed.

"Is there something wrong with you? I have enough trouble dealing with my wife, let alone that many hormonal loonies," Ed says and shakes his head in disbelief. Haley rolls onto her back laughing.

"Really, I do love working with them," I say. "I also learnt a lot about selling a business. That added to my business advising background and sort of set me up for the next chapter. I now help people groom their businesses ready to sell."

"So, what sort of clients do you mainly work with?" Ed asks.

"It varies, but I've worked with some very interesting people over the years. They seem to find me, and from there I work out if I want the job or not," I add, peering upwards again.

As the darkness settles I note the absent southern stars and their familiar patterns. “I’m working with an interesting small business at the moment,” I continue. “It’s been an eye opener. The business owner has carved out her place in a competitive market and she has built up a really successful niche business.”

“What do you do for her?”

Lots more hopefully, I think. She’s on the top of my hunting list. Callie’s scent is on the wind, I’ve been inhaling her, my seduction plan has been working and now it’s time to take that up a notch. I’m nervously excited; it’s been a while. First thing I intend to do when I return is test the waters.

“We’ve been grooming her business for just over five years and we’ve found a buyer. Now the time is right to have that component of the plan nailed,” I say.

Like nailing her and testing to see if she is a potential student, I muse in silence.

“Didn’t you say you had a farm as well?” Ed asks.

“Yes, I did have. Another guy and I owned an aquaculture operation. We started from scratch and recently sold,” I say over the night critters that are warming up for their evening performance. “I now work there casually as operations manager as part of the takeover process.”

“How do you fit in any time to go hunting?” Ed asks.

Ed’s observation creates a stir with Haley as her eyes widen to take in more.

“Don’t get me started, Ed. That’s a sore point. Re-education on the home front is happening you could say.” I fidget on the log, reviewing my bank balance of life credits. I stare into the flames, determined to make my dreams a reality.

“Yeah, I know what you mean. Do you have any kids?”

“None, but I love practicing to make them,” I grin and decide the conversation needs to end. “It must be bedtime.”

Over the next few days we view the mountains, spotting a lot of game; mountain goats in their white suits, bugling elk and high timber mule deer bucks. Our challenge is to locate the most animals each day and has us scouring the vast landscape.

I notice Haley is getting more into it with every story I tell, bug-eyed and on high alert for any chance to digest some wild stories from down-under. It is a pleasure to see a young lady interested in what is considered by many to be a male domain. I like to share my knowledge, awakening I have learned is the best strategy.

Looking high up to our right is a mountain pass Ed has never ventured over.

“Bet it goes down the other side with rolling grassy benches, be easy goat and deer country,” he suggests.

“Bet you’re wrong, probably a widow maker pass that drops off in all directions,” I suggest as we push up into the saddle of the next hill.

“Ed. Look ahead on the left side of that shale piece. Mountain goat. See it? Damn thing has just appeared from nowhere.”

“Yep. I see it. It’d be worth putting the spotting scope on that one. Look, he has a brother coming from behind the big rock further around to the left.”

Ed focuses his binoculars like an eagle.

Fixing their location, I perch the spotting scope on a near vertical downward angle. We spot two horse sized billies; long heavy horns, snow-white coats and large black scent pads indicate mature billies. We back slap each other in excitement.

"Okay master guide, how do we get down there without killing ourselves?" I ask. Everywhere I look appears to be sheer vertical drops with overhangs falling away to nothing.

"One thing's for sure, they are safe for today, there's no way we could get down there and back. We don't have the gear on us to start traversing either. Let's just watch and see. The weather forecast for the week is good, let's be patient and see what they do," Ed says, memorising their location as he squats lower to the ground.

Ed and I leave camp as the morning rays hit the ragged tops. I insist Haley stays at camp; today's trek will be too dangerous. I concentrate on fifty feet at a time; if either of us gets stage fright the consequences will be unthinkable. There are sheer drops to our right and left with hard rock chutes rendering insecure toeholds. We cling to the tiniest handholds and hang on tight, hauling ourselves downwards. My greatest fear is that we'll get rim-rocked and can't go up or down. Sweat pours out of me, it's as cold as ice. The slope is scarily steep and the altitude sucks my panting breath out of me. I don't look back for fear of losing my concentration.

Three hours later after a hazardous descent we perch on a rocky ledge. I am cringing in pain from the sheer stress and nervously splutter,

"We must be infuckingsane, what were we thinking?"

Adrenalin is surging through my veins and the aftershock has me visibly shaking as I look back up the near vertical slope.

"My wife would have kittens if I told her what we've just done," Ed stutters.

Catching our breath, we crawl to the spur's edge, peeking over. We can clearly see one billy, the other is tucked out of view by a small cliff, but it's a monster. Ed and I glance at each other, the billy is totally unaware of our presence. The stalk has been executed to perfection. I crawl nervously to the rim, struggling to get comfortable for a near vertical downward shot. Suddenly, I am in the zone, there is no escaping and it all becomes automatic, the rifle steadies, and the cross hairs align. I focus on my breath for concentration and squeeze the trigger.

Staggering back into mountain spike camp with our quarry, we celebrate our survival of the newly dubbed—'Widow Maker Pass'. Whiskey relieves the pain of sore feet, aching backs and tired legs. The spirit quickly spikes our exhausted bloodstreams. We relive our hunt several times. Haley is captivated. Perched on my camp log, my system is soaring. I close my eyes and lean back against a spruce. The euphoria is like that after a long weekend with a Protégée. I open my eyes and from under heavy lids look at the stars. The nearby stream bubbles, the night purrs with the sound of animals. Our presence is pure and undisturbed.

It is amazing how the days disappear and as morning breaks we gather around the campfire to warm up.

"Ed, we need to get some good pictures today," I say. "Did I tell you I was going to write a hunting article about this trip?"

"No, you didn't," Ed answers, surprised. He's holding the antlers of my mule deer buck. "So what are you going to say about me?"

"That's easy, you are a hopeless guide who makes his hunter starve to death by carrying all the big loads. That sounds close enough."

Haley and I are both laughing.

"Geez I hate Aussie's," Ed mutters.

"Truthfully, I like to talk about the experience and try to map out a plan for others to follow," I tell him. "I've been lucky, and if I can pass on my knowledge, I'm happy to share."

Haley digs into my pack to retrieve my camera.

"Are you a hunting teacher?"

"You could say that, I'd sooner think of it these days as making people aware of things, Ed. It's one of my three passions in life, I love writing even though I was hopeless at English at school."

"So, what are the other two?" he asks. "Obviously, one is hunting and fishing but what is the other?"

"If I tell you, you might not let me stay at your place," I say. We make eye contact and I am sure he understands.

The next morning as dawn breaks we start the long haul back and with each step I reflect on how hard we've hunted, the miles covered and just how much I love being out here. It is easy to relate my hunting passion to the art of satisfying a woman's desire to experience a total toe curling sexual experience. Developing a Student into a Protégée takes time and effort. Savouring her journey as she blossoms through pleasurable experiences, taking her into a realm of incomprehensible delights—it is such a pleasure to participate in her inner awakening. I sigh deeply as I reflect.

We descend into the main camp with full backpacks.

"Ed thanks for guiding me. I really appreciate all your efforts mate." I shake his hand and turn to Haley. "Think you might get yourself down-under for a bit of a road trip like we talked about? My offer is simple, get yourself down there when you can and I'll take you out for a hunt."

I grab a piece of paper from my pack and scribble my contact details on the top half for her. I tear it off and hand it to her. She does the same on the remaining piece.

"Let's have ourselves a whiskey and see what the slacko's back here have been up to," I say and push the cabin door open. Everything is shiny and clean. All the mountain critters are safe, unless they drop in for a coffee.

I fall into slumber, dreaming about the hunt for my next Protégée. They are all gettable; sometimes it just takes a little bit longer. Watching, waiting and knowing when the need within her has reached more than just curiosity, it's all about timing. Even if it's a brief break in the monogamy that possessively encircles her world. She wants to learn and experience what she has read. She knows there's something tantalising out there because she's not naive.

At sunrise the next morning, the familiar smell of bacon sizzling drags me from my slumber.

"Ed, this has been one of the best hunts of my life," I say. "Brad, can you book me in next year? I want to come back and see if we can find a big bull elk."

"We can try, but we have a limited number these days," he says. "I'll see what I can do."

"Send me some details. Thanks Ed. It has been awesome, you take care my friends."

Later, sitting at the airport I unfold the piece of paper with Haley's contact details; I grab a coffee and begin typing.

∞

Hi Haley,

How's the Rocky Mountain cowgirl?

I've attached a copy of a hunting article I've written about the wilds down-under.

Hope you can get your butt down my way, as the hunting is awesome.

If you want to be a master guide, I've got lots of things I can show you and am happy to do so.

Tom

Hi Tom,

That would be awesome.

Everyone keeps telling me that I need to get out of my little world and do some exploring before I'm hitched.

I'm going to save like crazy over the next year and hit the tracks down-under.

Promise me that you'll take me out on a hunt? I want to try your brand of outdoor adventure. It sounds unique, out there in the mountains backpacking around, OMG, you have the life. I want to learn from you so I can come back here and be the best guide ever.

Love the pictures.

Haley

∞

2

It's Friday morning and a little frosty; the leafy trees drip with dew reminding me winter is on its way. I leave a trail of footsteps on the stretch of grass between the car and the front steps of the local hall. Letting myself in, I smile when the creaky floorboards announce my arrival. I rent the rustic 1950s community hall a few times a week to teach yoga. Raising the louvered blinds to let in the natural morning light, the building wakes as sunshine flickers across the floor. The electric heater bars along the walls glow orange as soon as I turn them on and the enclosed air loses its chill. The kettle boils and I pour myself a cup of tea, wrapping my hands around the mug trying to extract warmth while I watch the first dedicated souls arrive.

"Good morning, how is everyone this morning?" I ask, keeping my tone low and meditative. "It's a bit chilly isn't it?"

I shrug my shoulders in a circular motion trying to keep moving. I rub my hands together to generate some heat to finish off my warm-up stretches. Students wander to their chosen space, a natural gravitation to the same position each time. It's silent time in readiness for today's practice.

Taking my place at the front of the class, I stand with the soles of my bare feet together at the front of my mat, my hands in prayer position at my heart centre. A serene feeling engulfs me in this stance. I feel grounded as if connected to the earth through far-reaching roots that twist and turn through Mother Nature's sacred soul and a wave of powerful emotion overwhelms me. Inhaling deeply, I turn within to focus on my breath. Time to begin.

"Placing your arms overhead moving into a little backbend, with a deep, long inhalation, joining hands together in prayer." My words are soft and designed to lull their senses so they are focused. "Exhale now, coming back to a neutral position bringing your hands to your heart."

The third round of Salute to the Sun centers my students. Their scattered minds have settled.

"Attune your mind with your breath, and without changing anything, ride your natural breath," I continue and close my eyes for a moment. Refocused, I look out at the sea of serene faces, and see they are completely composed. We continue working through the poses.

My devotees hang on my every word, exacting each pose with intention, "Feel into the stretch and breathe into any tight areas," I say, the flow of movements continue as we work through each muscle, joint and ligament. "Square off the hips to find the most benefit in your pose, and don't forget to breathe."

My voice remains soft and calm throughout, I'm in a reflective mood.

Picking up the pace for the more advanced students,

"Come into a forward fold, relax the crown of the head towards the floor to find some length through your hamstrings. Now, take a long lunge with your right leg to the back, sink into your lunge and breathe through the pose," I say and glance up to make sure everyone's alignment is correct. "Now take your upper body twist and hold your posture."

I continue, demonstrating.

"Let's repeat that on the left."

Following with ease, my well-trained students are fully focused and totally in the moment. The class flows easily and gently for the next hour.

With my voice to guide them, and soft music playing in the background, the student's sink into the meditation phase of the class and lie down on their mats. One by one I place heated lavender eye masks over each student's eyes to encourage deep relaxation. A wafting scent of lavender and nourishing words filter across the room. Those who need them, take them, those who don't, let them go.

Gently, I bring my students back into the world of the living. Moving into a seated position to feel more grounded, together we chant, "OM Shanti," bowing our heads in respect of our yoga practice today.

As the last student disappears through the doors, I pack up the few remaining items, rolling up my mat in a tidy roll so it fits snugly into the narrow cotton bag. I stash the spare mats and blocks into a storage cupboard and turn off the heaters. I grab my bag on the way out and retrieve my phone from the side pocket. My message bank registers three, they're all about tonight's event. How I'd love to turn the menace off and leave it off. My spiritual soul is telling me there's more out there, but I'm not sure what. I'm hoping with the sale of my business, new doors will open.

I have knots in my stomach when I push the door to my office open. Today we are gearing up to do my final media launch before the official handover to the new owners and I'm on a mission to make it a huge success. I have done some interesting jobs over the years: telecommunication companies, car dealerships and even the local accountancy firm, but tonight has provided my team with a doozy. Our preliminary site inspection of the venue created a stir as we dodged tradesman, obviously thinking we were part of the establishment's entertainers. Bev, my second in charge is in her element for this one. Her black pixie haircut looks so edgy with a splash of purple through the fringe and her bellybutton stud and hipster jeans make her look every part an entertainer. When she jumped up onto the catwalk to perform a few twirls on the poles, the tradesmen whistled in encouragement.

She is brilliant at her job. She exudes flair and imagination, and is a packet of energy. We feed off each other. I like to be super organised and in control to make sure it all stays together. Tonight we have bolted together a high-energy sexy media launch package for the opening of 'Pussy's', the new gentleman's club in town. Running my own business means most of the fun is had by others and I concentrate on the bottom line.

"Good morning Bev, are we all set for tonight? We can't afford any hitches. This is our final gig and everyone in town is going to know about it," I say, conscious the head of the company purchasing my business will be taking a vested interest.

My mind is now in organised business mode. I want this launch to be the best ever. Professionalism and perfection coupled with innovation, creativity and panache have been the hallmark of Cashin Communications and tonight will be no exception. I revise the program for the final time.

"I have tonight's event run sheet to finalise with you when you're ready," Bev says. Her confidence tells me all is under control, but I'm still nervous.

"We are due on site in an hour so we'd better get our skates on because I managed a quick drive-by this morning and the tradesman were still cleaning up," I tell her and grimace knowing how fine a timeline we have to make sure all the final touches are set ready for the television crew.

"I've confirmed everything and the foreman guaranteed they would be off site by the time we arrive," Bev says with confidence.

"Okay, hope he's right, didn't look like that to me. Anyway we will see when we get there I suppose.'

I am feeling a little edgy.

"I have a couple of calls to make and I'll meet you there, Bev," I add.

Arriving on site, Bev has taken the reigns immediately; somehow she has roped in two tradesmen and has them climbing ladders to assist with some of the high ceiling lighting. I chuckle to myself — she has them eating out of her hand.

"Good afternoon Eric," I say and shake the operation manager's hand firmly. He is excited but I can tell he is nervous; he has a lot riding on the success of tonight's launch. There is a twitch in the stocky man's eye. I remain calm. Thank heavens for my early morning yoga session.

"Callie, I'm impressed, the place looks amazing. Thank you for providing the extras for me, you've done a great job," he says, looking around. The seductive red drapes, spinning mirror balls and the striking silver poles for the dancers all come together. Our rent-a-crowd of male guests start to spill through the doors and Bev herds them to their tables issuing last minute instructions.

"I'm really happy with it. The place looks brilliant and if you would kindly sign off here, that takes care of all the paperwork," I say while Eric scribbles his signature to sign off for the added extras. I want no confusion at account payment time.

I cast my eye over the finer details and nod with personal satisfaction, this tempting house of pleasure is a flash joint:

dimly lit dens, voyeur's windows, pole dancers, and the endless flow of alcohol and tasty finger food should be a crowd pleaser for the grand opening. Tonight will be a bachelor party like no other.

Round tables swell with male guests and the club is soon filled to capacity. Captivating down-lights subtly illuminate each table centre, highlighting the ruby coverings and throwing a mystical ambiance across the room. The room looks alluring without the seediness usually reflected in this type of outfit and my chest puffs with pride at how well our scope of works has been executed. The entire room is charged with a palpable energy. I feel a little overwhelmed as I survey our work. My gut aches at the thought that this is my final contracted assignment. I've put all my energy into making this night a huge success. And, we came in on budget without a hitch.

I give the thumbs up and the television crew fire up the cameras. The dancers seductively grace the catwalk moving towards their stage poles to take their positions. The poles are intimately scattered throughout the seating area for easy ogling as the pussycat dolls twist from one sexy pose to the next. Sizzling hot and dressed to kill, these professionals exude sex appeal and know how to show off their art. Long slender legs wrap around the silver poles elegantly. Flesh peeps through where it should and it is just enough to tease the senses. I smile as I reminisce about my dancing days. Maybe it's not too late for me to give this art a whirl? I'm always up for a challenge, I think to myself.

"Hey Bev, aren't they amazing how they climb up there so effortlessly and descend like butterflies," I say, thinking back to when I was a professional dancer.

"I know, neat hey?" Bev says with a wicked grin.

"Bev, you know what, we should take up pole dancing, it'd be great exercise."

We both giggle.

"That's a great idea, Cal," she says. "I'd love to do that."

The entire venue is supercharged and the dolls continue to strut their stuff to the pumping beat. The film crew swivel and focus on the coloured notes being tucked into the ladies intimate apparel as the dolls continue to tantalise their male audience.

It's late back at the office. Bev and I break open a bottle to celebrate. We both look ragged after the intensity of the evening's launch and I'm feeling choked with sadness. My baby has grown up and now it's time to let it all go.

"You've been such an inspiration to me, Cals," Bev says. "And the best thing about you, is you wouldn't ask anyone to do anything you're not prepared to do yourself. That is your greatest attribute and one that I will take away with me and use over my lifetime."

We clink glasses and sign off our business relationship. I'm trying to hold it together.

"Thanks Bev. You've been an amazing colleague and friend and I will treasure our time together, always." I hold my arms out for a hug.

"Cal, you've taught me how to be tough in the face of adversity, yet you have a gentle strength, that's really admirable you know," Bev says, she hugs me tighter. "You'll always be a very special person to me."

Letting go, she drops her gaze as tears well in her eyes.

"I hope I have in some small way been an inspiration to you," I say, smiling warmly at Bev. "Inspiration to me is hard to grasp. Some days it is people who inspire, some days it is the work that I do and, some days it's a glass of champagne."

"I like your priorities," she laughs, "you've always been a great negotiator. I will miss that."

"My dad always said to me 'No' is just the start of the negotiation. I believe him, and that life is a journey, not a destination, so I try to seize each day. I've loved every minute of it," I say, then consider for a moment. "Well, almost every minute." I laugh to bleed off the stress.

"Me too," Bev concedes.

"We'll always be friends. Plus, we are going to be pole dancing buddies, remember?"

I pour another round.

"Hey, did you tell Tom the business has finally sold?" Bev asks. "He's in Canada hunting or something like that isn't he?"

"I've sent him an email to update him, but as you know, other than dotting the I's and crossing the T's, it was practically a done deal before he left," I confirm.

"God, that guy has a great arse," Bev says with a grin. "I could so eat it. Will he still be around after you go?"

I think the champagne has kicked in. She's fishing for information.

"No, he doesn't do much consulting work anymore. That's what he told me anyway. He has other interests." I shrug, hoping she can't read my face, because I agree — *yes he does have a great arse and I'd love to take a couple of bites out of it myself.* Tom has been our business consultant for the last few years and has helped me groom the business ready for sale. My exit strategy, he called it. Our monthly visits could get a little heated at times on more than just a business level, but all for the good of improving the figures, reaching KPI's and all that boring stuff necessary to get it all across the line. He definitely had me flushed in his presence on a few occasions.

"So, what else is on your agenda?" Bev asks.

"I'd really like to find more time to travel again. You know I love discovering new places and there's so much of the world I have yet to discover," I tell her, I can hear the excitement raise my voice.

“Wow, really? I know, you’ve told me before, and I laugh about your story of the hot houses in the Arctic Circle.”

“I know, that was a classic, freezing our butts off, working for peanuts so that we could make enough to sustain us for the next travel season,” I laugh, my thoughts drifting back to those days. A dozen backpackers from all over the globe, under one roof, we were cheap labour when we worked in the veggie hot houses in far north Alaska. Only one cassette between us and around and around it went as we worked like slaves all-day, and partied all night. The local home brew was our moonshine. It knocked our socks off till the taste buds in our mouths were numb, killing the effects of the freezing cold as the northern lights danced across the sky on a crystal clear night. It was a fabulous time. “Bev, it’s my passion. I want to climb mountains, trek through the wilderness and dig my feet into nature. It’s so awe-inspiring and freeing to immerse yourself that way. I’ve always been restless and find it hard to be tied down. I want to unleash my free spirit again. You can’t read in a book the experiences and knowledge you gain through travelling you know. I just love it.”

I take another sip of bubbles.

“You should consider writing a book Cal, you’ve done so much in such a short time, it’s amazing. Really you should.” Her enthusiasm takes her voice up a notch.

“I’ve never thought about it, but never say never. I certainly can feel a weight lifted since the sale was confirmed and I can’t believe this was my last event.” I hesitate, then look at her. “So my lovely, thank you for all your hard work over the years.”

“It has been my absolute pleasure, Cal. I’ve enjoyed every minute working with you,” she shares.

“I’ll Google up pole dancing lessons tomorrow and we’ll get started as soon as possible,” I say trying to change the subject. “How amazing were those pole dancers?”

“I know, I’d love to have half their strength, they made it look so easy, we’ve so got to take it up,” Bev says.

"I'll email you the details. Well, I think our job is done for the night, thanks again for all your help. Let's get out of here."

"Sounds good to me, I'm bushed." Bev throws her arms around me for a final embrace. Holding me tight, she sobs in my arms. I can't hold it together and tears stream down my face. I'm relieved and excited and sad all rolled into one. I can't stop the flow.

Pushing out the door, I wave goodbye to Bev. I slump in my car and the tears tumble. I can't believe I feel so emotional. This is what I wanted isn't it? I am usually so composed and in control. I sit here in the darkness with mixed emotions. I know I have done the right thing. New challenges are out there for me and I want to take every opportunity and open as many doors as possible.

"Morning, love," Rob says. He places a cup of tea on my bedside table." How did your final launch go?"

"It was a brilliant night and Eric was ecstatic at how well it all went, you would have loved the pole dancers." I take a sip of tea.

"How did you feel about it?" Rob asks. He senses my pain.

"It was a bit emotional for me to be honest, but it's time to move on."

"I thought it might be a little tough for you," he admits.

"It was, but it was an overall success thanks to all the planning and organisation that went into it. It was a great way to end. You should have seen Bev, she was in her element," I chuckle.

"A huge load off your shoulders at last."

"It is. Oh, and guess what? Bev and I are going to take up pole dancing together for a laugh," I say, reaching over the dresser for my computer, falling short.

"You forget you're not twenty-one any more, darl," he says.

"I know, but it's just for a bit of fun exercise and is all the rage at present," I say. "Pass me my laptop please, I want to Google the options."

I rub my eyes to focus in the early morning light. Let's see what's happening in the world…

Rob is my long-term partner and has been an incredible support over the years. His eyes smile when he's talking — they were the first things that attracted me when we first met all those years ago. He didn't carry a belly back then; those extra kilos have crept on over the years. Still his hazel eyes have warmth and a loving softness about them and his strong well-built frame is just right for his golf swing and getting him around the golf course. His favourite is the nineteenth watering hole of course. He settles in there after a round of golf with his chums and tells stories bigger and better than they ever were, each story growing longer legs than the last time it was told.

I Google up pole dancing, it looks amazing. I watch a YouTube video of last year's national pole dancing champion. She is lean and elegant and struts her stuff on the spinning pole. Her silhouette appears through the dim lighting, a black bowler hat casually pushed over one eyebrow. She wears a jewelled black push up bra, tiny briefs and a skimpy black jacket. With legs that are endless, she's toned and slender. There's a hush from the crowd as the routine begins, without a hint of strain she alights to the top of the pole. Every muscle streamlined, she elegantly controls each movement and flows from one manoeuvre to another. I'm in absolute awe. Oh my god, I am so taking up pole dancing with Bev. I email Bev attaching the YouTube link to the sexy pole dancer's sequence; she's going to love it.

"Rob, come and have a look at this."

I show him the upside down twirl.

"That looks tough, she must be as strong as an ox to do that," he exclaims.

"Don't you think I could do that?" I ask. I like the idea. It has been years since I've danced in a trained environment and the perfectionist in me is eager to tackle this sexy art. I'll probably be the oldest duck in the class, watch out babes.

"Well, I've just emailed Bev the details, this is going to be my new lease on life," I say.

"They wouldn't have classes here, surely?" I sense in his tone that he doesn't want me to do this, it's almost like I'm being childish.

"Let me see. There you go, two studios that offer classes locally." I feel quite smug.

"Okay, but don't break any bones," he says, before wandering off.

I like the idea of fun exercise and this will give me a chance to do something a bit different. Bring on the challenge.

3

"Welcome home," Chris, my brother, says. He grabs me for a bear hug.

"Thanks, it's always good to be back."

"How was your flight?"

"Great, but I'm totally shagged," I say with a chuckle.

"I'm sure, how long was it?"

"About fourteen hours," I say, flexing my sore back muscles, "have you been waiting long?"

"Nope, only about ten minutes," Chris says, "but what's more important, did you snag anything? Your pack looks a little light."

He picks up my pack to test the weight.

"I did, but left them with the local taxidermist."

"So, what did you get?" he asks.

"A monster rocky mountain goat and a big mule deer buck. I almost had a crack at a bull elk but I was a bit unlucky there." I sigh over the one that got away.

"What was the weather like?"

"Really good," I say as we step into bright sunshine. I grab for my sunglasses.

Chris sticks the ticket into the slot of the pay station.

"Fuck it's expensive," he swears.

I laugh at his definition of expensive.

"Don't worry, you make heaps, it'll hardly break you."

"It's a rip off, mate," he says, pulling the ticket out of the machine almost ripping it apart in haste.

Merging into the stream of city traffic, I sink into the comfortable car seat, Chris looks for a gap as we merge into the fast lane.

Chris is my favourite brother; mum always reckoned the girls loved him in his teenage years. Every time I see him I can't get it out of my head how he pegged his schoolteacher. A one off, but the story gets bigger and better every time we hit a bar, it's a bit of a legend event that stirs us. I'm a bit craftier. My 'Teacher' is a secret. "Do you realise it's been twenty-seven years since our sister died?" I say. I raise my eyebrows looking at the date near the clock.

"Really?" Chris replies a little shocked.

"Yep, I never forget it. Dad and I were there, holding her hand," I say. There's a pain in my gut; the image never leaves me. "Her passing changed my life. Once that light switch flicks off, it's all over. The challenge is to live life to the fullest, you only get one shot at it, and I don't intend to change that focus for one moment."

"Where were you the night dad died?" Chris asks. "It was his anniversary the other week you know. I tried to call you several times the night he died."

I didn't really want him to add this to the discussion topic.

"If I told you, mate, you wouldn't believe me," I say.

"So, you have secrets from your brother?"

I avoid the topic. I don't need to divulge, and besides my 'Student' at the time would be disappointed. What's more important is what I did after that. I got my arse on a plane and hit the mountains for a couple of years before coming back.

"I needed to escape for a while and do a bit of soul searching back then," I admit. "I needed to live my dream for a bit. Remember, I'm next in line on the family tree."

"Yeah, I know where you're coming from. I'm sick of working so much. Okay, I'm making heaps of money, but at the end of the month I have the same balance," Chris admits.

I dart a concerned glance.

"Only you can change that, Chris. You need to have goals and stay focused on what you want to do," I say, trying to inspire my brother.

"Well, I need to do that big time, 'cause how I'm operating at present, obviously isn't working," he says, his knuckles turn white on the steering wheel in frustration.

"It also helps when you start using the word 'No' with the missus," I snigger.

"You're game, mate."

"Remember, when you say 'yes', no-one expects a reason. It's only when you say 'no', a reason is expected."

"I know. I've been watching you and following your SPOT's on the GPS location system you send me via email. Every time I get one, it makes me jealous."

It's my tease. I just love it.

"I have three passions and they are my focus."

"So enlighten me?" Chris asks.

"Well, you know about my passion for hunting and fishing. Add writing and fucking to the list with the others."

"What? Fucking. I'd be lucky if I get one a week, mate," Chris shares with a laugh. "If you're getting it twice a week, you're really lucky."

"It's always a challenge till you get your head around it," I say, "it's so easy to stay in the same rut. Don't think I haven't had any challenges, I still have plenty of them to make it all happen."

I pause, reflecting on my current situation; Chris is concentrating on the traffic again.

Jess excited my addiction all those years ago, and fed it, and it was the sweetest wild berry I'd ever tasted. Everything I did or wanted to do in the bedroom, she was hot to trot, no training required. Then without notice her appetite for adventure disappeared, or was it on the way out when she hooked me in? I look in the rear vision mirror every day in hindsight, forever trying to get my head around it. The more I reflect on it, the more I'm confused.

This was a disruption to my marital sex life, like a lightning bolt, her biological clock went 'bang' on all levels, as did the horny hormones. Apparently I became an uncaring bastard and I thought our open relationship was consensual. My hot and horny Jess from the flower power era just petered out like a burnt out flame. Dreaming of a monogamist relationship after having more sexual encounters than I could ever dream of. Drifting down Jessica's belly, twirling my tongue, ready to explore her wet folds is now forbidden. Selfish man fucking has become the stalemate in our relationship. She knows my Sex Savant traits and sadly she has become possessive and worried about me being stolen. I have learned to live with the half-generation gap. If I look sideways, the husband rolling pin is waved in my face. I just wish she were like she was in the old days. In the generation where the precursor was a promiscuous interlude, I blitzed the pack. Now, other synergies are getting us through the rocky road of life. The habitual routine of husband and wife post honeymoon model has always worried me. She tells me I'm the best in the sack, I work like a Trojan and give her a completely open slate, but I feel as if she struggles to be happy with my efforts.

The time is now, as I contemplate the how. I need to do this for myself. I want some new, sweet honey to taste. One of my three passions is not a topic for discussion at the dinner table these days; the six o'clock news creates more interest. I would prefer to get a hunting license before venturing out onto the field, but I know that will not be allowed. Poaching will be easier in the current circumstances and much less complicated I figure, as I weigh up my options.

"Hey, Bro, can we pull over for a coffee? I'm parched."

I need a caffeine hit.

"Yeah sure, we'll drive through and get takeaway," he says, "so how's work? Last time, you mentioned your aim was to get down to zero clients. I'm impressed. What are you going to live on? Nuts and berries?"

Chris's capitalist household has him shackled.

"I'll find something. I always do. I'll find something totally different and from out of left field. I have no idea what, but things always seem to fall across my path."

"Good luck."

His preprogrammed world needs changing.

"Living more simply saves a fortune, and it's a great start I reckon," I admit.

"You sure you haven't lost it?" Chris jokes as we pull up to the counter and order our coffee.

"No mate, everything is on target, and the business I have enjoyed working with the most should just about be across the line and sold," I update, and a tinge of excitement surges through me.

"Weren't you working with that business for a while?"

"Yep, it's a good little operation," I say. "Callie, the owner has had me consulting there for about five years now; she's great to work with, and a really organised chick. So, with any luck, Cashin's will be sold. Another tick in the old box."

I stretch out to take my coffee, a waft of air from the air conditioner brushes my arm. It is keeping the confined space cool.

"Excellent. Callie sounds like a good sort."

"Fuck yeah. Black hair and luscious long legs," I say with a grin. He has no idea what I'm thinking. My Sex Savant brain cells are returning, surmising and planning. *Fucking good sort all right.* It's time I stopped just contemplating and being a bystander. I've felt like a boring old fart during this lull. It is time this hunter had an infusion of the addictive sex drug again. I tingle.

I recall in the early days how it was a continuous search for candidates to make my short list. Experience was a quick educator and when I discover a limitation, I wasted no time. A Callie was a rarity to find. I just knew it when I laid eyes on this type. I feel invigorated from my time in the mountains and my hunter instincts are sharp. My void of a Student has me eager to move in a little closer. For five years now I've watched and waited. Respect, sensitivity and understanding of the opposite sex's needs in the bedroom are not an automatic invite. A 'no' is a 'no', even if you think she's on the verge, so I can't rush it. My hunter instincts are attuned to detect the depths of her needs. It has made me a very patient hunter, striking only when I am confident of success. I love to take my Student deep into the realms of pleasure, satisfying her unexplored hunger, assessing the possibility of her attaining Protégée and maybe even Savant status.

I am hypnotised by the white lines disappearing under our vehicle as my mind wanders.

"The last edition of the hunting magazine had one of your articles in it, Tom," Chris says, pulling me out of my zone.

"What was it about? They don't tell me which one they're going to use, articles just appear randomly."

"It's the one about the South Pacific Fifteen," Chris says, adding, "I loved the way you gave an assessment of what's out there to hunt and when to get them. I didn't realise we had so many in our region."

"You know, I struggle to put the words together, but it's something I like doing. I like to hit them with an adventure of being out there doing it."

I'm a bit of an outdoor adrenaline junkie.

"You know Jess only has three left to get of the fifteen," I say, teasing my brother about my wife's hunting skills with this master guide.

"Really?" he asks. "I knew she had a few nailed but didn't realise it was that many."

"I'm trying to get her a whitetail deer buck, they're grey ghosts I reckon, they are the hardest of all to nail down this end of the earth. I've forgotten how many days we've spent trying to get one."

"I remember, you rated them something like fourteen out of ten in difficulty level," Chris says.

"Yep, the last few are going to be tough, she's sixty now you know. Still thinks she's twenty-one, and I keep telling her she's crazy, but she does what she wants to do." Jess has a gut-full of stamina and is a tough little woman. She has a personality that never leaves you in doubt about where you stand. I keep telling her I'm number thirteen on the list and the dog is her favourite, he's number one. I'll bet he's been sleeping on my bed.

"That reminds me, are you interested in doing a Canadian adventure? I was sort of thinking if we do those couple of trips across the ditch we will get you up to speed."

"Hell yeah. I'm in," Chris says already buzzing.

"I'll mention it to the guys over there that it may be a possibility. Leave it with me to organise that part. You can organise the flights when we get closer."

"Deal."

We pull into my driveway.

"It looks like no-one's home as usual," I comment.

"I think you're right, the gate is open."

"Need a pit stop?" I ask retrieving my pack from the boot.

"No thanks, I'd better make tracks, I've got heaps to do," Chris says.

"No worries. Thanks for the pick up, I really appreciate it mate. You travel safely, we'll talk soon."

I shut the car door and stagger in to find the key.

My first inclination is to wander up to the office and see what has been happening in the real world. My eyes might feel like they have sand in them but my brain is craving catch-up as almost two hundred emails flood the inbox. I scroll through them scanning for any of significance. Three pop up from the same person: the first is filled with excitement and elation, the deal is signed off and unconditional, the second is enquiring about when I'm back and how my trip went, while the third, invites me to a celebratory lunch.

Callie established a high ranking on my shortlist the moment I met her. The assessment process took about a millisecond. We had an instant synergy; essential and desirable elements on my list, she ticked one after another. I immediately sensed potential. I felt an instant surge of excitement to step outside the box and begin the exciting game of inveiglement. In her forties, she is the perfect target. An open cheque book to do what she wants, I gathered from the way her partner runs his life. Like me, she has no children and it is scary how alike our thought patterns and positive attitudes are. Sometimes the things she comes out with are as if she is reading my mind. She understands confidentiality; I know that from our dealings. We are equals on all levels of competence and organisation skills. I am unable to recall her ever being late for an appointment or waiting long for a response to my emails.

Our accords have only strengthened over time. She stirred my perceptive senses into overload as I determined if she could be a potential candidate. My focus narrows as I search to discover any hint of restlessness or void in her life. She's a loner, a bit of a gypsy; valuable clues to Callie's susceptibility. Each meeting was an opportunity to strengthen our connection. I tried to look beyond her dark intriguing eyes to read what was going on behind her magical stare. Her physical features are eye catching: fit, toned physique, long black hair kept simple, and luscious legs. I'd want to initiate a fuck plan on those legs even if they were detached from the rest of her body. Callie is one hot piece of flesh, a huge bonus I will be happy to accept.

Personality and chemistry are critical in my assessment. You can keep all those precious princess types, prick teasers and selfish ones. I like the hardworking, organised type, like the Callie's of this world. I discovered a long time ago they appreciate a good time in the sack. Callie wears no perfume, however, the natural smell of her body fascinates me. Each meeting we embrace with a light kiss on the cheek. I always imagine brushing her hair aside, parting those lips and diving my tongue into her mouth, deep and long. Moulding into her hips, melting her, tasting her need. The tone of our meetings lately has been a little spicier, with a constant, low voltage sexual banter trickling through. Now we have reached the end of our professional relationship, it will either happen now, or not at all. Callie is as close as I can get her to the barrier. I have used my entire bag of tricks to seduce this one. Driven by my desire for her, I'm salivating at the thought.

My number one concern is the fence she lives behind is wired awfully tight. I've been watching and waiting for the right time to step beyond the boundaries. Despite this, all the signs lead me to think she might have a chink in the fence line. It has taken five years to reach this point and it won't be long before I find out.

∞

Hi Callie,

Just hit the ground. Great news the business has sold.

Congratulations. You deserve it as you have worked so hard.

Yes, lunch would be appreciated. You name the place and time and I'll be there.

Kind Regards

Tom

P.S. Thank you, I did have a brilliant time overseas, and yes, I do have some bear stories.

∞

The upmarket bistro is on the edge of town and the smell of lunchtime cooking wafting from the kitchen whets my appetite, but I can do without the food. I would rather head straight to the checkout so we can find somewhere private and I have a Callie transfusion.

Don't get too cocky, I remind myself, it is so easy for the wind to blow your scent in the wrong direction and they are gone.

Callie walks in. She's wrapped in black and looks deliciously edible. One hot little number I think, unsure who's hunting whom. I let my imagination bounce a bit. The excitement of our success allows for intimacy and I enclose her a firm embrace and my kiss is on her lips. Our eyes meet. My plan is coming together and now I just need to make sure I don't stuff it up.

"Good to see you," I say, gazing down at her with a warm smile.

"Great to see you too, Tom," I say. I feel a tug on my heartstrings.

"The pleasure is all mine. Excited? I bet you are."

You look so unbelievably hot in that dress,* I think. *Can I take it off very slowly, one inch at a time and tantalise you with my tongue?

My mind is spinning.

"Can you believe the business sold so quickly?"

"I'm so happy everything has worked out, not many succeed at what we've achieved you know."

"I know. I can't thank you enough for your help and advice along the way, Tom. I couldn't have done it without you. Really."

I'm captivated; his eyes are luring me in.

"What's important is that you had the drive to see it through the whole way," I say. "You developed a great product to sell and you worked your arse off."

I'm laying it on thick to make her feel proud of her achievements.

"Yes, well, as you know, I don't like loose ends. Once I start something I have to see it to completion, otherwise it drives me nuts."

"Let's grab a table before they all disappear. Doesn't the food smell good?"

Placing my hand on the small of Callie's back, I steer her toward my target: a table for two in the far corner. Pulling the chair out for her, I inhale her alluring scent as she sits. It tickles my senses, I'm close, and a miss by an inch is as good as a mile when you are pointing the rifle, I remind myself.

"Thank you," I say as I sit. "It does smell great. How about a bottle of champagne to celebrate?"

Bubbles seem fitting for this occasion.

"Champagne will be nice thank you, Callie."

"Champagne please," I say, gesturing to the waiter.

I'm so excited Tom is here; he looks so edible in those jeans. The two of us alone, stabs at my breath making me nervous. This could be dangerous, my senses scream and my eyes wander over him. There is just something about him that turns me inside out.

The waiter returns and places a wine stand alongside Tom's chair and shuffles the bottle into the ice bucket. Two long stemmed flutes appear on the table.

"Cheers." We clink glasses as I try to tell her with my eyes what is in my mind. "Callie, it has been my absolute pleasure to share the last five years of this exciting journey with you."

***'I want you',* I call out in my head. I continue.**

"I guess the new purchasers will be getting organised to take over the day to day stuff?"

"Yes, they are. I have some training to do as part of the handover and then it's all theirs," I say. I try to flirt with my eyes hoping my nervousness doesn't show.

"That's the challenging part," I say sharing my wisdom, "the handover."

"They seem like really great people, so I'm hoping it all goes smoothly over the next few weeks. I've been preparing myself mentally." I sip my bubbles. "I've already started applying for jobs."

"Where?" I begin fishing for clues, feeling we are on a threshold of change. I sense she's gettable and I have a hot flush of my own.

"Our local physiotherapist has a vacancy at present," I tell him, "I'm quite interested in the position."

***I know the exact position I would like to have you in, I think*. On her back, legs spread, her hair messy on the pillow. Sitting directly across from Callie I contemplate running my big toe between her inner thighs and planting it directly on her bud. Gently shifting it into position to pamper her joy button, then teasing her till the air disappears from her breath while champagne spills from her lips.**

"Smells goods," I comment as the waiter slides the heaped plate in front of me. I look down, but can sense the shift and the possibility in the air.

"It does."

Although I would prefer to be taking a mouthful of you, I think.

"Anyway, enough about business," I say scraping my hair behind my ear as I lean forward to take a mouthful. "How was your trip? I've been dying to hear all about it."

"I had a great time in the mountains. I caught up with my old Canadian buddies. I just love the place. It gets me all excited."

Just like you do, exuding eat me.

"Sounds awesome. love those gorgeous pine forests—they're so fresh. I'd love to hit the mountains myself one day."

"Yeah, the buzz of being out in the wilderness makes you feel so alive," I say.

"Nothing like clearing the mind and surrounding yourself in nature," I say. "Did you see any bears?"

"Bears," I snort. "Everyone asks that question, you know."

"Well, everyone associates Canadian mountains with bears I guess," I stammer, trying to sound worldly. A mild panic engulfs me. I hope I didn't put him off.

"I saw heaps of tracks right through camp. Big, fresh bear tracks, but you hardly ever see them," I say. "But they are out there."

"So, you didn't feel like you were in danger?"

"Nope, never." I see a sparkle in Callie's eyes as I portray the big outdoors adventure guy.

"Wow, it sounds amazing."

I would just love to have an adventure with this guy.

"Imagine sleeping on the ground, it's as black as the ace of spades and you can't see a thing," I say, "but you can certainly hear them—they are not quiet, you can hear them rustle. They grunt like a dog barking sometimes, especially when they scent your campsite."

"Are they mountain dwellers in general?"

"They are, and they inhabit the most beautiful country," I share. "You should see when they crash through the alders and the bush simply swallows up a five hundred pound mountain grizzly. You wonder how they disappear."

"Do they smell your scent?" I ask.

"They sometimes follow in your footsteps," I explain, my hands working to expand the story. "Once they hit your scent line, they have to make a decision."

"I never thought they would follow the trail you leave," I say, intrigued by his story.

"The bear has to decide, should he cross the scent line, should he follow or should he go the opposite way," I say, my voice lowers as I picture myself there. "Remember, I'm there to hunt, not to shoot. There's a big difference."

Just like I have been hunting you, Callie.

"Wow, you make it sound so intriguing," I say, as he captures my gaze.

"I'm very selective, you know," I say. I continue my flirt. "I'm always very targeted with my hunt."

"Is that only with animals?"

"No, actually, I'm selective in everything I do," I chuckle. "Seriously, Callie, you would love it, the scenery is amazing."

"I know, I absolutely love trekking in nature and I bet the scenery *was* breathtaking." I rest my chin on the back of my hands, gazing at Tom. My nerves still flutter through me a little.

"That it was. You feel so alive when you're surrounded by majestic mountains and beautiful countryside."

"Did you take many photos?"

"Heaps of them."

"I'd love to see them sometime."

"I'm sure we can organise that," I tell her.

Her stare is intense and unbroken. Okay, time to begin.

"That would be great." I smile, so excited, my stomach knots at the prospect of future engagement. My pulse quickens with confusion, unnerved yet pleased at the thought of further contact.

"That would be great," I say, "I would love to see you again. Beyond business I mean."

I'm tingling with excitement.

"Well, I should have a lot more time on my hands now. My aim is to find a bit more balance in my life and have some fun. I've been working too hard lately."

"I agree. We've always been on the same page with that one."

"How about you?"

"Well, how about I start with…" I let my words trail off as my anticipation grows. "Callie, can I say you look stunning in that black dress."

I stare straight into her dark almond eyes.

"Really?" I am a little embarrassed and look away. "Thank you."

Here I am sitting opposite a guy who is as sexy as hell and I'm blushing already. *Better get yourself together*, I think, *he's moving in*. I know I want him and it makes me blush more. I fiddle with the stem of my glass to distract my nervousness.

"I want to explore your sensual side."

"What? I thought you were taken?"

"And I know you are too," I answer. Holding her gaze. "But, what the hell. If you don't ask, you don't get."

My silent stalk has been kept well concealed in the thick canopy of cover, until now. No more hiding amongst the rocks, it is time to drop down the ridge face and get into position.

I'm taken aback by the directness of our conversation and my heart is pounding wildly in my chest. I need air. Now.

"Well, I guess you don't," I concede in a brave tone.

"Our business is finished so I'd like to show you some of my other skills," I say, her nervousness encourages me.

"Really? Does your wife know about this?" I ask.

"No, she doesn't."

"And, you're okay with that?" I whisper.

"Yep."

The pounding in my chest grows more frantic with every word. I *have* to pull myself together, right now.

"I thought about you so much while I was away, Callie." I push just a little harder.

"You've been playing on my mind too, but I wasn't expecting this." I chew my lip. "Keep talking."

He is so hot. That beaming smile envelops me, pulling each heartstring, filling me with tormenting lust. *But I'm taken.*

"I want to kiss you," I tell her. "I want to lick you all over. I want to make every one of your nerve endings tingle, turning you into a state that you've never dreamed possible."

I sip my drink, and then before she can speak, continue. "And once I've done that, I want to show you other things that will make you wish that you had experienced them years ago." I lean forward so a light puff of breath goes down her cleavage. "I want to push every sensory button on your body."

"I've never crossed that line before," I say. My voice waivers and I hesitate as my hand sweeps across my heart. "I don't know if I could handle the guilt."

"I want to give you pleasure and amazing feelings," I say, moving in for the kill, "so you can experience your ultimate feminine highs."

"I think the champagne is going to my head," I say, catching my breath. "So, you want a playmate outside of your marriage?"

I want to make sure I'm hearing this correctly.

"I'm here to please you, Callie," I say, my hands open in a warm gesture. "Every inch of you."

"I've been reading those books about people like you," I divulge. I'm caught in his sapphire stare like a startled animal being hunted. I squirm a little. "I didn't realise they actually existed."

"So, you've been reading erotica?"

"I've just started. There was so much hype about it, I had to see." I twirl the stem of the glass in my hand, not sure if erotic literature is for me. Reading it makes me feel like I shouldn't be, like I'm not allowed. But why?

"Trust me, the reason they get such a following is because of the obvious," I say, adding to the tease between reality and fantasy. "It's what people want and don't get enough of at home."

Am I game enough to do this? I've always thought this guy was a good looker, but here he is, asking basic old me, Callie Cashin straight into the bedroom. He is tall, dark and delicious. His charm is dangerous—and tempting. So tempting.

I sense I have her; my stare into Callie's eyes means business.

I want to fuck you, my gaze says.

Dessert is served. Our intense flirt session makes my hot sticky date and her warm caramel sundae ooze with tease, the puddings echo our heated banter. The smell lingers to add to the sensory overload.

I pour the last of the champagne into our glasses. Gazing at each other, we try to guess each other's next move. With big smiles we toast again almost rubbing noses together.

It's game on.

"I'll be online tonight," I tell her.

"What happened to you in those mountains?" I laugh.

"I'm going to make you so wet and horny you'll have a wet patch on your seat. You'll be dripping."

My voice is husky as I taunt her.

"Bring it on," I reply with a show of bravado.

My heart thumps and I flush with guilt.

"I'm going to make you want what I have to offer so much, the only relief will be getting your hands on me," I say, "And I mean get your hands ON me."

I tease Callie with a departing hug that moulds her body to mine. I let my hand fall from the centre of her back to her arse and caress it. A simple twirl of my fingertip sends a message, *'wait till I really get my hands on you.'* Her kiss lets me part her lips and explore her delicious taste buds. My tongue dances deep and long with a fiery, passionate tongue tango. She pulls me closer and the anticipation builds. It's so sexual.

It will be my pleasure to devour you, just watch this space 'Student', I think as I watch her leave.

4

"Rob, could you answer my phone please?" I yell from the office.

"Rob Cashin here."

"Yes, hang on a second, I'll get her for you."

Looking up from my screen I mouth, 'Who is it?' Rob shrugs and hands me the phone.

"This is Callie… yes… Okay… ten o'clock tomorrow, that's fine… yes I know the location. Okay see you then."

I pump my fist as I hang up.

"Who was that?" Rob asks.

"That was the lady from the physiotherapists about the position I applied for. They want to interview me tomorrow."

"What if they want you to start straight away?" Rob raises an eyebrow.

"Well, the sale is through, it's a part-time position and I only have a few weeks of training left at Cashin's. It'll be easy to juggle," I reply, grinning with excitement.

Sprawled across the lounge with my laptop, my arm provides enough coverage to prevent prying eyes as I cross the dark lines into a potential zone of fatal attraction.

Jessica's favourite entertainment is crime investigation and with a Saturday evening lineup of so much CSI, I should be petrified.

"All criminals give themselves away you know," she says with a sideways glance.

"Do they?" I reply sounding about as interested as, 'I couldn't care less.' I roll my eyes when I reply, unable to pretend I'm interested. I hate the CSI channel with a passion.

"I reckon I could get away with a murder you know," she says.

"Is that right?"

"Yep," she says, obviously intent on enlightening me. "They show you everything in these shows. You know what most people stuff up on?"

"No. Tell me," I reply. I keep my eyes on my screen.

"It's the body. Yep. No body. No case. Just a missing person, you know."

"So, what you are telling me is when you kill me, you're going to dispose of me so no one will ever find my corpse?" I joke, fidgeting in my seat, my agitation clearly visible.

"Yep."

"How can you watch all that rubbish? It bores me to tears."

"Well, I love it."

"You're a CSI junkie."

"Oh shut-up, I can watch whatever I like."

"Yes, dear," I say.

She turns her focus back to the big screen and I re-focus on my laptop screen.

CSI Jessica's chair is a mere metre away and she regularly informs me of what's about to happen on her screen, before it happens. The constant reiteration of how dumb the modus operandi of the criminal is whilst proclaiming her skills as the ultimate detective is driving me crazy, should I be worried? Absofuckinglutely. I might be good at what I do, but it dawns on me this woman has been receiving an advanced education in forensic detection from her favourite channel. And for the last few years I've let my skills slip.

I never sought a hunting license for playing the field from Jess as I anticipated it would never be granted. If Jess took half an interest in what I was doing, the rolling pin would be out. If she gets a sniff of what my mind is thinking about, I will never hear the end of it. Seducing Callie online is already becoming addictive. I can't wait for my next instalment of infidelity.

The online messaging world of instant correspondence is my secret mode of inveiglement I have decided. Callie will soon learn to be an email addict. I intend to use it as our own private fantasyland. When we finally hit the bedroom, I don't want to spend the first hour warming Callie up for action—I want the degustation to start immediately.

Every time the inbox flashes, I want to respond immediately. I'm ravenous to taste her.

∞

Good afternoon, Callie,

My lips are still tingling from today's lunchtime tango.

It was divine. I've never been kissed like that before. You melted me.

Please use this email address going forward so we can keep this under wraps. I've opened my own account to keep it away from prying eyes.

I suggest you do the same.

Love the email code name.

'Gone Hunting'—It's perfect.

P.S. Make sure you clear your history files.

∞

"What are you doing?" Jess asks, glaring at me. My fingers stiffen immediately, and fear shoots straight through me.

"Nothing much," I say. "Just surfing the net."

"Seems like you are typing away to someone." She is peering over her glasses with curiosity.

"If it's annoying you I can go up to the office."

I need to get off this chair and move to somewhere a little more private. How stupid of me to think she isn't aware of what I'm doing.

"No, it's okay."

She turns back to her viewing.

"No, I'll go, I hate this stuff anyway." I make tracks to my office and my heart misses two beats as I hold my laptop like it's the Holy Grail.

∞

Champagne in a long stemmed glass with a strawberry immersed in the bubbles is my favourite. It makes for interesting kissing, especially when you bite and pluck a strawberry from my lips.

You have a way with words I see. I might throw in a few oysters to compliment the champagne to see what happens.

I'd be happy to pluck that strawberry from your lips, which I am dying to taste again by the way.

As you pluck that strawberry from my lips and bite it in two I will extract some back as I kiss you and let my tongue dance inside your mouth. I will use it as my weapon to explore your entire mouth, teasing you with new sensations.

Oysters? Yes, please, I love the way they slide down your throat all wet and moist and the thought of those delicacies fires my desire. I guess that's why they call them an aphrodisiac.

Kiss me please and let me explore your mouth further.

Your weapon sounds sensational, as does your intriguing email address.

'Bull Nuts'—Sounds more interesting than my code name. Does that relate to size?

I'm going to lick, suck and wet-kiss you. Every twist and twirl will make you beg for more. You'll be begging me to lick juice from your pussy.

I like the sound of what your tongue is going to be doing to my mouth. My pussy is pulsing in anticipation, imagining your wet tongue dancing between my folds. I might need a hot shot sooner than you think.

Beg? We'll see about that.

I'll wrap my arms around you from behind, nibble and bite you on the neck till you tingle all over. The tip of my tongue will dance up the side of your neck, through your hair and then dive deep into your ear, whispering hot talk. I will suck and lick you till you

fall to your knees. As I do this, I'll encircle your breast with my fingertips and gently squeeze your nipple. I'll squeeze it ever so softly and then harder and harder as you get higher.

Beg?

Yes, you will be begging for mercy.

OMG that ear suck thing sends shivers up my spine. My body is in overdrive. My nipples have shot to attention thinking about those strong hands fondling my breasts. You have picked my two most tender areas, both of which love to be stroked with the tip of a wet tongue.

∞

The hairs on the back of my neck stand up and my nipples harden. I have never dreamt of having a conversation like this with anyone, let alone writing it. I will have to develop my writing skills in a hurry to keep up with this raunchy stuff. Tom seems to be so switched on with this type of play. He's done this before, I'm sure of it. Am I the only one he is playing mind games with? Am I just a pawn in a wicked plan? What have I let myself in for?

Do I have it in me to unleash my wilder side, really let go and explore my inner sexual potential? Am I risqué enough for this? His charm has me hooked and I don't want to be unhooked. This is too heavenly for words.

I like the small circle tactic with a gentle touch in the most sensitive erogenous zones. I quake at the thought of touching Callie's female flesh.

∞

From behind, I run my fingertips down your spine concentrating on the lower reaches in the small of

your back. Standing you up with your legs spread wide, I run my fingers up your inner thighs. Up and down. I feel you tingling and let my tongue dance on the back of your neck.

You are making me weak at the knees. I have longed for your fingers to be dancing all over my body. I hope those fingers are as good at working their magic inside as they are outside my body.

Shivering in anticipation…

Just think of my lust flowing into you, mixing with your fluids, making a juicy cocktail.

Sleep wet.

Got to go. The 'Boss' aka my B is wandering around…

xxx

Here all alone—Better keep your B happy. Mine due home soon…

How can I sleep with that running around in my head, or should I say, inside me.

Sleep tight.

xxx

∞

In the sanctuary of my office, my fingers dance across the keyboard. I can't possibly sleep; my brain is hardwired on my newfound playmate. He's obviously surrounded on the home front and can't correspond further, not tonight anyway. I can imagine his 'Boss' would not be happy. Neither would mine for that matter. My mind is a blur with crazy thoughts and wicked emotions. Is this for real? Guilt is racing through my core. I've never ever contemplated crossing the line before. Can I live with myself if I do?

Sauntering upstairs, I climb into bed and try to rest. My eyes are wide open, my mind swirling with lustful thoughts. What on earth am I doing?

∞

Good morning,

Sleep wet?

Busy day cumming up.

Trust that the day treats you well.

Watch this space for your next instalment.

I did sleep wet now that you mention it—Thank you.

Busy for me too, no rest for the wicked.

Watch this space? I am intrigued…

And observant with interest…

I'd love to light your fire on this cold day and make you sweat as we grind our bodies together. I can imagine you riding my cock while beads of perspiration run down your body. I want to taste your liquid sex and manhandle your warm and steamy curves. I want to twirl the tip of my tongue all over your delicious body and suck you dry.

Want to play?

I would love to play. Let's see if you can make me sweat.

Light my fire… I'm all embers…

∞

My planning cells are taking over in calculated mastery, pushing the logical hardwired buttons in that sphere of my brain. My eyes narrow as I plan and think. This is my game. How could I have left it this long?

I'm excited. I'm going at a thousand miles an hour to keep up with this new component of my program. I need to rewrite my course to accommodate, but that will be the easy part. The need to continually be on the computer is the challenge every time I'm near it, I have to send further correspondence and Jess has already fired a shot across my bow.

My greatest concern is getting sprung in the wrong screen. It'd be so easy to have a set of unwanted eyes looking over my shoulder and not even know they're there. I must delete all traces to avoid a login and possible discovery of our threads as I try again to become a mastermind at deception. The sneaky adrenaline hit is getting me as high as a kite.

∞

You will have to wait and see what else is in my bag of tricks.

Ooh… So, you have more tricks?

∞

I'm far too brave online. This new way of communication has its advantages. I'm hooked on the screen and can't wait to get his next dose of hot spice. This is rapidly developing into more fun than I ever imagined. The intrigue is simply delicious.

∞

I could go a hot sticky date pudding with caramel topping as it dribbles over your tits and a glass of champers to make you tingle with bubbles. Feeling horny?

Always feeling horny, especially when you are teasing my mind. I'm wet and I haven't even tasted you yet. My mind is going crazy at the thought of what you are going to do to me. My body is like jelly with fuzzy emotions. I feel like I am sixteen again.

∞

I can think of fifty things that will be bliss for Callie's taste buds and none of them include jism. It has never been my style to make a women go down on me, especially day one. I think it's selfish, it goes against all my Teacher's guidance. Tasting Callie's nectar will be my reward as she convulses out of control. I lick my lips in anticipation; I can taste her sweetness already, it's like creamy white dipping chocolate.

∞

It's that time of the day I could go a bottle of champers and a carton of strawberries. Finger crushed, oozing juice, blending with the bubbles. Ever heard of a fuck plan? Think you can tell what's on my mind?

I'd like to join you in that bottle of champers; it's my favourite drop.

Fuck plan? Sounds extremely wicked to me; you might need to give me a hint.

∞

A *what* plan? What on earth? My mind explodes into a million shards at the possibilities. I'm convinced now I'm a pawn in a game, but I can't stop craving him. This is what I've been missing in my relationship and I didn't even know it. This is foreplay at its finest and we still haven't set up any fornication. This guessing game of lust-chess captivates me. Anticipating his next move has me crossing and uncrossing my legs, trying to ease the delicious ache he has created.

∞

Fuck plan. Watch this space.
Bet it makes you smile, I am.

I'm sure it will.

Smiling in anticipation…

∞

I'm being hunted. I am sure. He's hungry and it feels so bizarre to be courted in this manner. He has me totally captivated.

This is it. Time to go from the playroom to the shag pit. I hit the keys with purpose. My cock is hard; I hope Callie's pussy is purring.

∞

Home alone next Thursday. Want to come over and play?

∞

My heart feels as though it could pump out of my chest as I read and reread the email sitting in my inbox. Oh my god, this *is* going to happen. There is a hot wet squirt between my legs. Against all my morals, against all my values, I'm about to let another man take me. Am I really doing this? Can I really do this?

Next Thursday. I'm a nervous wreck already and it's an entire week away. My breathing quickens, adrenaline overrides my body, and I can feel my heart pumping through my chest. Breathe.

Forcing myself to be calm, I reply.

∞

Consider me there.

∞

I'm going to do this. I'm going to indulge in this sexual fantasy. If all those women in erotica book-land can get laid and be swept off their feet, why can't I?

Disbelief? Yes.

Crazy? Yes.

Hooked? Yes.

∞

I have a fuck plan that will rock your world. Do you think I'm anything but planned?

I'm in deep trouble, right?

∞

My eyes sparkle at Callie's acceptance. My initiation will leave her breathless, feeling complete, like nothing she has ever experienced. I am desperate to exceed all of her expectations and make her spiral out of control and fall off the precipice. I'm determined. I splash whiskey in a glass, filling my tumbler with a dash of water. I raise a toast to the screen. Thank you

Teacher. I'm about to take on a new Student. It has been a while. Please look over my shoulder as I tantalise this woman, she deserves to be treated divinely. I *will* succeed. I want to be the one who awakens this beautiful soul.

∞

Hey Callie,

Do you like smoked trout or chicken? You will need sustenance for high-level copulation.

Who needs food? I only want to drown in your champagne wet-kisses…

∞

If it is cold, hot chicken will be the ticket and if the weather gods turn on the sunshine, fish will be on the menu. It sounds procedural, but I want to make this interlude perfect.

∞

By the time I'm finished with you, you will be bow legged and ruptured and if you're lucky, only just capable of whispering for mercy.

Have no mercy, pleasure me till I'm numb and make me tremble. No special treatment required.

∞

I will use every part of my conditioning to impress. I want to explore Callie entirely to work out what physically pushes her buttons. Most importantly, the key for me is, 'Don't you cum.' Yes, Teacher, I am excited. I'm drooling. I take a large swig to calm myself.

∞

This is an invitation to an afternoon that will have consequences for you physically. Just giving you the heads up.

Well, is that right? Consequences, huh? Let's see about that.

So mister, what intimate piece do you like to see on a woman's body? Or, are you a birthday suit kind of guy?

Anything simple, less is more.

∞

Callie in her birthday suit, I'll be happy with that. My shag pit is vacant Thursday week. I'm not worried about an unexpected intrusion. That has already been factored into my decision. Jess is busy. That said, it would be a major catastrophe if it comes undone.

I'm so close to taking my quarry. Every nerve tingles and I find myself looking over my shoulder constantly. I prefer to hunt legally, but this type of hunting falls outside my licensing limits on the home front. My camouflage appears to be working. The thrill of the chase keeps me on edge. I've always figured, if you aren't nervous, you have lost it. If you get too cocky, you can die on the mountain. This is venturing into the territory of the badlands, and yes, people have been killed in this game.

I continually check my emails, the growing list must be making the hard-drive almost cum. Each message receives an instant reply as the banter between us accelerates. My gut tells me this one has been worth the wait.

∞

Less is more, I agree. I'm sure I can scrape together a little number that will be pleasing on the eye.

∞

I was hoping one day to dust off my lacy intimates that hide in the back of my drawer and find some use for them. I hope the moths haven't beaten me. I race upstairs and rummage through all the accumulated accessories. Ah, just what I was looking for, and they are black of course. This little number needs to be christened. It is sure to get his cock into gear.

It's the first email for the day and I'll bet Callie's inbox is gushing. Mine has a hard-on just like its owner.

∞

Good morning sleepyhead,

Early start at this end, the stars are still in the sky.

Would you like an early morning pussy rimming with hot sexy talk in your ear? I would like to feel your bud under the spell of my touch, while I softly whisper erotica into your ear. Kissing you till you can't breathe to take you on a morning high.

I want to roll you onto your back and have my selfish way with you, breaking you into a million bits until I shatter you. Then pierce you with a jolt of my cock as you die in the saddle.

Watch this space for your lunchtime helping.

∞

I'm ecstatic with the progress of my inveiglement plan on Callie. Getting Callie's knickers off is only half my intent. If I want to fully awaken her, it must become her obsession. I have to totally seduce her into a new way of thinking.

My goal is to form email threads. Threads Callie will see as intrinsic pieces of a puzzle. With each encounter there will be added seduction; each fuck plan will raise the bar.

My computer might be as quick as lightening, but everywhere I look, the beast has history files upon history files. My hubby might not be computer savvy, but he will only have to click on the wrong button once, and I will be part of the history files.

∞

You are going to have to contain yourself till Thursday. Watching this space for my lunchtime helping…

Ready for your lunchtime helping of pleasure? No light snack here, only a long lunch with hot music videos, champagne and strawberries.

For starters, I want to devour the side of your neck, nibbling and biting your ear while my hand explores your hot muff. I want to feel your oozing wetness. Your back will arch as my fingers run up and down your spine and bring you in so close that all you can feel is the heat of my body.

I would like to order the starter please.

My lips will be kissing and biting you all the way down to the top of your shirt. Using my tongue to wrap around each button, I'll spring them open so the tip of my tongue can dance around, making your nipples hard.

Your erotic tongue is sending shivering messages through my brain. And, yes, my nipples are hard in anticipation.

This is killing me.

The tip of my finger will tickle circles against your wetness and I'll run my wet finger between your lips so that you can taste what I'm about to taste… hot, wet pussy juice.

Now, I want to go down on you and melt kisses all over your vagina lips. Main meal is my specialty.

You are melting me here, you know. Do you always speak to a lady like this? You have a way with words and my body is responding with hot flushes.

All good to go on Thursday…

∞

He has me right where he wants me in his wicked little plan. I am head over heels in anticipation and we haven't even done the deed. How do I possibly sleep tonight? The suspense is killing me.

∞

Dessert? How about strawberries and hot dipping chocolate sauce? Now, my imagination is flowing.

Your fuck plan is set in concrete. Want a little taste tonight?

Absolutely.

Want to share juices?

I will massage your big toe between my lips as my tongue licks, caresses and circles. My teeth nibble and rub your toe as my fingertips run up and down your leg. My finger reaches your hot spot. I am inside your knickers.

I love a toe suck and massage along my inner thigh. Your plan will come undone if I choose not to wear any knickers. Hope you have a plan B in place?

I see you want to play in my shag pit?

Pushing the lace back, I want to explore your folds. Teasing your inner core, tantalising your senses and gently holding you there in a state of flux, letting energy flow from my fingers as you cum.

Yes, I want to play in your shag pit.

Stalk me.

Let the hunt begin.

∞

5

The kettle is on the boil as I sneak up to the office to fire up the computer for its warm-up phase. Coffee brewing in the plunger, I have to make this quick.

∞

Good morning, Callie,

Ready for a new day of adventure?

I am. Woke up with something you'll like, a glasscutter that will be your new best friend from today onwards.

xxx

∞

Butter wouldn't melt in my mouth as I trundle back to the bedroom with coffees in hand.

"Your coffee, dear," I say and place the steaming cup on her bedside table.

"Thank you," she says and takes in a deep breath. "What are you doing today?"

"Not much… working around here. I might slip over to the farm a bit later," I say, sliding back under the covers. I'm as nervous as a cat on a hot tin roof. I just know I am hunting a trophy. Trophy hunting always makes me super nervous because I know this one is a beauty and I don't even have to put my binoculars on it to prove that. I want Jess out of here, now, so I can organise the place just right. My cup wobbles and it feels extra hot.

"Well, I have my grandkids for the day, my usual Thursday," she says, her eyes lighting up. Thank god she has kids from her previous marriage. Now the grandkids keep her more than occupied.

"I thought so, what time are you going?" I'm anxious.

"I need to be gone by around nine."

"Anything you need done today?" The good husband says.

"Just hang out the washing if you could," Jess says as she touches my hand.

"Consider it done."

I peck her lightly on the cheek.

What can go wrong today? I don't even have to use my imagination—there are at least a hundred and ten things. Not one of them relates to my up and coming horizontal dance between the sheets. I'm excited. My biggest concern is that Callie will feel guilty. I will be disappointed and disheartened. Five years of patient watching and assessing, and at the point of executing my fuck plan, it could all come to naught. I haven't had a student for as long as I have known Callie and am anticipating that my void will to be filled. I clear my mind; it will be okay. Callie is hot to trot and my seduction is already beginning to imprint her. The only one who will be in tatters today will be Callie. I am going to deliver an earth shattering opening scene that is going to knock her into next week. I'm planning to have her walk out bowed legged.

I have hardly slept a wink, I can't remember ever being this aroused in my life. It's a heady mixture of adrenaline, guilt, and pure unadulterated lust. My mind is fluctuating between panic and anticipation.

My excuse for today's absence has gone down without a hitch. My excitement worries me; I'm not supposed to be this excited about going to work. My sense of deceit is overwhelming but doesn't change my mind. We *are* consenting adults. The secrecy tingles in my toes. I am ready to tango.

I snuck in a dummy run over the weekend to see where Tom lives. It's the perfectionist in me, always too organised for my own good. Pity he wasn't home alone. I could have surprised him with a preliminary rendezvous. I was feeling horny enough.

I leave the house in my work attire. My clothes for later are stashed in a shopping bag in the boot of my car. It's too cold for a little black dress today, so casual jeans and a low-cut fitted top with a leopard print chiffon scarf will have to do. I only hope his arse is as hot in the flesh as it looks in his jeans.

"Rob, I'm off to work," I call, descending the stairs.

"What time will you be home?" he asks. "I'm not sure. I have heaps to do today, it's going to be a busy one." I hope he doesn't drop in to work to see how I'm going. It has crossed my mind, as have a million other complications that I have tucked away for now.

∞

Can't wait to see you.

On my way…

xxx

∞

Sent. This is it. You are on girlfriend. I can't stop shaking. I take a final glimpse in the mirror. Holy hell, keep it together and stay calm. I must remember to breathe, slowly.

The space I feel as the screen door closes behind me is a cure to hide my fraudulent mask. Eyes that read me so well, how haven't I been asked further questions? It's all in my guilty mind, it must be written all over my face. I can't quite believe I am doing this; I'm fighting against my morals.

My mind is skittering as the anticipation eats away at me. I am willfully walking into the danger zone, deliberately treading into forbidden territory. I just hope my conscience can handle the aftermath. Fire and passion are drawing me into his shag pit. I can't wait to see his face light up with his delicious smile and I get to kiss his lips all day long.

The car disappears down the drive, thank goodness. I thought Jess was never going to leave. Time to get myself into gear and get organised. Callie is going to be arriving in an hour and the window between total disaster and my fuck plan initiation is a mere fifty-five minutes away. I finally have space, and it is all systems go.

Last night I programmed my playlist in sequence. I hit the play button and my air guitar joins in. These songs will be playing in the background while we make other classic noises.

Champagne is plucked out of a hidden box in the back of the bar cupboard and stashed into the freezer for a quick chilling. I mustn't forget it and blow the bottle to smithereens. I can do without glass throughout the freezer compartment today. Retrieving the fresh strawberries from behind the office desk, I sample one. Divine. I place two long stemmed glasses from the bar on a shelf in the fridge to chill. I arrange a plate of morsels including: bell peppers, finely sliced smoked salmon and marinated olives. I dip in to have a little taste test and add a few crackers on the side.

The firebox requires stoking and I will need to get an armful of wood. The heavenly ambiance of the fire is why I wanted this to be our shag pit for the first takedown, although it's a big risk. Callie will be walking into my house; I need to make her feel comfortable. I refuse to consider the other obvious scenario, Jess arriving unannounced. So far, all has been managed with ease and my scheme is coming together without a hitch. Did I mention timing is everything? I love the thought. Feeling a little cocky, my air guitar swings wildly.

The work mattress is positioned in front of the fire with fresh satin sheets and a luxurious New Zealand possum fur-skin rug for us to roll in as we sip bubbles. Shuffling the furniture into place, moving the soft padded monster lounge chair, (heavy damn thing), I struggle trying not to mark the polished floorboards. I want it placed on the edge of the mattress facing the fire. I push everything close to the slate surrounding the fire. This is going to be my opening scenario. I'm going to plunge in and take Callie apart in this monster.

"Shag pit, ready, set, go," I crow aloud, grinning as my excitement bubbles over.

Sitting in the chair I gaze at the flickering fire, just the slightest breath of heat hits my groin. I feel like a whiskey. That's a BIG NO, I remind myself; even if it's only to toast my Teacher, I can't let Callie taste alcohol on my breath, not on the first date. A cup of coffee is what I need. Kicking back listening to the beat of the music has the desired effect. Ready? Absofuckinglutely. Bring it on, Callie, because I'm going to do you like you've never been done before. That is a promise, as I remind myself of the plan.

Once Callie enters the house there will be no smoochy warm-up session. I'm going to hit her clit straight up with my tongue and take her out. I suspect she hasn't had a big hard cock to impale herself on for a while and to be able to ride it like a wild cowgirl, without it doing her within fifteen minutes. I know it sounds cocky but she wouldn't be coming if she were being well taken care of.

Rubbing my crotch I feel my knob throbbing. A little tease is also in my plan: I want to make her cum by sucking her tits off. One out of left field I like to deliver so she wonders what else there is. I must stay calculated because if my excitement gets too high, I will lose my load. I must control myself. My NEW Student will have a virgin fresh taste, and I want to enjoy every mouthful.

Callie's subjugation is my total desire and purpose for today. I want her to know there is something else out there. I want her to start looking for it and become my Student. I can almost taste it; she's ripe for the picking.

I will work out a timeline of activities after today; each will build and take her just a bit further. At every interlude I will introduce something new, all in preparation for her Protégée status. I can't wait, and I'm sure Callie will make it to Sex Savant. Now I'm dreaming. Give me a Sex Savant any day, an equal in the sack. That would be like diving into a forty-four gallon drum of honey and coming up all covered in sticky drizzle.

The dog alarm sounds and excitement butterflies flutter inside this Sex Savant. My Teacher's words and lessons repeat themselves 'You are to deliver, not receive.' I *will* have a new Student once I blitz Callie in the saddle. I can think of nothing less, she will be addicted and failure is not an option. I want this woman, badly.

It is natural to have last minute doubts isn't it? I pull into a rest stop for a quick pit stop to change my clothes. My nerves are on edge, tightened to the point of snapping. Turning into his street, my heart thumps hard. Pulling into his driveway, I step out of the car to open the gate. Looking up the driveway, I see Tom's house on the top of a slight hill, it looks like a mansion through the trees. Peering up to see if I can see any sign of life. Is this shag pit going to be safe? I'm operating on remote control; adrenaline kicks in to my system as I drive along the dirt access road. A still pond sits to my left surrounded by a large grassed area where sleepy sheep graze. To my right is a large green farm shed. Up ahead the driveway curves around to one side of the house. Tom's truck is parked in the bay. Pulling up alongside the garage, I take in a big breath, and somehow I calmly step out of the car. The backyard is manicured to perfection and his puppy bounds towards me with a welcoming bark.

Clean-shaven and hunky as hell, Tom closes the distance between us in less than five seconds. Without a word he grabs hold of me and sticks his tongue straight into my mouth. Our lips latch together with pure intensity as he wildly begins to discover my tongue. The furious kiss torments my taste buds, his tongue dances back and forth coaxing mine to do the same. Exploring every groove, he consumes me; I'm melting into him. All my nervousness disappears.

"Good morning," I say finally wrapping my arms around Callie's neck. "Find the place okay?"

"Good morning to you, not a problem at all," I reply. My hands grip around his waist and I try to calm my nerves.

"What have you been up to?" I ask, cocking an eyebrow.

I take her hand and lead her inside. I don't want to hang around out here, I want to devour her gorgeous body.

"Not much," I answer with a grin. He knows damned well what I have been up to. Emailing him every goddam minute of the day and night, getting all sexed up over his erotic words and tantalising scenarios.

A weeklong cyber-seduction has laid the foundations and I'm not going to waste any time. We both know what we are here for and it isn't sugar lumps and coffee. Rehydration is two hours away and we can talk then.

Inside, I embrace Callie, bringing her in tight, teasing her lips. Diving deep to taste and torment her taste buds, a prelude to what I will do to her entire body. My tongue is like a rattlesnake, licking, flicking and drawing her in. Moulding against her, I send a 'fuck me' energy transmission. My rock hardness jams into Callie's belly as I hold her close. I feel a pre-cum patch in my jeans and my balls tingle. It's not every day you get into a new set of pants. I want them off.

I tremble with excitement. It's coming off Tom in waves and warming me through. Nobody has ever wanted me like this before. Before I can open my mouth to speak or get a real sense of location, he grabs me around the waist, lifting me off the ground. I feel the head of his cock pressing through his jeans; my knickers are soaked. Without breaking his grip, he lifts me off the floor and my legs wrap around his waist as he carries me across the room. He settles me into the soft cushioning of the lounge chair. Wet-kissing me, he kneels down in front of me. The ambience takes my breath away. My heartbeat is violent, out of control; my nervousness is fierce and overpowering.

Time to advance to stage two. The secret little dream I had about those legs clamping around me like steel wire is now in fruition. The next part of my fantasy is when she parts those luscious legs of hers and impales herself on my cock to hit her sweet spot. Patience.

The lounge chair is where I want to begin but I'm not going to just climb on top and nail her to get my rocks off. No way. I'm going to take her most sensitive point, wrap my tongue around it and make it swell. Flick over the top, clamp down and nibble and swirl across it, placing

direct downward pressure. After I have done that once, I'm going to do it again. I'm calculated. I have a job to do.

We linger on our kiss. With maddening slowness he leaves a trail of kisses down my neck and along the low neckline of my top. Delicate brushes along my skin tingle as he works toward my breasts. He peels the chiffon scarf from my neck and tosses it aside. I gaze into his eyes in anticipation, holding my breath. My chest is pounding with adrenaline overload. I feel soft bites curl the rim of my top as his teeth prise it away from my body to take a peek at my tits. My nipples are piercing through my top from over swelling breasts. Gazing up at me with wicked blue eyes, I can see his hunger for me, his hunger to taste me, hunger to take me, hunger to devour me. His gaze lowers to the button on my jeans; his fingers glide the zipper down with gentle care. Lifting my arse off the chair, Tom eases my jeans down my legs collecting my shoes on the way to fully reveal my black lace underwear. His insatiable tongue toys with my inner thighs tracing the outline of the delicate lace encasing my mound. Tantalising the edges to leave a delicious trail of wetness. Entranced in every movement, I'm breathless and overcome with pure pleasure. There's no rush in Tom's deliverance as his tongue continues an excruciating and delectable dance through my pussy folds. I grind my hips to the rhythm of his erotic tease. With slow, skillful deliberation he peels the black lace from my skin, dropping it on to the fur rug. He returns again for a long lick along my inner thigh and then … I feel him there. He has latched on, his tongue dancing across my bud. Jolting wetness escapes in a rush as he teases and taunts my pulsing clit. My head drops back on the chair-back. I close my eyes. Carried away to another place, the feeling of pleasure is overwhelming. Incredible. My fingers clench the armrests as I feel my bud ignite. An almighty orgasm feels as though it will rupture every part of me.

"Ohhh … God …I'm cumming."

My entire body vibrates as he licks up my juices and moves up to deposit my wetness into my mouth.

I gaze into her eyes and let them tell her: I'm here to do you like you've never been done before. I will take you higher than you have ever been taken. I lower my eyes and admire her. With the tip of my finger, I massage her bud while the tip of my tongue explores her soaking folds deeper. Another hot gush as a second jolt of sex energy hits me like a pulse. The throb of her clit is swelling like an erection. Again, I nibble, clamping down on her bud, my tongue grooving the ridges on either side. My digit inserts like a miniature cock into her snug wetness, pushing against the flow. Fondling her G spot, I feel her spasm out of control as my finger torments her ridges. My tongue dives into her to extract her dripping essence.

I see a flash of fire, a streak of light and beyond that, no more as my eyes close. Luxuriating in the tease. I'm in heaven. It is the only way I can describe it as I ride waves of arousal through peaks and troughs. I am floating. Each time the peak is higher and more intense, he is bringing me closer to another climax. My breath is sucked out of me as I try to inhale and recover. My heartbeat is out of control as my body erupts. I have never, ever…

His tongue continues to explore. My senses are heightened even further. He slows his pace and takes a long slow lick of my opening. I pry my eyes open trying to move the weight of my head so I am looking down at him, feeling a change of pace. Tom's impossible big blue eyes meet my gaze, his mouth wide open, and his tongue lapping a long intentional, sensual stroke. His eyes lock onto mine the entire performance, melting my inner core, tantalising each cell around my pussy.

This is only the audition. I have only just begun to determine how much potential you possess, Callie. This is

going to be my pleasure. I like what I taste. I'm giddy with motivation to make this one count.

It's crucial I don't blow it. I ease back on my eagerness and taste the damage. A long, slow, gentle flat tongue lick to relish the spasms I feel pulsing against my tongue makes Callie climax again. My hardness tingles as my brain shoots a surge along its length. I'm in dangerous mode. This is what I live for, the scent of a woman.

Tom continues to lick my mound before making his slow ascent to my navel, teasing each inch of my midline with succulent mouth dribbling kisses, leaving my skin shivering. His demanding stare doesn't leave mine as he nestles into my cleavage sucking along the line of lace covering my bosom. He reaches around behind my back to unclip the single clasp. He slips each strap down my arms and tosses my bra over his head toward the makeshift bed. I am now fully exposed. He cups one breast, sucking the nipple of the other. Erect with arousal, they engorge even more as his tongue circles each one. I watch each deliberate lick and stroke of his expert tongue as the heat between us builds. I feel a delicious twist through my core… oh please… don't stop.

I've spent so many hours checking out these tits, dying to finally see and devour them in the flesh. I'm going to use this as an interlude for abeyance. I don't want to break my new toy by overloading her pulsing bud. That is for another lesson, overload and beyond is for another day in the shag pit.

Licking, sucking, nibbling and gently working out how much pressure I can leverage on each nipple, I feel Callie building up to climax and I'm tempted to make her cum again. Not yet. I decide to keep this exercise in mammary intimacy for later today. Saliva dribbles from my mouth as I taste her nipples ooze and I pull off to savour her gooey flavour.

My fuck plan is right on track. I'm in control mode. I'm drawn back to Callie's pulsing clit. The tip of my tongue dances to a tune that is playing on the pulses she surrenders. As the energy pulses amass, I increase the intensity to meet her need. I don't want to make her pass out in the first hour. I feel her vagina convulse as I ingest another sample of her divine juice. My mouth cups up like a funnel. I want to be drowned in her nectar.

Searching for the right blend of movement and pressure, with each twirl, I feel a corresponding pulse. With each nibble, Callie shivers. My finger delves in exploration to find her G spot and I tease it with a snake like twist. She squirts hot wet juice and I lap through the aftermath.

Pumping with fuelled excitement I'm not even contemplating using my own hardness yet.

It is so intense; I'm soaring. Tom is decimating my body. Somehow I understand I'm teetering on the edge of what he has in store for me. The maestro moves back down to my clit, his tongue working its magic around my swelling lips. Without invitation, I feel a finger insert into my wet hole, I release a moan of pleasure deep from within. He massages inside me, and the combination of his finger strokes and licking sends me over the edge. A hot explosion rocks me and I gush all over him.

"Ohhh… My… God…" I moan.

My pussy convulses and contracts. I'm immersed in ecstasy. Lying breathless, unable to open my eyes, as if drugged, I sink into oblivion.

I sense the time is right to start on the insertion phase. Lifting Callie from the chair, a flashing red light goes off in my head—DON'T YOU CUM. I visualise my Teacher standing next to us waving her finger like a cross nun.

I still feel drugged and a little out of it when Tom peels me from the chair, his strong arms effortlessly lift my tingling body and he gently lies me down, slicing his hands from underneath, he runs his fingers along my flesh. Tom shifts the fur rug to one side before I reach the soft mattress. The fresh satin sheets feel cool on my clammy skin. Adjusting the pillow under my head, he aligns my body along the length of the plush cushioning. I feel his cock against my thigh, pushing hard. I gasp as I take him inside me for the first time. I feel his pulsing penis pierce my wetness, sucking me breathless. I feel the blood rush to my lower lips, engulfing him as he thrusts into me.

He begins to stroke in and out with deliberate, slow strokes. The sensation of him entering and leaving me with such intention is so good it's excruciating. Waves rocket through my body, the vibrations make me groan; he is ravishing all of my senses. My arousal amplifies and I am totally immersed. I begin to move in rhythm. My body screams with pleasure. He is draining every molecule. He holds me tight—his delight is obvious.

I roll onto my back; it is time to let Callie ride me long and hard. I need to explore how hard her body can ride and grind me. I watch as she takes my penis and holds it in her delicate hand. With her juice all over my length, she feeds me into her slit and lowers herself into position. I watch my throbbing cock disappear into her and how I don't shoot, I don't know. I have to suck this one up. I stare into Callie's eyes. I'm transfixed by her aura of beauty. Perspiration drips from her forehead as she mines the sensations for pleasure. Staring into her eyes, watching her thrusting, I'm mesmerised as she pulses, spasms and gushes all over me. Her nectar is a sticky mess running down the sides of my hips and my arse crack. I raise my hips and wrap my hands around her waist to hold on tight. There is no chance of escape.

Tom is watching my every facial expression. I settle into a rhythmic movement as my natural instincts take over. My bud is in full arousal. He pushes his pelvic bone against my mound to tantalise me further. Feeling his cock deep inside me, a thrilling sensation sweeps through me. It's intoxicating, real, and raw. Feeling my inner lips begin to clench and convulse, the crescendo builds. So intense, so rapturous, so exquisite. I'm mesmerised as I continue to glide on top of him, seamlessly floating along the length of his body. Sweat glistens on my skin. I luxuriate in this sphere of pleasure. I can't stop. Readjusting my body, I sit up slightly higher and my bosom gains his attention. I arch my back to enhance my sexy position, taking him deeper at his root. He feels so deep inside me, my tender folds totally engulf his dick. His smell is intoxicating and lures me deeper. With my hands upon his chest, I continue my rhythmic dance, his hardness so deep inside, it is impaling me with agonising ecstasy. My fingernails dig into Tom's chest flesh as I throw my head back, gasping for air. Surging to unimaginable heights, my lips swell and pulse as I reach my peak and feel my convulsing inner lips grip the base of his cock as my spasms take over.

Breathless and exhausted my body falls to his, my heart in raptures. My ear to his chest, I hear the violent pounding of his heart. Or is that mine? I'm not sure. Sinking into a morass of satisfaction, I bury deep into his chest, entranced in the afterglow. Contentment. Bliss. He leaves me lying there basking in the sensations pulsing through my body, giving me time to recover without rushing me out of pleasure. I sense the inevitable, it is my turn to tantalise his cock. I take a deep inhalation and try to ground myself. I want to take Tom's essence deep inside me.

Callie consumes me, holding my shaft deep inside, guiding it into her depths. Her head lolls back, her mouth open, and she groans. I swell with a pulse of anticipation, I'm going to cum, and my balls contract. The tempo is building and I know it is time to fill her. I need to readjust

my focus. My balls are tingling, the tip of my cock feeling her contractions pulling and massaging my cock as she pumps me harder.

"Fuck, you got me," I moan. I shake and clench her hips, driving her even harder as my knob rattles her depths. My cock explodes upwards. My head tosses to the side, my eyes clamp shut, my hips push up as a pulse shatters every nerve ending. Pins and needles make my entire body shiver. Callie collapses, her sweat-drenched body covering mine. I wrap my arms around her holding her tight. Callie's internal muscles consume my knob as her cunt sucks the last of my semen.

My first erotic interlude is exquisite. I am limp. I am breathless. I am in heaven.

My initiation program of sexual annihilation is complete. I lost count of how many times she came. My senses consumed as we devoured each other. I kissed, licked, sucked and tasted every morsel of her I could extract, reigniting my fire.

Teacher, I have done you proud. It is the start of another candidate entering the Sex Savant tradition, welcome Student. Round one down. Round two in an hour.

6

With gentle tenderness, my fingertips trace the length of Callie's spine. I lay a gentle kiss on her forehead.

"Champagne?" I whisper.

"Yes please," I somehow murmur, still in a haze. My eyes are closed. I am still impaled and my whole being is tingling. *Pinch me.*

I shed a warm smile. My fingers fondle Callie's shoulders tracing her freckles. I kiss her crown, caress her dark hair and inhale her beauty.

"I have died a divine death," I sigh as the warmth of Tom's body infiltrates through me.

"The pleasure is all mine," I murmur as the warmth of the fire soothes our exposed bodies. Callie is relishing the moment. I lay a soft kiss on her mouth, trace her lips, her breasts and down to her bellybutton.

I unravel in the warmth of the fire and our embrace. My eyes are closed, the touch of my illicit lover tantalises my nerve endings. I soak up the aftermath. I can feel sweat trickling down my body, cooling my skin. My inner core is coming to terms with what has happened. Never have I experienced such passion. I have never been annihilated like this in my life. I try to appear relaxed and in control, while wondering where this has been hiding. Is this what I was made to experience?

Immersed and twisted in the cosy fur rug, mesmerised by the fire, I feel barely conscious, only able to focus a little. I gaze at the ceiling. First impressions? His house is amazing. High exposed timber ceilings seem to go on forever. Floor to ceiling windows overlook a sea of trees and lush green gardens sprawl for acres. The incredible ambience has me stunned. I want to steal this fluffy fur rug. It is as if I'm wrapped in cotton wool. Wow, he really meant business when he mentioned shag pit, never in my wildest imagination did I think of a bed on the floor in front of a blazing fire, adorned with a fur rug. And, this is all for me?

"Who built your house?" I ask.

"I did ninety percent of it," I say.

"Really?"

I blink a couple of times and run the back of my hand across my brow.

"Yep, it took me seven years, but I eventually finished it," I continue. "The roof and high timber ceiling I had builders do. It would've taken ages on my own. The weather would have beaten me. I installed the windows, laid most of the block-work and what I couldn't do I contracted to a retired bricklayer and worked as his labourer."

"You must be incredibly proud."

"The floor was a massive job. I had the plumber install the flue of the firebox, which was required under local government rules, only to have it leak like a sieve. He's a good mate of mine, so that provides a bit of entertainment when we catch up."

I look at the firebox and back at Callie lying there. I smile and adore, taking in the aftermath. The temperature in the room is just right for nakedness as my eyes appreciate the taste my mouth consumed. I always knew the body under that skirt would be something to behold. I am not disappointed: she is stunning. Callie's olive complexion

is slick and toned with curves in all the right places, she's a feast on my eyes. The energy she expended was impressive. It kept me as hard as a rock, matching her pace I used my training by an older woman to satisfy a younger woman.

"So, how did your first couple of days go on the new job?" I ask, as I run my fingers through her hair.

"I like it, it's close to home and so convenient," I say.

"That's great, is it a casual position?" I ask, watching her hair drop through my fingers. I lean down and steal a tender kiss.

"Yes, I'm the fill-in person, so far, so good, I quite like it."

"Sounds perfect for you, for now."

"It's only a stepping stone until I work out what I want to do, I need to readjust after running my own show for such a long time," I say with a shrug.

"Well, it'll bring you in a few dollars and keep your mind active."

Leaning forward I inhale her essence and place another gentle kiss on her parted lips.

"That's the plan."

"Let me go and get some bubbles."

It's time for a break from the physical pit. Rehydration is needed while I prepare Callie for the next round. I head to the kitchen to retrieve the bottle of chilled champagne and strawberries. Grasping the neck of the bottle I ease the cork from the opening, the sharp 'bang' echoes through the extensive room. I return and settle on the mattress. A light hint of sweetness from the bobbing fruit looks hot and sexy as I fill the glasses. I take a whole strawberry and run it through Callie's glistening honeypot, twirling it in her juices. Holding the strawberry above my mouth I lick the collected drop with my tongue, devouring it. I know I am beaming. Call it reminiscing.

How good is this? Champagne and strawberries in elegant long stemmed crystal flutes. I'm sold.

"Cheers," I say with a smile as he places a glass in my hand.

"Cheers."

We clink glasses and seal our deed.

Welcome, my new Student.

Totally naked, we sip on bubbles. Way to go. The first mouthful is refreshing and cool. I realise my mouth is parched. Every drop must have leaked out of me. I notice the music, which has been playing all along. Sexy songs. I like his taste in music.

Lowering my gaze to those gorgeous tits, I admire her. Sweat leaves trails on her skin as Callie sits against the lounge sipping bubbles, elegant as she fondles her glass, her slender fingers graceful as she seems to cherish the stem. Those legs are the luscious legs of a dancer, I am sure. I have a trick or two for those legs and it involves more than wrapping and curling them around me. I want to make Callie cum through her toes with the gentlest of touches. "You have a beautiful body," I tell her, admiring the feast before me, I raise my glass in a toast.

"Thank you."

I am a basic guy trying to keep some level of fitness with work and mountain treks. It's hard work but worth it when it comes to this sort of activity. Callie is the same age and common sense tells me she eats enough for a sparrow and works out to keep her shapely figure. The champagne is going down smoothly. The eye candy entrances me. I am in heaven; I have found it, right here, right now. I want to press the pause button for a while to slow down the minutes ticking on the clock. I steal a kiss from Callie's lips as a whir from the kitchen reminds me of food.

Buzzing comes from the oven. "Hope you like satay chicken wings?" I tell her and heave myself up.

I really can't think about food at this very moment but there is a smorgasbord of delicacies Tom has gone to a lot of trouble to prepare. I must partake, although my appetite doesn't agree.

I sing to a tune, twirling my hands in the air. Closing my eyes, bobbing my head a little to the beat. I feel so relaxed in Tom's company.

"Enjoying yourself I gather?" I refill our glasses, immersing another piece of fruit.

"Of course." I shoot him a flirting glance.

"I love the cyber-sex sparring." I reach out to take a chicken wing.

"So how long have you been contemplating pursuing me?" I ask and roll onto my side taking hold of my glass.

"I never hesitated," I admit.

"Interesting," I muse, tasting a morsel of chicken.

"Since we first met."

It's too early to disclose the Sex Savant hunter side of me. I don't want her to discover any of it until the timing is right. I need Callie to mellow in the delight of being totally obliterated.

I have never strayed before. It has taken me a lot to step out. I peer down into my bubbles feeling a little guilty.

"You went to so much effort," I say, "you sent me so many flirting signals but just didn't hit on me like most men would. I could tell you were waiting. I just needed a bit of time."

I lift my glass to tilt it Tom's way in a little gesture of thank you. If only he knew how much he has stirred me, and my sex juices. Once he broke through my armour of self-protection, his cyber-play tactics finished me off.

"Top up?" I ask, bottle in hand, leaning toward Callie.

"Yes, please," I answer, extending my glass.

"Pleasure."

The champagne bubbles overflow and dribble down my hand. Without warning suddenly he snatches my flute, and his lips savage mine. Desire and passion explode between us, his strong hand against my back pulls me in close. My naked breasts press against his chest. Lust surges through me. Sensing his desire, I perceive his eagerness. His cock presses into my thigh, I can feel it hardening again.

'I wonder if anyone has made you cum by kissing your tits?'

I keep my voice low and calculated as I concentrate on those edible nipples. I'm going to turn you inside out, Callie. I like this challenge. I will make you squirm in pure ecstasy until your body can't take it any longer. This is not going to be a twenty-minute take down. I want to feel your sex energy as you lose control. It gets me high. I need you. I will tease you with my hardness keeping it out of reach. That would make my Teacher smile.

Taking a mouthful of bubbles, I spread my fingers wide and pull Callie towards me. I attack her lips as she accepts fizzing bubbles from my mouth. Swilling back and forth the bubbles mix with our fluids making our own distinct flavour of passion juice. With each deposit there's leakage, making a track to my next destination. I snare the soaked strawberry in between my teeth and thrust it into her mouth. Then take one nipple into my mouth. It hardens like an erection as the tip of my tongue swirls around its luscious contour. I smother it with our passion juices before targeting the other. A moan escapes Callie's lips and her body jerks. This is going to be sensational. I'm going to get so much pleasure tasting the elixir that will drain from each of her nipples. The goo is light and hard to detect till she hits sensory overload. I suckle like a purring kitten.

Whirling the tip of my tongue over the nipple in my mouth, I increase the pressure. I begin to work on it like a clitoris and nibble with lips, mouth, tongue and teeth all in unison. I change the direction and motion of my dance,

like a drumbeat and it's growing louder. I am captivated by her rhythm. I squeeze the other nipple in my fingers and follow her body as she arches.

Increasing the speed and hardness of movement I taste the delectable flow of tit juice.

"Oh. Oh. God, I'm cumming," I whimper as I buck. An orgasm pulses right through my clit.

I want to make her cum again and taste more juice. Callie's body is in total submission, but I want more. I move into overdrive, switching from one nipple to the other. Dribbling mouth juices all over her nipples. I am relentless in sucking and whirling my lips and tongue in various motions till I hit the precise combination. I don't give it any peace. I test her limits of pressure in increments, staying just below her pain threshold. Each time I feel her level of pleasure increase through my searching tongue, I increase the encumbrance between my fingers. I am turning her body into a shivering pleasure pot and I just love it.

What's happening to my body? My nerve endings are pulsating, uncovering areas I didn't even know could be satisfied. Absorbing each new sensation, each jolt, spasm and erotic explosion, my mind is barely functioning. Each caress of my most intimate body parts from his capable experienced hands leaves me desiring more. My eyes remain closed in bliss as I groan in pleasure.

As I work my way down her body, it's time to build another crescendo. My eagerness is fuelled by my desire to taste more of her sex; this time it will be our mixed cocktail of juices. The alluring smell draws me towards her pussy. I want to swallow her juice. I suck and tease her folds in my mouth, drawing them in like a lure; her viscous squirt feeding my frenzy.

A little voice cautions me, 'Don't break her first time around.' I need to keep that level in the kit bag for another

occasion. It will happen, but not today. Control yourself. Don't make her a train wreck; she still has to be capable of driving home. I bring myself out of my selfish zone. Be gentle I tell myself, nibble, suck and stroke her and keep the delight blissful. Work away at all her pleasure points; breasts, clitoris and G spot and devour those passionate lips to imprint her desire.

Rolling between the soft furs, I'm barely breathing. Holding our embrace, the passion increases in rhythm and intensity. It's a feverish discovery of what we each have to give and receive. Strong hands caress my curves, constantly revisiting my wetness. I will him to put his fingers inside me. Stroking, playing and teasing my G spot, his firm confident strokes melt my inner being. Circling, rimming and massaging, he moves me through highs and lows. He ventures with a strong grip back to my breast, the warm wetness of his tongue flicks over my nipple. He sucks and caresses every inch of my swelling flesh. He moves across to the other breast to bring it to the same aroused state, while his other hand continues to work its magic between my legs.

"Oh... my..." I scream. I convulse and spasm beneath his fingers. He doesn't stop. Continuing to suckle on my breast he tantalises and teases my swelling bud, building the intensity, ensuring my erogenous zones tingle constantly.

I feel the blood pumping through me, pooling and throbbing around my opening, flushing my skin and making me shiver. His tongue grows more savage, ever increasing the intensity, sending ripples of ecstasy through my body.

Finally he pulls back to give me space. I wallow, floating in disbelief at how my body found this place, lingering and enjoying this incredible moment. Leave me here forever.

The sexual connection is intense as I test out how far I can take her, exploring her limits and venturing into unchartered areas. Callie has reignited my addiction. I need

my hit and this Student is going to be my new sex syringe. Her overwhelming potential is pushing all my buttons.

I drink in a shivering, spun out, breathless body. Her heart is pounding so hard, bursting to escape. I'm entranced at the sight. No words are exchanged. A telepathic power is interlacing us.

I have one more phase. I want Callie's pussy to be dribbling. A physical reminder of where she has spent these precious few hours.

I want to conclude with my most challenging position. The sensations that grab my cock as it goes in and out at this angle, tips me over the edge every time. Only if I use supreme control do I stand a chance. When I do rise over the peak, there's nothing like a long session caging a body from behind to deposit deep and direct. I roll Callie over and envelop her delicate frame.

Nibbling and biting on the back of Callie's neck, I grasp her hair, wrapping strands through my lips. Exploring her ear with my tongue, I hear a moan of satisfaction. The tingle of fingertips and smooth long strokes along her naked back comfort as my dancing tongue withdraws and my lips kiss every inch of her delectable flesh.

Flipping me onto my stomach, his breath tickles my ear as Tom blows warm sensuous breaths from behind; it brushes down my neck sending shivers down my spine. His tongue probes my ear as his body pins me down. I turn my mouth towards his, devouring a savage kiss before he kisses the length of my spine, working his way towards my arse cheeks. He spreads my legs wide open and with long slow licks his tongue deliciously teases, strokes and flicks. It feels so erotic from behind. My pelvis rises up to meet his hungry tongue, giving him easy access. His chest slides up my buttocks, his weight fully on my back.

My cock enters Callie from behind in one deep thrust. I want to take her now, I want to lose control and drain

my ball juice. As my cock penetrates deeper, I feel my knob poke at Callie's depths. Overcome with greedy lust, I thrust forward, pushing my hands to the mattress to raise my torso, ramming my cock deep. Her head thrashes from side to side, her fingers clench into spasming knotted balls and her husky moaning sets me off. My balls tighten and sperm spouts out of me at full force, pulse after pulse until I am totally emptied.

Ever thought you could suspend time? Impossible I say, but if it were possible, I would be doing that right now. Our time together dissipated in the blink of an eye. It's time to shake myself back into reality and wash away the love juices we have exchanged. The incessant smell lingers on my senses, but if we don't get organised, it won't be the only human smell around here. It will be my blood all over the floor.

Taking my hand, Tom leads me down the long hallway to his en-suite. A large open window overlooks a lush garden outside. I admire the greenery. A single glass pane encloses the shower with double shower roses. Large marble tiles underfoot complement the light airy feel of filtered light peeking through the open windows from the shimmering afternoon sun.

The water is warm and refreshing as we soap each other down, fondling each other clean. He hugs me close, gazing down into my eyes for a long moment. Water cascades where our bodies meet. How wonderful it feels to be embraced with passion. Kissing him, I feel his tenderness.

But I will have to leave soon.

The cleanup is something that is always the final nail in the coffin. In this case, I had better get it right because this explicit venture of mine is illicit. It seems a shame to hide everything, but I don't have a permit. It's too late to feel guilty now. Besides, I have had the time of my life and it felt fabulous. I don't regret it for one single moment.

We towel dry and wrap up before retracing our steps back down the long, dark hallway to the open fire. Gathering my pieces of clothing that are strewn from one end of the room to the other, I redress, straightening myself up. I scoop up my far-flung shoes and chiffon scarf. I dare not leave any traces behind if I want to play this game again.

Time to put this all in a box. I don't want to even begin to imagine the possible implications and ramifications that may follow. Best I get this over with now. I'm going to sound like a calculated bastard, but there is no other way to do it. It is not my intention, quite the opposite; the positive to take out of this is the opportunity for us to move forward. I just hope that is what I convey. My fingers are crossed.

Tom takes a seat in the large armchair, tugging at my hand, steering my body to sit on his lap. My arse lands on his legs, my legs swing to dangle over the armrest. I sling my arm around his neck, stealing a kiss.

"Now, there are rules," I say as I stare into Callie's eyes.

I am taken aback. *Rules?* Tom stares me down.

"Rule one."

I immediately think, he has done this before; I really am a pawn in his game. How can this be after the most amazing love making session?

"Rule one," I repeat. "This is only between you and I and to be kept totally in a box."

I nod. *Well, I have figured that out already, next?*

"Rule two, this will only ever be fun and will not lead to anything serious."

I nod again. *Okay. I can handle fun.*

"Rule three, you can never ring or text me, we will contact each other by email only."

I consent. *I sort of figured that one out as well.*

"Finally, if either of us wants out, no questions asked, out means out."

Tom has definitely done this before; he even has rules of play. I sit a little embarrassed and totally speechless. My gaze lowers in retreat, nodding in agreement, my heart pounds uncontrollably. I am astonished.

Best to move the program along and not dwell on my lecture. Callie is smart, nothing more needs to be said. A site visit of my place is the best opportunity to change the subject.

Time to go I sense, I offer to help clean up, but he assures me all is under control Tom gives me a tour of his extensive house, from wing to wing. I am totally overwhelmed by its grandeur. The trophy room is an eye opener, I have never seen anything like it, and it's impressive, with antlers hanging on the walls and an enormous bearskin taking pride of place. I feel like I have just been mauled by my own bear encounter.

Walking hand in hand towards my car, Tom swings me around to face him, grabs me and lifts me off the ground. He hugs me so tight I can hardly breathe. Kissing me, I sense he doesn't want to let me go.

"Thank you for a wonderful day."

I am elated.

We share a tender kiss goodbye. It is long, sensuous and lingering. I am completely melting into the ground as his strong arms lower me gently back to earth. Opening my car door to leave, he kisses me again. I sense neither of us wishes this day to end.

I am already thinking about next time, because I can sense there is going to be a next time. My journey with my Student has been initiated. I am swelling with pride. This one is a keeper.

I make my way down the driveway, where only five hours ago I entered, not knowing what to expect. As I pull away, I know I will be dreaming about this day for a very long time. I am in dreamland the entire trip home.

There is no one home when I arrive.

∞

Thank you so much for an amazing day.

Still floating…

XXX

∞

I finish cleaning up our trail of destruction. Callie has the same size feet as Jess, so no need to worry about footmarks. Though, I wipe down the glass and tiles of the shower to dispel the excess water. I throw a lamb roast into the oven and once it starts cooking I open the oven door slightly so the sweet smell masks our afternoon delights. The flutes are washed and sparkling back in the bar cabinet and the dishwasher is humming with two days worth of dishes. A quick trip to the bin to stash anything suspicious, I hide the bag under the other rubbish. The sheets and towels I stash under the mattress in the spare room for a wash tomorrow. Replacing the furniture, I make my final inspection. A whiskey is a smooth way to end this perfect day and compliments how I am feeling. My Teacher would be proud. I raise my glass.

Logging on before I call it a total close, (1) immediately flashes into my inbox. Opening it hastily, I am totally hooked; the desire for ongoing communication is imperative.

∞

A pure pleasure and it was all mine. Thank you.

XXX

∞

7

The logical side of my brain is trying to temper the excited side without much luck. The excited side is winning by a mile, until I roll over. On the other side of my bed is a reminder why I must keep all this in a box. I wish she would let me do it my own way, I sigh.

"Morning, would you like a coffee?" I don't know why I ask. It's a habit; every morning I get Jess a cup of coffee.

"Yes, please," she replies.

"Okay, I'll get you one." I am trying to get motivated.

"What are you doing today?" Jessica asks. I feel like Hercule Poirot has entered the room, I am already looking behind the bushes.

"I need to get up soon. I have about an hour on the computer to tidy-up a business submission."

It's my first lie for the day. Callie starts work in about an hour and I want to get her all wet and horny before she leaves. I hope she will be online as I fuel my need for a cyber-hit.

"After that, there's that pile of mulch you had delivered ages ago, and haven't done anything about. I'm starting to get cranky looking at it every day. It needs to be moved before the cattle scatter it everywhere by playing in it," I say. A job is a cure for my excitement and makes me feel like I am absolving myself. “So what have you got planned?”

“I’m not sure, I might visit my aunt today. She likes me to go the same day each week. It helps with her routine.”

“That will be a challenge.” I raise my eyebrow; the tone in my voice is skeptical.

“What are you saying?”

“You are in town at least three, if not four days a week. Why would it matter which day?” I shake my head, sliding out from under the covers before I get kicked out.

“She is old, and it does matter.”

Why did I go there with that comment? I must be dumb.

“Up to you how you manage that one. I am amazed she is still alive,” I admit, heading towards the door in my birthday suit.

“I know, the number of things she has wrong with her is incredible.”

“How is her skin cancer?” I call out as I head down the hallway to the kitchen.

Returning with coffees in hand.

“Here you go.” I hand the cup of steaming coffee to Jessica and slide back under the covers.

“It’s getting larger, but it won’t kill her, the fluid around her heart will. Once the defibrillator battery shuts down it can’t be replaced.” Jess gazes into her coffee.

“Okay, you do what you have to do, but she is a tough old bird and I reckon she will still be alive after I am gone. The genes on your side of the family are almost perpetual.”

“Everyone has lived to ninety plus, except my dad,” she says.

“I rest my case. On my side, especially the males, have all died by fifty-five, except dad, he made sixty-five. My ticket won’t be for the long haul, I don’t reckon,” I say. The thought makes me more determined about my Student and

to get out and follow my passions. I've been reinvigorated to make that a reality.

"Don't say that," Jess says with a sigh.

"Well, history is a good guide, anyway I need to get started."

I don't want to get into a negative frame of mind to start the day. I need to get online and get my Callie fix to get me through the day.

I am abuzz thinking about my newfound playmate. I haven't slept a wink; my mind is playing games with me, recounting every minute of ecstasy. I'm feeling as naughty as a schoolgirl. Once the euphoria wears off I will need time to reconcile my moral values, until then, I want to keep a lid on things.

I resist the urge to slip downstairs in the middle of the night to see if I have any emails. I can't risk a midnight peek, it'd look too suspicious. It's gripping me, something so stimulating that is affecting my every waking moment and I am still shell shocked. I have been totally and utterly obliterated and I want more. I never knew I had so many fruits that just needed bearing. I can't recall the last time I screamed in ecstasy.

Those rules. Who the hell has rules? How do I deal with that? I have a huge learning curve ahead of me I sense. Everything happens for a reason, I have no idea how long this will last or where it is taking me, but I want to go along for the ride. It's making me so horny. I had no idea my body was capable of such intense feelings and endless peaks, reaching one after the other. Why have I never experienced this before? I have been totally mauled and I loved it.

The bedside clock shows me I have two hours before I need to start my morning shift. Rolling the sheets back, I slip out of bed, and once on the stairs, I race. I feel like a child sneaking about in my own house. While the computer warms up all I can think about is what's on Tom's agenda for the day. More plans I hope. I am craving a cup of tea, but it will have to wait, my usual morning routine is being tossed into turmoil as Tom's emails take precedence.

∞

Morning, Luscious one,

Ready to cyber play? You will get RSI. Do you know what that is?

Repetitive Sexual Inclinations.

Morning to you, too and a good morning it is. RSI? I like your take on that one. Thank you again for yesterday, I haven't stopped thinking about it and neither has my body. A little tender in parts as a reminder, I thought that might make you smile.

I was totally blown away with our session yesterday. I hope I can play the wild card to keep up with those overwhelming testosterone levels.

A woman can handle so much more than a man. You are doing a brilliant job. Just let me play with you and keep you high, it gets me off, not just physically, but in my mind as well.

Oh, well, all right, if you must. Keep me high and please do that to me again, what's a girl to do?

I just get off making you cum and enjoy the experience. Now you know, we just have to plan as much as we can to be together.

Do you want a bonus one?

Well, I have a project for you.

Let's call them fuck projects.

Bonus? Yes, please

Fuck project? Sounds enthralling… Do tell.

When you go to work today, I want you knicker-less thank you. I mean bare-arse under your uniform. It gets my cock hard thinking of you walking around like that.

Bare arse? You are joking. You know what it will do to me don't you? The seam of my work pants will rub on my slit all day making me wet and horny and wanting more of you. You are such a tease and I can imagine your smutty smile as you read this.

Your challenge is accepted and I will update you in my lunch hour, as I will need to come home and change into another set of work pants.

I do however need a hint of my reward for taking up such a challenge.

Want your reward described to you?

Yes, please…

I am going to spin you into another world.

Are you ready?

You'd better be.

You will be dressed in a black lace G string, stockings and suspender belt, your choice of heels

and a black lace bra. I will lay you out flat on my mattress covered in purple satin sheets whilst out in the warm sunshine.

I will gently warm massage oil to squirt all over your body. I want you to squirm and tingle and as I remove each of those garments, one at a time, you will spasm. There will be oil all over your lacy intimates.

Damn. And, all I have to do is go to work half naked for one day and the reward will be a warm oil massage on purple satin sheets in the sunshine? Choices… Choices… you bet I am in on this one.

Clue number two?

I will be manipulating the massage oil so you are slippery and warmed by my sensual touch. I will be working from your head to your toes. You will feel wetness ooze between your legs as oil runs down and makes a mess on those purple satin sheets.

You expect me to be able to work today with thoughts like that running around in my head? My crotch is already wet and the day has only just begun. You are making it extremely difficult for me to concentrate on anything else.

Totally naked, you will feel the power of my eyes penetrating your skin as I inhale your beauty and explore every inch of your delicate curves. I want to massage all your spasm points; starting with your

toes, your big toe in particular. Then I will move up to your hips, to the small of your back, your shoulders, and down your flanks. Finally, I want to cup your breasts and massage your nipples into erection.

OMG. That sounds spellbinding. My body is yours to pleasure, when do we start? Big toe? Mmmmmm… Sounds divine and cupping my breasts? Well, I have had a taste of that already and if I can recall, you made me cum as you sucked my nipples, sending an arousing signal straight to my clit.

Stress and tension disappear, replaced by pure pleasure as I work on the base of your neck. I will be totally naked and will be inches from your face. You will not be allowed to touch, only look and use your imagination, no matter how tempted you are to touch.

No touching? Come on now, that's not fair. You are allowed to work your magic on my body and get me all hot and horny and I can't touch the goods?

How is that possibly a fair deal? I want to negotiate.

My fingers and thumbs work your muscles slowly in a circular motion. Back and forth, repeating until I feel all the oil has penetrated your sensual skin. Rolling you over, using fresh oil, which has been warmed by the sun, I will be massaging the oil into your luscious curves so I can explore every inch of your beauty with my hands.

Okay, so you are a masseur as well? Is there anything you can't do to make a woman weak at the knees and tremble in your wake?

By the way, you have overlooked my inner thighs...

Working your ankles and each leg, I am moving up to your inner thighs coming within centimetres but not quite touching you there...The strokes increase in intensity, polishing up your entire being, both breasts are cupped and your nipples massaged. As I feel you cum, I increase the pressure delving you into a continuous stream of orgasms.

Okay, what's the catch? This is way too rewarding for wearing no knickers to work today. I can barely contain myself with this body exploration. I know how those strong expert hands feel upon my skin, but a complete oil massage and body bliss is all too much for me to take at this time of the morning.

I don't need to read the fine print, where do I sign?

Turning you back over, you are going to love this. Have you ever had a hard-cock back massage? Well, it will go like this; your back will be covered in oil, my chest will massage your legs, arse cheeks and back. I will be tenderly biting you on the back of your neck as you feel my penis tantalising your skin. I will move up to the centre of your back and stop at the base of your neck. The action will be long and slow.

I feel a need building in you as I run my shaft between your arse cheeks and down through your enticing

hot wet vagina lips. Tormenting your need, but not penetrating, teasing all over the small of your back, up to your neck and back down to your pussy lips again. I will leave you hanging as I glide back over and retrace my path.

Torment? That is an understatement. No penetration? How could you? How could you not? I am so wet with anticipation right now I am willing your words, and you, right inside me. I want to feel your oil-laden body encase my frame and pierce me from behind in one slick penetration. Your cock can then discover my inner world as I swallow your pulsing cock-head with my warm, inviting glove of quivering folds.

Ready for the final phase of your reward?
Watch this space.
I will leave you hanging for more...

There is still more? You've got me right on the edge now. Wait till I get my hands on you.

Do you think that was fun? Have I still got you hanging? Now it's your turn to do me. Not with your hands, not with your elbows. No. With oil. Yes, ride the small of my back. I bet that has your imagination running wild?

Now that sounds like a cumming session waiting to happen. I promise to be a good girl and go to work without my knickers on today.

Got to go, start work soon.

Shower time.

Chat soon

XXX

∞

Jumping into the shower, I wash away my wetness, hopefully enough to disguise the sex smell that seems to be continually oozing out of me. I can't believe I have to be at work in fifteen minutes, where did the morning go?

"You haven't had any breakfast."

"No time for breakfast today, I don't feel hungry."

I will have to live off air.

"You should really have breakfast, Callie," Rob tells me, giving me a stern look.

"I'll be okay."

I smile. I have no knickers on and feel naked and very mischievous.

"What time will you be home?" he asks.

"Whatever time I finish," I reply, reminding myself I need to start keeping this vague. I'm going to need some escape time.

∞

How has your day been? Busy here, always the way. I've been working away at the ten-ton mulch heap that needed to find its way into the gardens. I've been looking at that heap for a while and I finally changed that today. Sweaty, hot and ready for a champers?

Just in for lunch and a change of uniform thanks to your little challenge.

I have had a smile on my face all day.

My day has been busy as well, a million phone calls and fires to put out, but nothing out of the ordinary, except for sinfully parading my bare arse around the office, going totally unnoticed and feeling rather fiendish my friend.

I think my sex smell might be a giveaway.

I can smell your womanly scent from here. It's written on your forehead and it will be my pleasure to taste your pussy and relieve your need for a licking and a sucking.

Yes please, I just had a little gush.

Do you wear clothing to bed? If you do I will cut the garments off you and throw them out the window. I don't care how much they cost, flesh only in my bed. These are my rules.

It is going to be oily next time we meet and if you have your wicked way with me on those purple satin sheets, I will be happy to discard any clothing unless otherwise requested.

Back to work.

Chat tonight.

xxx

∞

The last thing I need for my article is a title. Scrolling through the pictures of Ed, Haley and I, there are two that stand out. The mountain vista and Ed and I gazing back up Widow Maker Pass. I type 'Rocky Mountain High' in large bold font. My first draft is complete and I hit print.

"Jess, can you have a read of this for me?"

I wander into the bedroom.

"What is it?" she asks, her eyes glued on the CSI channel.

"One of my hunting stories," I say and push it in front of her with a pen for corrections.

"When this program is finished, I will."

I saunter back up to the office.

I wonder if Callie will have a look and make some comments.

∞

Good evening, Cals,

How are you this evening?

I have attached an article I have written. When you have a few minutes can you have a look and make note of any suggestions or corrections?

I'd really appreciate any feedback you may have.

xxx

∞

Minimising the screen from the emails, I begin to scroll again through the pictures I want to submit. There are just fewer than two hundred to choose from and I narrow it

down to thirty. The whiskey in the tumbler is smooth and the relaxing sensation goes down warmly.

∞

Good evening, gorgeous arse,

How are you?

Received your attachment, will do.

Good evening, Luscious one,

I am well, thank you.

How has your day been?

xxx

It has been very naughty and so much fun. Who needs knickers when you can go bareback?

What are you up to?

Dinner is done.

Okay, got to go for a bit. I'm dying to have a shower.

Back soon.

xxx

∞

I am in my office without suspicion, so I may as well stay here and wait for Mr. Gorgeous to take a shower. The article Tom has sent through is interesting. He is a hunter from the badlands, in and out of the bed. Fifteen hundred words and only a few minor corrections and additions and I have finished editing his article. I wasn't aware he was into writing.

Another string to his bow, and a bit of an insight into what he does in his down time. He has me fascinated. The light bulbs are flashing in my head. I've always wanted to do something different, contemplating a photography venture in the wilds once tickled my fancy, but I never thought about writing. This skill of Tom's has me intrigued.

I place Jessica's coffee on the bedside table, page one is done and the black moustached Poirot is consuming the big screen as a deterrent.

"Don't you ever get sick of Poirot?" I ask.

"No," she says and the biggest smile ever appears on her face, "he's so clever."

"Whatever you say," I say and shrug in dismay.

"I've started on your article," Jess blurts out.

"Thanks. I'm going to have a shower and then going back to select the pictures for it."

I hate CSI more than ever. A shiver passes right through me as I divulge another lie, but I need to talk to Cal again.

∞

Howdy, Luscious one,

Showered and sparkling clean.

Would you like to grind me?

I'd love to grind you…

Did you have a chance to read my article?

Yes, I have read your article, and it is brilliant. I loved it.

I can't believe you have covered so many miles.

You made it sound as if I was looking through your binoculars. I could feel the mountain freshness and I could inhale the seasonal change.

Where did you learn to write like that?

That's a rare skill; wish I had the thought process to put my travels into words.

I'm glad you liked it.

I failed English at school you know.

I find that hard to believe, you seem to have a stylish way with words in my opinion. You could write a book on your adventures, it would be a best seller. 'Out There Doing It in the Wild' by the Mountain Man.

Is that right?

Well, I love writing and get excited about doing those articles; it is another one of my passions.

I don't get paid, I just organise free subscriptions for friends.

I should get you one.

That would be great if you could, I would get a buzz out of reading your published work. I'll bet those pictures you have will look awesome with it as well.

Just make sure you get it sent to my work address otherwise I might be turned into bear bait.

It would be my pleasure. Consider it done.

Thank you very much.

Do you have any back issues I can savour?

Okay gorgeous, I'd better sign off and make an appearance upstairs.

Sleep tight.

XXX

Yes, I will get them out of the closet.

Same, Poirot is probably just about finished.

Sleep wet.

XXX

∞

The Rocky Mountain article sparks a little smirk; I wonder what Haley is up to? Time to drop her a line and find out.

∞

Howdy there, Haley,

Attached are the pictures from our hunt and a hunting story about our Rocky Mountain high adventure.

Still thinking about how good it was.

How is the savings planning going?

Tom

Hey Tom,

Wow. I love it.

When it's printed, can you get me a copy of the magazine please?

Saving already, your tip was the first deposit into the 'Haley Heads Down-Under' fund.

Haley

∞

Tucking myself into bed, it feels good to be horizontal. I could do with a sensual love making session to put me to sleep. I will have to be satisfied with my new bedtime book. The single girl in the office lent me a book today. She's totally into erotica and recommended this new series. She's thirty-two years old and still lives with her mum. I might learn a trick or two and spring it on my illicit lover. I can't have him with all the advantages, especially since he has started giving me challenges. He has me thinking even more now.

"Rob, you need to read this," I say, revealing the cover.

"What?" He asks, sleepy eyed.

"It's about sex," I say.

"Okay, once you have finished," he says rolling back over with a sigh.

I scan the first couple of pages. I close the book and roll over, dreaming of penetration by my mountain man.

∞

Good morning my Luscious Legs,

Sleep wet?

I slept like a log; I think I must have been executed. I went to the dead and it was very quiet. I woke up with a hard log. Want to be splintered?

Morning, Hot stuff,

Splinter my insides with pleasure.

Do you have a busy day ahead?

A busy day ahead I have indeed. I have a long shift today with plenty going on to keep me well entertained no doubt.

What's on your agenda for the day?

Yep, the same at this end, there's always lots to do. It's a beautiful looking day. I have to spend the first half of my day in my office on the computer researching the last segment of a business plan someone shot me through to have a look at.

This afternoon I will be on the farm, they are short staffed today, so I'll be in the mud and water till late. I'll be online after that if you can chat.

Anyway, have a good one. I'll be watching my icon here till lunch to see if you can sneak me a reply. Watch yours, 'cause I have a wicked thought to hit you with to leave you gasping. Heaven help the next person who comes to your desk, they will see a sparkling set of mischievous eyes and smell you are on heat. Sex crazy heat.

Sex crazy heat is making me sweat already and you know what happens when I perspire? The salty clear beads need to be licked from my body one bead at a time. Think you can handle that?

Then it will be my turn to make you sweat and I think I know how I am going to do that.

Have a good one…

xxx

∞

A voice comes from around the doorway.

"I'm going to go and spend a week up in the Kimberleys, there is a vacancy with the bird club up north."

Holy fuck, my computer screen is wide open and another message flashes in and one pops up.

"What's that?" she asks. She might be at the doorway, but she isn't blind.

"That's our email account, I'm in the back end of it rather than Outlook. I wanted to clean up all the old messages."

I can't work out how this excuse comes to me, but it does and slips out easily.

"Oh, I thought you did everything through Outlook," Jess says.

"You can, but it takes heaps longer. The Internet reception is so poor here, you know." I turn back to the job at hand, adding, "Not a problem dear, the Kimberleys will be a great opportunity for you."

"You off to the farm this afternoon?"

Jess continues to hover.

"Yep, Jed has organised for me to keep an eye on his work exchange student from the States. She arrived only a couple of days ago. I'm yet to meet her."

"Wasn't he doing that?" Jess asks.

"He has to be back at his office and asked me to do it."

Jed loves his farm but the office job pays his bills and keeps it all turning over. Presently stuck behind an office desk, he has a plan to retire into farming life, a chance to knock off a few extra pounds and smell the fresh air, while still maintaining a commercial flavour to keep his business brain ticking. Jed is the right person to take over Big Nipper operations. His timing couldn't be better.

"What's her name?"

"Christine. She's only here for a couple of weeks and is doing a paper on the variations between how we do things here and how they compare in Louisiana. Should be interesting to analyse her notes."

I might have sold the operations, but I'm still intrigued by the critters.

"Okay, whatever, I'll be away next week anyway," she says and leaves.

I will need to become sneakier. Stalking around the danger element, the hunter must leave no trail of scent to become the hunted. It will remain like that till my mind adjusts and it becomes routine, it has been a long time between drinks. That is what it takes to live one of my three passions. The excitement element revitalises my core, each time the effect is the same. Intertwining the logical process, which underwrites my passions. It helps eliminate detection and emulates success as I reconcile my in-fucking-curable urge to have a Student.

It's the excitement of survival. I am elated. I type fast using every finger.

∞

What are you doing next week?

You are not going to believe this, but the boss has just told me she is going away for a whole week.

I'll be batching for the entire week. I kid you not.

The weather chart is looking good, and what I have in mind won't be affected by the weather. It'll be more like hot sunny days for washing and drying the sheets.

Interested?

Interested? Are you kidding me?

Bring it on.

I am brewing my excuse as we speak.

OMG. I'm wetting myself.

You are serious, aren't you?

I wouldn't joke or tease you about something like this.

You are kidding me. This is unbelievable.

Booked in, mattress and purple satin sheets, my fuck plan you already have, I might have to include a little surprise, can't have you knowing everything.

Bring it on.

∞

Why do I think this is the start of some incredible stroke of fortune? How is it possible within a week of our first roll in the sheets, we are going to be flung together for a week? We might have to work, but who cares. I have to pinch myself to believe this is happening.

8

It is critical to get Callie back into the sack as soon as possible. She's hot to have her brains hammered out again and I want to keep the momentum pumping. I was planning where we would have our next adulterous encounter when good fortune bestowed itself. A full week together within a week of our first sexy interlude will be fabulous. This is crazy. This has to go down in the classics as far as I'm concerned. I am pinching myself again.

This is going to be our equivalent of the Olympic Games. We have three days to get it together and this Sex Savant better get moving and have a pile of fuck plans in place. With a horny Student in the passion pit, I doubt there will be much sleeping.

'Lucky me,' I crow as I wander around my trophy room punching the air. I haven't felt this high since my last Student. It brings a devilish smile to my face.

∞

Good afternoon, Cals,

Can you believe we've scored a week to nail each other's brains out? Senfuckingsational is the only word that comes to mind. Are you ready to be totally and completely hammered?

Good afternoon to you, Hot stuff,

Bring it on, my bags are packed with air, I won't need clothes. I just bought a carton of champagne and stashed it in my boot. I have a horny pussy and will travel.

Leave it with me to organise the catering for the week. Anything in particular I can tantalise your taste buds with?

Yep, I want your delectable lips for kissing, your tits for sucking, your bud for nibbling, your pussy for fingering, your legs for stroking, and your toes for teasing… that's a start to the menu.

Consider it done.

P.S. My excuse has been bought and I have a week to play.

∞

Our greatest strengths will shine for this lucky break, organising a week of mind-boggling indulgence. I recheck Jess' air tickets and departure confirmation countless times. I am expecting my computer to grow devil horns and ejaculate all over the keyboard as Callie's erotic responses flood into the hard-drive.

∞

All systems are go, let the week long party for two promiscuous consenting born again adolescents start. I'll be in around 7 once we finish at the farm.

I'm fuelled up and ready to hit the road. Ready for my invasion?

Key to unlock the door is under the pot plants on the left hand side as you walk into the outdoor area. The rest I am sure you can work out.

Got to run…

xxx

Okay, see you soon.

xxx

∞

The drive up takes no time, I am excited. I let myself in, peering through the darkness to find a light switch. I dump my bag in the nearby bedroom and wander back out to the car to retrieve the case of champagne and goodies for the week. My first job is to start chilling the champers, a necessity to rehydrate the system, because I know I am going to need it.

Time for a quick shower so I can freshen up. How about a little mauve lace ensemble for tonight? This ought to get Tom's cock hard and my purple heels should get his testicles tingling.

There are so many light switches in his place, I might have to phone a friend. I need mood lighting to provide intimacy and I know the switch will be here somewhere. A glass of champers in hand, the room glows with dim light as I await his arrival. Draped along the kitchen bench in my heels and lacy French knickers, the self-service lane is open and my hot spot is brewing.

Driving up the driveway, I see the lights are on. Callie's car is here, now I can relax. It has all come together and I am about to enter the ultimate shag pit. Bring it on.

Last night I sat on the lounge in my trophy room looking at the antlers on the wall, all memories of my adventures. A bear hide hangs on the wall behind me, a wolf skin

under me. Life has been good. With a tumbler of whiskey in hand and my fuck plan circling around in my mind, I twirl the amber liquid. What would my Teacher have done this soon? I recalled how she just let me explore and nail her some more the second time round. I will use this week for Callie to explore her confidence in the sack. I'll just let her go wild and monitor it and adjust accordingly, her tasty nectar flow will tell me. One thing's for sure, I'm going to be relentless in seducing her. I want her brain to be thinking sex twenty-four seven from now on. My inveiglement strategy is coming together perfectly, maybe a little too perfectly. I've teased Callie relentlessly this week, our first session was mind blowing and all I have to do with this one is hint.

Entering my home, my eyes almost pop out of my head.

"Holy Fuck," I exclaim.

There, in the kitchen, is a sex goddess. I'm speechless. Swathed in mauve lingerie, draped to those curves, Callie's dark olive skin contrasts with the softness of the overhead light. Her 'come fuck me' heels complete the image. I have an instant urge to devour her and I don't care to take my time right now.

"Sorry, Teacher," I whisper, "I have to have her."

I lock my lips on Callie's—all day I have been tormented with wicked thoughts as our hot emails kept my cock tingling. I finger her through the lace, quickly finding her entrance. I hook my digit between the fabric and her soft skin. With a long swipe I sever her seal, feeling her folds throb and her slit pulsing. My finger dives in deep and moulds into her G spot.

Callie spasms, I watch her eyes close, her hands grab the bench-top for support and I feel her rush as she arches back and cums all over my hand. I am delirious as my need to deposit a load takes on a new urgency. Standing back I drop my shorts and underwear, they fall in a heap on the floor and I kick them out of the way. My cock is ramrod hard. Spinning Callie around, I hitch the lace to one side and pierce her drenched opening to massage her lips with my cock-head. I tease her clit with my wet knob. Holding my cock across the length of her velvet entrance, Callie gushes all over me. Collapsing onto the bench-top, her arms spread wide, her gorgeous arse raises high in a raunchy arch. I am going to take her as the lust for my own release takes over.

Pulling back, I go straight for penetration, almost lifting Callie off the bench with the first thrust. The next thrust lifts her as I hit her deepest depths. Pulling her down hard, I hold still, I want to feel her cum on the end of my cock-head. Callie's scream goes straight through me, it triggers me to fire my essence into her, pulse after pulse, matching her climaxing highs.

The edge is taken off. I withdraw as our mixed juices dribble to the floor. My eyes roll back as relief overwhelms. I needed that as if it was the only thing on earth that mattered. The planet could have blown up and I wouldn't have cared one little bit, I was having my own explosion.

I scrape Callie off the bench-top giving her a passionate tongue entangled kiss.

"I needed that," I tell her. "Welcome, you look unbelievably gorgeous tonight."

"You nearly killed me with that entrance."

"Man, what an outfit. And those heels... You are one hot sex kitten on luscious legs."

I'm impressed and I know this is going to be one very dangerous Student, I am sensing all round, and we have hardly begun our journey.

"Find everything?" I ask. "Looks like you managed to light the fire okay."

"Yes, thank you, I made myself at home," I say. "Let me get you a glass of champers."

At the fridge, I bend in a little as I open the door. Exaggerating my pose, wiggling my tormenting butt in Tom's direction. I sense he is admiring the tease.

"I need a shower, but I have to stay here for a while and admire the view. You look exquisite tonight."

Leaning on the bench I see the dribble I created and the chilled glass coming my way.

"How was your day at the farm?"

"Excellent, we have a research student from Louisiana visiting at the moment. She is really switched on and loves it. It's been good to show her around so we can compare notes, especially the science verses the practical," I tell her.

I change the focus, not wanting to let this pass without absorbing the splendour. I'm captivated by the image before me and now it's time to take Callie all the way.

Tom holds me around the waist and guides me back into the deep lounge chair. The fire creates a soft glowing light. An allover body caress tingles my senses as his kisses drop to my toes. Tenderly, he arouses the flesh on my legs as he awakens my inner thighs, I feel cum ooze between my legs. My eyes close. I want to behold this sensation and wallow here for eternity. I feel a gentle pressing of his lips to mine with so much passion I feel like I am going to erupt with raw emotion. Soft licks of his tongue explore my every inch, melting me with each kiss and caress. He is merciless with an intensity that lasts for what seems like hours of pure indulgence.

His tongue reaches my nipple. It's electric, tongue to nipple, nipple to tongue, massaging, kissing, caressing and sucking. Agonising and deliberate in intention, he kneads my breast with passion. It is a slow, gentle arousal from deep within my core. I am awash with delight, climaxing in the pit of my sex. Overtaken with a flushing of perspiration upon my skin, I take his growing engorged knob. Pushing into my flesh, he lays on top of me, the full force of his shaft yet to be infused. Holding me tight, bound in passionate embrace, strong and safe. Tom's lips toy with mine. His tongue is masterful, he wants me, and I want him. I want him buried deep inside, filling me.

"Oh, god… take me… take me…"

Tom's penetration is deep and his strokes have me clenching my spasming flesh. I am being annihilated as the physical energy is sucked out of me.

Withdrawing, my fluids glisten like a thick glaze on his length. I want more.

"Do me like that again, please," I beg.

"I want you so bad, I need to taste you," he says, descending for more.

Tom's ravenous tongue trails down my skin cresting my curves and crevasses in its wake. Wet-kissing my erect clit and as he goes down on me, I begin to shiver. The intensity builds until I am engulfed in a constant series of multiple orgasms. My entire body is tingling, writhing and flexing. His soft, wet tongue coaxes my swollen clit again. I grasp his hair as he sends me into Nirvana. All I can manage is "Tom…" in a whisper.

Gathering me up in his strong embrace, he relocates me to the bedroom. He is gentle as he lays me on the sheets and his masculine body hovers over mine. He inserts his cock like an arrow, propelling straight into me with one lash. He is embedded deep with gyrating possession.

Gazing into my eyes, he makes deep, passionate love to me, stroking every inch of my internal being. I am lost in ecstasy, my moist opening eagerly swallowing his throbbing tool. I take in every inch of him as my internal folds pulse and suck his entire length. My body starts convulsing as he pins me down tight and pushes deeper inside me, hitting my bodily limit.

He loosens his tight-hold, and without a word invites me to merge my body with his. He aptly holds me, giving me permission to grind my clit against his flesh as our love juices ooze onto the bed and I gush in convulsing swells.

With heavy breathing, he invades me, possessing my whole being. His balls tighten as his cock pulses in my depths. He roars as the last fierce stroke sends his senses soaring. I take his jism, every last drop. Clamping harder, using my spasms to stroke and squeeze his shaft, he fills me with his nectar, pushing me over the edge. I moan in ecstasy.

The morning sunlight filters through to our final resting place. Callie is wrapped around me like a cloak. I am totally embraced. I don't want to be extracted. A selfish urge grows; it's my morning habit. My day breaker pulses as I roll Callie over and plant an early morning load of semen into her to start the new day.

Sex, coffee and a bubbling hot spa is our morning protocol this week. Naked, we climb in to enjoy a warm soak.

"Have you ever used a firearm?"

I know the answer. Callie's only touch of a firearm is what hangs between my legs.

"No, why?" I ask, excited, biting my bottom lip in curiosity.

"I have planned a few activities this week and one of them is teaching you to shoot. And, I don't just mean my cock."

The way her hand is around it now, is a good first start. A nice firm grip massaging up and down my shaft, I steal a kiss.

"Sounds like fun," I say, "can I hold your cock when I squeeze the trigger just like this?"

I take my hand up his entire length, running my finger through his hole to push my fingertip in.

"Only as long as I can have my finger on your target." I lean forward and flick her folds, placing my fingertip on her bud.

"Sounds like a deal to me." With a jolt, I release his cock, slipping and half drowning in the process. The spa water splashes over the sides.

"Anytime you are with me I will always be taking every opportunity to place my finger, toe or tongue on your bud to make you cum, in private or public," I declare.

"Now you have me scared," I say, "you would have me collapse on a street corner?"

I twinge in anticipation.

"How about we set up a target range and put a heap of holes into it? I like to use oranges as they explode in all directions."

We rub noses staring into each other's eyes as the water laps.

A mattress lies on the grass nearby and the firing range is set. Oranges are strung to the wire fence alternating with full cans of cola for maximum effect. A pillow rest in place, prone, we both lie there naked as we line up the first target. The safety instructions and technique are preliminaries, like sex education, you should be wearing plastic. We had that honest conversation day one. The thrill of the first explosion is what it is all about.

I whisper,

"Squeeze the trigger, don't pull it, just squeeze."

Callie squints, lining up the first orange through the telescopic sight. The end of the barrel steadies for the critical moment as she squeezes the hair trigger.

"Look, look, I got it."

I'm already hooked. I didn't expect orange pieces to scatter everywhere.

"Excellent shot, right on the money. You got it, that's for sure."

Cute arse.

Mastering technique and balance, oranges and cans disappear as Callie piles up the empty brass cases. Reloading the magazine with fresh food for the rifle, the whip-crack starts again. The way Callie has mastered the use of a rifle doesn't surprise me. She's a natural in and out of the bedroom.

As the last shell is extracted from the breech, Callie sprawls on the mattress and I sense the outdoor bed is about to become a sponge. I see the look in her sparkling eyes as I anticipate another nailing is about to happen.

"Fun, wasn't it? You are like a kid that has found a lollypop in the candy shop and wants to suck it for all it's worth."

I retrieve the rifle to make sure it's safely unloaded and out of harm's way.

I feast my eyes, taste her sweetness, smell her hotness and soak up her aura as I feel my flesh on hers. It is divine.

"One last thing we need to do before we knock off. Would you like a bike ride? Let's go and put those sheep away."

This job needs doing before it gets too late in the day. The shadows are starting to descend.

"Of course, I love spreading my legs around you," I tell him and we stride to the shed, hand in hand, wearing nothing but our naked butts.

I'm having the time of my life. I mean, who goes bareback on a quad bike, rounding up sheep? This is the best day ever. *Pinch me.*

The outside spa is our shag pit for tonight. Situated on a large elevated timber deck overlooking a tropical garden. We are in an oasis of birds of paradise, beautiful plants and palm trees towering above the lower canopy, silhouetting against a stardust sky. It's my favourite time of day. There is a slight breeze swaying the elephant ears and various blossoms emit nectar attracting the night critters. The Milky Way turns into a spectacle overhead, levitating us with awe. It touches me greatly.

"Did I ever tell you where I think we come from?" I ask Callie.

"No."

"I lost interest in the Almighty from above when my sister died at twenty-one from the big C. I thought if there were an Almighty, he would have tapped her on the shoulder... That didn't happen," I say. I survey the starlight and visualise an image of her in my mind.

"I'm so sorry to hear about your sister. It does make you wonder why, doesn't it? It's all part of the journey and some journeys are longer than others," I say, conscious of Tom's haze and deep sadness.

"Discovery channel had a series on how scientists think the world all started. I just loved it. I can relate to it so much. The star dust theory, I call it," I continue scrutinising beyond our realm into the illuminated night sky.

"Stars have always amazed me, too."

I feel the connection, staring into the never-never.

"They explained it simply, pieces of everything close by collided and swirled around till it formed our planet. Then more stuff collided as another planet hit, and what was left created the moon. Everything here came from the stars. As a result, the bits we are made up of are from the stars. We are all stardust."

I raise my glass and toast to the stars. A tear trickles, I know it's a simple explanation, but doesn't need to be any more complicated.

"I love your theory. Thank you for sharing." I wrap my arms around Tom, snuggling in close as the water glistens. I hold him tight.

"We only shine for a short time," I say and another tear trickles. I believe both my sister and father are stardust again.

"So, what's your greatest dream?" I whisper.

"I have three passions; more time in the mountains, doing all the things I love like hunting, fishing and climbing those peaks while I'm still physically able," I share. "I don't want age to beat me. I need to make changes to make it all happen."

"That's why you want to go to New Zealand to live?" I ask, "And hunt more bears?"

I sense a real desire.

"Yes that's exactly what I'd love to do," I say. "I also love to write. I was dumb at English at school, but it's something that pushes my buttons."

I turn my head to look Callie in the eyes. I place the rim of my glass on her lips, tilting it up gently.

"What are you going to write about? I loved your Widow Maker Pass story," I say as I move my legs through the water and wrap them across his. My fingers twirl Tom's chest hair as I stare into his eyes. "You are just like a big cuddly bear with a secret cave of treasures."

"Probably a hunting book or something like that," I say, caressing Callie's legs. "Something that maps out a real adventure and the difficulties along the way."

"Oh really? I still think whatever you write will be a best seller... So, what's the third thing Big Bear?"

"Fucking," I say, creeping my fingers towards her tenders, "because I love to make a woman cum endlessly."

"Maul me then… Bear," I say with a tease.

"I'll give you a bear hug and mauling alright." My eyes become beady.

Stealing a kiss, Tom swoops me up through the water without a moment to take breath. He perches me straight on his knob, filling me with his hard-on. My body reacts with synergy, my pelvis moving in unison with his dangerous thrust. Eyes burning, I'm ensconced in his solemn stare, entranced and overwhelmed in unadulterated lust.

Lying on top of him, I kiss him again with long, slow, mesmerising kisses. I slide off him and come down to earth for a microsecond. His finger inserts deep inside my sodden entrance, massaging my folds. Extracting his finger, he parts my folds for a climaxing bud massage. He's there, straight on my sensitive clit, and the rimming is relentless.

Shifting me above the water with gentle care, he places me onto the spa cover. He drops his lips to corrupt my clit with greed. His mouth attacks. My bud is throbbing, my breath is faint and my body is limp as tears trickle from beneath my closed eyelids. He is determined to finish me off.

It is incredible to think it is Sunday evening already.

'Where has the time gone?' I ask myself.

Tonight, I have been put on notice. My Student has issued me with instructions. It's a scary thought. I've been letting her feel her way around the shag pit and Callie is already demonstrating why she will be my ultimate Student. When you find your ultimate student, you let them grow and bloom naturally.

"Sit on the lounge and don't move an inch," I insist.

A wooden chair is less than a metre from my line of

sight. Placed to ensure the viewing distance is perfect. The generous lounge chair allows me to sit comfortably and relaxed. I am anticipating a raunchy performance.

Callie enters the room, the timber floors echo with the sound of delicate heels. The dim room, whilst massive, only features the two metres surrounding my chair at present. The music begins, it has a heartbeat base, and speaks out with hot desire. It is a timeless and seductive piece.

In the dim, hazy half-light I feast on Callie's edible curvaceous silhouette. Exposed in fishnet stockings, a suspender belt, sexy lace knickers and matching bra, she's beautiful. I sit aghast. Callie's flesh revealing body stocking barely covers her arse and has me salivating. Killer six-inch heels, free flowing hair and feather boa floating over one shoulder, all in wicked black. My heart races as my Student begins to weave her magic across the dance floor. This time, it is the queen-bee who is looking for honey and my role is to satisfy her need for sweetness as she injects herself with my cock.

Now it's my turn for the kill. I'm going to bowl him over with this little number tonight. My heart beats faster as I set the scene and make my presence known. Lifting one leg, I place my toes on the seat of the chair, casually resting my elbow on my bent knee. My mating dance begins.

Alluring. Sensual. Sexy movements with a blown kiss and a wink are all part of the build up. I want to be well rewarded for my efforts.

Legs, flesh, and flirtatious invitation, I have my prey captivated and entranced. Stunned in my spotlight, enticing him into provocative entrapment, his eyes ravish my body. The floor providing a platform for my clinching finale, I slither towards him in a cobra-like gesture, slinking up his body. I bite his tongue in scorching possessiveness, my greedy hand fondling his cock. He is all mine tonight.

It's a late finish at work tonight as I clink onto my mobile phone to send a text message.

∞

On my way

Looking forward to making your wait worth it

Feeling fit as a fiddle…

Ready?

You better believe I'm ready.

See you soon Big Bear.

XXX

∞

Tonight, I have scattered tea-lights from the front door to the fireplace. There's not a light in the house, only seductive fire flames and soft light from the dotted tea-lights. My romantic setting looks sensational. Champagne in hand, I casually swathe myself over our well christened chair, my legs spread wide.

Tonight, I am wearing stiletto heels and barely there intimates, all in black of course. I have set the romantic scene. I wait for Tom's car to beam lights up the driveway.

Tonight, my heart is frantic.

Ascending the curved path of the driveway, I peer to my right at the expanse of building. From my car window, I see the reflection of the fire, roaring in orange fury. The main lights seem to be switched off. I walk towards the glass door, my eyes feast on the array of food carefully

laid out on the kitchen bench. Before I register any specific ingredients, I am lured in like prey by hundreds of small flickering candles amassing the room. A chain of flames leads to the chair in front of the blazing fire. There, in black lingerie, draped across the chair in stunning sexy heels, my goddess awaits, her legs spread wide open in proposal. Like a dog tied to a knell, I am drawn to the end of the chain.

"You look simply divine tonight," I whisper, kneeling in front of her sharing a kiss, "but I'll need a quick shower before I devour you."

In record time, I am refreshed. Feeling a surge through my cock, I pause for a moment. I feel the stare of my Teacher. 'Yes,' I mutter to myself, 'I know. You are right, that is why she is here breaking all the rules. I promise not be selfish.'

"I'm battered, shattered and legless. That was intense, Cals," I exclaim rolling in her arms.

"That was unbelievable," I gasp.

"Refreshments and spa time?" I suggest.

"Sounds good to me."

"What time did you get here?"

"I got an early mark from work and was here around three."

Pleased with my timing so I could setup the candles and get ready for Tom's invasion.

"Here, let me pour you a drink."

The first one disappears and the bottle is discarded on the second round.

"I'll go and get another one, back in a second," I say, getting out of the water.

I return with more supplies.

"Did you know your phone is flashing?"

"Shouldn't be, I'll just go and grab it."

I'm a little wobbly, a Tom dusting and a couple of glasses have gone straight to my head.

"There's something wrong, I've had several missed calls and a dozen messages."

A massive hit of panic sends shivers through me.

I can sense all is not well by her body language. Her naked body is shivering. I take a couple of deep breaths.

"You are not going to believe it but where Rob was playing golf, someone was hit by lightning last thing this afternoon and it was on the news. He has been trying to call me to let me know it wasn't him. He has called everyone he knows trying to get hold of me."

We stand in stunned silence.

"When was the first call?" I say, trying to get some semblance of order about the situation.

"About four hours ago." I am bewildered, shivering where I stand, my phone still in my shaking hand. "Best thing for me to do is to text Rob and let him know I'm okay."

"Sounds like a plan to me, what are you going tell Rob?" Tom asks.

"I'll say I was out with a couple of friends and I left my phone in my car."

How quickly all this can turn south.

"He'll buy that okay?"

"Yep, I'm sure he will. Though, in future I'm keeping my phone a little closer at hand. I guess I had better go home and make sure he is okay," I say.

Getting caught isn't in my plans.

"Of course not, we are having way too much fun."

"Lucky this happened at the end of our time together, it has been an amazing week, thank you."

"Will you be okay to drive?"

“Yes, thank you for your concern and thank you once again for a fabulous week, I’ll email you when I’m home safe.”

∞

Thank you for an amazing week. Every minute was simply to die for.

Home safe and all is well.

Don’t really understand what all the fuss was about, but I had to sit through the stories anyway. His mate is okay, so everyone is relieved. He didn’t even ask about my week. It has been a good distraction.

Thank you again.

Can’t wait to c u xxx

∞

9

Hungry for one another, our obsession and infatuation for each other has been growing exponentially as we steal any opportunities for an interlude. Callie's body is covered in sweat, her hair a saturated tangled mop, and her eyes are bloodshot from the euphoric high of our sex romp. It is amazing her speech is not slurred. Her coordination is a bit wobbly as I help her into the hot tub.

Relaxing in the spa, I'm feeling very chuffed with myself. Nibbling away on freshly peeled king prawns, my drink of choice in hand, I would regard this as the most inappropriate time to be discussing any potential work project. Have you lost it, Cals?

Did I interpret correctly what she has said? I haven't had a sip of my bubbles yet. Hasn't she been listening to me? Did she have a brain snap? Doesn't she understand my future vision? Is she infuckingsane? Somehow Callie mentioned the words 'project' and 'work' in the same sentence. I need to do her again, this time without mercy.

I'm going to place my big toe on her clit to remind her why she is here. I direct my massive foot along Callie's inner thigh in a direct line to her bud, gazing directly into her eyes.

Her swollen bud is still erect and there is an instant connection. Her bud rolls and massages itself and in less than a minute an aftershock is officially recorded. But I'm not finished, applying more pressure as Callie almost climbs over the edge of the spa trying to disengage. Her hand grabs my foot holding it firm, now I have her pinned. The multi-flow of orgasms is intense, her face twists, her lips curl and eyes spasm as every muscle in her body contracts. Callie is spun out.

My eyes are glazed with tears, my awareness is somewhere between conscious and barely cognisant. Admiring the naked body floating opposite me, I am in dreamland. Conversant with the familiar surrounds, I have been taken to new highs with skilled seduction. I am scarcely managing to detect the lingering shivers on the curves of my skin.

Taking a deeper breath in order to find a touch of reality, my brain talks to my hand as I administer a sip of bubbles without spilling any liquid down my bare chest. The effervescent sparkle tickles my nose and tantalises my tongue as I savour the familiar palate.

The day is stunning and the outside surrounds enrapture my senses as the leaves gently dance between wisps of wind. Birds come and go, settling from time to time for a drink from the stone birdbath. A trio shuffle in to nibble from the seed tray nestled into the fork of the tree directly in front of us.

I have been toying for a while about the possibilities of a shared project with Tom. I think we would work well together. With our mix of skill packages and can-do attitude, we could make anything work. If passion and drive are core ingredients, we are on our way. Who knows the outcome, inevitably that is our future, I hope. It is all about the journey, we have no destination, and I would love Tom to be part of my journey.

"So, horny bear, as I was saying, I've been thinking about an undertaking and it might be something that pushes your buttons," I say, "before you rudely interrupted me with your toe trick. You are the only one I know who would have the skills to make it happen with me."

I chuckle, knowing we would make the ultimate team.

"Really?"

"I was thinking we should write a sex manual," I say and can see I have his attention.

"Do you really think anyone would be interested? Or, should I say, give a fuck?"

I'm caught off guard and a little dumbfounded.

"Hey, the stuff I've been on the receiving end of would be the ultimate manual. You will have to change your identity. There will be so many women after you."

It's my turn to get the puzzle in his head working. I know he is good at this.

"I know exactly what you are up to."

Callie is cooking up something and my skepticism is turning to suspicion very quickly. This could make everything ten times more complicated.

"Is that right?"

"Absolutely."

She thinks she has me hooked, the bait is there.

"You know me too well, it will be interesting and challenging, but I think we could do it," I say, acting blasé, letting my arms hang over the sides of the tub.

"You are targeting two of my passions," I say. I am intrigued.

"I know," I say, "and not by accident I might add."

"I suspected. Another glass of bubbles please, and let me think about it."

Callie knows exactly what pushes my buttons.

I recline and submerse myself deeper into the warm water, resting my head on the side, surveying the clear blue sky for further inspiration. Tom caresses my leg with tender strokes.

We both share some silent thinking time. I know I have his brain engaged—I can see it in his eyes.

I am infatuated. I can't imagine life without my bear now. My day is filled with sneaking in raunchy emails in the hope of a returned response, a captivating word, and a tempting dare. What started out as taking a playmate has taken precedence over all else, nothing else matters.

I feel like I have borrowed a new book from the library. The old one on the dusty bookshelf at home is looking tired and worn. Over the years it has gathered dust and is a little tattered on the corners. The new one I have my hands on is exciting to read. Every word is novel and engaging. I can't put it down.

Inhaling him in, I sense his big blue eyes piercing my soul. I know he is pondering the options. Tom's business analyst side is ticking over. A smile gathers on his face. It's uncanny how alike we are, always on the same page. I love his quick wit and cheeky personality which has been so much fun to peel open layer by layer. Our relationship has developed so quickly. It makes my heart swell with happiness. Tom drops a hint every now and then of how he really feels when he lets his guard down. We are kindred spirits in a parallel universe and having met, I believe, is fate.

"It means we will have to keep this secret society life going as a minimum, till it is completed," I say, my tone serious.

"Sure. Want to give it a go?"

I beam a sly grin his way.

"Be patient, let me think about it," I say. I need to change the subject. "So tell me more about your yoga?"

I need to give my brain a chance to think all this through.

"Yoga I practice for my wellbeing, I like to keep fit and healthy. It's so good for you."

"I'd like to give it a go," I tell her. It sounds very refreshing, I must do some research.

"You will have to come along to a class one day," I jest. "When Rob is away, we can wing it. I'd like you to have a go, it'll be good for you."

"Only as long as I can come to a pole dancing lesson as well," I challenge.

"No males allowed. Sorry."

"If I told anyone my fuck buddy was a yoga guru, pole dancer extraordinaire and is one hot, horny woman, they would think I'm on drugs." It all sounds too good to be true, but somehow I have stumbled across the most delectable Student.

"It's a weird mix, I know."

"I know, and work makes it hard to balance all these things, plus me in the picture," I acknowledge, titling my glass.

"Juggling is my forte."

"Yogi, it takes both of us to make this happen," I say, as 'Yogi' somehow enters my head. I guess this comes from yoga, though I do cackle about the character Yogi Bear.

"It does," I say, surveying the gardens beyond. "It isn't always easy."

Yogi, how cute.

"The challenge is for both of us to manage our relationship and yes, we are going to have a few bridges to cross. I know we will. We would be naive to think we wouldn't," I add.

"Well, I never thought I would go this far, but here I am, so go figure?"

Lying back I close my eyes and contemplate. This is definitely a break in the rules department. I weigh up the pros and cons. As I have grown older, I have been focusing on making my life simpler, divesting. The capital that makes me tick gets less and less. My life expectancy of capabilities to roam the mountains is dissipating. The

mountains are timeless and they are not going to wait for me. This project can work, an even bigger plus. I'm thinking about this objectively.

For twenty-five years this desire has been my core dream. Until I started making major changes it was like the wind, everywhere all around me, flirting with my imagination, yet impossible to grasp. I'm not there yet, but I can taste it. This project ignites my passions, the more I think about it the more I like the idea. I take another sip of my drink as my mind whirls in thought.

I have no children to follow in my footsteps. I have my trophies on the wall, but I want to make a mark in the world beyond this space. I can see how clearly this project and my desire to live closer to the mountains can bolt together. I can travel with this project and still realise my dreams. There is a synergy that could bind my passions and the light bulbs are coming on. My entire being is being revitalised. I hope I am up to the challenge. If we can bring this together, it would be incredible, but it will be a massive task for both of us I'm sure. Not every day will start as a diamond but the challenge will be for us to make every day finish like one.

"Okay, back to your sex manual, Cals. I've never really thought of doing anything like it, but as you know I am at the end of a chapter in my life and passion number one could bolt nicely into the plan. I was always wondering how the other two could be blended," I say. I feel a tingle of inspiration as the relaxing warm water swirls around me.

"Change is a good thing and if we get our thinking caps on, we could massage around some ideas and really make this work. I think we have the skills between us, don't you?"

I push a wave of water across and over Tom's chest, touching his cock as I glide my hand past.

"Skills to do it? You are kidding me. We have a package of skills between us that are capable of doing anything."

I know we would make a formidable team.

"You think we could pull it off?"

"The biggest tick in the box is our organisational skills and we will need creativity, lots of creativity."

"I think we can do it." I stroke his penis and run my finger along the centre, cupping his balls in my hand.

"It doesn't mean anyone will want the end product, they will probably think it is rubbish. You have to remember, I failed English."

"No pain, no gain."

"Okay, I'm in," I concede. She's got me.

"Really? You like the idea? Best to chew off one bite at a time and see how it develops from there. Two heads are better than one, they say."

Callie leans her head forward and turns to face me with a diamond twinkle in her eyes. Our relationship has been kept in a box. We are contemplating starting a project, a sex manual of all things, what are we thinking?

This will add a new dimension I had never even considered. It is so different to any other type of assignment I have undertaken. This one has side benefits, Callie in the sack. And no, I'm not thinking with my dick.

With a change in direction of conversation, my mind swings back into gear.

"Now, what is more important? Doing it or talking about it?" I ask. We tangle like two octopuses, arms and legs meshing together for the remaining hour.

We share a long sensual kiss leaning against Callie's car. As she bends to get into the car I take the liberty of fondling her arse and crotch.

"That feels so good," I say.

"I wish I could stay longer so you could insert that tool of yours back into me," I say, feeling a wet trickle.

"Okay Yogi, get your arse out of here, travel safe. I'll be online tonight."

"I will be too, if I'm not surrounded."

"Excellent."

"It will be my pleasure," I say, blowing him a kiss.

"Thank you so much for this afternoon and thanks for travelling up here today," I add, pushing the car door shut.

"It has been my pleasure, enjoyed every moment Mr Bear."

We struck it lucky with this space, both of us managing the day off work to sneak in an afternoon of indulgence. Departing from our fantasy pad, reality bites again as my mind tackles the mayhem of frantic traffic in front of me. It deflates me. We need a weekend of play. I must devise something so we can share another overnighter. I send a sneaky text. I hope he looks at his mobile before he gets sprung.

I want to fuck u all night long.

My mobile lights up.

Bring it on...

xxx

My analyst functions are in motion. We are going to need a business structure. It is no longer if, but when. The wheels are in motion. It didn't take much to hook me in. Callie knew this would grab me. I know I've been outmanoeuvred, she has definitely inveigled me with this one, but that's okay as this could be serious fun.

Evening chores finished, I am busting to log on and check my inbox. There are a hundred things floating around in my head. I want to start right now. I am almost jumping out of my skin. I had better get a handle on

all this excitement otherwise the only thing that will be exciting around here will be the undisclosed disposal of my body.

This is a black project and the half shadows created by the semi darkness get my mind into the mood.

There's a (1) in my inbox.

∞

Thank you for a wonderful day, I am still spinning…

Thank you, it was my pleasure. Awesome afternoon and I can't wait till next time.

xxxxxxxxoooooooxxxxxxx

Bet your mind is in overdrive.

You bet. I was thinking, we have to set up something at the front end. It will end up being a business, so we should have something in place from day one. It will be easier to do now, rather than later. We probably have things we will need to register too.

I agree, I will research some options and let you know what I can find out.

The problem to do this is we will need to engage an accountant, and once we do, one extra person knows about us and is in the loop, and 'we' will not be a secret any longer.

I know and it does worry me as we have done so well to keep 'us' under wraps. We will have to outsource some things and I don't think that can be avoided if we want to make this happen.

Okay, I will think about it. I do know someone I can talk to and we can possibly use his address as a registered office to keep everything away from our home addresses.

Sounds like a plan. I will leave it with you and I will work on the other side of things.

I will look at the simplest structure. I have some ideas on that one, but since I haven't done this sort of thing for a while, I'll need some extra help.

I will secure a post office box for any correspondence.

I agree. A P.O. Box for mail makes good sense. Any idea where?

I'll choose a location between our homes I think.

It's exciting, in more ways than one. Bring it on.

It is exciting and I have a good feeling about it all.

The best thing is, we can use technology to make it all work, and we don't need stock or any physical stuff. We can do it anywhere on the planet, just as long as we have Internet connection.

We'll end up being computer nerds. You got your nerd hat on yet?

Suits me, don't you think?

The power of the Internet is amazing and the way in which social media interaction has taken off, it's like a new way of life. It will help us I reckon.

It is a new way of life and our challenge is to keep up with the technology.

And it's only going to get bigger.

We need to keep ahead and up to date with the latest social media ideas as well.

You got pole tomorrow night? Can I come and watch? I'd like to be the pole.

Yep, pole tomorrow night. No males allowed in the viewing room. I keep telling you, you'll have to wait for a private show.

Sleep wet.

Sweet dreams…

∞

It takes me half the night to let my mind settle and rest. Tackling a project with Tom is overriding my natural sleep patterns as I toggle with the endless possibilities. I am quietly excited. More time with Tom will be fabulous, and with an extra challenge thrown in, a change will raise our relationship to another level.

My morning habit is coffee, computer, coffee and back to my computer for my email fix. I hope Callie is online. I have free time at this end as Jess has her coffee and chills out at the other end of the building.

∞

Good morning, Luscious one.

xxx

Good morning to you,

My mind kept me up all night and I have come up with some great ideas already. I'm excited.

My mind has been spinning and I'm excited beyond comprehension. I'm full of ideas. Get your head around a name. We will need something catchy.

I will. We'll brainstorm it tomorrow afternoon, if I am not too broken.

It will be the next day for sure.

Ha, ha. So cool and calmly said…

I've been thinking, we really need to map this out heaps. There is so much to cover and we will easily get sidetracked.

I agree, it will be a huge learning curve, but I think we can do it.

Hit it like a well lubed, juiced up sex romp, which is the thought process behind it all. That will drive it big time and make it a success.

It will, with us in the drivers seat.

We are both passionate about our chosen subject.

We have the skills to keep plugging away at it.

Who knows where it will take us?

This is just the next phase to add to the mix, to keep it different.

Yep. Probably in more ways than we realise. I have to say the intensity is about to go off the planet and into outer space. Awesome.

I agree and we don't really have to add anything to the existing chemistry.

Okay, have a good one. I'm off to the farm.

XXXXXXXXXXXXXXXX

∞

"Good morning Christine, how are you today?" I say.

"Well, thank you. I'm finally accustomed to the time change and the accommodation is awesome," she says.

The second floor of our workshop also serves as accommodation and even though it's basic, it is comfortable.

"So, what's on the program today?" I say, to let her set the agenda.

Christine's freckly face beams a willing smile, her long red hair is scraped back neatly for a day out on the field. She might be a bit vertically challenged, but there is a country girl's toughness in her movement. She's a mature aged student trying to reinvent herself for the next chapter of her life.

"I want to go out and check my experiments and do some more water testing to compare my data," she says.

Two days of rain have made the place muddy. My gumboots gather five inches with each step. I'm accustomed to staggering around in the mud, but Christine is a bit of a greenhorn in tow, like a staggering drunk. It's hilarious to witness. She is really enjoying being out here in the elements. Huge earth walled ponds contain two million litres of water, aeration systems and predator protection. I'm enjoying sharing my knowledge. I'm not concerned about competition or intellectual property and we need more students with working knowledge to give the industry a better chance of survival. The thought brings a wry smile to my face as she trips over and her notepad tumbles over the bank of a pond.

"Are you okay? Leave it, I'll get it," I say.

I slip down the embankment. She blushes and laughs

as she dusts the dirt off her hands and brushes the knees of her jeans that are filthy with brown clay mud. Her jeans are snug as she readjusts them and her tits are just a bit more than a mouthful. Her jeans ride up into her crotch, I'd be introducing her to the naked pussy dare one day, it is my male genes and I can't help myself and look.

"Here," I say, brushing the dirt off her notebook, helping to steady her.

"Thank you, Tom." She grins.

"That's, okay. It's easy to fall over out here, be careful," I add.

"I love it, I'd love to get a job here," she says.

"When you finish your studies, you never know."

We head towards the processing shed.

"How about we go back over how we manage our product once they are caught," I say, sidling up to the holding tanks. "The first twenty-four hours are the most critical."

I stare at the trays of crayfish and only the whirl of pumps from the aeration system is heard. I reach down inside the tank taking hold of a column of trays. Lifting the stack to the rim of the tank, the crayfish display their displeasure at my intrusion as I pry the lid off an enclosure.

"Think of it like this, I've just snatched you out of your house, not just snatched you out, I've also ripped your house down in the process and dumped you into a cell with a whole heap of strangers," I say and let the image sink in for a moment. "You remember why we catch at night? These guys are at the bottom of the food chain and everything wants to eat them."

"Because it is when they are most active?" she asks.

"Yep, that's definitely part of it and the cooler air prevents their gills from drying out."

It's no different to hunting. I've applied so many of my hunting techniques to the day-to-day farm operations and that's why it works so well. Their entire existence is how to avoid being taken out and it's like a game to me.

"Can we do a night survey? I was thinking of seeing if we could go around the edge of ponds once it gets dark to see how much activity there is."

Her excitement makes the suggestion too good to refuse.

"We can do that, and how about we have dinner afterwards?" I ask, trying to be smooth. She looks at me with a twinkle.

"Sure, what time should we start? And only as long as I can organise dinner, you've done so much for me here."

"How about we start at six?" I say. "Make sure you wear your oldest clothes and bring a raincoat. The forecast for tonight is rain."

10

"Rob, I have a little project for you," I say, tracking my eBay order.

"What is it, Cal?" he asks, leaning towards me with interest.

"I'm expecting a delivery," I grin and place my hand on his thigh. He knows I want something.

"And?"

"It's my new pole," I disclose, my hand clutching his morning chubby.

"Have you lost your mind?" he asks. He thinks I'm trying to be a teenager again.

"No, I haven't. I want to be able to practice at home so I can improve and keep up with the young chicks. You know I can only manage one lesson a week with my work timetable," I say, sliding my grip up and down his shaft. "I want to get better at it."

"All right, I guess so…"

"What time are you finishing today?" Rob brings me a cup of tea in bed.

"Around six and then I'm off to my pole lesson."

"So, what time can I expect you in?"

"I'll probably be home around nine," I confirm.

"Okay, I thought you might be in a little earlier," he sighs. "What would you like for breakfast today?"

"I'll just have toast as usual."

I'm not really hungry.

Peeling myself out of bed, I head for the kitchen to start my morning ritual.

"So where do you want the pole to go?" Rob asks, walking into the living room.

"How about here?" I gesture to the main overhead beam in a space that will allow me to twirl and strut my stuff without knocking anything over.

"Okay," he nods. "So, how much was the pole?"

"Two hundred, that's all," I say, defending my purchase. I'm paying for it, so I don't know why it's a problem.

"I thought it would be heaps more. Still sounds expensive though..." he says, "for a pole."

"I know, but it has a mechanism that allows it to rotate gradually as you swing on it," I explain.

I sneak down to my home office for a quick peek at my emails. I'm dying to tell Tom about my pole.

∞

Good morning, gorgeous,

Excited, my pole is arriving today.

I can't wait to get your pole just as hard and spin around on it.

XXX

Good morning to you too, Luscious one,

Just beat me, I was typing as your email flashed up.

Awesome stuff, I can't wait to push you up against my pole.

Does it mean I can have a performance now?

xxx

Absolutely.

What's happening today with you?

It's a busy one today. Plus I'm at the crayfish farm tonight, means getting down and dirty in the mud.

How about getting down and dirty with me?

Hell yeah.

Sounds like a deal to me.

Okay, got to go to work, talk at lunchtime if you are free.

xxx

Have a good one.

xxx

∞

I'm first at the office today. I switch on the urn, wash the cups and clean the kitchen surfaces to begin the new day. I arrange my portion of the front desk in readiness for today's onslaught. The computer blinks twice, the calendar for today is full with each of our therapists booked with back-to-back appointments. It's going to be a busy one.

"Good morning, Callie."

"Good morning, Al," I reply.

I peer over the counter as the cleaner moves closer to lean over the desk. Al is a tall gawky sort of a fellow, he's going through a tough time at home and the circles under his eyes are beginning to show the stress. He shuffles around the office going about his morning duties. I make him a cup of tea in the mornings when I remember.

"How are you this morning?" I ask. "Like a cuppa?"

"Better, now that I've seen you, lovely lady," he says. "Yes I'd love one thank you."

He smiles, besotted. Al has asked me out several times but somehow he doesn't get the hint. I head for the tearoom to make the morning cuppas.

Returning, I hand Al his brew.

"How is your lovely wife?" I enquire. I need to distract his attention otherwise he is going to get into trouble from the office manager.

"Thank you. She's not well today. I have her booked into the doctors around lunchtime."

"I hope she's okay, Al." My concern is sincere. The poor lady is suffering from dementia. "I have to go and get the mail and milk, I'll be back soon."

I head out the door.

"You have a wonderful day, Callie," Al says. He opens the front door for me and I feel his stare as I depart on my morning errands. All harmless, but I really wish he would take the hint.

There is a small queue at the post office as I wait my turn. Outside, the heat of the day is already starting to bear down as I head towards the supermarket. It's only a twenty-minute circuit. I re-enter the office, luckily Al has moved out to the back offices and finishes soon. The girl who sits next to me is already giving me a ribbing about his infatuation. Apparently I'm not the first.

"Good Morning, Callie," Ruth says.

"Good Morning, Ruth," I reply.

She nods as she takes the first call of the day. Ruth is fun to work with, always jovial in manner and happy to share a joke or two, mostly ribbing the patients who visit the practice regularly. She is large breasted with a lovely face and pretty green eyes, her hair usually scraped back in a braid for work.

"Get your early morning AI helping?" she smirks as she answers a call. I head straight to the kitchen to deposit the milk into the refrigerator and begin sifting through the mail.

"Callie, when you have a second can you take these files downstairs?" Ruth says. I nod as I take call number four and the waiting room begins to fill with the first patients arriving for the day.

"Good morning, Mrs. Nash," I say. She is here for her weekly visit. "Yes, I have you booked in for your regular appointment."

I gesture for her to take a seat in the waiting room.

"Ruth, I just have to run down to storage to grab a file, are you okay to hold the fort for a minute?" I ask.

"I'll manage."

"Ruth, what a morning," I say, tucking my hair behind my ear, unwrapping the plastic on my sandwich.

"Get used to it, it happens all the time," she says with a smug look.

"I love being busy though, the day flies," I add as we sit down for our lunch break.

"Who are you texting?" I throw out, fishing.

"Look at this one," she says.

It is an illicit text from her boyfriend.

"Aren't you married?" I ask.

"Yep, but this guy was my school sweetheart. We ended up going separate ways and he is married to a bitch," she snarls.

"You be careful, Ruth," I caution.

"My hubby is hopeless in bed," she says, "and for many other reasons, I want out."

"So, have you done the dirty with this guy yet?"

I'm curious.

"Once, we did it in the back seat of his car," she says with a snort, "I loved it."

"What, girlfriend? Are you are insane?"

"Look, another message, he's coming here again after work today and we are going to meet."

It's a basic message.

'Want a fuck?'

"What are you chuckling at?" Ruth asks.

"How about we send him something back to get his pecker really hard?" I offer with a snigger.

"What do you suggest?" Ruth hands me her phone.

Together, over the next hour it gets hornier and hotter. Ruth is hooked.

"Callie, have you done this before?" she asks. I've been far too excited and have too many one-liners.

"Nah. Never."

"Yes, you have, I bet you are getting a bit on the side as well," she says. She's right onto me.

"Is that right? I wish," I reply, trying to deflect the challenge.

"Yes, you have, I knew it. You are one of the quiet ones, I bet you have."

Ruth is defiant.

"It's time we went back to work, girlfriend," I say. It's back into the lion's den.

I laugh myself senseless as I digest Callie's email about Ruth's extracurricular activities. It's a classic.

My inbox is getting more than a little servicing as a message from Haley hits my screen as well.

∞

Hi Tom,

What's the best website I can look at to find out about trekking in New Zealand? I know you will know.

Haley

Hi Haley,

Where I will take you, there are no tracks, we make our own.

Tom

Tom,

I want to look at flights as well. Where would I fly in?

Haley

Haley,

Auckland is where you should hit southern soil.

Tom

Tom,

Thank you so much, it's snowing here.

I started an extra job at the diner and it's all going into my down-under account.

Thanks, Haley

Haley,

Lots of laughs, it's sunny and forty degrees here.

Take care.

Tom

∞

The afternoon shift is in full swing and at least the telephone has backed off a little. I sneak into the loo to check to see if I have any emails from Tom. A text from Rob flashes in.

Pole here, installed.

Thank you. I punch in.

It's a constant stream, one in, one out as the day drags on. Armed with the banking and mail I head out the door for the afternoon run. I can't be long as Ruth has the front desk to oversee and it is so easy for it to suddenly become busy beyond control for one person to manage.

Mission accomplished, I return.

"What are you doing tonight, Callie?" Ruth asks.

"I know what you are doing," I giggle. "I'm going to pole lessons with my old colleague, Bev."

"Many in the class?" she enquires.

"You would be surprised. Mostly all young girls, I think Bev and I are the oldest ones there," I attest.

"What made you take up pole dancing?" Ruth asks, interrupted by the phone, she takes the call. Still looking at me, concentrating on both.

I wait for her to hang up.

"It's all the rage at the moment, I thought it would be good fun."

"I bet you get a bit on the side too." Ruth is as direct as they come.

"You are incorrigible, Ruth," I say shaking my head.

I log on to see if Tom is online before I hit the pole studio.

∞

Hey, Bear,

I'm going to ride your arse off soon. I'm learning a few new moves tonight that will spin you out.

My pole was installed at home today.

How has your day been?

xxx

Howdy, Yogi,

Long day in the trenches, but what's new, got to go and do crayfish surveys tonight.

Gather yours has been the same.

Excited about the pole.

xxx

Okay. What are you doing Friday?

Nothing planned at this stage.

You got a window?

Well, I will know tomorrow if my B is out and thought you might like a yoga lesson and then return here for a quickie before I have to work my afternoon shift?

Fuck yeah.

I'm in. You don't need to ask me twice.

Is it an 8 a.m. start?

Yep.

I'll be available and yes, I'd love to.

∞

Texting:

C U at pole, Bev x

Yep, I'll be there soon.

XXX

"Okay girls, tonight we are going to do some climbing and gentle rotations as we descend," Candy says. Candy our pole teacher alights the three metres to the ceiling with ease. Her sexy body wraps around the pole, legs tight, she lays back, twists and turns, gracefully unwinding. I am impressed at how elegantly she has executed her move. I glance over at Bev and she's in awe.

Candy is sex on legs. Her tiny hot pink skirt barely covers her knickers and her heels are at least six inches high with hot pink soles. She just oozes sex appeal out of every pore. Her long blond hair floats over her shoulders. She is sophisticated and simply stunning.

Hot pink sequins and bling is her thing. Even her logo 'Fit 'n Sexy' sparkles. Satin pink drapes float down the walls of the pole studio with sparkles throughout the fabric. Floor to ceiling mirrors line the entire front wall while mirror balls fall from the loose spangled fabric dotted across the ceiling.

Hot pink cushions are scattered along the black leather lounge in the far corner while a dozen poles make up the bulk of the room space. It is a very girly and rather sexy space.

The session begins and the sweat drips off my entire body after a few minutes. This is harder than it looks. Candy made it look so simple. My inner thighs are aching and pinched from holding on for dear life. Surely it's not ladylike to have bruises on my inner thighs?

"How good was that, Bev?"

"Unbelievable, Cal's, we're going to be so fit if we keep this up," she says, still a bit breathless.

"I know. I'm sore all over."

"Me too, okay, see you next week?"

"Okay, bye."

Driving home, my upper arms wearily hang on the steering wheel, just managing to guide me home.

"Hi Rob," I say, bright eyed even after an exhausting day and night. "Doesn't it look fantastic? Thank you so much."

The sleek silver pole glistens in the light, I do a little twirl, even though my arms feel like they have been stretched out of their sockets. I swirl to the ground, lying out flat.

"It was fairly easy," Rob gloats as I lay there. "I just had to bolt a top plate in and it has an adjustable shaft."

He is proud of his technical building skills.

"Thank you so much."

I'm stoked with it.

"I'll be back around midnight," I say, my headlamp in one hand and raincoat tucked under my arm, it's pouring down rain.

"Okay, happy surveying." Jess wanders over to the plasma to snuggle down as a gust of wind hits the building rendering a creak or two. "You be careful out tonight, the weather is awful."

"I know, but this will be the final component Christine needs to do to complete her work."

I shiver, knowing it's going to be cold.

"Great night for it," I note, more than a little sarcastic.

"What effect do these conditions have on them?" Christine is rugged up like a snowman.

"Actually, you're not going to believe this, but this type of weather is like a magnet to bring them out. They feel safe in these conditions. The cover of darkness and rain provides them with the ultimate freedom to move around."

"Awesome, can't wait," Christine says.

We fire up a quad bike each and we head into the mud and rain.

The darkness around me bears down. The light behind me disappears and I immediately look over my shoulder to see nothing. Fear belts straight through me as I slam on the brakes, performing a one hundred and eighty degree turn. I power the bike straight towards the last bend in the road.

Christine is buried in the mud underneath the upside down bike. My first thought is that she is dead. It looks bad—all I see through the hammering rain is a tangled mess.

My headlamp just adds to the haziness and uncertainty. Somehow, her body is on the roadside ditched and the bike is suspended over her. I flip it off her. She is lying on her back but there is life; tears of stress are streaming down her face and she is in shock. I heave a massive sigh of relief.

"I want you to move your toes and fingers for me," I say. I need to make sure she doesn't have any major injuries. She nods her head—there is feeling.

"Any pain?" I ask.

She shakes her head.

"Okay, let's get you out of here," I say. I place my arm around her to help her up. She is giddy and grabs hold of me. "We need to get you warmed up and dry."

We are both covered head to toe in mud and wet to the core.

"You feeling okay?" I ask as we enter the building. The relief from the rain is welcoming.

"Tom, I'm so sorry, I hope I haven't wrecked your bike. Yeah, I'm fine, but your bike," Christine stutters.

"Don't worry about it, the most important thing is you're okay."

The stress is starting to bleed-off.

"Count that one as a lucky escape. We need to get you out of these wet clothes and washed down, you are covered in more mud than I've ever seen. And then we are taking you down to the medical centre."

She is still clinging to me—a sign I need to make sure she is well enough for her homeward flight.

Turning the shower on, she still has symptoms of stress and anxiety as a plume of steam begins to fill the room.

"Thanks Tom, lucky I wasn't here by myself tonight." She disappears into the shower.

Thank heavens, it could have so easily have been a catastrophe.

Completing the incident report I breathe a sigh of relief.

It's five to eight and I make my way into my introduction to yoga. I've never done a yoga move in my life.

"Hello," I say. I wander over to Tom. "I have a spare mat right here for you."

"Thank you, Yogi."

This is hilarious, I giggle inside. They are all so serious. There are just three men out of the fifteen. I take my position and a sleek athletic sort places her mat parallel to mine.

"It's silent time," I whisper in Tom's ear. "Just watch me up the front and go with the flow and follow those around you."

I head back to my mat. I bet he gets a hard-on with Pearl next to him. She is my most flexible student and she is hot even to another woman. She has lean muscles, soft curly blonde hair and a body to die for. He will be in his element once she bends over.

I lie on my mat chilling out, already enjoying the downtime. Callie begins to focus our minds. It suddenly hits me like a hammer: now I know why Callie has been able to master some of the higher-level erotica control so quickly. I've been teasing her, taking her to the limits, I was wondering why she was handling those advanced techniques so well. She now has me even more intrigued at her level of skills. I have to do some research on yoga.

"Tom, it's time to wake up," I say, giving him a little shake.

"Callie, I loved it," I say, sucking in a deep breath, pushing myself up while the hall empties.

"Did you see the guy over there, the older one, did you see what he did with his leg? I thought he had detached it when you had us bring our leg to the chest. I'm still shaking my head."

"He's good at that posture, he's been doing yoga for a long time," I explain. "Did you like Pearl?"

"Which one was Pearl?" I ask. I was surrounded.

"The hot piece on your right," I tell him. His face flushes a male hormonal surge.

"Oh yeah, when she put her hands down on the ground her arse almost poked me in the face, I could have just run my tongue through her slit," I cheekily suggest. "It was so funny. As she was going down I was watching and I suddenly realised she would have a direct line of sight to my focus, I tucked my head down before she saw me take a peek. It wasn't fair to make her feel uncomfortable."

"Thought you might like that one," I laugh.

"Seriously, the older guy with grey hair and stringy features impressed me the most, I'm sure he had a detachable leg." I raise my eyebrows. "He looked like he could bend inside out as he went through the routines."

"He's been practicing for a long time, just like you in the sack, you get good at it."

"Never seen a guy so flexible, especially for his age."

"What did you like the most about the class?" I enquire.

"I liked all of it. Honestly, I did," I answer sincerely.

"Time for a quickie?" I ask, grabbing Tom's hand, I have an hour before I need to be at work.

11

My Student has devoured all the basic lessons with an insatiable appetite. I am ecstatic with Callie's performance in the sack. She is proving to be exceptional. I have not revealed to Callie she is my Student. I do think, however, she suspects there is a logical methodology to how this is unfolding, manipulating her participation in the horizontal position. She is becoming a clever, sneaky vixen. After I have levitated her, I will reveal my Sex Savant status. Until then, I intend to remain silent. Experience has taught me early disclosure may inhibit a Student's potential. Scrutiny of their performance and comparison with others doesn't necessarily inspire. I don't want to do anything that may inhibit Callie's continued attainments. At the appropriate juncture of time, I will disclose all.

In my office I ponder the question, my Teacher would have challenged her Student to think outside the square and display initiative. So far Callie has demonstrated a lust to stimulate her sex as she becomes more open minded. Her awakening has been a pleasure for me. It has been such a long time since my last student and it might not have been so easy for me, but with Callie, I have a quick learner. Showing her once, maybe twice and she has taken the ball and run with it, so to speak. I need to challenge her further.

Callie has never wrapped her virgin lips around a joint and smoked the 'hootchie' stuff. There is some in my freezer suffering from frost-burn. Infusing the biological mind with a dash of smoky aphrodisiac is not necessarily everyone's cup of tea. It is definitely not my every day of the week substance. I'm almost falling off my chair with laughter. It is going to be interesting when Callie opens this email.

∞

Good evening, Cal's,

Ever smoked the promiscuous stuff?

∞

Inbox (1) What? Absolutely not. I have always been too scared of the stuff. I have somehow avoided it until now. Tom is really stretching the boundaries. I have broken every one of my moral rules to date. Now he wants me to get stoned. Is there anything he hasn't tried? How far does he think I will go?

∞

Nope, never tried it. Another conspiracy in your bag of tricks I suspect?

You want to get me drunk on bubbles, completely violate my body and now you want to get me high as well? You are out of control…

I am in.

Well, that was quick. I thought you were sleeping? Can't let sleep get in the way of naughty talk and

play, now can we? Do you need some spice to make a long night wet and wild?

I have a new challenge for you. I want to get you high on champagne bubbles, mixed with a wicked purple concoction of Pornstars, share a joint with me and then I will totally have my wicked way with your body. A Pornstar is my favourite cocktail and weed we will need for my next fuck plan.

∞

I rub my hands together like a fisherman with a large haul. I do have a deep bag of tricks and I am only starting to reveal the contents, piece by piece. I'm having the time of my life. Callie is flexing my imagination to make this more delicious, intriguing, captivating, and exciting. The chill-out affect will empty her mind so she becomes totally uninhibited. I love it when I finally get a woman to the mind control element. My joy is to literally smoke them and obliterate them to release my own hormonal high. I take them into the realms of ecstasy and hold them there in a state of euphoria. Then, the trick is to do that on impulse. Callie is a fast learner, she will master this in no time. I still have other lessons I want to deliver before getting her hooked in this advanced state. I'm just teasing her around the edges for now. My Sex Savant cells swirl from the taste of her euphoric highs, like a drone attending his queen bee.

I have a naughty schoolgirl feeling. A cigarette behind the toilet blocks was always out of bounds for me. I sniggered at all the girls who were caught doing that silly stuff. At least there are no teachers watching me. This is completely crazy. I love every minute of it, swept up, challenged and taken out of my comfort zone. The transformation in me is surreal. I am opening up to things I would have never dreamed of doing. Tom has a manipulating effect over me. I am so captured by this drug like feeling. I want more. It is hypnotic. I see myself thinking more laterally every day. Accepting dares and challenges I would have never imagined I would take on. This has become my all-consuming obsession. I am totally infatuated.

I have no idea where to look. Smoking weed? I don't know anyone who would even know where to get it. I rack my brain till it hurts… and still nothing.

Hang on a minute, what about Asher's boyfriend, Tristan? He is a cool dude who might have a connection or two. He's a real surfy guy with a constant tan and a buff body, no wonder Asher fell for him so quickly. If I make a call and drop the hint, with a little flirting, I might get what I want.

"Hey, how are you?"

"Good, Cals." He recognises my voice. That's a good start.

"What have you been up to?" I say, trying to sound casual.

"Not much, just hanging around here, watching the waves," he says in a droll reply.

"What are you doing for lunch?" I enquire.

"Who me?"

"Yeah."

"Ah, not much,"

"I'm going to be coming out your way today."

"Sounds cool."

"Okay, I'll meet you at the surf club around twelve?"

"Awesome."

"Hey dude, are you still into that hootchie stuff?"

"Ah, maybe, why?"

"I'm going to a party and want to get my hands on some."

"No problem, I'll bring some, see you at twelve."

Well, that was easy enough. Let's hope he turns up with the goods.

My urge to log online is insatiable. I have to update Tom.

∞

Okay, I've sourced a contact… Confirmation pending…

A friend of mine has connections.

This should prove to be an interesting little adventure. Have you discussed payment terms in detail? LOL.

No, I haven't discussed exact payment terms. Cash is his currency no doubt.

Go girl, go.

∞

There is a buzz in my head. The weed is infecting me and I haven't even laid my hands on the stuff.

I am in love with Callie's sex manual idea. The right side of my brain has me excited and the scope for potential is endless. The business analyst side of my brain takes control. We have to identify marketing opportunities, operational, organisational and financial considerations in a timely manner. We need to begin a document to keep track of all our thoughts.

The estimated timeline bolts into my future vision. My mountain hiking adventures will give me the energy and inspiration I need to do my side of the project. When limitless peaks surround me, my notepad will get a

hammering. Reminiscing, it will be timeless.

It will be our glue in the low times, keeping Callie and I focused for the long haul. The urgency in my keystrokes gives way to my excitement.

∞

I am as excited as a teenager on my first date.

My mind is working away at what we are about to undertake. Remember how we did the business plan for your business and then developed action plans to keep us focused? We need to work along similar lines.

It doesn't need to be complex. We can work through it logically to come up with the most suitable business plan for our needs.

I have contacted the accountant to work out an entity structure. He has a couple of ideas that sound like they will work to keep this low key, and at the same time, above board. What he is thinking would almost amount to a partnership structure. Since we don't want to register anything out in the public arena, we can use a particular type of entity structure that technically stays off the system. We need a name for our entity.

Sounds straightforward and simple enough. How exciting is this? So we need a name for our entity? Leave it with me and I will see what I can come up with. I love a challenge, as you know…

Okay, I will leave it with you. You are the creative one for that sort of thing I have noticed.

BTW, I have secured a post office box.

∞

I can feel Tom's energy and enthusiasm escalating and it is infectious. I desperately want to make this work.

∞

P.O. Box, great stuff. If we need registration numbers etc. it will all take a little time, but it is all in the pipeline.

It will all come together in no time.

I have confirmed we can use the accountant's address as our business address, that way when and if we need to use a physical address we have one.

Excellent. It will start to gather steam shortly and then we will be in the thick of things and gasping for air.

That is not the only thing you will be gasping for…

Feeling me on top of you, pinning you to the bed as you envelop all of my cock. You hold on tight, squeezing your internal sinews, muscling and massaging my pulsing need. I'll feel your powerful orgasm and when I extract my cock, I feel a hot gush of juice leave your body. Then it will be your turn to rock my world by climbing on top and impaling yourself on my cock for a clit ride. Ride me hard, bringing yourself to climax as many times as you desire, whilst I hold my knob hard, just keeping it from the brink…

My pussy lips are swelling as you work your magic touch along my central line, I can feel you arch your pelvis, transgressing my entire body…

Hold that thought. Got to fly, I have a weed man to visit.

∞

Since our weeklong annihilation of the sheets, we haven't been able to score another overnighter. It is eating away at me. It gives me a chance to feel Tom's hot shot first thing in the morning, and I love an early morning pussy rimming with hot talk that only he can deliver. It's bad talk and I should be blushing, but it makes me gush, sending me over the edge. I'm hungry for more.

"Hey, Cal, how was your day?" Rob asks.

"Long," I say, staggering in from a day's work and a weed run. I am exhausted. "We had an extra helping of injuries which really put the day's schedule out of whack. What's for dinner?"

I'm hungry and mentally drained.

"I don't know yet, I was thinking we might cook a couple of steaks and vegetables, how does that sound?" he asks.

"Okay, sounds good to me, I'll do the veggies, can you handle the steak?" I ask.

"I'll fire up the BBQ now," Rob says.

"Have you decided if you are going to do the tournament up north yet?" I say. Not wanting to force it and look like I am pushing him out the door.

"We were talking about it at the club tonight, we are all keen, so I reckon we will."

"What dates are you thinking?"

"Fifteenth till probably the twentieth next month for the local one and yet to work out the dates for the other. Why?"

I sense Rob is a little ruffled.

"Just so I know what you're doing, that's all," I lie, blush, and hope I haven't let it show what just went through my conscience.

I have been praying Rob's week away with the boys would come off. They have been procrastinating and finally a decision.

My side of things is set, I need to give Tom the heads up. He is going to need to come up with some sort of plausible excuse to spend time here. I can't wait to feel his boner in me all night long. I am already gushing, anticipating him piercing deep, spearing me completely.

It's my turn to excel. I am going to create my own inveiglement strategy to lure him out of his home and into my shag pit. He will to have to come up with a really good excuse not to be wetting my sheets in acceptance of my invitation, for at least some of the time. I'll send him home drained and nailed, but more likely, it'll be me who will be totally obliterated. I can't do much to help him with an excuse. I have to leave that for him to devise. I'm sure he will work his magic. Together we always seem to make it happen.

I am in dreamland, a potential whole week together, surely he can scam a long weekend out of that. Oh. My. God. How fabulous would that be? I might see if the other girls on the roster can swap days. The planning never stops. It eats at me every minute of the day.

I have to make this look incredible. I'm going to make it hot and heavy. Inserting raunchy pictures and sexy kissing lips, along with a program of full-on sex. That should get his man juices going. I want to get Tom's mind drooling, leaving him with uncontrollable desires. I crave for him to take me the moment he walks in the door and pin me against the railing.

My mind is spinning. I only hope he can free up the same dates. It's time for me to compile my winning email.

∞

Hey there, gorgeous,

I have a break in my schedule and my mind has been going nuts.

Please find attached an invitation, just for you.

I'll be home alone for a week, hope you can join me for some of the time. Perhaps for a long weekend of pure indulgence, followed by a couple of weekday interludes of lust. See what you can do from your end.

Interested?

xxx

Fuck Invitation

You are invited to a party for two.

When:	**Anywhere between the 15–20th**
Where:	**My place**
Why:	**To fuck your brains out**
Bring:	**Hot pussy poker** **Licks for wet kissing** **Appetite for juice** **Tongue to explore cavities**
Supplied:	**Hot wet pussy** **WEED...** **Copious amounts of champagne** **TLC on tap** **Massage oil**

FUCK Program

Arrive at 9am for our first explosive fuck

Tits, naked arse, wet juice, more juice

Sheer fingering, licking and sucking...

Followed by a champagne spa bubble bath

Gourmet lunch for two

Pornstar cocktails

Porn and toys

Dinner for two on the balcony sharing fine wine
and music

Pole dancing display and a pole fuck

All night long fucking

Early morning fuck

Long, luscious morning fuck for hours tangled
in the sheets

Champagne in the spa

Delicious hot breakfast and coffee

Fuck talk and fingering.

A country drive and a special surprise for you

Lunch by the lagoon

Back for more fucking, sucking, licking and fingering

Seafood morsels and a candlelit dinner

Fuck each other's brains out all night long
till we drop.

Want to get your hands on me yet?

Let's fuck, play, sing, dance, fuck, pole, suck, fuck, finger, oil slide, massage, eat, drink, pash, bubbles, cum, cum, cum, fuck me, fuck you, suck bud, suck, fondle, erotica, porn, pole, fuck, cougar, pre-cum, hot juice, licking, ball stroking, arse fingering, fuck, fuck, and fuck some more...

Come up for air if your dare...

INTERESTED?????

RSVP ASAP

∞

I'm glued to my computer, reading Callie's Fuck Invitation over and over. A shot of adrenaline goes straight to the head of my knob. I feel a chubby coming on. I suspect it will be there all day in some shape or form. She's such a tease, how am I going to concentrate on anything? This is a very clever tactic, the only way I won't be there, is if I'm dead.

∞

Fuck Invitation accepted. Bring it on.

I'm going to have a wicked time with your mind and make you so horny that by the time I get my hands on you, you will be dripping.

When I walk through that door I'll pin you up against the wall, you'd better be wearing a short skirt and knickers, yes, knickers. Your arms will be spread wide and you'll be hanging on for dear life. Your legs I will spread. You will be standing there spinning, pinned hard against the wall and your tits will leave an indent in the wall.

Your neck I will kiss violently, I'll search out your ear and dip my hot wet tongue deep into your earhole with a hot breath. You will try to flex your head away as the intensity will be too great. You will buck and squirm under my stronghold. All the while my hands will be running over your body with firmness in their touch, sending you a message of desire; I want to take you to another world with my transmission of lustful energy.

Biting your flesh through your dress, my mouth will go down the centre of your back, nibbling, kissing and teasing. Reaching for your skirt, I will lift it up and tuck it into your bra, then dribble my mouth juices down your tummy so that you feel me drooling.

I'll bite the inside of your thigh and run my fingers like a scratching stick over your back as my searching mouth moves lower, finally reaching your knickers. I'm going to bite them, making a hole in the lace, and you know what I'm going to do with that hole.

Rising up behind you, the hardness of my body is pushing you harder into the wall as you feel my playmate against you. It will be the launch pad to lift you off the floor at least six inches so that you are fully suspended. My rod will be the pole you will be impaled on, nailing you to the wall.

Day one. First impact. One nailed Yogi.

∞

Well, that surpassed the kind of reply I was after. Hot, heavy, hungry and even a sample of what to expect when he walks in the door. This is so crazy and fabulous. I can hardly contain my dizzy excitement.

Thank heavens I have been taking pole-dancing lessons. I am going to have to get my creative thinking cap on and choreograph a personalised routine, for Tom's eyes-only.

Raunchy music, one hell of a sexy piece of lingerie to flaunt it, with enticing moves to keep his eyes locked to my body. I can't wait for him to deliver his plans on my body, blowing me into oblivion as I spasm with a toe-curling tingle of excitement.

Not being able to have each other makes my life one of anticipation, captivation, obsession and pure lust. I want him in between my legs, in between my tits, in between my lips, in between everything.

We have to make this rendezvous happen. Coincide our calendars and milk every minute we can. We are extremely organised in our daily lives, so it will be planned within an inch on both sides. No wonder we are a hit, we are like two peas in a pod, we both want it badly, what can possibly go wrong? Our illicit sexual relationship has turned into an affair like no other, longing to liaise, please and tease.

∞

Day one, first impression looks rather tantalising.

Still deciding whether to wear any knickers or not. You will just have to wait and see...

Glad you can make it Bear. x

∞

I have no idea how Callie has freed up her swanky shag pit, though she did mention something about her B being away on one of his golf tours. I have my own challenge to make it happen. This is the tough bit, coming up with an excuse so I can be absent. This will take extraordinary scheming to get past Jessica as she isn't dumb. My eyes blink a couple of times as I think.

My planning has begun and I'm totally consumed with hundreds of ideas. I want to completely blow Tom's cock to bits. I want it to be the most amazing weekend he has ever experience in his entire life. That is my objective. I need to make it a mixture of fun, fantasy, erotica and exquisite catering.

I scroll through my list of possible songs to start creating my pole dance routine. I need time and practice to perfect my spellbinding performance. Narrowing it down to a few sexy and seductive songs, I choose a kinky number. It's perfect. A good tempo for seduction as it builds up through the chorus to entertain and enhance my sexy moves. I want to see a hard-on in his pants after my opening scene and suggestive moves. I want him drooling, so he nails my arse to the pole.

Six and a half inch diamanté studded black heels, a fishnet body stocking and a lace G string will leave a tantalising taste in his mouth. My aphrodisiac will be my finale when I open my legs and drop my pussy two inches from his face.

In a hidden file on my computer, I start detailing my weekend plan of events. I design a menu incorporating a shopping list. Champagne, wine, shots and Pornstars are added, as these are our favourite. I can't forget the strawberries. They are a necessary accompaniment to our bubbles. Our trademark now, as an addition to our drink of choice and I can't think of having a champers without them anymore.

On Sunday, I'm going to treat Tom to a hot rock massage, followed by a light lunch by the water's edge. I will need to find a secluded place. The main street of my local suburb will attract prying eyes to my weekend bedfellow. It is critical to keep our togetherness under wraps. We are having far too much fun to be detected. Discovery now would catapult our obsessive razors edge living to a grinding halt. Neither of us wants that. I can't imagine living without this infusion in my life. It would feel like my right arm was cut off. The thought of anyone or anything intruding into our space makes me cringe. It can't happen, it won't happen.

∞

Planning in full swing, fabulous you have coverage your end. Mark my words… This will be the best weekend of your life. It will be filled with passion, intensity and pure indulgence that will rock your world.

Ready for one hell of a ride? Let's share the magic and discover every inch of each other's bodies, minds and souls, and together we will rock this world…

Bring it on, Luscious legs,

Now, I need to confirm your shoe size? Intrigued? I have a surprise coming for the hostess with the mostess.

I'm very intrigued… hostess' foot size is a ladies, six. Looking forward to my surprise, a foot fetish I have.

∞

My mobile lights up, the display screen revealing the caller. It's Asher.

"Hi Asher, how are you?"

She asks me a question.

"Not much, I'd love to " confirming I have nothing happening for the afternoon.

"Give me an hour and I'll be there."

"Hi Ash," I say, embracing my best friend.

"Hi Cal," she replies.

"How are you?" I ask, knowing her smile already answers my question. Asher is a gorgeous blonde bombshell with wicked green eyes, a real down to earth girl with no hang-ups about makeup and designer clothes. I guess that's why we are besties. I hope Tristan didn't mention our midweek luncheon and weed collection.

"I'm well, thanks."

"Hi Callie, good to see you." Tristan hugs me. "Let me get you a drink."

Tristan places a chilled long stem glass in my hand as we wander out onto to the deck to indulge in the afternoon sun. There are four loafers and somehow I end up lying next to Tristan.

"Before we get too settled, can you show me a bit of yoga Cal?" Tristan begs.

"Tristan, Callie didn't come here to give you a yoga lesson, for god's sake," Asher says, with a frown. Tristan looks at me in tease.

"Just a couple of moves then," I say, placing my drink on the outdoor table setting. "Okay, let's start with the cat posture and move into a downward dog position."

He arches his back and places his hands and feet out in position.

"Now, I want you to close your eyes," I say and as he does, I throw my leg over his back.

"Giddy-up cowboy." I ride him like a bronco. Asher is falling off her seat in hysterical laughter.

"Go Callie," Asher whoops. "That will teach you, Tristan."

Tristan collapses onto the deck, diving nose first.

"Okay, Callie, you win," he grunts. He lies sprawled out on the deck. We laugh, picking ourselves up to retire to our loafers.

"Where's Rob?" Asher asks.

"He is out competing in his Saturday comp, I call it his man-cave thing."

"When does he go away up north for his annual tournaments?" Asher sips her drink and Tristan lies back like a cool dude.

"Soon." I tilt my sunglasses.

"Why don't you go?" Asher suggests.

"I don't enjoy it. All that ends up happening is I spend most of the time on my own. I end up putting my joggers on and searching for the best walking tracks and spend my day doing that," I say looking towards the setting sun. "The boys come in and expect dinner and I have to relive everything they did for the day, several times over."

Tristan starts laughing.

"Sounds good to me," he chuckles. Asher elbows him to behave.

"So, it's easier if I stay here and do my own thing," I muse taking another sip.

Tristan wanders off for another bottle.

"Tristan wants me to marry him," Asher confides.

"Does he?"

"Yeah, I don't know. I've been there already. I don't know if I want to do it all over again."

I can't tell from her eyes since her shades hide them, but the twisted lip confirms her tone.

Tristan returns.

"Chip Callie?" he passes the bowl around. "So, you like your new job?"

"Yeah, it's great. Keeps the bills paid, but I want to do something different. Something will come along. It always does."

I already know what it is but I'm keeping my cards close to my chest.

12

"Do you have everything, darl?" I enquire, glancing at the clock.

"All set to go. What are you doing this weekend?"

"Not much, I might go over to Asher's house tomorrow night," I mention.

"That sounds good, you always have fun over there."

"She's having a couple of girlfriends around, so I thought I might join them."

"You watch Tristan, he's got the hots for you," he growls, jealous.

"You are kidding me. Anyway, he's not my type," I say.

"I'm serious, he's got the hots for you, big time."

"Don't be silly," I laugh. "He's in love with Asher. She's beautiful and they are getting married."

"Anyway, I have to go, you have a good time and I'll see you in a week," Rob says.

"Don't forget to send me a message to say you are there safe. Okay?"

"I promise, I will," Rob says.

Our goodbye is a hug and a kiss and a peck on the cheek for good measure.

∞

Good morning, my divine goddess,

Sleep wet?

Hope so. Are you ready?

xxx

Good morning to you,

I'm hot and horny and ready to do you.

Drive safe and be here sooner if you can.

Home alone, ready and waiting.

Get your Bear arse into that truck now…

xxx

∞

I'm trying to remain cool. My backpack of hunting gear is packed in my truck for illusionary purposes. A box with basic staples for the weekend completes my charade. Who do I think I am kidding? I have been on the email system for the last twenty minutes under the guise of work. I should be more careful, it feels like a dead giveaway. There's a little voice in my head saying, 'you're insane. You don't have a hunting permit'. My Sex Savant logic kicks in to save the day. Free passes should be mandatory. If Callie had a cock it wouldn't be a problem, I try to convince myself with my mere male logic.

"What are you up to for the weekend, my dear?" I casually enquire.

"I haven't decided yet. There is a bird sale on in town, I might go to that," Jess says with an equally casual response, "or, is there any chance I can come with you? It's been ages since you took me anywhere."

Her voice sounds disappointed. She looks at the ground shuffling her feet.

"Jess, it's just the guys, you know what they are like about a woman coming along. You know I don't care, I'd be happy for you to come but they get shifty about it."

I am really feeling like a cheat and a liar. I should just stay home, this one has really taken the edge off me.

"Let's have a coffee," I say.

"It's okay, I don't feel like one, I'll be fine. You have a good time and be safe won't you." Jessica waves as the dog does three sixties excitedly around her legs.

"I always do," I say as I plant my arse into the seat and shut the door. At least now I'm on my way and the escape is a sense of relief.

I have finished racing around making last minute preparations. I've cleaned the spa and remade all the beds with fresh linen, adding a couple of drops of lavender oil. It smells divine. I could roll in them. I suspect Tom will have a coital plan for every couch in the place. I'm so excited to have him here, a whole weekend of scrumptious wickedness. We will destroy my entire dwelling. "Yes, please." I raise my fist in the air, willing it to happen.

Our game is a blaze of intensity. I recall our lunch and how Tom ran his hand down my back and twirled it around my arse. Then, dipped his tongue into my mouth for a kiss that sent me over the edge. Secretly, I left there with wet knickers. Every time I think about him I get a spasm in my loins. Our chase is developing into a wild hunting game. Exploration, hounding and pursuit as we venture into each other's lives. It is my escape from reality. I'm discovering how perfectly we are suited as players in this game of lust.

A 'no response' or a 'no show' to Callie's initiatives sends the message I don't really care. It is when you do something like this, that you appreciate the effort that really goes into making it happen. I wouldn't dare miss it. I am infatuated.

I'm tingling like a teenager again, albeit with an old head, 'Thank you Teacher' I muse. Callie is hot to trot and the coast is clear. No pesky partner to worry about for an entire week, but unfortunately, I am only able to commit to a weekend of lust. However, the coming week may well incorporate a few more site visits, so to speak. We must take advantage of our limited opportunities, they are way too precious to pass up. I am half way there already.

Texting…

There in 30 :)

Her reply is instant. I knew it would be.

Ready and waiting…

Indulging in fantasies and enjoying all the pleasures we can discover. No outside influences, just the two of us and all the fun we can create. I know we will make the most of every second, minute, and hour. I want to be totally indulged with every whim and fantasy with this one amazing individual.

My whirling emotions make me nervous, excited, high and desperate; wanting everything to go smoothly, wanting to feel those amazing feelings, wanting to see that lustful smirk on his face when he gets sexed up watching my pole performance. Simply wanting to be with him.

The entrance door is slightly ajar, Callie has tied a blown up picture of hot red ruby lips with red satin ribbon, smack in the middle of the door. Slowly I push the door inward, my lioness is waiting. Barefoot, wearing a short denim dress, flesh exposed from the tip of her toes to the two inches

of hem and her tits are oozing in my face. There is a thirst in her lustful eyes. A surge pulses through my body. I am as horny as a deprived Bonobo chimpanzee on his first meeting. I am going to hammer Callie till she is obliterated.

There is no way we are going to make it to a bed first up. I want to plough it straight into her and nail her with my cock. My Teacher's voice screams at me, 'don't lose it. Passion yes, but you have a long day in front of you. Stick to your fuck plan.' Callie pounces straight onto me and wraps her legs around my waist and her tongue prods down my throat, thrashing my tonsils. I wrap my hands tightly around her arse to make a platform.

'No,' I say to myself. Control, take advantage of the fire and spin her out. I continue to kiss her lips with violence.

Our lips remain locked, our tongues dance, swirling around, in and out, frantically searching for each other's tip, flicking back and forth, replicating in advance the frantic fuck to come. I can feel her pulse pumping faster and faster. I slide her onto the second step and hungrily expose her breast. Flicking across her raised nipple, the hardness intensifies as her hips grind upwards seeking a source of relief. Fingering her knickers to one side, I fondle her and immediately begin to tease.

Placing the tip of my finger on her swollen bud, it twitches uncontrollably. I follow Callie's clit with my fingertip. Her body convulses, she releases a plea, "Don't stop," squeezing through clenched lips. Her fingernails dig into me, holding on as she arches upwards. Without changing the position or pressure she cums in convulsing waves, each time soaring higher. The echo in the stairway is loud and the smell of pussy juice fills my senses.

As tears of pleasure flow, I lick Callie's sweat, lightly kissing her tingling lips. Her starry eyes say it all. I continue to wallow in her wickedness. I lower my gaze. Her body

squirms in anticipation as I rip my shirt off, unbuckle my belt and let my hard cock jerk out. I drop to my knees and push her scant dress up high. My tongue and lips ravish her groin with nibbles, gentle bites and long, slow wet licks of pleasure.

Instantly I'm rewarded with her scream. Three climaxes are blended into one, her clit throbbing violently.

"Good morning." I give her a cheeky grin. My eyes are sparkling.

"How are you?"

I lean down and place a gentle kiss on her lips. No more words are needed.

I have been annihilated at the base of the stairs. Tom burst through the door with vigour and purpose. My heart is only just settling after pumping like mad to maximum capacity, having almost leapt completely out of my chest and onto the bottom step.

"Good morning and welcome, gorgeous." I smile, catching my breath. "Ready for an awesome weekend? I am."

"Hell yeah. You look so edible in that dress."

"Why thank you, fabulous start I must admit, you didn't even make it further than two steps into the house," I say. If this is what the entire weekend is going to be like, not only will we like it, we will love it.

My mischievous grin assures him there is a lot more in store.

"I'll gather my things later, they can wait," I announce.

"Sounds good to me."

"There are still a couple of things I want to do involving pure pleasure of flesh first."

Time for the wall, I need to deliver on that one and seduce Callie into oblivion and deposit into her snatch.

"Champers? Why not."

"Yes, please," I say; now I've taken the initial edge off.

I am overly organised. I have the double spa half filled with water and sensual foaming bath oils with a low table neatly tucked by the side of the spa bath for our plate of delectable nibbles.

My nerves have settled since his arrival and now I can concentrate on immersing myself in a weekend of pleasure. The atmosphere is relaxed as we delight in our familiar nakedness. My eyes devour Tom's roughly sculpted body, feasting on his manliness.

Steam and bubbles are beckoning as I plunge in. Callie has a small table strategically placed within reach. Two empty champagne flutes only need to be filled as she retrieves the nibbles to complement the bubbles.

"Does it get any better than this?" I say. After a hard physical week I need this.

"Absolutely not. I mean really."

"How was your week?" I ask.

"Good, same stuff, you know how it is," I say, our legs intertwine beneath the balmy, invigorating water. Tom's hand fondles my calf muscle and occasionally wanders up and down my leg. Hmm... Love touches... Feels so heavenly to be caressed and pampered. Tom does it so naturally and with such sensitivity.

"So, Rob's away for a week?" I double check. Since I'm about to nail his wife in his bed, I need a little reassurance. I know it is all clear, no reason but a nervous flutter. There is a massive amount of trust between Callie and I. This is really venturing into territory of the badlands. Confidence in your partner is paramount.

"Yep, I asked him to text me when he gets to his first overnight stop."

"That reminds me, two things. First, I must send a message to my brother and thank him for the weekend

coverage. I will do it a bit later. And, secondly, there are a couple of things with our project I would like to discuss. No rush, just as long as we do it before I have to leave."

"Okay, I have a couple of things as well, they can wait till later. What are you supposed to be doing for the weekend, anyway?" I am curious.

"Hunting with my bro."

I explode with laughter.

"Hunting. Did you tell him you were hunting my bit of bacon?"

"No, but I suspect he has it worked out I am hunting something close to that."

We chuckle.

"What's your brother's name?" I roll onto my side, swirling the water.

"Chris." I enjoy the view. *You have beautiful legs.*

"Don't you have four brothers?" I ask. The champers tastes sweet as I let my lips linger on rim of the glass.

"Yep, I'm the eldest and he is next in line."

"He sounds like a nice guy. Is he the accountant?"

"He is qualified like me, but hates doing numbers."

"Is he into the hunting thing as well?"

"Yep, he's just starting to get into it. He's bought himself a couple of rifles and is now learning the basics. I have him organised to come across the ditch with me to show him mountain hunting," I say, my eyes wander down through the bubbling water to see the outline of Callie's map.

"He will love it. Where does he live?"

"About an hour from where I live. He picked me up from the airport when I came back from Canada last time."

"That was good of him. I assume he is married?"

"Yep." My eyes are feasting. Callie is in all her glory, now where do I start?

"Kids?"

"Two sons and a daughter, but it really upsets me, he is forbidden to even allow his kids to ride a quad bike."

"Really?"

"I kid you not, it's ridiculous," I say with disdain.

"What's his wife like?"

"She seems nice enough. But from what he tells me, she spends more money than he can make, and that is an achievement I must say. He makes heaps and he is at the point of cracking a wobbly."

"How old is his wife?"

"About the same age as him. It was funny last week when he bought himself a hang glider. He said to the guys at the shop, if you can have it in my garage before lunch, it's a deal. That was so it was there before his wife came home."

"Why?"

"His wife cracked the horrors and was really angry."

"Why can't he own a hang glider?"

"I don't know why, he might fall out of the sky and not keep making money, I guess."

"That's ridiculous."

"Tell me about it, anyway, he is the only one who can do anything about that. We've had the discussions."

"So, he's your protégé?"

Tom is reclining back with his head resting on the soft neck rest. His Herculean shoulders bulging out of the steaming mist like a giant edifice. He is so edible. His muscular arms rest along the bath rim as the water ripples over his chiseled chest. I know what his sculptured body does to me. Butterflies. Heart flutters. Spasms. And those lips are so goddamn edible.

"Not really, just being his big brother. The main difference is he has kids and all the responsibilities that go with that. It puts a totally different perspective on the things I can do and the things he can do. He needs to get

the balancing act sorted out. I am biased, and he is to blame as well, but it has been a total over indulgence in his household. Though, from what I observe, he is a really good dad. He simply needs to get the work, money and expenditure equation more balanced. He's a smart guy and the light bulbs are flickering."

My eyes are closed, and I enjoy the water as it soothes me.

"Tonight, Yogs, we will consume copious amounts of champagne, purple Pornstar chasers and a joint or two and I'm going to screw your brains out till you are senseless," I confirm.

"Absolutely, I have a surprise or two of my own that will rock your world Mr Bear," I squint and look back with mischief.

With the most profound seriousness, I know Callie is more than in. I can feel she is letting me play this part of the game for her own delight and her seduction has me completely captivated. The stage is set for one hell of a session, one that would intimidate most, filled with lust which will power us through to the early hours and beyond. I'm thriving on it with such a willing Student.

Our banter is fun, flirty and titivating as we discuss how we can share more time together, his ideals, my interests and so on. He is so easy and playful to be with as we banish the world beyond and focus on ourselves. Our fun seems to always lead to hot talk and when the intensity increases again we can't keep our hands off each other. A wink of an eye, a sly cheeky smile, satisfied, we are both on a high for hours savouring the aftermath.

I duck out to the vehicle, retrieve all the extra necessities for the weekend plus a special little present. Callie's story of cold toes and feet while working in the snowfields of Alaska gave me the inspiration. A snuggly pair of woolen ugg boots will warm her toes and feet. I've also included a

black sheepskin, made into a bear rug. I have a plan for its use. I don't want to get the real one too messy.

"Howdy."

I am leaning into my vehicle when the familiar voice scares the daylights out of me. Nick the maintenance man has sprung from nowhere.

"Saw your vehicle Tom, knew it was yours straight away," he says with a grin. The towel wrapped around my waist looks suspicious.

"How are you going, Nick?" I extend my hand trying to look calm and collected hoping my towel doesn't drop. He is an associate, but a nosey one. "I had to do a plumbing job. I had to crawl into a cavity to try and get my shifter around a loose joint. Damn thing ended up drenching me," I say. "My clothes are in the dryer."

"I was just doing some hedges across the road and I was sure it was your truck and when I saw you come out, I knew it was you," Nick says with a cackle.

He almost sounds like he is in cahoots with Jessica as a CSI plant.

"You working Saturdays? Man, you must be busy. You into plumbing now?"

"Yep, busy as fuck, mate," I reinforce. "Sorry, but I have to go, I was just down here to get some tools I need to finish the job," I say. Luckily there is a wrench in the cab.

"Okay, no worries," he nods, "good to catch-up mate."

The thing that worries me is he mows my mother-in-law's lawn. It's a small world, damn. I'll just keep this one to myself even though my day has been a bit destroyed. Callie doesn't need to stress, but I am, just quietly.

"Oh My God. I'll never have cold toes again. Thank you so much, you didn't have to," I say. My mind boggles with the black bear. "You have plans for this don't you?"

Don't you love a man who takes charge and leads the way? I do, and although I have set a basic outline for the agenda this weekend, I know the horny male in this heated room will take the lead. It is exactly as it is supposed to be, in my books anyway. My job is to make him feel at home so he is relaxed enough to take liberties when he feels the timing is right.

As we luxuriate in the spa, I casually take in, at a glance, my Adonis in all his glory.

If she only really knew what was running through my mind, this is all getting a bit too close and my rules of play are disintegrating in front of my eyes.

13

The stage is set. The silver pole catches the dim light, a hint of a silence beckons as my private dancer takes centre stage. The first beat pumps through the stereo speakers, her body awakens, she begins to move, simply oozing sex. Her cavorting sends shockwaves through my pleasure vision stimulating my pulsing cock. Embellished in risqué threads of lace, my imagination cuts through to her mound beneath. The 'come fuck me' stilettos and black G string exude sex. Callie's sensual routine knocks me off my chair and spins me out as she seductively hooks her feather boa around my neck and lures me in for a kiss.

I gaze to the heavens, thank you Teacher, if it were not for your training I would have lost it in the first twenty-seconds. My cock is on high alert and the urge to plough in is deliciously tempting. Squeezing her arse and leg muscles together, with the strength in her arms, she spins upside down. This woman is one fit, sexy outfit. My eyes are agog drinking in her provocative sequence. Perspiration glistens like watery diamonds sprinkled all over Callie's flesh as she channels her whole heart and soul into her routine. I pinch myself, *this isn't a dream, this is really happening.* The last beat is perfectly timed. Straddling my lap she sucks my tongue.

Plugging my lips into his, it is my turn to dominate his body. Leaving him sunken in the chair, I peel the lace from my body, piece by piece leaving my heels in place. Re-straddling his legs, I arch my back and skim my breasts along his chest and past his lips. I sense him inhale me. Curving my arse in the air as I delight in my mating dance, I want to take him. Seductress at play and horny as hell, I feel like a bitch on heat. I part my opening and sink onto his pulsing erection. *I am ready to have my way with you.*

Dancing on his pole, my breasts bounce in his face, each nipple having a turn on his salivating tongue. Amalgamating in climax, I gush juice all over his immersed rod.

Regaining my breath I lift her light frame off my cock, delivering her back to the pole. Using her feather boa to softly tie her hands around the base, her body lays along the lush carpet. I totally savage her boundaries, pushing her limits. A quaking, sprawled seductress is splayed on the floor as I climb off her. I've turned the tables and hammered her into submission.

Wandering out onto the balcony, I place the cutlery and napkins on the table. Sauntering over to my man, I hug Tom from behind. Dusk is in the air and Tom's aroma is inescapable as my arms wrap around his torso snuggling my head and smooching a kiss into the back of his neck, his warmth radiates through me.

The ambiance is divine as I feel Callie wrap her arms around me. I feel a mystical sensation of inexplicable feelings. Her warm face nuzzles into the pit of my neck, blending with the intake of visual arousal, I am mesmerised. Throughout the millenniums, our species have gazed with the same quest for enlightenment, I am certain.

"Callie, doesn't this make you ask, what is it all about?" I ask dreamily. "When you look out into the night sky it really does have a mystical affect."

"It does, it really does. We are all so obsessed with material things. Just look at that beauty and all it entails."

"It is simply magical tonight."

"I don't understand why more people don't take the time to stop and smell the roses. Hold me, you feel so warm," I say, placing my arms around Tom's neck, bringing his mouth to mine. It is a perfect night to stargaze. Chilling out on the deck we enjoy the view and share in each other's company.

"Hey, Sexy arse, can you see if you can fire up the BBQ for me?"

"Not a problem, Luscious legs, if yours is anything like mine, it'll be easy, we have everything that opens and shuts and I am sure it can't be much different," I say, the black cover hides a replica.

Firing up the outdoor BBQ, Tom takes charge of grilling some juicy salmon steaks. The smell wafts across the balcony as I finish preparing the side dishes. It will be a pleasure to share this evening with my dream lover. I sense he is in his element.

The afternoon session from lunch till now has been intense and with only a quarter of the champagne bottle to finish, the mood for experimenting is welling up. Variations and imagination are our cocktail ingredients for over indulgence. The circular dish in the sky has started its climb and the radiating light is alluring, shedding over everything. Dark shadows disappear while familiar shapes return from their hiding places and the red eyes of the night

critters become visible as possums and koalas grunt and grumble. Their chorus is harmony to my ears and reminds me of being in the wilds.

The moon is golden orange as it crowns over the horizon, gradually revealing its glorious fullness. It is bewitching as we sit in silence witnessing its magnificence unfold to highlight us in its glow. The darkness excites me, mischief stirs as I snuggle in close and run my hand down and along Tom's inner thigh.

"Ready for a Pornstar?"

"Let's do it." I grin cheekily. "I have the purple concoction ingredients. So what's the story behind this purple stuff?"

I am more curious than ever.

"A couple of years ago when I was in Canada, I was at a bar when two wayward girls with punk rock hairstyles came in. You should have seen their hairdos. They knocked this country boy for six. Anyway, they sat next to me, we started talking and before long we hit it off. They were drinking this purple stuff. It looked like one of the sexiest cocktails I had ever seen and after two hundred dollars we rolled out of there into a cab."

Sexy and dark purple, just like my Teacher's stockings.

"I am looking forward to tasting this wicked little purple devil. You do the honours." Tom confidently picks up each bottle. A heady mix of red, then blue swirls together to form a potent deep purple. It reminds me of his purple satin sheets. One headache coming up, I register. The ice cubes playfully dance in the swirling haze and my first sip is sweet and delicious.

Giggling like two juveniles, we sip and chat as if we have no cares in the world. We playfully unwrap the plastic bag of weed and add Tom's freeze dried stuff. Now it's time to blend our efforts jointly. The strong odour of dope hangs in the air. It is the forbidden that has been ingrained into us that makes the shadows larger than reality. The challenge we've set is unfolding and we are eager to step across the line, just this once.

I'm feeling pleasantly tipsy and the alluring purple drink is tipping me over the edge. I take another gulp.

"How good is that?"

"Call it a hydraulic leg opener," I say raising my glass, taking a sip.

"My legs will be open, that's for sure. You are going to nail me, aren't you?" It tastes sweet and smooth. Oh… My… God, it's sublime.

"You got it in one. I'm going to have you chilled out and take you into the realms of ecstasy."

Callie's body will be a spasming, quaking mess as I hold her there giving her a taste of a whole new level.

I couldn't care about tomorrow. Nothing else seems to matter but the two of us sharing our purple potion and rolling a joint. I am relishing the transgression into forbidden territory. I want this man to take me there, I feel secure in his hold. I know he will bring me no harm.

It has been so long since I have rolled a joint, I must look like an amateur. I am making this up as we go. A pair of scissors will render it fine with paper wrappers to hold it all together. The strong smelling greenery is chopped and cut. Rolling weed into something resembling a 'joint' is definitely not my forte. We are not here to get plastered, so one should do the trick. We are enjoying this task together as we egg each other on like peer-pressured teenagers.

"Looks like a professional job. What do you think?" I hold it up to the light for closer inspection.

"It looks like a bought one."

"Okay, do you have some matches and a candle?"

"Give me a second, I'll get some."

All those childhood memories spike up and tease my mind. A tick off the old bucket list; drunk, stoned and fucked, the big three combination of teenage naughtiness.

Callie takes her first puff and she almost chokes. There is a splatter, a raised hand to wave off the smoke that is hanging and a guttural cough to follow. A swig of the purple devil clears her throat, ready for another draw. This time she inhales fully. Health conscious Callie is right into it, giggling, slurping down purple devil and puffing on weed.

"How do you feel?" I ask.

"It must be a dud," I say, sounding impatient. "I don't feel any different."

We fall about sniggering.

"Wait," I caution. "Give it a few minutes."

Five minutes come and go, but nearing seven minutes, the concoction of purple devil and weed take over and we are locked into a haze, kissing, licking and devouring each other like we are possessed. I can feel it is time to blow Callie to bits and scatter her in all directions. I'm floating away, but not enough to forget my Teacher's instructions for moments like this.

I feel young and frisky. The weed is starting to take effect and my brain begins to blur, throwing any inhibitions I have right out of the window. This is going to be sensational as every part of me is surrendering. Feeling amorous and down right lascivious, I want to experience it all. A surge of flushed cheeks warms me into sublime relaxation and a deluge of lustful, horny thoughts sear through my fuzzy consciousness. There will be no secrets tonight. Our spirits will be dancing on the table. Isn't he gorgeous? My cheeky devil has perched on my left shoulder beaming its little red horns and winking, tonight there will be no inhibitions. The night is all ours to disgrace.

The garments hanging from our bodies are discarded in all directions and as the air grows cooler I gather Callie up in my arms lifting her off her feet to carry her to the bedroom. She is wrapped tightly around me. Together, we collapse onto the bed, burrowing beneath the cool sheets.

We are like two kittens playing, clawing, biting, licking and fur-balling.

It's from the instant we lock our lips the transfer of energy is hot. Skin to skin, lips to lips, thrust to thrust. The passion is so deep I feel I could just burst with the fullness of my heart. Tom's burning desire, mesmerising gaze and irresistible scent all wrapped into one emotional filled aroma. It is intoxicating.

We lie breathless and intertwined for what seems like hours. My head sinks into his chest as drowsiness takes over and sleep is imminent. I feel warm and secure cradled in his arms. He holds me tight as if he never wants to let go. My heart melts.

I roll over and wrap my paws around my purring kitten like a big cat. My kitten immediately responds with a kiss. The blankets are an absolute mess and it is amazing we have slept at all as the air is biting. I feel selfish at three o'clock. There is no warm up, just a quick and frantic mount like an old tomcat.

A strong hand gently traces the curves of my body as I lie on my side. I feel a sensitive brush under my breast as his fingers sweep down along my midriff to trail over my bellybutton before diving straight down to part my mussel. It is so stimulating. Slow, deliberate strokes outline the folds of my lips, working closer and closer towards my vagina. His fingers rim my slit then slip inside. Wet from the very first brush of my breast, now my nest welcomes his prying advances. Tender, gentle strokes arouse me even further as I groan and arch my back like a stretching kitten.

"Oh, that's divine."

Without warning, I am swept onto my back and mounted. He spears me with one fierce, provocative thrust. Instantaneously he growls with pleasure as he gasps for breath. I can feel his arms pinned to the side of my breasts shaking as the aftershock shivers his senses.

The moon has disappeared while we've been intertwined in slumber. The new day is welcomed in with another coital collision. Lying in each other's arms, we are looking forward to today's activities.

"I have a surprise for you today," I confide. It is something Tom would never have dreamt of doing.

"I can't wait. Does it involve more nailing of your luscious legs and sexy arse?" I respond with a wicked smile. Callie has planned a surprise for me. Something I have never experienced and very different I am informed. She has me intrigued, but I am not going to guess. I want to be surprised.

"Wait and see." I know he is going to love it. "Feel like brekkie in the spa?"

"I do, I'm famished."

"It'll be ready in a flash, the tub should be nearly full now so jump in and I'll bring it in."

The goddess of luscious legs has struck again preparing to indulge me with coffee, a hot spa, scrambled eggs and buttered toast. I can feel my body recharging. I am in heaven immersed in the warm tub.

"There, how does that look?" I say. A delicious smell wafts through the bathroom as I arrive with our hot breakfast.

"Amazing, thank you," I say and beam a smile Callie's way.

"Pleasure."

"Honestly, how is your head this morning?" The effects of last night's exploits are negligible.

"My head is surprisingly fine, thank you," I admit. It's not very often we get to wake up together, my smile broadens as his face lights up. I slither into the water to join him.

"It must have been all the physical activity that drained the toxins away. That is the benefit of doing things in moderation as we still have today, and half of tomorrow to

go. We don't want to spoil it all by being totally whacked out."

"I couldn't get over how high you took me. My internals were in a constant state of rapturous tremor," I radiate, settling back into the warm water.

"The pleasure was all mine. I was into you as if I was an extension of your body."

It is my divine pleasure feeding on Callie's body and incredible energy flows. I feel honoured to be awakening her daring soul, as we play uninhibited. She trusts me. I must respect and honour her trust as I nurture my Student. Pushing the boundaries, I constantly assess to ensure I don't break her limits and totally ruin her.

"Well, you can do that to me anytime, anywhere you like. It was unbelievable. I was upside down, around about and spinning out of control. Are you sure you didn't inject me with something wicked?" I playfully add.

"I did. My cock," I say, giving my crotch a rub, showing off.

"You held me in a constant state of flux. Seriously."

I might have taken her a bit closer than I thought.

I have planned a little pampering, followed by a picnic lunch and have deliberately chosen a secluded place for this exploit. I will be in constant surveillance mode searching for any familiar faces that may have the potential to totally spoil my day. It is not as if my playmate can be passed off as some sort of stranger. The last thing I want is my secret lover to be public news. Rob would be furious, and I'd be out on my ear. I am having way too much fun for our infidelities to be discovered. It must remain our secret.

"Point me in the direction you want me to drive. I have no idea where we're going, remember," I say, looking left, then right as I back out of the driveway.

"Taking your utility is much safer than my car. Half the people around here know my car and your utility will go unnoticed," I say. I peer out of the window, looking for anything obvious.

"Why do you think I have a tradesman's work utility? Because no one would have a clue as to my existence, they are everywhere."

Except fucking Nick, I think.

Pulling into the driveway of a day spa and beauty establishment, I shoot a shocked look at Callie.

"This is definitely a first." I am just a plain basic model, but this one has won me. "Do you realise they will need a week to work on me? One look at my nails will make them go to the garage and search for a horse file for starters."

"No, they won't. Once they look at your hot arse, they will want to drop your pants and mount you. I know what's inside those pants," I say, I smile trying to be innocent.

"Rubbish, they will run and scream," I say, rolling my eyes.

The aroma of incense sends a spicy essence that radiates throughout the air. I inhale the enticing scents. I love the relaxing effect it sends to my brain. Ushered into a heated room with instructions to change into white gowns, Tom sticks his hand into my crotch with a cheeky grin.

Massaged from head to toe with supple hands, I lie there totally oblivious to my surroundings. The sweet young thing delivering my treatment is at least seventy years of age and reminds me so much of my grandmother. I'm glad she isn't my Teacher. I'd be on my back in between strokes. She is gentle and softly spoken, gliding around the table effortlessly with little waste of energy. Words are not necessary as the steam from the volcanic rocks gently heat the room.

"I think they are ready," my 'grandmother' whispers.

"I am going to place one rock in the middle of your back first, it will be hot, I will tell you when I am lowering it."

Her gentle hands begin to place hot, volcanic rocks along my back, then along the backs of my legs, shoulders and neck. I hear the door close. I am left alone to absorb the radiating heat. I am transfixed by their power. Powerful is the only way I can describe the feeling. It very nearly turns me into a comatose state.

I cannot recall the time the door re-opened, but I feel the now cool rocks being removed from my body one by one. It takes me time to recover enough to peel my body from the table. What a treat, I don't know what it costs, but it was worth every cent.

I am a converted cynical male hot rock therapy junkie after one session. I might even lash out and treat myself by finding a pile of flat rocks and try it on Callie sometime. This is a must, I have to learn it, and I want to add it to my bag of tricks.

Callie is in the waiting room, having finished her own plunge into the rock pleasure pit. She smiles and asks the obvious.

"Like it?" I can see Tom has enjoyed the indulgence.

"I loved it, if you told me how good this was going to be, I would have never believed you. Thank you so much for organising this, it was unbelievable, we have to get some of those hot rocks," I say with a kiss on the cheek as a thank you.

"Pleasure, you spoil my body, so I wanted to treat you to a little indulgence."

I am chuffed.

"Thank you, I seriously enjoyed every second of it," I say, my whole body feels limp.

Across from the day spa is a park by the edge of the water. Carting fold-up chairs, a bottle of bubbles and a picnic lunch, we plant ourselves under a leafy tree. Feeling pleasantly subdued, taking in the vista over lunch, we casually chat admiring the view.

Ducks know picnickers are easy targets and a pair try their luck with us. We reward them with tidbits for their efforts to amuse. This idyllic setting stirs us into courting activities again. The innuendo and flirting is always omnipresent as our bodies begin to stir. The relaxation session is finished. We are hungry, not for food but rather the passion of flesh on flesh. The hunger is taking charge again and I already have a fuck plan for this afternoon that is going to reward Callie for her special surprise. It will be long, slow and sensual. I intend to deliver it with an intensity that is powerful, just like the hot rocks that originated from their volcanic environment. The exchange will ignite a pit of pleasure, molten heat will run and it will be a hot sticky explosion decimating her bed.

Returning home, our things are packed away. We cuddle on the couch.

"You've outdone yourself today, Yogi." I am still chilling out. "Thank you, you are an angel."

I am besotted. There are no words to describe the throb in my heart.

"It was my absolute pleasure, Bear," I say. Never let this twilight vanish. We share a tender kiss as we wrap our arms around each other, embracing in silence. "Make love to me."

Tom bestows a slow, passionate kissing session manipulating every inch of his sensual tongue and a gentle teasing of my taste buds. As I slowly caress his back he pulls me closer to his body and massages my breasts, I feel my nipple draw erect against his fingers. My hand reaches down as I massage his cock feeling pre-cum ooze out of his crown.

I work the stickiness along his shaft, massaging him as he hardens in my palm.

My pussy tingles as he strokes my edges dipping closer to the wetness he has created inside me. His tongue is reaching further down my throat as he lifts the intensity of his kisses and strokes my neck. I shiver in anticipation.

We move into a sixty-nine position. I am dying to taste every inch of him. One touch of his tongue on my bud and I melt like butter. I slowly lick the entire length of his throbbing mass, swallowing him inch by inch. We delight here for several long devouring minutes.

Taking his time he lays me on my back. I am hungry to take him inside me. Slowly, inch after sensual inch, I feel his pulsating length enter me. He presses down. I rub up against him, grinding him from underneath, pulverising every inch of him while he pounds deeply into me.

He begins to ride me harder and harder and as his vigour intensifies, with one final thrust we explode together, filling my entire slot with hot desire. Breathless, we reel in the moment. I want to stay here forever. He holds me tight to feel my heart beating. Don’t let me go, not tonight. Hold me. Hold me.

14

I feel as deflated as a pricked balloon. Returning to reality, I open the front gate. It is this return to the enclosure and the apparently normal system of the day-to-day cycle that has me stifled. I am so conditioned. I immediately look at the roadside lawn. It is in need of attention after only three days. It is this thinking that creates my entrapment. I shake my head. It's back to reality, or else. I am more determined than ever to break out. My life is ticking by, my three passions are not going to stand by and find their own fill. The groundwork is laid, I just have to keep focused, and I can taste the inveigled web. Callie's sex manual is the final link in the thread of temptation.

Sitting in the seat of my car, the vehicle is stationary; I look in the rear vision mirror peering into my own eyes. I see a change. I'd let myself physically slip into a pit before my dad died of a heart attack, it was time for me to shape up or ship out. I am next in line to drop off the family tree. I don't want to see any of my brothers go first, but I don't want to give my body the early excuse for a quick exit plan either. Changing my eating habits, a flexible part-time job of hard physical work and a fuck buddy are all paying dividends, big time. I've shed thirty kilo's and am reaping the benefits now, being able to totally nail Callie's brains out in marathon long

sessions. I am grinning. It is the sex drug infusion injected into me making me want to devour Callie's convulsing spillage. It has me hooked. At least I have made one of my three passions into reality. The next two, here I come.

Loud music is pumping through my stereo. All the neighbours know I am home. I know it is safe to text Callie as she is still home alone for the rest of the week.

I want to maul your sexy arse.

Laughing, I put the old truck into first gear and re-enter the constricted zone. Shutting the gate, I leave my demons in the background. Just shut the gate and drive, I instruct my brain, it's back into remote control.

A forbidden text dings on my phone.

'Ooh you are a little naughty… are you texting me?'

My little voice inside chuckles. Rules *are* meant to be broken.

I respond.

Maul me anytime Bear.

I will need a week to recover from the onslaught.

My mind is scattered from the takedown. Tom screwed me senseless. The house feels lonely without his company. We laughed, danced, ate and drank and played with every molecule of each other's bodies. From head to toe, tasting, touching and exploring, it was orgasmic. I had my entire body turned inside out in pure lust.

Reclining in a deckchair in the sun, I stare out at the view. I recall how Tom chopped the weed that almost turned me green. We had so much fun as the purple devil entered my system and it is all a little blurry after that. Why have I lived such a sheltered life? My mind flutters over memories of hot raw, passionate sex, the spa baths, the endless flow of champagne, his smile, and his body. God. His body. Why has it taken me so long to discover this cache of jewels? It is like unclasping the lock on a long lost treasure trove and clutching at handfuls of the sparkles within. Each time we meet he reveals a few more of his secrets. The way his tongue moves into my grooves, pinpointing pleasure zones on my body, shooting missiles into my brain. Timing his rhythm to take me out at his whim. My treasure is there to be unshackled. I hope this is only the beginning of our journey into the trove of attraction. Our debauched tangle in the sheets has me yearning for more.

Sauntering back inside, I begin to piece the house back together. Everywhere I look is a reminder. The pole has smears from our bodily fluids. I will need to air the mattress and wash the sheets on a long cycle. Everything has secretions of our love juices all over it and the place smells of sex.

A soft, black feather lies on the carpet. A smile brushes my face as I relive my pole routine. Tom's look was priceless.

Parking in my driveway, the place is obviously empty and a wicked smile smothers my face, I should have stayed longer.

I must thank my brother. Scrolling through the list of contacts I select his number.

"Chris, how are you going?"

"Good TB. How was your weekend?"

"Excellent, thank you," I chuckle. "Thanks for the coverage, appreciate it, mate."

My thank you is sincere.

"Not a problem, anytime, but you owe me one."

I deflect the conversation.

"I know. Now, we need to get some dates organised for your trip across the ditch."

"Yeah, I was wondering when we were going to lock that in. I want to get it programmed in so I can block

out my calendar," Chris says, sounding like he is on a mission.

"Okay, well, what makes the most sense to me is, how about we do a Thar hunt?"

"Sounds good to me, just sign me up. I'm keen."

"I'll email you the details after I discuss with Jess what she's doing."

"Sounds like a plan."

"Okay, and thanks again," I end, hitting the red button.

I look around my surrounds, my subconscious is calling me a bastard. I don't have a hunting license. My application to acquire one was eliminated several years ago and I continue to justify, 'what she doesn't know, won't hurt her.' How wrong are my male brain cells? I'm just hoping over the next couple of weeks Nick, Jess and her mum don't end up sharing a cup of tea together. The thought runs through me like an overdose of salt.

Dragging myself around the house my shoulders slump in depression, I need another fix. My junkie status with my thirst for annihilating Callie levitates my thinking as my inveiglement plan blows out of proportion. I will do anything to have another hit at the risk of an overdose. Turning my computer on, my need to partake again is already calculating a next time. There is an instant flow as our ritual of cyber-play grabs me by the balls. There are still site visits this week. My week looks like it is planned. Planned for fucking.

∞

Thank you again, Luscious one,

You were right, it was the best weekend ever.

The Pornstar drinks, champers, exquisite food, hot rocks and weed were all amazing. I'm still having orgasms over your pole routine.

Like to mess those sheets up again? Yogi site visits cummminnnn uppp…

The pleasure was all mine. I am walking around my empty house in a daze, not knowing quite what to do.

Thank YOU for sharing such a wonderfully intimate and erotic weekend with me. I will never forget it.

xxx

P.S. Site visitor register is open for Bear registration.

∞

Pouring myself a tumbler of whiskey, I am in my own land of bliss.

I send an email.

As I read and re-read through Tom's emails, I know we have both been bitten. The love bug has dug in so deep, we are reeling from the sting.

∞

I am in trouble. I can't stop thinking about you.

I can't eat, I know I won't be able to sleep and I can hardly breathe…

This formidable distraction is all too consuming making it very hard for me to concentrate on anything else but you.

∞

My glass of whiskey quickly disappears, as does the next. The smoothness is mellow. I am chilling out. The smell and taste quench my thirst helping me to forget about pussy juice, briefly.

I hear Jess' car coming up the driveway and decide I had better get my Sex Savant arse into gear and get dinner organised. Sex Savant or no Sex Savant, dinner thank you.

"Evening Jess," I say in a husky voice.

"You feeling a bit horny?" she asks.

"I'm always horny," I reply.

If only she knew what I have been up to.

"I know. Let's have dinner first. I'm starving."

"Sure." I might be in, but there is a process I have to adhere to, I always have to wine and dine this one first.

I'd better start manufacturing ball juice. Now.

I lick, suck and slide her knickers down. It's amazing how a bit of competition spurs my cock to new heights. I can't believe she didn't get a sniff of Callie on my breath or cock. First thing I did was lick her pussy to get her flavouring and then ran my knob through her slot for an extra coating. I was scared in those first ten minutes. The covers and sheets are left in a tangled mess. One nailed happy wife. The morning air smells of our creamy aftermath. I think I might plant a quickie into her to really make sure there is no suspicion.

"I am going to get a coffee and breakfast. What would you like?"

"If you are making, how about scrambled eggs?"

Extracting myself from the sheets, I have three tasks; coffee, emails, eggs, all in that order.

∞

Good morning, Luscious one,

Raining like cats and dogs. A snuggle up day...

You would be a mess all over the bed sheets by now, I would have rolled you over, kissed you, rimmed you, while talking hot talk into your ear…

Good morning, Sexy,

Snuggle up with you any time.

Did you mention rimming me? Yes, please, I can't possibly have dry sheets now can I? They were wet for three days while you were here… Let's do it all again in the rain.

XXX

How about a spa, coffee and then a session in the warm water?

Champers in the spa, followed by a wicked little purple sweet treat to start the day, now that's our sort of breakfast.

Want to sneak in a phone call today?

XXX

All of the above and more would be my wish for the day. Would you like to cause mayhem on my body? It has recovered overnight and is ready for another onslaught, as only you know how. Want to come over and play in the rain? Still home alone. Cum and get me…

Phone call, yes please. That's breaking the rules isn't it?

∞

He is such a tease and I love it. These mind games are endless as we weave our web of lust. We have created our own unique language in our own wicked world. More and more of his rules are being broken… it is very interesting.

"Okay, Jess, breakfast in bed." I beam a reconnection.

"How is your coffee, like some more?"

"Yes, please," she says. "You are a good fuck. Not just a good fuck, a bloody brilliant one."

And that's a compliment from the woman from the flower power era.

"Liked what I did to you, did you?"

"I did."

"Well, if you let me, I could teach you a lot more," I say. It slips out before I can shut my mouth. I should not have said a thing, big mistake.

"Is that right?"

"I'll be back in five, I'll get your coffee." What was I thinking? I escape to the kitchen.

The kettle hisses and the plunger wafts caffeine as I fill it. I return, recomposed.

"Chris and I were discussing our Thar hunt."

"So what does he want? A free guide."

"No, he will pay the costs," I say, back peddling already.

"I was just trying to bolt the timetable together so it works in with everyone."

I have opened a Pandora's box. Why didn't I just say Chris would be coming over with me on a certain date? I am so dumb.

"You know what happens, every time you help someone out it costs us."

He is my brother, but she is right.

"I know you are right and I'll set the ground rules before we do anything. I promise."

"Okay, I don't care what date, as long as it doesn't cost us anything, things are tight at the moment," she says. There's sadness in her eyes.

"Just make sure we have time for another go at a whitetail deer if we can," she adds.

My eyes are agog at the endless possibilities. My mind filters back to our sex manual. We are extremely audacious having never taken on a business of this dimension or style. It will be challenging and confronting I have no doubt. This doesn't come easily or naturally to me, it is outside my comfort zone completely. What was I thinking?

The perfectionist side of me is saying you can do this. My realistic side is contemplating all it entails. Words like gargantuan, Herculean and overambitious come to mind. Are we insane or just plain crazy to take this on? All of the above and, I have thought of our name, I can't wait to share it.

The forbidden number hidden in my phone I can't resist, and I dial it. It only rings once and Callie is on.

"How are you?"

"Awesome, gorgeous, and you?"

"Awesome, I'd like to nail you, right now."

"What are you waiting for, come on over."

"I wish I could."

"I have a surprise for you."

"You do?"

"Yep. You ready to go boot scootin'?"

"Anytime with you, Yogi."

"We're booked in for the Country Music Festival, it's going to rock your world."

"Are you serious? I like your thinking." Pinching myself. "What's the lineup?"

"All your favourites," I say, my voice filled with excitement.

"That's going to cost heaps."

"Don't care, you're worth it."

"You sure?"

"Yep."

"Okay, I'm in." I have to be in, who wouldn't. We definitely have a double dose of planning genes between us. "Make that a Hell Yeah. I'm in."

I wave my free hand in the air, practicing my air guitar swing.

"It's ages away, but start getting excited, gorgeous."

"I know it's still a long way out, but those are the risks we take."

Assuming we are still together. Next year's calendar is filling rapidly, we have more planning happening than the Pentagon.

"Okay, you have a good afternoon, you just made my day, thanks."

With a definite commitment to plan our future, the lineup pushes my buttons. I like having things organised and that is a trait Callie and I share in abundance. We both know we will be there on time, on target and with all guns blazing.

It never ends. I just hope doing the actual work on our project is easier than doing the administration.

∞

Cal,

What a challenge. They have lodged all our information so we can acquire our tax numbers, but apparently the taxation office is running a couple of weeks behind and it will take up to three weeks to issue. There's nothing we can do till we get a number, puts a bit of a spanner in the works.

No drama, we have patience. In the meantime my creative juices have been flowing. I have a name for our entity, how about something meaning the quality or state of endlessness or having no limits of time, space, or other quantity? I thought that sounded like us, one word captures all of that. What do you think? It will be our secret.

I like it, let's go with it. It is in my calendar to follow up the tax office in two weeks and I will keep chasing them each week after that if we don't have any success. I know it is difficult, but we can't move any faster, the system is the system.

I've been thinking about our marketing plan. We are going to need to get a YouTube snippet and set up a blog site.

Might have to film your sexy arse.

Is that right. Gee, that will scare them.

How about we just film your legs?

Your arse, I could just eat, so will lots of others.

Funny one, we will see.

You wait till we get started.

∞

Hundreds of emails a day plunge into my inbox, my replies, just as many to keep up with Callie's hunger to satisfy my deranged mind. Unrelenting in desire, we want to get into each other's pants. We are hot for each other. A week of site visits will leave Callie's 'holiday hole' weak from our bed sports. We are so into each other, I'm surprised our infection hasn't landed us in hospital with an infatuation virus.

∞

Good morning to the Luscious Legs that pushes my buttons…

My mind is going wild with the thought of you. I'm about to clear my desk, and once it is clear, I could use it as a workbench to drive you senseless. I'd like to take you apart, bit-by-bit. Starting with your clothes. I want to eat them off, then devour each leg and then kiss the entire length of your arms. I want to suck the life out of each nipple and then drink you dry. I could really dish out a mind blowing, leg bowing session—ARE YOU INTERESTED?

Now let me think about that for a minute? Actually I only need a few seconds… Interested? EXTREMELY… I am on the verge of a terminal illness; it is called bonked to death… Borderline breathing, knows no threshold, limitless boundaries… YES, I AM INTERESTED…

I will be there in an hour, Luscious Legs.

One whole hour. I am hanging out like you wouldn't believe.

I'm having withdrawals as we speak and this feeling is unfriendly. I need your hands to rupture my body apart, your tongue to live on my skin and to feel you inside me with raw emotion. Dreaming…

I'm going to lick, suck, and devour you.

Are you ready for me?

I'm always ready for you.

∞

Tom pushes through the door, the bulge in his pants visibly swelling. He probes his hand straight between my legs to rub my thigh. My hand slides down inside his shorts. He gasps when he feels my fingers curl around his cock. I rip down his shorts so he is uninhibited and his throbbing cock thickens in my hand. Desperately, he reaches down to feel my wet pussy.

My heart races as his rigid cock spews pre-cum. Frantically, he rubs fast between my parted wet lips and over my swollen bud. Both aroused, we masturbate each other to find some relief.

Eager to taste her gorgeous wet slit, I force her back against the wall. I kneel before her and discard her wet knickers. I spread her legs to open her pussy up to me. I

devour her till she can take no more.

A trail of destruction wreaks havoc through my body as we both soak up the gooey aftermath. I love these daily site visits.

∞

Thank you for visiting site today. Same time, same place tomorrow?

Yes, I wouldn't miss it for the world. While the cat is away, the mice will play...

I have a new song for you to add to our collection. Download the video, now. You are going to love it. The film clip shows a pole on the back of a truck and I know you are going to want one. Now that should raise some eyebrows when I get my cowgirl boots on and climb that thing. Want to cum boot scootin' with me?

Be awesome fun...

xxx

Awesome song. And yes I want to boot scoot with you.

xxx

∞

"What? A pole on the back of your utility."

Jess looks at me like I'm on weed.

"Yep. A gold bastard, it'll look hot."

"What part of your brain is not engaged? Add that to the broomstick you have on the front of your vehicle and everyone will think you have a problem with your manhood. Driving around with that, you'll look ridiculous, I won't be getting in your truck with you, no way," Jess says.

Don't judge a book by its cover, don't they always say? I could easily have one fitted that is removable, wouldn't that be fun? I am thinking of a future fuck plan. Callie, watch this space.

My brain cells expand to take in what I am contemplating. I am lost in my faraway thoughts, almost in a trance; it keeps me amused, Callie upside down and inside out. That's an awesome sight.

A hot summer night parked somewhere private in an open paddock. A party for two with loud music, a few champagnes, we inhale the bubbles and each other. A hot passionate session follows.

The countdown is on as we badger each other with anticipation.

∞

Hell yeah. We'll be dancing up a storm together. I'm definitely going to get one of those poles installed on the back of my utility.

I want to play with you so badly, it's a shame we live so far from each other.

We DO live too far from each other, 'cause I could get lost in you right now for hours.

That is for sure. I miss you…

One of the problems with this game isn't it?
I miss you too…

Just one minor one, yes.

You set the rules…

I know I did.

Ever considered breaking your rules of play?

No.

Why?

There has just been no reason to go that far.

∞

Following a week of lust, passion and raw, nonstop sex has left me all but frustrated. I am disillusioned by his last email. I am falling for him more than he is for me, I fear. He did tell me his rules of play from the onset.

I hate his rules.

15

Unearthing ways to light Callie's fuse, I've been scrutinising her body to further explore her switches and toggle her buttons. I already have most of it contrived, but I want to make sure I don't overdo it and burn her out. I am identifying how to make her juices flow constantly. From the moment she jumps in the car till I manhandle her out the door I want her oozing and craving sex. It raises my testosterone levels ready for her sampling.

As I sit at a blank screen, my challenge is to develop imaginative ideas to fuel the fire-pit in her belly as she anticipates our next encounter. It's time to increase the dose. Everything I have added to the concoction has merged nicely, exposing her to lewd acts of fornication. My inveiglement craft will totally transform my Student to Protégée status. I just need to keep uncoiling the pile of rope. Then I will really get my dose of sweet salt into her veins.

Callie's next buzz is obvious. I'm very surprised she hasn't already experienced the thrill of this one. Her mossy mound is as black as midnight on a moonless night. I relish the sight as my twisting tongue dances through the strands feeling its way through her hairy bush. As I unfurl her inviting underwear, her vagina sucks my chin in like a vacuum, surrounded by her fur. It is time to change the sensation and taste a naked mound, exposing her bud in all its glory. All my students have shorn their pussies and fallen in love with the sensation. Once they exploit the slip-slide along my back it is like getting humped by a reckless pup as their clit grinds into the small of my back. Callie, it's your turn to get down and naked.

I'm going to frame this as a dare. My eyes narrow, I can already taste her slickness. I imagine her hot, wet juice of ejaculating cum ooze from her bare lips.

I type faster.

∞

Ever been TOTALLY NAKED Yogi?

I am not talking about strutting around in your birthday suit.

Your furry mound will have a new realisation providing a sensation of attractant for my pussy licker. Your black hairy magnet will be immaculately groomed and fuzz free.

Smoothness adds an enhanced dimension. Long dark fibrous knoll turned into a cue ball, smooth as a baby's arse, clean as a whistle. Are you ready for your naked hair free session?

∞

I am cackling to myself. My lips are salivating at the aphrodisiac of my own tease.

"What's so funny?" Jess says and pokes her head around the office door. "Can I have a look?"

I flick the screen to minimise, it flashes like a red flag.

"You've been looking at stuff you don't want me to see. Are you online with someone?"

I've been sprung.

"No dear, Chris sent me through a great picture of two people screwing on top of the arch of a bridge. It was a progression; first she mounts him, and then rides him and finally she produces a bottle of bourbon in her hand. She waves it about after taking a swig. It's so funny."

Chuckling to hide my nervous twitch. I tab on the minimised icon in the corner bringing it up to full screen. I'd already planned for this very circumstance after my last near miss.

"I will send it through to you." I look over my shoulder as she leans against the door jamb.

"Okay, you do that. Like a coffee?" CSI is on patrol I sense. I can feel her piercing stare.

"Yes, please, dear."

I hope I'm not going to get screwed over here.

A new email appears in my inbox, the sender changes my focus.

∞

Hi Tom,

Been to the camping store, I'm all confused, there are too many things to choose from.

Can you help me?

I want to start collecting. I received a bonus and half went into my savings account and the other half I want to use to get stuff for my travels.

So excited.

Thanks, Haley

Howdy, Haley,

I've attached my gear list and an article I wrote on gearing up for mountain hunting. I'm already planning where I might take you.

Tom

Tom,

Thanks for the gear list, with each pay cheque I will buy a little bit more and save the rest.

Do I need to bring a gun with me?

I've been trying to practice here, but no one has any time to show me. It's frustrating. I've been targeting cans and fruit like you told me, when I can.

Thanks Haley

Haley,

No need to travel with firearms. You can use mine. Keep practicing; the only way to get better is practice, practice and practice a bit more.

Tom

Tom,

Everyone knows I'm coming down-under next year; they are all excited for me.

H

H,

Not half as excited as I am...

Yes, won't be long before you book your ticket. It is exciting for you.

I'll hit you with some dates before long so that you can organise your travels around our excursions into the mountains.

T x

T,

Awesome.

Hx

∞

Totally naked? Ouch. Sounds arduously distressing to bestow upon my mound. Where do I start? It is a jungle down there surrounding my bower of bliss. Tears flood my eyes thinking about the pain to be inflicted. I will need to take this over several innings to bear the onslaught to my undercarriage.

Beads of perspiration scatter my brow. How do I explain my bald patch to Rob? He will think I'm having an affair with a lesbian. I know how he ticks. I will have to come up with some excuse like I read about it in a magazine or it is the latest craze for pole dancers.

∞

Do you mean totally naked? Ouch, it sounds so painful. No pain, no gain I guess. Don't hold your breath on this one…

My tongue and pecker are tingling with anticipation. Your Luscious Legs I will be parting, wide.

xxx

You can foretaste my naked button and hairless mound already, can't you? I'm not sure if I can go through with this one, it will be too suspicious to unleash at home.

Leave it with me… I will not divulge my secret right now.

You will only know when you possess me.

Bear me as you will…

Yours in lust,

Cal xxx

∞

My Teacher would be animated with excitement. My motivation rivets through me. When she impaled me totally naked, I was gone. The hotness of her cum seeped through my skin as she ground into the root of my shaft. Her clit gripped my pelvis sending her spiralling.

Now, I have an insatiable appetite to devour Callie with a naked pussy. My fingertips dance along her slick legs exploring her inviting opening. The tip of my tongue massages her silky skin. Get ready to be slurped and sucked, Callie. I'm hungry to taste your nakedness.

All day my mind has been darting in several directions trying to figure out the best way to prune my topiary. Shaving will look and feel good for one day only, plucking will take a year, and waxing? Double ouch. There's no time left to go and have a Brazilian. My epilator should do the task. Surely a little pain down there will be manageable?

∞

Morning, gorgeous,

How's it hangin'?

Sleep well I hope? How fabulous is this weather? It'd be great for an outdoor romp in your spa.

xxx

Good morning, Luscious Legs,

I slept very well, thank you.

Awesome weather here, sun is shining, not a cloud in the sky.

I have a busy day at work with heaps of physical activity.

I'm feeling fit as a fiddle, keep up the physical activity as you are going to need it to keep up with me. I'm feeling like a long, hot, intense all day session with you. Want to feel wet from sweat and gushing juices?

Don't forget you have your challenge to complete by tomorrow.

And… Yes, plans I have for your body.

It's all a work in progress. I haven't disappointed you so far have I?

Of course you have plans. I never doubted that for a moment, it makes my job so easy. I turn up, get my brains screwed out for an entire day, share hot and cold bubbles and fine food, what else could a girl possibly ask for? I'm still pinching myself to make sure I am not dreaming all of this.

I'm going to massage the entire length of your spine with my hard cock. Once I have finished your back rub, I will let my rod slip down and search out your lube from your freshly plucked silky hole. Then I'll ride your back and bite your neck until your body tingles all over. Holding you down, pinned tight, with one thrust; I will make you squirm and spasm out of control…

By the way, that is item number three on tomorrow's list.

xxx

∞

Tom is so fiery and it does things to my brain and leaves me hardwired. He has me totally worked out and the more he taunts my sex drive, the hungrier I am to eat him and dive into his shag pit. His raunchy words haunt my every waking minute. He is so hungry to tear me apart; he has no mercy, he is fearless and he goes hard at it, leaving me in the midst of euphoria. His instinct is god given and his primal attack is as hot as hell.

∞

Item three on the list is sounding rather erotic, one and two will be equally as blistering I suspect, leaving me sizzling, smoking and sweltering no doubt. I know your back massages make me tingle all over. I can't see you so it leaves me impassioned with anticipation…

∞

I have run out of time to test the sensitive skin around my hairy mound. Plugging my magic machine into the wall, I flick the switch on and hover over my pubic hairline. This is not going to be easy, inch by inch I take it from different angles, trying to get some relief from the raw, swollen, bitten areas. The combat is sending shock waves through my body, piercing my brain with torture.

How do women do this? This is excruciating. I collapse on the hard ridge of the bath, holding on to the edge to take a breather. Lying at my feet is a mop of black wiry growth. Is that all mine? I snigger. I am only half way there and I haven't even attempted my undercarriage. I really should have gone to a salon.

Reluctantly, I stand again and feel a hot rush surge through me. Looking down I see my raw skin flaming with aggravation. 'Damn you, Thomas' I curse. With half an hour left to go, I must complete my pursuit.

My stomach is a knot of nerves as I take the last turn into Tom's driveway. Love drugs pump through me with violent palpitations. I'm feeling foxy with my bare tenders. This is going to be one hell of a ride. I can just feel it. I run my fingers over my slit surrounds. That feels smooth.

Now familiar with the gate's lock and chain, the pond to my left and the affectionate puppy that greets me. I chuckle as I pat his crown and tickle under his neck.

I scrutinise Callie's sparkling almond eyes; I sense it, I feel it, the anticipation is palpable. Locking lips, my hand wanders down her stomach and over her curvaceous hips to tantalise her inner thighs. Her flesh is as smooth as silk. I stop short in tease. I am searching for a hint. Is her

dare done? My fingers flick over her knickers, there's no bulging mop. Yes. Pre-cum oozes in sticky foretaste.

My nerves soon dissipate as his welcome embrace wrings me out like a lovesick sponge. I am infatuated. Tom's strangling muscular arms choke my frame. My lips are seized and possessed. I accept his wandering hand exploring my inner thighs. His foreplay of carnal desire is reaching fever pitch.

"Good morning," I say, greeting Tom with a warm smile, I lower my eyelids sheepishly. His welcome kiss is passion filled. My heart skips a beat as my feet retouch the ground.

"Good morning, Luscious one, how are you today?" I whisper.

"Better now I'm here."

Down in the trophy den, I've strategically positioned the lounge. Draped with a silver-backed wolf skin, it sits directly under the imposing bearskin that hangs on the wall above as I lower Callie into the fur-lined pit.

In front of me is an oversized high backed armchair, draped in a fur of some kind. Tom sinks me into the soft, lush fur meeting my gaze with his dilated pupils. I beam up at him through my lashes, lured by his charm. He is in his element. His taunt begins. He strides around the chair without a break in skin contact. My sultry eyes flirt, accepting his dangerous advances as the mood sharpens.

Her dress hangs limply over her thighs. There's no subtlety as I finger my way up Callie's luscious legs to find her knickers. My hand scoots in like a hawk. My talons attach and twirl. I remove the elastic from around her hips with one claw, pulling them down her legs. I toss them aside. I lower my pupils within an inch of her vulva, she is stripped naked, her virgin skin is pristine, her smell intoxicating.

Froth gathers on my lips. My eyes absorb her raw, beautiful sex. Adrenalin oscillates through my body. My dare has been executed; my Student has scored

impeccably with her execution of baldness. I am going to make Callie love her newfound chum as I sensationalise her senses by running my knob through her slit, pulsing a pre-cum trail.

Tom's eyes beam wide gesturing a nod at my accomplishment. All the pain was worth this precious, cheeky moment. I know I won't be disappointed. He is going to take me to infinity and back, testing my level of resistance. I feel seductive revealing my nakedness.

I had the closest of shaves this morning. I removed four days of wiry growth to give my facial skin the smoothest of finishes. Flesh to flesh; I begin exposing nerve ending to flinching nerving ending. I start my grand tour down low, deliberately climbing from there. My tongue flattens out like a cobra's hood, licking each tasty morsel. I lap at her clit, breaking open her seal with ease. It's time for a female blowjob. I want to guzzle her cum as she squirts through the annihilation. My mouth clamps down on her throbbing bud, my tongue engorges to relish her swollen female penis. I snuffle deeper into her, sucking on her juicy peach nectar. Endowing a trail along her erect button, I salivate in oral intercourse. Consecutive orgasms obliterate Callie as I snake my digit, hooking it into her pit. Hot, wet cum gushes profusely as I withdraw my finger, ingesting viciously into her fleshy folds. Her cum forcibly squirts between my teeth as I eagerly drink every drop of her juice. Curling my lips, like a bull testing for heat, I fuel my lust.

I am cherishing each amorous moment; completely succumbed to his sensual touch, entrusting every wicked word, and lavishing in his masterful presence. I feel honoured to partake in his captive ritual.

I want Callie to explore the sensations of hairless clit grinding. I need her to indulge her bald surface and experience new pleasurable sensations. My indulgence

fuck plan is simple; there are no new tricks or variations. Callie's comparison is to be unmarred. My will to please intensifies. 'Don't you cum,' I hear my Teacher's voice echo inside my head, 'your Student has delivered with a ten out of ten. Reward her and let her ride you. Don't be an idiot and sperm her too soon.'

"Now, I'm going to lie on the mattress on my back. I want you to mount me and ride me for as long as you can." My cock feels like a steel ramrod. My crown is quivering in anticipation as Callie spreads her legs wide, climbing into position. Clenching my hot meat in her fist, she lowers herself to swallow me whole, impaling herself on my cock. I feel her hot velvet glove slime me as she sucks my knob and shaft deeper into her depths. Easing my hips upwards, my pelvis is positioned perfectly. I whisper into Callie's ear,

"Ride me hard."

I am in awe with my own liberty. Every peripheral nerve ending is tingling as my vagina relishes in overload. His saddle pushes up to meet my every thrust sending shivers in overwhelming rushes through my entire body. I abuse my position, pushing down harder to encompass my ultimate pleasure zone, grinding my clit into his mound. Rising and falling in rhythm, the sensations at our union point feel magnetic. My clit throbs in a sequence of ripples until a quake bursts under the sizzling pressure. My nails clutch Tom's chest, tearing at his skin, my entire core convulsing. The surge leaves me completely breathless and panting hard.

Perspiration is dripping from my brow and beading from every pore of my skin. My brain oscillates from this drug overdose.

"Oh. My. God. Bear," I gasp. "That was intense."

It is a pleasure I struggle to explain; a spent woman rests on top of me gasping for air, her bodily fluids all over me and the air smells of sex. The heat from her body

covers me like a thick blanket. I am still buried deep inside her pussy, while my fingertips gently float along her spine. I long for her to feel celestial.

"So, did you enjoy your first naked ride?" I whisper.

"You have no idea how amazing that felt I am still spinning... Seriously."

"You did a good job on the hair removal, Yogs. Was it painful?"

The redness still shows.

"Painful is an understatement. It hurt like hell." I grimace.

"After lunch, be ready for the next session, I am not finished with you yet."

"Great, I am famished after that overhaul and a bit of rehydration wouldn't go astray either," I say, lying lifeless. I can't move a muscle.

"I'll give you a hint of what we'll be doing next."

"Oooh... do tell." An excited giggle escapes.

"Well, next I'm going to lie on my stomach, and you are going to trickle oil all over my back. It's your turn to massage me with your hands, tits, belly and that hot, wet furless pussy of yours. I want you to use your silky smooth bare tenders to ride up and down my spine and grind your bud into the small of my back and grind me hard," I say, staring into Callie's eyes with passion.

I push myself up to extract myself from the shag pit; returning with a tray of goodies in one hand and a bottle of bubbles in the other.

"Hope you're hungry?"

The champers is poured; we relax, laugh and chat so easily together. I love our effortless pillow talk; it flows with an undemanding change of pace. Carefree in each other's company, it is spontaneous and uninhibited on both sides. I am tranquilised in his presence.

"I have to tell you, Jess almost caught me emailing you. I'm sure she got a sniff of what I was doing," I warn.

"Well, I have this naked pussy I'm going to have to explain," I say pointing towards my hairless mound.

"I think we should look at relocating our activities from here," I say.

"I've been thinking the same. It's only a matter of time and we will be busted here. The same at my end," I say, lowering my gaze in setback.

"Any suggestions?"

"I'll check out a couple of alternatives and email you some details. I've been thinking about this for a while. We need our own shag pit," I hint.

"Our own shag pit?" I repeat. I like the idea.

"Yep, that's what we need."

Tom places a strawberry to my lips.

"We should look for a short term place where we can play. If it works out, we could find something more permanent. What do you think?" I say. "Something for a couple of hundred bucks a week?"

"It would make it heaps easier as most places have after lunch check-ins and it cuts our day in half. Coming home late all the time will raise a red flag," I say.

"The first half of the day into midafternoon suits us better, leave it with me I have some ideas..." I sink into deep thought.

"Okay, I'll leave it with you. Send me some details so we can discuss it."

"Will do."

"So, tell me, how *are* you going to explain your naked pussy?" I snigger.

"I'll just ride my way out of it. I wanted you to be the first to indulge," I say. I smile raising my glass.

"A great tactic, honestly. Whack your flexible friend in there and give it a whirl and don't let him go down on you. He'll taste sex."

"That'll work for sure." I laugh.

"Let's up the security. I'm having uneasy feelings," I say, a sixth sense sweeps through me.

"Remember, you are dealing with a woman, and we are the ultimate CSI's."

"Don't I know it." Feeling glad a potential shag pit alternative is in the pipeline.

"I love the animals in this room, they look so real. Every time I come here they fascinate me." I look around the walls full of mounted heads.

"Yep, I have some neat ones. I don't have them mounted these days. The cost is prohibitive. I just keep the antlers and horns," I admit proudly gazing around the room. "Do you want to know something? It isn't the trophy on the wall that pushes my buttons; it's the memory it evokes. It's the whole adventure, the planning, the hunt, the journey and the thrill of the chase. I can recall every one as though it was yesterday."

"Do you screw in here much?" I ask with a smirk.

"I'll fix your smart arse comments," I snarl, grabbing Callie, I wrestle her onto her back kissing her with passion. "Okay, it's your turn to spoil me, the oil is ready and waiting."

I point to a side table by the lounge.

"Cockless time, ride my back with your naked pussy."

I lie prone in readiness. Callie's clit grind into my back is divine as I feel her hot sponge slide back and forth.

I luxuriate in the oil massage and indulge all my senses. I come to a grinding halt, my clit pressed deep into his sacrum. Oh... my... I'm there...

Cal slides off me and wraps her arms around me. We cuddle. I gather my breath and whisper,

"I want to nail you every day, Yogi. Did you say Rob was going away again?"

"He usually heads north in winter with a few of his mates each year. Why?" I reply, still in a haze.

"Do you think you could wangle a couple of weeks to come to New Zealand with me?" I toss out there.

"I'd really love to." I plant a sloppy kiss on his cheek.

"I'm working on dates to go over right now. My brother Chris is coming over for a visit and Jess usually comes over a few times a year as well. I just have to do a little juggling to fit you in," I say. My brain cells are wickedly planning.

"I'll find out from Rob and send you the exact dates, I won't even need an excuse. I'll be home alone for a stint, so it will be easy." I smile, loving the idea.

"Okay, leave it with me." I suck on Callie's left tit. I want to bite it and leave my mark on her breast.

Our parting kiss leaves me disappointed to be going home. Driving away I smile in amazement. Oh, my, god, he wants me to sneak across the ditch with him. A couple of weeks in his playground, just the two of us, I can hardly contain my excitement.

I still can't believe this is happening to me. I have never felt so intensely high in my life. The bare orgasm took my entire world apart. My inner thighs are still tingling.

∞

Naked is the new black. I am completely sold.

Thank you for an amazing day and one hell of an experience.

Naked bits. Yeah.

XXX

Thank you for a wonderful day, I absolutely loved doing you naked. Consider it ticked off the list.

Ready for your next fuck project my Luscious one?

xxx

∞

16

"What's happening today, Jess?"

I roll off from my early morning indulgence.

"I'm staying here today, I want to spend the day in the garden," she says, still lying facedown.

"Would you like a coffee?" I ask pulling the sheets back and extracting my body from the covers.

"Yes, please, I'm going to lie here for a while, I can't move," she says, the bump under the covers remains still.

The first orange rays of sunshine highlight the wall behind our bed.

"Here's your coffee, my hands are full, you are going to have to move all the stuff off the table so I have somewhere to put it."

"It'll be okay, just put it on the book."

"Okay." I wander back around to my side and prop my pillow against the bedhead.

"I might see what Chris is up to this afternoon. I want to get our New Zealand trip organised. That also means we need to fix some dates." Taking a sip I put my hand on Jess's behind, resting it there.

"I was thinking of going over for about six weeks," I say.

"Keep talking, I'm listening," she replies sounding dazed.

"I was thinking you might like to come over towards the end of that for a couple of weeks and fly back with me."

I'm trying to keep some space free to sneak Callie over for a couple of weeks in the middle of my time away.

"I want to make some bookings so it's all bolted down," I add.

"Okay, sounds good to me."

Approval from the boss in principle delivers a wry smile to my face as I take another sip of my brew, my mind calculates.

"How's your coffee?" I ask.

"I haven't had any yet," she mutters, still sprawled out on the bed.

"Well, I'm going to have another. I'll be back soon."

As the coffee brews the beast is already warmed up from my first coffee break.

∞

Good morning, Luscious one,

How are you this beautiful morning?

Sleep wet I trust?

Woke up with a rock breaker that I'd like to sink into your honey hole to stir your nest. That would've been a fine way to knock the top off it.

NZ dates are confirmed—We can book your tickets.

XXX

∞

I wander back to the bed to find Jess perched up sipping her coffee.

"Ready for another?" I ask and she nods in reply.

I travel back to the kitchen and return.

I dial the telephone next to the bedside table.

"Who are you ringing?"

"Chris."

"It's too early," she scorns.

"Don't worry, dear, he's like me, he'll be up and at 'em."

Three rings and we are organised for a beer at his place this afternoon.

"Told you he'd be up," I sneer, feeling a bit cocky. "I'm out of here. I'm helping out at the farm today."

"How are they going over there?" Jess asks.

"Really good, another eighteen months and I reckon I will be redundant," I say, sounding confident.

"Don't bet on it." Jess shoots back.

"I've massaged my way out of all the consulting work and this is the last major thing on my plate."

Except for Callie's 'sex manual', which I wouldn't dare reveal. Anything to do with Callie stays in the box in my head.

"What are you going to do after that?" Jess puts out there.

"We still have enough cash from the farm sale to keep us going for the next two years if we are careful. You want to take a trip to Europe don't you?" I pause.

"Of course, I would love to go."

"I want to keep working away at having more time across the ditch and doing some basic stuff to keep the cash register chugging. I can't do it till I've finished my contract." I sigh.

"Anyway, I have to go," I say standing up to head for the shower.

∞

Good morning, gorgeous,

I did sleep wet thinking about having that rock breaker pounding into me.

That's awesome news about NZ. Have passport, will travel.

Have a good day.

I'm working all day, will try to be online tonight if I'm not too surrounded.

xxx

∞

I bite my bottom lip. Rob is heading north for his annual tournament and I'm going to disappear for a couple of weeks. No explanation needed, I just need to get it slotted into the work roster.

"G'day, Chris." I knock and step through the open front door.

"Hi Tom, come in, I'll be out in a sec, let me switch this computer off. Go to the fridge and grab a couple of beers will you," he yells sending an echo from his home office.

"Where's everyone?" I ask sensing an empty house.

"They're out shopping," he replies in monotone.

"What would you like, full strength or light?" I yell from the kitchen peering into the overcrowded fridge.

"Full strength, mate."

"Okay."

I grab two beers.

"So, what have you been up to?" I hand Chris his beer.

"I've been busy. A screw-up occurred and the accounting info we've been receiving has all been rubbish. Now I have to give this idiot the boot and fix it myself."

"Like that is it?"

"Yep, I hope your news is better," he says.

"Well, I'm getting New Zealand organised and working a bit at the farm. All my consulting jobs are done and dusted," I reply.

"Lucky bastard," he says. He sucks down three quarters of his beer in his first pull. "I wish I could do that, I'd love to get rid of these morons I have to work with."

"Just so long as you get some miles under your belt for fitness before you come across, I don't care."

I'm serious.

"I'm booked in with a personal trainer."

I look at him surprised.

"Awesome arse on her, too," he chuckles, "yep, she whips me with no mercy."

"Are you cool with the dates?"

Getting down to business.

"Not quite, the second lot is fine. The first, nope," he says.

His mobile rings.

"Chris Banham... Terry, I don't care, this will send you broke. He has to go and Darren told me to get on the plane and be there tomorrow to fix it."

He hits the red button.

I know exactly what he is doing and where Chris is coming from. I guzzle my beer, retrieving him another. I was once a hired gun.

"Terry's the local manger and likes this guy, he feels sorry for him. Darren owns the company and I get my instructions from him," he says. He is so angry you can almost see steam coming out of his ears.

"Forget about it, let's get down to our trip."

"I can only do seven days, not ten."

"Okay, where I want to go we will need a chopper ride in, otherwise we will spend too much time hiking."

"What's the cost?"

He is in that frame of mind.

"You, two thousand, me nil."

That gets a laugh.

"Okay, you got me. What do I need to bring?"

"Just hunting clothes and hiking boots. I have everything else already there." I confirm taking another swig.

"It is neat you having a house over there," he says unable to hide his envy.

"It was the first thing I did when we sold the business, as you know. Otherwise the money would have been spent long ago. At least this way we still have something to show for it. Now let me have a look at your boots."

I want to check the tread, mountain hunting starts at ground level in my books, the same way I look at potential students.

"They are toy boots, mate. They will last a week, if you are lucky."

I frown.

"They cost me heaps," Chris defends.

"They might have cost you heaps, but they are useless. See how the sole flexes easily in my hands."

Chris watches as I push the toe and heal up.

"They need to be heaps stiffer. They are okay for molehills, but once you get into the rocks they will roll under your feet," I advise, passing the boot back.

"You have any binoculars?" I ask.

"No," he replies.

"You have that hunting magazine around here somewhere?"

I look over my shoulder at the magazine rack.

"Yeah, over here."

Flicking through the pages I find what I am looking for.

"See these," I point to an image. "You need a set."

"Okay, good. I was wondering what the old girl could get me for my birthday. I'll buy them, wrap them up and give them to her to give me," he says with determination.

"Anyway, you look busy," I say, swallowing my last sip of beer.

"I am and this one is a major screw-up I got to deal with right now."

I see stress on Chris' brow.

The mobile flashes again.

"Tom I'll need to take this mate, sorry."

"That's okay, I'm out of here."

I gather another couple of beers, a roady for me, and another for Chris. Cracking the top I hand it over, he raises the bottle 'cheers' and turns his back in frenzied conversation.

He needs change, he has high blood pressure and taking on everyone else's problems isn't helping. Been there, done that and I am not going back. I hope I can help when I get him into the mountains. I am genuinely concerned.

I wake with a tingle so deep it aches. There's no one here to whisper into my ear with his deep husky voice, sending shivering messages through my soul. He has me impossibly aroused, his index finger pressing on my tumescent mound to feel its throb. This is his foreplay to warm me up for our morning shag with tantalising licks that wisp at the cortex of my ear.

The manly flesh beside my body is so delicious. A turn-on any woman could not reject first thing in the morning. His pulsating cock forcibly humps at my thigh in growing anticipation as his hot sexy talk continues to tremor through me. His finger further pierces through my wetness to taunt and tantalise me with skilled temptation, continuing his alluring dance, circling around my bulging clitoris, a moan runs out of my mouth like a flow of pre-cum.

His mouth engages mine as my climax shudders my insides. He drifts his wet finger across my tongue parting the union between my lips allowing my own flavour to bite my taste buds with lust. His body smoulders on mine as he rolls over and heaves into me with one commanding, virile push. Domineering, yet dynamic in proposition, the inertia is unstoppable. My slit is prised open to take in his throbbing cock. His thrust is sumptuous and imposing as I luxuriate in our wicked tango.

He ascends, inflating his surge before breaking through his release, moaning with exhilaration. Chest heaving, his mouth gasping for air, he towers above me thrusting in to magnify the intensity and release every last drop of his spunk deep into my pit. Planting a kiss on my parted lips, his tongue delves in to find mine.

'Good morning,' he would say, 'how are we today?'

I miss that morning glory and all it entails.

Reality bites hard as my notion disappears into thin air and the snoring body next to me lies like a log. Scraping my hair back and refreshing my face with a splash of warm water, I smile in eagerness to upload my online inbox.

∞

Feel like dancing? I want to tango with you and dance on your hot manhood riding to your rhythm. My tongue dancing with yours, pashing long and slow… Swallowing your taste…

Takes two to tango… Awesome day for a horizontal dance, then a spa…

Wish you could jump into my bed with your majestic tool so we could play.

Want to horizontal dance with you till the sun goes down and feel you all over my body.

Inside, outside, hands, tongue, fingers.

My whole being tingles under your spell.

Horny as and want you BADDDDDD…

Mmmmmm my wish for the new day… is to be with you. xxxxxxx

What a great way to spend a day.

Hungry? You bet, to eat your arse off and devour your sexy legs.

My throbbing clit for entree,

Wet pussy nectar for main meal.

Nipples for dessert,

Arse for afternoon snack.

Can't wait to hammer your brains out.

Thursday—Noon till?

For as long as you can play.

I have all day to play.

Bring it on, ready and waiting.

Is that right?

Yes, you rock my world. You make me create fuck plans and then deliver them like a tornado, I have a plan coming your way… can't wait till tomorrow.

I love rocking your world.

And you want more, not just more, but a total screwing.

I'll send you home with a pussy and arse that are both gaping wide and dripping sex.

I am in trouble. Shaking in my boots.

P.S. NZ dates booked.

xxx

Now we are on the same page.

Have a good day, got to run.

Awesome.

xxx

∞

How do I possibly concentrate with emails like that running around in my head? Another day behind my work desk and one more sleep. Unable to risk home soil invasion too often, I have researched and located a nook half way between our abodes. Early check in is an advantage as our limited time is precious. Booking essentials, king sized bed, sunken spa, and a secluded location. I have my feelers out for a longer term shag pit, but this will be suitable in the interim.

Breakfast? Oh yes, I had better eat before I go to work. Staring into the pantry blankly, not really feeling remotely peckish I grab some crackers from an opened packet, this should fill the spot. Firing up my laptop with a few minutes to spare I attach a picture of me on the pole at my last pole dancing lesson. Sent.

The inbox flashes (1) and there is an attachment. I look over my shoulder to confirm the isolation of my presence. Jess is nowhere in sight. The screen begins to transform in an instant, the curvaceous form that appears is inverted on a silver pole. Legs entwined, body suspended with hands and hair free flowing. The picture disguises the face. I know in an instant the form hanging, like ripe fruit, a mango to be picked, broken open and devoured.

∞

Now, do you want a good cyber session? I'm horny and will be having wet dreams after looking at the picture of you upside down on the pole. I'd like to lick and suck that honey hole and taste your sweet juices.

Thought you might like that pole position.

It is easy access for you to enter at your own risk.

That is on the list next time I have a chance to do you on your pole.

I will have a few new moves by then I'm sure to try out on you.

No, I will be trying out new positions on you while you are spinning around and around then screwing you as you ride the hell out of me while I am on my back.

I'll screw you hard and deep till I gobble your balls completely as you sink into my folds. I will drain cum out of you as you shoot deep into my hot hole. My juices will drip down your arse crack while I lay my head on your chest and I inhale your glorious manly smell.

I've been thinking about what I'm going to put your body through tomorrow. I want to see if I can make your tits express juice. When I have you spun out, I'd like to be shooting a load deep whilst biting you hard, leaving a trail of destruction.

No mercy I sense.

Absolutely none.

∞

I haven't slept a wink. I have confirmed our early check in and now I have to get through the next few hours and I will be on my way, I am gushing already.

∞

Good morning, Luscious,

Did you sleep wet? I slept hard, ready for today's play.

xxx

Good morning to you,
Excited and wet as. See you very soon.
Room confirmed. Number 10.
xxx

Bring it on...
xxx

∞

Arriving to check in, keycard in hand, I enter through the white slatted door, the room is beyond stunning. The spa is sunken into the corner of a large en-suite surrounded by clean white tiles. Fluffy towels drape over the rails, the stone vanity has plenty of bath gels to soften the senses and wipe away our secretions.

Stashing our goodies into the fridge, I pluck two glasses from the overhead cupboard and chill them ready for champagne cocktails. My nerves are fiery today, even after all this time together, I still get knots in my stomach that I can't possibly control. The anticipation and build up to these interludes is so intense, a bite of fear grabs me every time. Still.

He is never late. The door is ajar with one minute to go.

The car park is well hidden from mainstream traffic. I park and make my way to room number ten. 'Okay, here I go, bring it on,' a little voice in my head echoes.

Entering the shag pit, the air is super charged, what an amazing place. It's time to make you squirt everywhere, Callie.

One mauling after another seizes my body time after time. Rapturous tongues delve deep, discovering, taunting, tormenting. The room is filled with screams and moans of ecstasy. The onslaught is intense. Two sweaty bodies heaving to find the next high and softening to taste our next sensuous kiss, it is simply blissful.

Six hours fly by like they were minutes, relieving our bodies in between with flowing champagne and body soaked bubble baths. These precious moments in time will fuel our next divine interlude. We are obsessed and both hooked.

∞

Thanks for an afternoon of simple pleasure, Luscious Legs,

I enjoyed it soooooooooo much.

P.S. I've got two hours spare tomorrow, let's meet half way and have a car shag @ 9am?

XXXXXXXX

I must thank you. It was so good to see you again. The pleasure was all mine. How good is room ten?

Home safe

xxx

P.S. I'll be there…

∞

The two-metre white bull aerial screwed through the bull bar finally comes to a halt, as does our shagging. The

seat underneath me is like a seeping sponge. Callie pulls off my stalk and the mixed juices drain down my shaft infusing the seat beneath. It smells of sex. Callie's funnel has a long glistening thread of cum dripping down as she extracts her mount, like a spider's silk line, it clings to her folds as she lifts off. We are high on our fixation.

The dark tinted windows fog as the car park overcrowds. My head hits the roof as Tom's shaft spears deep into me, sending me into shockwaves. My breasts swing back and forth as I grind my clit and shoot down his cock as I cum.

Hitting multiple hot spots simultaneously, Tom prods a single fingertip into my belly button sending energy through my internal A spot far into my vaginal walls. I drop like a rock, my head almost ploughing into his face as he grabs me to prevent collision. My eyes roll back, my lips twist inside out. My central core explodes. I'm totally wrecked.

"That was your bonus, you can now tick that one off your bucket list, car fuck, done," I snigger.

"Thank you, I needed that. Do you realise we've been at it for nearly an hour? I am totally spent. I need to get out of here, I have to go to work."

Plucking my bra from the back seat, I redress in a hurry. I don't think I should be driving.

The car assault with a lethal weapon is over and the old utility smells of our passion. I'm as happy as Larry, whoever he is. My jeans have a moist sticky patch like candied honey as my balls sought a double coating.

Texting:

Got u begging for more?

Don't see enough of U to beg.

Pounce on each other like lovesick rabbits.

That we do, hump and hump some more.

Awesome, I love it.

Obsession I would say.

Not a bad obsession.

Keeps us going so strong.

Beyond anything I imagined.

Same, it has been a fantastic experience to find such energy.

I just love it. Lots more to cum…

Ohhhhhh yeah.

I have plans for us… we have mountains to climb.

I am sure you do, bring it on. I have heaps of juice for the task and my own plans to match.

I could eat your juice with my lips every day.

And… the rest????

I'm still hungry.

U?

Always hungry for U.

Already hanging out for your touch like u wouldn't believe.

Have a good one.

Talk soon.

xxx

The drive back goes unnoticed, my mind recapturing the last couple of hours. We are so insane. This is crazy fun. I am so in love with this obsession.

Switching my fuzzy head back into work mode I feel comfortable that the procedural stuff is happening. Wrapping my brain around our business plan is the next phase.

I am going to use a very different mindset with this business model. I have no choice, I am not just cuddling my business partner, I'm in her pants—big time. Time has come for the how and why I do things to make some changes. I can sense the same from Callie. The little hints and innuendoes keep coming and I do notice them. It is more about a journey and turning it into an adventure, a very different adventure.

∞

I've received an email from the accountant, we are now on the system at long last and that has almost been a project in itself. The Taxation Office had a system crash, you can only begin to imagine the confusion, it would have been a bit mind spinning I am thinking. Anyway, we have what we need. Let's run with it.

Hell yeah, we are on the map. Let's make this a reality.

The next critical thing on the list we need to knock over is a bank account.

Let's go with an institution that neither of us have an affiliation with. Start afresh and leave little to be traced.

Okay, sounds good to me, let me know where and when you want me to meet. I will collect our business documents from the accountant tomorrow so we have them when we reach the bank. They are going to want them I'm sure, let's get this out of the way.

Agree, I will organise an appointment time and let you know.

Sleep tight my angel with precious wings, as that is what you are to me. You are very special to me. It is the honest truth. I keep telling you, you are a beauty, yep you are.

xxx

My head just swelled.

I love working out exactly what pushes your buttons. You don't realise how many plans I have for you, oops... one too many whiskeys, my tongue has slipped, only slightly—DON'T ASK ANY QUESTIONS.

Sleep well my angel.

xxx

∞

I'm armed with all the necessary paperwork; I hope it is all the bank needs. A discrete kiss in public, where we are never seen, we look at each other with big grins. It feels weird, our first tangible interaction. We should not be standing here like two embarrassed school kids; we should be jumping out of our skins with excitement. Keycards and accounts set, we are out of there like two scalded cats, back into the sea of faces.

"How easy was that?" I say. "Our project just grew legs."

We sip cappuccinos at a nearby coffee shop in celebration.

"Brilliant, how good are we? It's all coming together, well at least the business structure side of things. Next step, let the hard work begin," I say as the froth touches my nose. "Ticking the boxes, we have to be like a dog with a bone with most of these things, nothing is ever easy, but it feels like a win."

"Easier said than done, but it does feel good to tick the boxes as you say. How exciting, you never thought you could ever play with your business partner now did you? Best job in the world, coming right up."

I am tingling with excitement.

"I like this frothy coffee, I'd like to inhale and devour you like I'm sucking up the froth. I'm going to have another one, that way I can pretend at least. Would you like another?"

"Thank you, yes please, half strength for me." I smile.

"Next thing we should do is a mini business plan. I appreciate that we are all excited, but we need to brainstorm the potentials, the why's and how's. That way it will help us to have a clear path." My analytical cogs are turning.

"Absolutely, that's a necessity, haven't we been there, done that already? It doesn't seem all that long ago that we were on opposite ends of the table deep in discussion, now we are on the same side and both our skills are merged, so watch out." I gaze at my new dream business partner.

"Okay, I will write up the key items to help focus our thought process a little. I'm so excited, this I think, is going to be good." I gleam. It has potential written all over it. Let's not trip and end bottom up.

"I know it's very exciting I must say. It gives us great scope to fire up our creative juices," I say, shrugging my shoulders, my hands clasp my knees together in excitement beneath the table.

"Much happening for the rest of the day?" I want more from today, but it isn't going to happen.

"Not really, you?" Cal asks.

"Same, another day in the trenches, it never ends, it'd be so good if we can make this into a drip feed system, no expectations, but it would be excellent," I say. A little buzz swells through me. Though, if I'm going to make it my passion, I quietly pray, please.

"No expectations, best way to be, then anything additional will be a bonus in my eyes."

"It's all good, where are you parked?"

"Down the other side, it's not too far to walk."

"No worries, will you be online tonight?"

"Sure will, chat then."

"Okay, have a good one. Looking forward to it."

"Bye." His hug feels divine.

"See you later, Luscious."

Strolling back, I feel a little flat. We should have been having lunch and an out of control brainstorming session, followed by a full on afternoon romp in the sack. This black project stuff is not really my style, but that is what it is and that is the way it will have to stay. I sigh.

17

I'm trapped, the computer is in the office, I'm down here in the lounge room and if I start sneaking up there, it will be curtains. Unexpected guests have dropped in and I wish they would disappear. They are staying for dinner and the only feed I am interested in is a dose of cyber with Callie. I am an addict. I begin to hatch a plan, even if it's only for a snippet. I hope my limp dick excuse cuts the ice.

"Look, I just need to check my emails quickly, I've been expecting an urgent proposal all day, I'll be back in five," I say, but it sounds unconvincing, even to me.

"What are you expecting?" Jess asks. The sort of question I didn't want.

"An answer from government funding for the business plan proposal, it was supposed to be here today and they promised me an answer by last thing this afternoon."

Another lie.

"Can't it wait? I thought you weren't chasing up any new consulting work?" Jess scolds, frowning directly at me.

"Yes, but this email lets me know what I'm doing tomorrow." I skulk off to the office. This needs to be quick.

The beast takes forever to boot up and damn, it doesn't want to talk to the Internet first go. Tapping the keyboard in frustration until finally I am connected.

∞

Feeling wet and horny?

Could do you in a heartbeat, nail you to the wall as I climb behind you and pin you out flat. I want to lift you off the ground with one push upwards and hold you there suspended on my hard cock. You will be totally impaled on my spear so deep that it hits your A spot like a bayonet and makes you capitulate in total ecstasy. You will be dripping hot juices uncontrollably.

Surrounded tonight, got to run.

xxx

Damn, I'm home alone till 8 and want to be dripping with ooze.

Good night…

xxx

∞

"What are you doing? We are waiting…"

I was unaware of the intrusion; it scares the living daylights out of me. I must remain cool and calm. I should have been expecting it, but I'm so in love with the obsession, the mind-bending obsession.

"Just logging out. I'll be less than a second," I mutter closing everything down in urgent mode. I shut down immediately.

"Any news?"

"No. Typical government department, and it took ages to log on to the Internet, it didn't want to talk to me tonight."

At least one part isn't a lie.

"Okay, well hurry up, we have guests, Thomas," she sighs.

Almost sprung, that was close and a little reminder of how quick all of this could unravel if I'm not extremely careful. What was I thinking doing this now? How dumb am I? Is this what it is like to have your basic sense of judgement clouded? Fuck.

The first rays hit the horizon and the machine that runs my life is abuzz. I can't help myself, even after last nights close encounter. I have to do something about this urgently. I need my fix.

∞

Good morning, Luscious one,

Feel like a day breaker? The sun is coming through the trees now.

Would like to spin you out this morning and then have a hot spa, coffee and a toe spasm...

xxx

That sounds rather inviting... a spin out in the spa and a toe spasm, spasming my bud into a pulse and tantalising the tender flesh of my inner thighs? Yessss please...

I am going to get an updated phone. Almost got sprung again last night when I was closing down the computer. The B hasn't said anything or made any suggestions or noises, but her eyes are watching...

You seriously need to organise tnat.

Best to just play it cool and spend less time on my computer and work with something more discrete.

I agree, it will be the best thing you'll ever do. I juggle both constantly so it doesn't look too suspicious.

I'll work on getting the Internet on my phone ASAP.

Have a good one, Luscious,

Talk soon.

xxx

K, chat soon.

xxx

∞

Sex Savant's timeline is on the horizon as I up my dosage of allurement. Callie impales herself on her flexible friend in her down time. She is no stranger to flexible plastic. Now is the time to bring some additions into the shag pit. It needs to be dangerous; a bit different, unexpected and something unusual comes to my mind. Callie will be squirting with anticipation.

My Teacher never used novelties; it was flesh on flesh only as she delivered her erotic invasion. It was all about touch, feel, smell and taste as she demonstrated a woman's endless pit of seductive fantasies that so easily inveigled me into my life obsession. Using her building blocks I have created my own teachings. My intellect is turning; I have a responsibility to bestow upon my Student with robust discipline. I will concede to the manufacturers of plastic, adding my own touch. My eyes narrow with a sly glint, Callie, your luscious legs and arse are all mine.

My new smart phone is idiot proof and I'm in love with it. Why haven't I done this before now? What have I been thinking? My first communiqué is an illicit email.

∞

I want to kiss you long and passionately, my tongue deep inside your mouth, probing as I replicate the twisting and twirling motion of breaking your seal. I want to climb over your body still twisted amongst the sheets as you feel my tease pushing against your flesh. My hand finds your eager wetness, fingering your leaking nectar. I devour your kisses, pashing you back. I feel you push hard against my finger as it goes deep into your slit. You groan with pure delight.

Slowly descending, I begin sucking, licking and nibbling your nipples and surrounding breast with long slow slurps. Moving down your belly I inhale your hotness, anticipating suction on your altar of love. You feel my tongue part your folds as I spread your legs and my finger finds your G. I mouth your erect bud and tantalise its throb.

You roll me onto my back and indulge me as you suck my cock, my finger hooks inside your slit to

feel your honey nectar ooze as you place your dripping hole over my mouth. Together we pull each other in tight and ride wave after wave of oral passion.

With my swollen cock in your hand, you hover above me, guiding my torment straight into your pit. Your soaking velvet glove is twitching as it engulfs all of me with one plunge. You ride me to stillness, I hold still until I feel you cum in one huge continuous orgasm, gushing sweet nectar along my shaft.

Time seems endless at our united root. I feel your need to take me. You place your hands on my chest and ride me again, grinding me hard with powerful clit gripping motions. My cock is deep inside you, I feel my climax growing ever more irresistible. Then with your final explosive shudder in unison we spasm, ejaculating hot essence of love deep into your depths. Still spasming after what seems like minutes I place a gentle kiss on your neck. Then we fall asleep wrapped in each other's arms...

OMG. That sounds absolutely divine. All my senses will be ravished with your delightful invasion.

That's the idea.

∞

The content I've typed attracts the attention of the Internet search engine crowd. Sex advertisements appear, the thing has it's own brain; it's scary. It is like the damn computer knew I was thinking dirty and there it is—my inspiration, a new sex toy for Callie.

∞

I have a present for you, Yogi. I'm going to send you a link for a new toy. It looks like the best thing I've seen since sliced bread. Thursday, be ready, because I'm going to buy you one and have it charged ready to perforate your folds.

Now that looks relentless, a welcome distraction from my daily chores to fire my flume and send me spinning no doubt. Excellent to see a toy made for two, love to share my spasms rather than going it alone, so much more fun.

Thursday, same time and same place?

Ready to play? Early check-in arranged for noon. Favourite room requested.

Want me to bring anything?

Desire, passion and your insatiable rod. That's all.

Done... That's easy.

Excited. New song for you on its way...

Love that song, you really have my taste in music sorted.

Glad you like it. It has a great beat and is right up your alley I thought.

I will play it heaps, Ohhh yeah…

I'd like to saddle up on my Bear right now. I'm going to choreograph a pole routine for your eyes only. I think you might like cowgirl boots on the end of my legs, a short-fringed skirt, my midriff exposed, cleavage thrust out and not forgetting my cowgirl hat. That should do the trick, what do you think?

Bring it on. Do you have your pole lesson tonight with Bev?

Yep, after a long one at work, it will be fun to let loose on that pole tonight. Bev loves it too. Great for stress relief, sexy dancing on a pole does that to you. It has been a busy day, it'll be great to unwind I must admit.

Awesome, looking forward to that little number. Busy day here as well. I've been boxing and packing crayfish today, trying to train the staff so I can spend more time in the mountains. That's my plan.

Sounds like a good plan to me. My mountain man turns this cowgirl on and that arse of yours is to die for. I'd like to get my fingernails into those arse cheeks and pull them close to me for that extra ounce of satisfaction.

You've given me a cock tease, now it's shower time. Can I cum over?

Any time cowboy, come on over just the way you are.

I'm dreaming of that.

You have a good one.

xxx

You too, talk soon.

xxx

∞

Oh my god, I'm falling in love with this man. He has taken over my thought process. I'm at that point in life that most people must at some time reach, when they really start to wonder what their life is about and the direction their steps are taking them along the un-trodden path into the future. The restlessness I constantly feel has probably contributed to the ease with which one man, whose inestimable sexual extravagances overwhelmed me so completely that I became infatuated beyond my wildest desires and snatched me out of my mundanity.

With a fascination to unearth my greatest pleasures, my secret life has given me a freedom to discover my individuality and sexuality to its outer limits and beyond. I know this journey with Tom has only just begun and it is a benediction of relief. With only a handful of partners in my sheltered existence, it seems I have been given inspiration and courage to explore my newfound fun with the ultimate playmate.

I can tick the black man off the bucket list. Despite his horse like appendage, he was a total disappointment between the sheets. He was a selfish man who thwarted all those fantasies I dreamt about. An Italian Adonis was next in my travels and I learnt to have my arse screwed night after painful night. A couple of other semi-long term dud relationships which ran out of steam and left me empty and hungering for something much more romantic, intangible and satisfying. I think I have found him.

Play time. I'm showered, my face is freshly shaven, and I feel smooth and slick. I ooze excitement, my mouth waters at the thought of tasting Callie. I want to taste every little morsel my pussy eater can lick and suck. I take a couple of seconds to reflect on my strategy and clear my thoughts. In the side pocket of the car door is our new fully charged toy and an eight-inch blade knife. It's about as sharp as the end of my dick as I hacked away at the blade mercilessly. I was sweating turning it into an edgeless weapon. It's so blunt it would hardly cut butter. My fuck plan requires just that for a back and forth severing motion.

The door is slightly ajar. Hot water is filling the spa bath with oils wafting a sensual aroma throughout the room. Bottles of champagne are chilling. A scented candle flickers enticingly, while mood music plays in the background. A hot to trot lace number sets off my sexy purple heels for my killer long legged look. I'm ready.

Grand finale time and there's no time for flutters, it's game on. This is my type of pursuit, there's not a nervous bone in my body. I'm here to do my business of pleasure, Callie devouring style.

I am behind closed doors in an instant. Callie is draped over the lounge. Her high heels look wickedly sexy, her thighs spread open, and knickers hitched up her slit barely camouflaging her naked velvet door as they disappear inward. Her head tilted back in a 'root me' pose. Bosoms visibly taut, her nipples stand erect through the lace covering.

I bite Callie's neck like a wolf. Growling with fangs set for the kill. I swoop in, my hand brushing her cock teaser as I slip it down under her arse till my forearm is trapped in her wedge. I throw her heels off with my free hand; they are in the way for my plan. I manhandle Callie to the wall, flattening her like a squashed bug. I push her tits into the panelling, her head pressed sideways.

Pushing my shaft into her back I dry root her, one, two three humps, sending a surge into my ball bag as pre-cum pools in the fork of my crotch. I pull back and stick my finger between her trembling legs, and am rewarded with a squirt. My fingers are hot and messy. I poke my fingers covered in sticky nectar straight into her mouth for tasting.

"This will be salty next time," I whisper in torment. I insert two fingers into Callie like a spear, lifting her higher up the wall as she tries to climb. Arms spread like a crucifixion with impalement as my palm hits bone. Her tippy toes don't quite touch the ground.

Juice covers my hand with a puddle of cum. I lower her to the floor so the soles of her naked feet touch the tiles; there is a trickle of wetness leaking to her ankles. I place the knife along the side of Callie's cheek and with one hand on her neck I whisper, "You know what I'm going to do to you?" I pause licking her face and then along the blunt blade edge.

"I'm going to sever and dissect your knickers."

My tone is serious.

Callie's eyes are focused totally on the blade till it disappears down below. My hand clamps vice-like, I feel her neck pulsing with shots of adrenaline. I twirl the blade downwards between her hip and knickers and saw with the blunt instrument to sever her panties off.

I'm literally gushing juice. I feel warm fluid pour out of me. The cold steel slivering my skin is shaking my core as I try to dig my nails into the wall for support. My sweat is making me stick like glue to the hard surface.

Undoing my belt, I whip it out in one slick movement. I glide the leather over Callie's back like a cat of nine tails master. Folding it in two I swing it into her arse. The crack is like a whip, rendering a red welt.

I whisper in Callie's ear, "You are at my total mercy now."

I spit on my hand to wank my cock. The blood pumps like a hydraulic ram and I feel my thickness hit its maximum pre-cumming surge. I take aim, lubing it through Callie's pussy lips and up her arse crack, pushing in an inch.

"No. Don't you stick that cock in my arse. You will split me in two," I whimper, shaking, "it's too big."

"Next time I'm going to push it in more than an inch," I growl as I feel her tight little arse hole bite the head of my cock. Her arse grip teases as I start pumping inch in inch out. I look down at my knob as it disappears, I hold Callie's hips, and my balls tighten, my cock nearly spunks.

I pull out.

"I'm not ready to cum yet," I snarl.

Reclaiming the new toy from the table, I am ready to dish out a flogging. The plastic horseshoe vibrates into life, humming like a swarm of wasps; it slips straight into Callie's nest. I wrap my arm around her torso and position the stinger on her clit, while it mashes into her

G spot simultaneously. With my cock in my hand, the throbbing meat is sucked into Callie's pulsing moist folds. The vibrating plastic almost knocks me off. I wheeze as it spirals a charge straight down into my nuts. My forehead hits Callie's head. I gasp, my eyes water, my brain is in sensory overload. My cock holds the oscillating cock-cunt killer hard into Callie's G spot. I hold dead still. My knob hitting deep into her pit, her internal muscles wank my cock as they ingest my shaft.

My arms are sprawled across the wall, my fingers are locked in deformed tightness, the palms of my hands are sweaty, and my legs are pinned to the wall vibrating out of control. I feel like a smashed atom against a solid mass, exploding till I can hardly breathe. My lips are twisted and I'm spluttering. I am unable to make a sound. I am in a state of one continuous delirious orgasm.

This little device is relentless, massaging with a snake-like swerve, Callie's knees buckle, I hold her tighter, and her convulsing jolt sends me over the edge. My balls climb-up under my penis with a punch, I just lose it and shoot my jizz. Pumping in and out, each thrust is a jolt in my scrotum as I empty totally. My final thrust pokes in, I hold Callie in a cable tight grip.

Callie's rag doll body slumps in my arms. Her severed knickers hang mangled around her ankles.

I sink Callie into the lounge with a passionate kiss watching in awe as she begins to recover. How high a woman can go has always fascinated me.

"Like phase one?" I ask.

"I loved phase one. No complications. No hesitations. Just straight in for the kill. I love your knife skills. Does that mean phase two is X-rated? Should I expect a machete next?" My eyes widen at the prospects. "And that new toy is a killer, it makes me tingle everywhere."

"There'll be no mercy for phase two," I snigger, sucking her nipple.

My flesh shivers, his husky, lewd voice entrances me. His peering eyes sting me and my body grows limp in his lustful stare. He is masterfully unhurried. Fuelling my fire with hot talk and a dangerous tongue flicking into the cleft of my ear, igniting my passion further.

"Bring on phase two," I demand. "After a little dip in the spa of course."

It's time to rest from our sex assault. Immersed in the warm, oil soaked bath water, jets of bubbles add to the mix.

"So, tell me more about your place in the mountains? I can't wait to see it," I say. I want to know more, I can sense it is Tom's dream to be there.

"It's my exit strategy you could say," I say taking Callie's foot in my hand, massaging her sole, I rest my head back closing my eyes.

"My plan is simple." I start massaging one toe at a time. "Ideally I'd like to live six months a year over there to be in the mountains and six months a year here. That's why I'm so excited about our project, it bolts in so perfectly as a moveable job."

I continue.

"The more I mull it over, the better it sounds."

I feel the softness as Callie's foot relaxes into my palm. "The house is simple. It's in a small town in a quiet little back street. The entire house fits into our living room here, with ten square metres to spare. I kid you not. It's three bedroom with a standard sort of layout."

I'm picturing it all in my mind.

"A clad shed for the boat and car. But, you want to know the best part about it?" I ask as a rhetorical question. "The mountains are so close you can look out of the front windows and there are five thousand foot peaks to stare at every day."

I pause. The warmth of the water is making me purr. I prop my head up and take Callie's big toe in my mouth, sucking the pad tenderly between conversations.

"Blink and you'll miss the town. I think there's only something like fifteen hundred people living there. The hunting and fishing are awesome and it is a mecca for walking. It's the only place on the planet I want to be. I feel so free there," I tell her.

"I can't wait to go there," I say. "What do I need to bring?"

"We just need to get you a pair of hiking boots and we'll fit you out with some basics. That will be a little project for us. We can do all of that here and other than that, you don't need to bring a thing, the place is totally kitted out," I nod. "With a bit of luck we can make this happen and get you across the ditch for a taste."

I look across at my Student knowing that we have escaped out of the box. All my inner fibres are telling me this is inescapable. I don't want it to end. I can only feel it getting stronger and I know that I'm captured in this web. We are becoming the centre of each other's world and the links we have created are meshing.

"So, you liked your little wall passion session?"

He is smirking.

"It was sensational, thank you. That new toy is out of control. It adds a whole new dimension like you wouldn't believe," I say. Tom is inspecting it closer as he dips it into the water to wash the sticky implement.

"So I noticed. It rocked my boat too, let me tell you."

"Does it get any better than this?"

"I don't think it could get any better than this, I mean really, could it?"

Our eyes are glued to each other, hand in hand we kiss and then embrace.

"I know this isn't in the rules, but I think I'm in love with you… is that okay?" A tear rolls down my cheek as I hold Tom tight.

"It's okay," I admit. I hold Callie in a tight embrace as my lover.

My mind is resisting the urge to blurt out my response, but I know I am in love with her and it's futile to think otherwise.

He doesn't have to say anything. I can see it in his eyes. My heart melts, tears now streaming down my face. I'm overwhelmed. I will never forget this moment. Ever.

Salty tears well in my eyes, I feel them, it is a memory I will soak up for eternity. We are intrinsically linked. Our insatiable lust now deeply binds us. We are in love. I wonder what this all means for our future.

18

Wiping each other's tears away Callie rolls over snuggling her back against my chest, I open my legs to accommodate as she nestles in. She feels as smooth as silk.

"Well, I'll be on the plane soon," I say. I'm excited.

I wish Callie could be my bag handler for this trip, but Rob's timetable doesn't bolt into it. Next time.

"I know, not long now, you excited?" I spread my arms out swirling the water.

"I'm always excited to get across the ditch." I lean back a little and take hold of my glass spilling a splash down Callie's lips.

"Hopefully, by the time you are back I might have a more permanent arrangement sorted out for us. So far everything I've tried to source requires bonds and references. Most places want a long term commitment."

"I'm sure you will find something for us," I say.

"Well, I've been in contact with a village of units and they don't require any of that stuff. They are building a couple of small villas and I've put our names down. By the time you are back they might be available." I am hopeful.

"That sounds promising. It'd be great to have our own place," I say. "It'll be cheaper than coming here a few times a week and we can use it any day or time we want."

"For sure, it sounds like a plan."

Callie is her usual super organised self and I love it.

"Now that leads me to where we are up to with our project," she rolls over, swings her arms around my neck and plants a sloppy kiss on my lips. Then sliding back, her head just out of the water and her eyes glisten.

"Now. Our business plan," I say, placing my knee in her crotch as she settles, her thigh resting in between my loins. I wrap my arms around her submerged shoulders. "Our first objective, before each work day starts is to have a fuck."

"Ticked." I giggle. I already love this business plan.

"Agreed, now, just refreshing, the key components of a business plan; goals, marketing, operational, organisational and financial. Let's get a few thoughts in our heads and keep it all fairly simple." My tone is formal.

"So, goals; I want to be your perpetual playmate. Marketing; let's have fun and keep that flexible,' I say and slide up to kiss Tom on his chin in slow motion inhaling his scorching stare. "Operational… How about you make me cum endlessly."

I lick his lips with a slurp. They taste divine.

"Organisational; well, I'll be on my back whenever you want," I admit, planting a wet-kiss on his edible lips, lingering there, "and financially; I'll always have champers chilling in the fridge for us. How does that sound?"

I slide back, grinning from ear to ear.

"We'll, that's the business plan done. I'm happy with that. Never played with my business partner before. I love it already." I nod my head in agreement.

"My first thought is, we have to get you with the program and have your computer updated, it's the only way to go. That's our first purchase out of the slush fund," I insist. "I've been researching how we can share our work in real time, it will change your way of thinking, believe me."

I fix my focus on Tom. I slither off his chest and lie back

against the edge of the bath.

"That's good, because that aspect has concerned me. I was thinking we could use email, but if we can work together through an online network that would be fabulous."

I must get with the program; it's time to change my way of thinking.

"That way we can both work remotely but still keep in touch with what each other is doing. A small outlay for such integrated technology."

"Okay, that'll be a project I can manage over the next couple of days before I go away. I'll get everything the same as you and we'll be set."

The business development is starting.

"Any chance you can set the basics up for me?" I plead.

"You source the computer and I'll set it up. Let me know when you are thinking of going in, I might be able to come," I suggest as Tom massages my foot.

"Well, enough business strategising, I guess we'd better call it a day before we both get in trouble."

"I guess we should, lover."

"Today was fabulous, thank you so much."

"Always a pleasure to be with you, wouldn't it be great to stay overnight? Seems such a shame to have to return the key tonight when we have it till morning."

"I know, it's unfortunate, I'd love to stay but I will be in serious trouble if I do."

"Same… oh well, perhaps one day…"

I'm dreaming.

There'll be no trouble falling asleep tonight for me, I think wickedly to myself as I snuggle into my bed and rest easy. I've had the most amazing day.

The early morning traffic is bedlam. I manage to find a parking space quite close to the main entrance and head towards the footpath near the front door. I see Tom waiting. He's so punctual, unlike most males I know.

"Good morning, gorgeous. How are you this morning?"

I sidle up and wrap my arms around him.

"Good morning, Luscious, well thank you, how are you?" I say, stealing a kiss in public view.

"Better now that I've got my arms around you. Love you." My head snuggles in and Tom's hand encompasses my arse with fingers spread and draws me in closer to him. We make our way towards the store.

"Love you too." I know it's creeping in. But I can't help it. "Look at the people here, isn't that something?"

I'm impressed at how many people are ready to besiege the store. There is about to be a stampede as the team leaders are having a final briefing, they all clap hands, the doors open and it is operation business for Callie and I.

"Okay Yogi, she's all yours."

In the box in Callie's hand is our new toy.

"Leave it with me. Do you have time for a coffee?"

Not very often I can hold Tom's hand and wander. It feels totally foreign; my eyes beam wide for any onlookers I may recognise. I'm feeling very nervous out in public.

"Absolutely," I say, "that's what I'm here for, a morning outing."

I perch at my kitchen bench, depressed. The next few weeks are going to be testing. But it's more than that. I'm going to miss 'us'. Day one and I already feel like I've had an amputation. The things we do together are so much fun, the emotions overriding me are overwhelming as I unscrew the wine lid. Desire, agitation, ecstasy, despair, passion and sadness are all going around and around taunting my mind and gambling with my heart. I fill my empty glass. I'm in emotional turmoil thinking about the what ifs, the maybe's and the buts. The distance is frustrating. I have to get my head around these passionate emotions whirling around and causing me total confusion.

"Callie, what would you like for dinner?" Rob asks.

"I don't mind, anything will be fine," I sigh.

I stagger to the pantry, my legs are a little unstable, and up in the corner I snatch a packet of blue pills and toss it to Rob.

"Want to play?" I am in need of some relief and this will solve two problems.

Rob smiles like a dog sniffing on heat and the blue tablet is bitten in half and swallowed down. Our foreplay has started with a glass of water and in forty minutes it will be bait the hook time.

I tuck into my bed after logging off the Internet. There were no Tom emails. He must be in transit. I am even more depressed.

"What's wrong Callie? You have been distant all evening." Rob senses all is not as it should be.

"Ah nothing, I've just had a terrible day at work," I admit. I use my poor work as a cover for just about everything now.

"You sure? You have been acting strange lately. I'm worried about you. Do I have reason to worry?" He looks at me. I know he loves me.

"Why are you worried about me?" I give him a blank look.

"Just that you haven't been the same since you started work with this new crowd. You are working harder now than when you had your own business." He shrugs.

I want to work so I have my own independence. And, it gives me my cover to play with my lover.

This is the place I love most and it's time to collect on that promised flight. The call gets stronger every time for the wilderness of the South Island of New Zealand; tramping, trout fishing and hunting the unspoiled wilderness before I get too old is my plan. My frustration has been that each year my time spent over here has diminished due to house projects and the endless list of chores and work commitments that keep me West Island bound.

"Your brother up in business class sent this down to you, Sir." The flight attendant places a spiffing glass of burgundy red wine on my tray.

"Tell him thanks, mate." I take a slurp. I'll have to tell him the el-cheapo seats down the back have better wine in miniature plastic bottles. This is terrible. I slur, trying to look posh, as if I have friends in high places.

The local transit bus service is pure heaven as we stagger in through the door after two hours of road travel. Relieved that our long day of commuting has concluded.

"I don't know about you Chris, but I need a beer," I say.

The sun is just about to drop behind the jagged peaks and it looks absolutely stunning. Standing on the deck I inhale the view, this is where I belong. I am free here.

"Sounds good to me. Where are they hiding?" Chris says. He looks in the fridge oblivious to the beautiful surrounds.

"Not in there, mate, out in the shed you'll find them," I say, walking over to the bench-top I throw him the key.

"What? Out in the shed, don't you keep beer in the fridge?"

"No, it gets cold enough here that it isn't a problem for nine months of the year. Anyway, the fridge is turned off when we're not here."

"Found a six pack, what is this?" Chris takes a swig and gargles it around like mouthwash. "Tastes good, I like it."

"It's the local drop," I say. I take my first pull, wiping my mouth with the back of my hand.

"Chris, do you want to sort something out for dinner while I get my beast configured to the local system?" I say, plugging the stick into the slot, the software starts its transfer of downloads.

"Yeah, what are we going to have?" he says. He looks in the fridge with a blank look. It's empty.

"Out in the shed you'll find a freezer. Grab some bangers and there should be some frozen bread we can toast. And, start the barbie while you're out there," I blurt.

He curls his bottom lip up and heads back out to the shed.

Logging in, I'm a happy camper. It's all done. That's the easiest configuration I've ever done.

∞

Evening, Luscious one,

All good, safely here, it has been a long day.

How was your day?

Champers would be the stimulant to complement the beautiful view as I have you perched on my lap with my arms around you, taking in the view together.

After the sun goes down I'll take you to bed and consume your nakedness...

xxx

P.S. We'll be out for the next ten days. Watch Mr. SPOT.

∞

The whine of the departing helicopter is replaced by pure silence as Chris and I stand at the foot of towering peaks. A crystal clear stream bubbles and the north-easter rattles the red tussock heads like giant swaying mops.

"Okay Chris, let's get our tents set up. What a ripper of a day, not a cloud in the sky," I say. I head towards my old camp under skies so blue, it's opalescent.

"What a place, how did you find this spot?" Chris says, staring in disbelief, he is gob smacked by the vista.

"It took a lot of boot leather to find this place, it was just like finding a cherry girl when I stumbled into this system. No one ever steps foot in here, it's nearly impossible to get into. It takes a big day's haul on foot up that canyon we flew over you know. And, it is right on the edge of most people's budget to get a machine drop off."

"It's a cherry girl alright. Bet no-one's ever been in here."

Assembling our gear we have a pile that will make our camp feel like a home away from home. I normally backpack in here with minimal gear, but we have a few extra luxuries this time thanks to the convenience of the chopper.

"A virgin place, just like you, in need of a lot of training," I joke, setting up our camp chairs. We are able to view a massive piece of country right here just sitting back and looking, without even taking a step.

We have three tents, one for surplus gear and one each, pity we don't have a couple of playmates. I know one that would like to be here.

"Got those binoculars handy?" I ask, placing the strap around my neck, I focus mine on the hillside and begin scanning.

"Yep, got 'em," he says. Chris sits in the chair besides me. I don't take my eyes away from my binoculars, sweeping the mountainside.

"The key is to look, and search slowly and methodically," I say. "Often you will only see the tiniest piece of animal to give you a hint. What happens is your brain's software will hone in its deciphering skills. It takes time and patience to master the identification process. You would think they'd stand out like a neon light, but they don't. Mostly they are hidden, waiting to be uncovered. It takes practice and patience to find them. You always have to be looking. And, once you have found one, there's no guarantee it's the one you are after."

It's exactly like looking for a Student.

"The weather forecast is mostly for clear skies. We should be able to get out and cover some country," Chris suggests.

"Hope so, one thing about this mountain country is never assume. It can change here in less than fifteen minutes and will be trying its best to kill you. Mother Nature in here is very unpredictable," I caution.

I recall several times when storms hammered in like hurricanes. Lessons never to be forgotten, my survival skills are now imprinted.

"Found one, under the bluff, just off the main ridge line near the gutter to the left. And, there's another to the right of that one." I steady my hold, trying to make sure I don't lose my positional fix.

"Where?" Chris swings wildly across the sightline.

"Wait, I'll set up the spotting scope for you," I say, darting over to my daypack I break out the tripod and scope.

"I don't think they are what we are after, but we still need to check them out," I recommend. You never know if you don't look. I'm always in search mode.

"Look in here." I move away from the lens. "Now, this is on twenty power and see how small they are?" Chris places his eye to the scope turning the focus knob.

"Okay, I've got 'em. Man, how did you see them there?" he questions. Chris changes back to his binoculars. "Okay, I see, they're just black dots. Hey, one just moved."

Chris trembles with excitement and his finger continues to adjust the focus dial compensating for his nervous shake.

"Now you know what to look for, the next couple of days we will sit here and just observe," I whisper. "No use putting our scent all over the mountainside, everything will disappear because we are, how could you put it, being loud mouths and advertising our presence. Keep your voice down, sound travels along way out here. Be patient and observe."

I sink back into my seat. I have a methodology that works.

"Why don't we go after them?" he blurts, keen as a billy goat sniffing a nanny.

"Because, how long do you reckon it will take us to get up that face and above them?" I growl. "I reckon it's a full day's climb. And, there might be more suitable ones elsewhere, they are just young ones. Patience, Bro. They won't even have pubic hair."

After two days I feel an urge to get some boot leather on the ground. My plan is simple; we climb up the vertical face and hunt along the tops behind our camp. Digging our toes into the steep shale we hold on tight to the tussock and mountain snow grass to pull ourselves up. Peering over the slightest terrace I come face to face with a bull, it stares at me. We are in gridlock. The bull has not heard or scented us, but he has seen movement, his attention has been attracted. Chris is twenty metres below me; I slowly sink to the ground signalling to catch his attention. I mouth, 'We have company,' pointing towards the bull. It stands stock-still.

"Let this one go," I murmur as Chris moves up alongside me.

"He's not what we're looking for, he's not ready to be taken, see the horn size?" I gesture. "We'll keep him in the memory banks for another day."

I wink. Chris nods in agreement. I think he is getting the picture.

"Whacking and stacking them is not my style, selective hunting is what pushes my buttons, you know," I admit. I wipe the sweat from my brow before rising up slowly to eyeball the bull. It's still motionless. He stomps his hoof, spitting out dust. Alarmed, but not frightened, he makes his way to higher ground.

"How in the hell did we get that close?" Chris pants, trembling with excitement, sweat rolls down his forehead.

"Easy, we selected a zone to make our approach that allowed us to take advantage of the wind thermals. At this time of the day, the sun is yet to hit these faces. We've been able to sneak in close, but that doesn't mean we have to pull the trigger. Always remember, when you pull the trigger the tranquility out here will be shattered and everything in the valley will know there's an intruder. That's the best way I can describe it to you, it's like being an idiot at a party; you get drunk, think you are god's gift to women and hit on the wrong one. Suddenly, they are all on the defensive."

He gets my comparison.

"Been there, done that," he jokes.

"Don't worry, we all have. The most important thing is to learn and apply," I sneer, raising my eyebrows. "Remember, they are all gettable, just like women. You just need the softly, softly approach."

The mountains span for miles as the sun beats down, sweat pours off us as we climb higher. We are in the zone where eagles soar and angels dwell. It has a spellbinding affect; everywhere you look there is endless grace. It washes through me like a cascade of ripples on a sandy beach.

"Lunchtime," I call a halt.

"Good, what a great place for a sandwich. It's unbelievable out here," Chris says, surveying the view. "If you told me that we were going to climb up here, I would have said no way. Now I know why you love this stuff, Tom. It's amazing."

Chris is breathless, not from the climb, from the vista and being out here in the wilderness.

We continue our mountain assault, crossing a steep shingle chute until I signal a halt. Focusing my attention to a bend in the stream down at the bottom of the main river. There, feeding on succulent grasses the spotter turns one bull into three, then six. I can clearly see there's a cracker amongst the herd. There's a beauty in the pack that anyone would take, any day of the week.

"Okay, Chris, you're not going to believe this," I say, turning to face him. "We have spent all day climbing our arse's off up here and down in the main valley we have ourselves a couple of rippers."

Chris looks at me knowing it's game on, even after a big day.

"Mate, we only have about three hours of daylight left. Those big bulls are what we are after. We have one of two choices, we either try to find them again tomorrow or we give it our best shot, now."

"What do you think?" He looks for guidance.

"Well, experience has taught me that when you find one that is ready to be nailed, if you let it go, there's a fair probability it won't be there tomorrow," I admit, shrugging my shoulders.

I peer through the scope again to make sure.

"They'll move on and there's no guarantee we'll find them tomorrow. That means we won't be back in camp till well after dark. Bring your headlamp."

He nods.

"It's up to you, if you think we can do it, let's go."

I survey the route. Some of it's ugly.

"Okay, I want you to watch my boots. Don't focus on anything but. We have some difficult stuff to cross and descend through, don't do anything else but follow me. Give me your daypack, I'll put it in my backpack," I say. He looks insulted.

"Don't argue. You want to do this?"

I want to taste pink meat in the pan now the decision has been made.

We begin our descent and sidle downwards on a direct path. Wedging slots in the hard surfaces to find purchase holds. Slipping and sliding we fall on our backsides, grabbing pointy plants that leave puncture wounds in our hands, and our legs ache with exhaustion. We peer over a ledge, hidden behind a big rock, they are only one hundred metres directly below us.

"I can't find the ones we want," I say. I'm caught off

guard; they should be here, the others are. Patience, I whisper to myself. One appears.

"Look, straight next to the third one on the right. It must've been hiding behind that bush."

We remain undetected, exactly how I like it.

In position, the one I really want Chris to nail has vanished. I scan and there is no trace of the animal. Patience, I mutter to myself.

"Chris, I want you to drill the one on the left next to the dark one."

The master bull has materialised.

"The one moving?"

"The one broadside, a metre to the left of that one."

"Oh," he chuckles, unable to hide his nervousness.

I'm focused through my binoculars keeping totally fixed. We've got this one in the bag, now it's time to pull the trigger.

"Take your time, it isn't going anywhere," I whisper.

The rifle belts into his shoulder and the valley echoes like thunder.

"You nailed it. First shot, what a ripper," I shout, punching the air.

Hugging, we release to shake hands. What a hunt. We are buzzing, who cares if we have to boulder hop all the way back in the dark. The moon shines over the crest as a silvery light falls across the valley. Gathering clouds begin to blank out the mountainous outlines. Mother Nature's uncertainties make mountain hunting one of the most challenging pastimes. Her moods are as diverse as the landscape she encompasses. Her annual rotational clock is ticking and there's no guarantee she will be kind. The environment she shrouds should never be underestimated. To successfully negotiate her moods and bring home the bacon or antlers takes a unique package of skills.

"Chris, see those swirling clouds starting to blanket the tops, see how fast they are moving, bet we'll get a dump of snow tonight," I say, I can just feel it in the air.

Hey Bro, look outside, did you ask Santa to pay us a visit?" I pull my head back into my tent.

"What do you mean?" he mutters through the coverings, he's totally wrecked, he hasn't moved out of his tent, not even for a leak since we arrived back late last night.

"It's snowing. I kid you not."

"You are kidding me," he yells, poking his head out in disbelief. The landscape is totally white and there's an inch covering our tents. "Lucky we did that deal yesterday."

"Don't I know it, mate, you did a brilliant job. I'm still running the whole thing through my head," I say. I'm as proud as punch.

I continue.

"Where's that sat phone of yours?" I ask, knowing he travels everywhere with it, even though I hate it. "Call us a pick up for tomorrow, let's go and get a big fish, what do you reckon?"

He looks at his shredded boots and nods in agreement.

∞

Howdy, Luscious one,

Back in for an overnighter. Bro nailed a monster. Going to see if we can get a double dose and crack a big fish as well.

Trust all is well with you.

Thinking how I would like to roll you over and kiss you to bits.

Love you.

xxx

∞

I'm not expecting an answer, as I'm not due out for three days, though, Callie will be tracking my SPOT messages and will see one appear housebound.

∞

Just logged on to follow your SPOT and saw you were home.

Just in for a bit, had a great time. Want a fuck?

Great minds think alike; want to be there ensconced in your sleeping bag in front of the fire with you.

I'm missing our horizontal dancing.

xxx

Eyes are closed thinking about it.

Mine too. I want to make love to you so bad…

Yes, please, I could handle that, copious amounts of hot sex in front of the fire.

One day?

Yes, please, one day.

Okay.

***Deal**.*

Sounds promising, aren't we breaking the rules?????

***Rules are meant to be broken, but we have a long road to go yet so let's see where that takes us**.*

For sure, we can't rush these things, having too much fun as it is.

That is one hundred percent so; we have been going so well.

Yes, let's not reinvent the wheel quite yet.

Agree; let's keep it turning at a nice comfortable pace.

DEAL.

***I should be there doing you and doing you**.*

That would be simply divine…

Now you have me jealous. What I would give to have the day, make that the entire weekend, make that every day whilst we are on the subject to play with you.

Sounding better all the time to me. I'll take everyday, thank you.

Patience… but not forever I hope.

The sooner the better, we can dream in the meantime and be together as much as possible.

Agree. Let's work away at it. It's amazing sometimes how things suddenly change, it all happens when you least expect it.

Nothing more certain than change, the more flexible you are with it, the easier the ride of life's journey becomes.

Yes, change has been something that I am constantly challenged with and accepting it definitely makes the ride easier, otherwise you end up bitter and twisted.

For sure… I have a surprise for you when you get home from your travels. I have sourced us an interim shag pit to play in. Can't wait to see you on Boxing Day.

You're amazing. That's brilliant Cal. I'm so excited. Christmas is around the corner and Boxing Day we will play, for sure.

You know what? I've been thinking I've never had so much fun in my entire life. With you in my life, it has completely changed my world and my thinking and I have never been happier.

We needed to get the spice of life happening again and I'm glad we are sharing it. We are so successful because we have so many things in common and that's why it is working so brilliantly. Who knows what the future holds, but we are giving it the best chance to succeed. Otherwise, it will blow up.

I've been meaning to sincerely thank you.

You have given me so much pleasure; it has been an experience I'll never forget—Really it has.

We've shared so much fun and a truly amazing journey.

So, THANK YOU so very much for everything.

I'm looking forward to our next chapter.

Now you go and get Bro a fish, a big one.

xxxxxxxxxxxxxxxxxx

∞

19

The keys are in my hot little hand, the place is just right for our needs, and all I need now is for Tom to get himself back over here so we can decimate the bed sheets. I have set a lustful scene in the small unit I have sourced and our shag pit now needs to be christened. We've always joked about going to the next step and securing our own pad. We will be able to steal away together to our own haven, any time of the day or night. This is simply perfect. I've created an 'Interim Shag Pit' sign for the wall that'll hit him between the eyes when he enters along with the remnants of my knifed knickers hanging off one corner of the frame in their tatters. Ruby pouting lips are splatted across the walls as an inviting lure, all a bit of a pun between the two of us. It looks great.

Another surprise I have tucked up my sleeve is a blowup pool, we love to indulge in a spa. It fits snuggly in the shower recess. I've filled the top drawer with our play toys and the refrigerator with dozens of bottles of champagne. Now I just need my illicit bedfellow home.

I've spent weeks in devious thought about a Christmas gift that will go undetected at Tom's end. Anything that can't be hidden will be suspicious. My gift must be consumable. Jess, he tells me, is an unrelenting CSI. We're unable to do the deed on Christmas day, but there is a break in holiday festivities at both our ends the following day, so Boxing Day will be our Christmas day indulgence.

I decide to design a ticket-sized book of tear off vouchers with explicit sexual favours on each. I title my booklet, 'Luscious Credit Vouchers.' The list grows; Have your way with me for a day, BJ while driving, sunset picnic for two, naked outdoor session, dance the night away, one hour body massage, oil massage—your choice of body parts, selfish man sex, 69'er, tie me up ...The list is endless.

Fifty vouchers scrawled with divine, indulgent things I'm going to do for my lover. I'm going to wear his arse off. I throw in a couple of fishing and camping vouchers as well and wrap the entire bundle in green gloss paper tied with a large red bow and include some iTunes gift songs I know he will love. I'll be dressed in tiny red intimates; my tits and arse will be his for a couple of hours. It's going to be a tight squeeze, but I've lined up my excuse. Our venue is decked out and will serve as a trial run for a longer-term shag pit down the track.

∞

Luscious one,

Watch your Christmas emails for a Santa present that will have you dripping all day. Your Christmas dinner will be hot, hot, hot...

I'm sure I'll be delighted when I unwrap Santa's present.

Intrigued...

Excited? You bet.

P.S. Interim shag pit secured and set up; I've left Santa a key under the mat in case he needs to make a visit.

Watch this space.

I thought I'd been a naughty girl??????

Naughty girls get naughty presents.

Oh goodie.

XXX.

Hell yeah, hanging on the door handle it will be. Plus some other surprises...

Looking forward to it. I have a surprise for you too. You had better be good now.

Another win for us, it's all confirmed, I have a vacant swanky shag pit for the new years break. Want to cum over and play?

I will work on my excuse right now. I'm sure my B mentioned something about a few days away with the boys, that'll give me the out I need.

I can't believe our luck, again...

∞

Driving along I feel very pleased with myself. With a key left under the mat and the close proximity of the place, I have to check it out. Especially since my next phase of Callie's teachings are going to enter a new dimension. I've got a whole bunch of stuff in my kit bag as I string out this sexy interlude. There hasn't been one thing that she has knocked back and I intend to keep my A class student at the top of the leader board. I'm getting her accustomed to variety, my inveiglement strategy is working superbly, we have a long journey ahead of us and there's no need to rush any part of it. I'm going to introduce her to something out of left field, every man's fantasy is two women and, well, maybe it's every woman's fantasy to have two men. After intercepting the mailman for Callie's new bedfellow, a plastic man will be her Christmas surprise package as I lure her into getting comfortable with the idea for the real deal. Yes, I've got wicked plans. I took delivery of the twenty kilo beast I ordered online, having tracked its every movement to avoid Jess getting her hands on it at the front gate. Hung like a horse, I can't wait to initiate my Christmas threesome fuck plan on Callie. My imagination is running wild with Callie dancing the buttocks jig with the plastic man poking her and my cock inserted from behind. I just about cum over the steering wheel and drive past the turnoff, I'm now looking for a place to hang a U-turn as I swear and curse.

Fishing my key out from under the mat and armed with Callie's bag of Christmas delights, I enter our personal shag pit. Cal has set this place up like a brothel. It looks amazing. I'm so impressed. I almost split my sides with laugher. Pool, champers, sex toys, damn, I've taught her well. I shake my head at the decimated knickers dangling off the sign.

I hang her present bag on the doorknob between the kitchenette and bedroom, attached with my plan that's sure to get her wet. Back out to the car, I retrieve the lump of plastic man, he's heavy, and at least twenty kilos plus. He is now the focal point on the double bed. I dump him right there in the middle, his cock looks dangerous.

The door is ajar and there is a tap on the timber panelling, frightening the living daylights out of me. I almost have a heart attack. Who in the hell is this? It rips straight through me and I immediately close the distance to ensure limited viewing. I'm not expecting visitors.

"How are you going?" I casually drool. "Is there anything I can help you with?"

"Hi, I'm Paige," she says, flicking her dark locks behind her shoulder. I extend my hand to greet her, while continuing to bar her entry.

"I'm here testing keys, we can't seem to locate the spare set to this unit," she explains, gathering a new bunch in her hands.

"Oh really?" I raise my eyebrows.

"Yep, I'm just testing to see if we have keys to each door," she says, flicking her hair again and grabbing the door handle to try and insert the metal object.

Equipped with a plastic four litre ice-cream container full of keys, she appears a little flustered. The heat of the day is obviously adding to heat under her collar. Sweat trickles down her neck into her cleavage. Nice set of hooters I note as perspiration patches cling her flimsy cotton shirt to her midriff, exposing her pierced belly button. I could fix that sweaty problem by licking it all off, she's a little stunner for her age. That hot and horny late thirties, early forties I just love. My appetite gets a tease. My imagination needs to get back in the box otherwise we will get an eviction notice. I refocus on the problem at hand.

"Okay," I say.

"Yeah, dad wanted me to do this job. Look at this container, there's hundreds of keys. I have to have them all sorted out before I can finish today, he said. He's a cranky bastard you know," she says in a huff. I'm red faced, the tables are turning, and my brain whirls around at a million miles an hour as reality returns. How do I get out of this? It is obvious that I have a key. My mind is blank, panic is setting in, I know precisely what she will see from the entrance and if the landlord is a cranky old bastard, we will be evicted before we even christen the place.

"We don't seem to have one for your unit," she shrugs. "We are testing all the locks to make sure that we have keys to all the on site units. Your unit is the last one. I have just about been through every key in the place, twice. Do you have one?"

I stand there dumfounded.

She looks at me, and then at the lock, I'm busted. Caught, judged and sentenced, it is a subconscious compliance. I'm captured; there is no way out of this one. Guilty, I'm unable to think on my feet about the brothel that lies before her.

"Also, there is an internal door that I need to check as well," she says, grinning. "It's a compliance thing with council fire regulations, we have to have keys for all the locks in case there's a fire."

She knows she's got me.

"I have to have this job finished today, or dad will kill me, he's pissed with the council inspector and he's in a bad mood," she adds, reiterating the urgency.

The internal door? Now my brain really gets a hit of 'Hell No'. Yes, that internal door does have a lock. My mind runs through the countless sex objects all over the place, there is no hiding them now.

Cal has planted so many devious items within eyes view; she has a knack of being creatively kinky. Hundreds of ruby lip pictures are pasted all over the walls with the central focus on entry, a sign reading, 'Interim Shag Pit,' secured to the wall right in full view. To top it off, a set of severed knickers hang off the sign's corner in all their ragged glory. Black stockings are tied to the corner of the bedposts ready for an erotic congress tie up affair. Champagne glasses at the ready on the bedside table with a flashing toy charger indicating the wicked little device is ready to play. Cal's iridescent flexible friend is on the dresser ready to be inserted into some wet slot at a moment's notice. It's amazing it doesn't spring to life telepathically. The blowup pool for two in the shower cubical neatly blocks the entrance into the bathroom. And on centre stage in the middle of the bed is the virgin plastic man with a nine-inch shaft standing up handsomely for all to see. His cock will probably poke her in the eye from this distance.

I'm down to two brain cells… Fuck. Me.

Paige, the now key mistress, is staring at me like I'm hypnotised.

"Here, let's try mine and we'll get this one copied." Amazingly, the key in my hand slips straight in and with half a turn the audible clunk of the internal mechanism responds instantly. It must be my slight tremble that has made all the teeth grind.

"Yep, I'll get this one cut for you, I can't help with the internal ticket puncher, and you'll have to try each one in that container I guess."

"That'd be really appreciated. If you could do that for me, I'll owe you big time," she says.

"Okay, I've got to run if you want this key cut today. I'll drop it into the front desk."

"Thank you so much."

Stopping at the front gate, I have to call this one in with a quick email. I peer into the rear vision mirror to check our unit, the door to the interim shag pit is wide open and Paige peeks out for a momentary glance and disappears back in. She is onto us, our deranged Santa tactics must be making a stir, bet she's going to take her time with that key search.

∞

I'm at the front gate of our shag pit. They needed to test the keys; a girl is in the place as I type this to you checking out the internal door lock. A light just turned on, I'll bet there's going to be some gossip at the front desk now. Expect an eviction notice.

Hope they don't damage my virgin present.

I put your bag of surprises on the door handle inside with a glossy Christmas fuck plan hanging on the outside of the bag. I then bolted out of there. She will have to move it to test the pile of keys she has.

∞

Sneaking up to the ladies to take a quick break to retrieve my emails, I read that our shag pit has been invaded. That poor girl will wonder if she's pregnant by just walking around our wicked pad. The lips, the sign, the toys, OMG, she will be ruined for life.

I gather my wits about me and return to my work desk, looking as flushed as the Christmas shirt I'm wearing.

It's Christmas Day and for the first time in ages, we are going nowhere, other than me sneaking out tomorrow to our interim shag pit.

"Happy Christmas, Jess," I say. I lean across to give her a kiss and stroke her inner thighs that are still tingling.

"Merry Christmas, Tom," she replies.

"Thank you for driving last night, I don't think I would've been capable," I admit. Christmas Eve at mum's place is a tradition in our family and I always eat and drink too much as Chris and I share a few ales.

"Would you like a coffee?"

"You know I would," she says, her face lighting up.

Heading down to the kitchen, it's an automatic process, kettle, laptop, kettle, laptop and coffee.

∞

Love you lots, Luscious one,

Merry Christmas to you xxx

Merry Christmas Lover Bear,

You have received a gift song from Yogi.

Awesome. Thank you.

Listening now, thank you soooooooooo much.

xxx

You are welcome.

Just a taste of what's to come.

Cumming you will be as well, check your attachments…

<u>Yogi's Christmas Threesome Fuck Plan</u>

You are invited to a play in my shag pit

IF YOU DARE

LET'S MAKE A LOVE TRIANGLE

Ménage a trios

Vaginal

Anal

Oral

It's all yours to taste...

No condoms required...

That's brilliant.

Yogi accepts your invitation to taste two cocks.

YES, Please…

Christmas fuck plan, I will be there.

xxx

Excellent. All good for tomorrow?

Yep,

All good to go for tomorrow.

Planted the seed, I'm out of here.

I'll be there, will only have a couple of hours, it's the only window I can manage over Chrissie. Bells will be on, make them ring and chime.

Still laughing about the key mistress, every time I think about it. Got an eviction notice yet?

∞

It must be the day for Christmas presents, the time zone difference gives Christine the illusion that she has completed her draft thesis with a day to spare.

∞

Hi Tom,

How is it all going? The crayfish should be going crazy this time of the year, but ours are all asleep.

I have attached a draft copy of my thesis and would really appreciate if you could have a read and provide me with some feedback.

It looks like I might get back down again next year if my funding goes ahead again.

Regards

Christine

Hi Christine,

Merry Christmas and Happy New Year, attachment looks like it is all there. Will review and give you feedback.

Awesome stuff, if there is anything I can do to help with your funding submission, please don't hesitate to ask.

Regards

Tom

∞

I must arrive at the shag pit first. Armed with my skimpy Santa outfit, pieced together for my lovers eyes only are a few lacy bits, in red of course. Finally, everyone is organised and out of the way as I hot foot it, darting out of the house like a rabbit catcher.

Arriving at our shag pit, I'm welcomed by a decorated bag hanging on the internal doorknob. My jaw drops when I see what is on the bed.

'Holy hell, what is he thinking. I'm in double deep trouble,' I mumble to myself, my eyes water in anticipation. Lying in the middle of the bed is a pliable mass of moulded rubber in the shape of a six-packed manly torso, designed to be a girl's best friend no doubt, a tartan bow around his tool. My hand finds its way around the base of his shaft, it's so close to the real thing it is frightening. A twinge of excitement shoots through me as I stare at his impressive pecker.

Attached to the bag is my invitation. I wonder if there are key mistress fingerprints on it. I grin. Placing Tom's present on the small table by the bed, I throw in a couple of bonbons and reindeer antlers for fun. I scurry to change into my red lace G string. Jumping on the bed I sprawl out in an appropriately inviting pose draped over my rubber mate to await real flesh arrival. Leaning over I practice my blowjob skills on my new bedfellow. My lips are doing the wild thing getting into rhythm when the door opens to reveal Tom's cheeky smile. His eyes drink in the package on the bed.

"Ready to unwrap me, Santa?" I ask.

Without a word he swoons down, slides my knickers aside and slurps on my slit as a welcome treat.

My cock is instantly erect as I swoop into Callie. I unzip my jeans and pull them down tossing them to the side. I whisper, "I'm going to rub my cock up and down your slit, then stop at your bud and hold it there."

I take my cock in my hand and hold the head of it on Callie's bud. I feel her climax and as she does, I sink it into her in one thrust.

"Grind me," I say as I position myself over her so she can ride me upward.

I slowly begin to deep stroke her, my cock massaging her G spot and poking deep into her sweet spot. I feel her internal muscles grip tight around my shaft, teasing me.

I roll onto my back. Callie rides me in frenzy as I grip her hips down tight. Her Christmas present is ready to be taken.

"Go girl go," I huskily stir her.

"That was awesome, Santa," I say, panting. "I'll be naughty more often if you nail me like that."

I giggle.

"Merry Christmas, Luscious one, how are you?"

I wink, looking at the plastic man. We are covered in sweat from the already thirty-five-degree day; I hit the air con switch.

"I was really good till I saw plastic man. Merry Christmas, gorgeous," I beam. Extracting myself from the bed, staggering over to Tom's parcel with a wobble in my legs.

"That was just a taste of what's to come next week, and we'll be utilising our new playmate. Feel like some bubbles?" I head to the glassware.

"Of course, it's Christmas." I flop on the bed, my legs spread. I feel our juices flow out of me.

"I don't feel like anything to eat, if I do, I reckon I'll explode. How about you?" Tom says. "I will struggle with a glass or two."

"Same, this time of the year is insane," I say, rubbing my swollen Buddha-like tummy.

"You got nothing to worry about, look at my porky pie." I stick my belly out to exaggerate the pose. "How long do we have today?"

I take my first sip of the day and it isn't even ten in the morning.

"Just over an hour," I sigh. "Want a swim?" I gesture to our makeshift spa.

"Absolutely," I say turning the shower on, the water cascades in. Jumping back on the bed, I unwrap my presents.

"Thank you so much."

I lean over and caress Callie with the gentlest of touches, licking her lips.

"Like your Luscious Credit Vouchers?"

"They are fantastic, you are so creative, lover. We will be using every one of them."

"Thank you so much for the hiking boots voucher." I plant a big wet kiss and snuggle in closer.

"We need to have you fitted with some good hiking boots, let me know when you have a window of time and we'll go and have them fitted."

We lie on the bed together, chatting, sipping and smiling. These are such simple pleasures we are sharing. I could roll over like a kitten and just purr all day long in Tom's company.

"I love your plan, I've worked out the threesome thing now. You had me worried there for a minute, I thought that you had a real playmate to add to the mix," I chuckle. "And the hiking sticks are perfect, I can't wait to go to New Zealand to try them out."

"Pleasure. That plastic man is a classic," I say, rolling off the bed to move the lumpy frame over to make a bit more room for us to relax and spread out. "What a story getting him, I had to cut the mailman off at the pass to make sure I took the delivery."

"His cock's a doozy," I say, my eyes widen.

"You will handle it, we are going to christen him next week at my place," I say, "I sent Jess away to a day spa for her Christmas present so we could play."

"Awesome. You will have to get me drunk before I can take both of you, ouch."

"I'll get you drunk, stoned and horny and you'll be begging to be nailed."

I raise my glass.

"We have to give him a name, what do you reckon?"

"How about Eugene?"

"That's funny, Eugene it is," I say, nodding in agreement. "How is everyone at your place?"

"Good, I enjoyed not going anywhere yesterday for a change." I'm pleased about that. "Yours?"

"Same, except we had everyone around," I say, raising my glass for a sip.

With just enough time to wallow in our makeshift spa, we relax in the warm water with antlers on our heads and champers in our hands. It's so simple We giggle about the key mistress. Hearing the story face to face is always better.

On the landing Tom wraps me in his arms in a great big bear hug. My mouth parts and my legs quake reveling in his passionate embrace. His hands twirl along my spine, his arms over my shoulders, he devours me with one final kiss goodbye. My eyes close, inhaling his every molecule. I don't want to go, but I must.

Callie departs and I head to my vehicle parked around the back. Paige pulls up in a golf buggy towing a trailer for rubbish collection.

"Your old man got you working today?"

"Yeah, too costly to have staff today so he roped me in."

"No rest for the wicked you know. You get that key?" I ask. "I dropped it into the front desk, no one was around so I put it in envelope and I knew you would find it."

I'm throwing a little bait out there.

"Thanks for dropping it in. Bet you been busy as well," she says, her cheeky grin has a sparkling flirt attached.

"Is that right?"

"Yeah, made yourself at home I see."

I've got lots to do if I want to treat Callie to a variation in the delights of the flesh. Her participation from the ground level up in the planning, execution and taste test will stretch her limits and our plastic man, Eugene, is just the beginning.

20

Lounging in the chair under the bearskin, I take refuge sipping my coffee. Jess is in a mad flap, stuffing the last few things into her twenty-kilo bag for three nights away. Hair rollers and makeup are last minute additions that are putting her flight schedule at risk. As much as I'm tempted to push this along and sit in the car and blow the horn, I'm not that game. I will have that horn stuck right where the sun doesn't shine and that would be for starters.

I use this break in proceedings to gather my thoughts while I chill out and wait patiently. Callie, whilst she doesn't know it, is just about to finish basic training. It's so crazy, she's one awesome lady and this is complicated. I'm not supposed to fall in love with my Student. It's only going to get more complicated once Callie gets a taste of Protégée status. Plus, we have our project that's growing legs. It's definitely a convoluted web we have woven ourselves into.

I'm hungry to taste the eroticism of a threesome. If anyone had ever suggested a threesome to me previously, I would have choked. The idea has grown on me since Tom has planted the seed in my head. Tom doesn't pressure me. He encourages me to take my time and use his sexual appetite, opening up my naivety to a world of fantasy and titillation. What has struck me the most is that sex is such an important part of his life. He makes so much time for the experience and entertains it at every moment possible. And that is only his sexual qualities, there's that whole other 'us' package I'm in love with too. I'm hooked. I get a kinky twist in my mind every time I think of our rendezvous' and my mind is in this mode twenty-four hours a day.

So, how about a little dress-up for this threesome? I like to stretch the boundaries and add my own take on the plan at hand and it's imperative now that I have two cocks to please. Thigh high black boots, a black satin garter, coupled with a black lace negligee. That will get him hot to entirely devour me.

Disrobing, I place my leg on the edge of the spa bath and begin grooming my essential elements. I want to be slick and totally fuzz free as I venture into threesome impalement.

"Callie, where are you?"

"In here, Rob."

"I have to go, the guys are waiting," he informs me. My rump is in the air, legs spread with my vagina lips exposed. I score a kiss on my naked butt.

"Nice arse. Good to see you are going hairless again, I love that look on you," he comments.

I chuckle.

"Goodbye, darl, make sure you have a good time," I say.

"Oh, your mobile was ringing before," he informs me.

"And?" I look up.

"It was Asher, are you going over there, again?"

Damn, why did she have to ring?

"You watch that boyfriend of hers." He points a finger at me, half in jest.

"It's fine, I told you that Tristan is madly in love with Asher, not me." I shrug my shoulders and turn back to the job at hand. *Better watch that Tom*, I snigger to myself.

If only he knew.

I finish grooming.

"Hey, Ash, how's it going?" my mobile pressed to my ear.

"Good thanks, Cal, how are you?"

"Great. Have you had a good week?" I ask with interest.

"Not too bad, I've been pretty busy at work, but other than that, not much to report."

"Tell me about it, work's never ending. How's Tristan?"

"He's good, busy surfing and running as usual, he fits work in there somewhere too," she updates with a chuckle.

"We'll have to catch up soon, I haven't seen you in ages."

"Let's make a plan," she sings.

"Are you free on Saturday? Rob's away so you should come over."

"Yep," she says, she sounds excited to catch up.

"Okay, well, let's have a cocktail party and I'll contact the other girls and see if they can make it too," I say, my organising voice is quite excited.

"That'd be great, okay I'll bring a spirit and we'll see you around five thirty?"

"See you then, okay, bye."

This is working out to perfection My next three days will be with Tom, then Saturday with the girls. Talk about packing it in when the cat's away.

A flutter of nervous anticipation passes through my core as I prepare myself for three days of extracurricular activities. I can't think of a better way to spend my three days off work. Visiting my illicit man's house for the next few days with the sole purpose of fleshy erotic interaction. If I'd told Rob what my intentions were, I'd be in deep trouble.

It's time for a quick shower; the dip invigorates my mental preparation. I'm anticipating an onslaught today, flicking my hair over my shoulder to tease it through my fingers, I like the way it's starting to gather some length and fullness.

I'm out the door.

No one is home, as expected, when I arrive at Tom's pad. I know he won't be far behind me; we had planned his B's airport drop off with my arrival down to a tee. Jess has only been gone a few minutes and I'm on their doorstep as instructed.

Tossing my bags in the usual place, I choose his trophy room to position myself for discovery this time. Slithering onto the pool table in the middle of the dark room, I casually recline with flirtatious attitude. A small cushion from the lounge snuggles under my head; my legs sheathed in thigh high patent leather boots, and seductively crossed. I know Tom is only minutes away. My insides twinge with a shiver surging down my spine. I'm ready to play, lover…

Arriving home, I dart straight down to the main bedroom lumped with Eugene in tow. Struggling with both arms to balance his dead weight. I need a wheelbarrow to carry this hunk of rubber. Pulling back the sheets, I plonk him down in the centre of the bed. We are going to be very naughty. This is Jess' domain. Callie will be laid in my boss's bed today.

Tom sniffs out my presence; he roughly parts my legs, admiring my boots. He licks my slit the entire length wetting my pulsation. My head tilts back as I groan…

Before I can utter a word he bites me directly on the vulva sucking my breath away. He's aggressive and hungry and my knickers are torn to one side as he ploughs into me.

"Holy hell," I scream and his tongue canes across my clit like a whip. His finger slithers in seeking my G spot like an instrument of animalism. My hips buck in response to his invasion. His hands cruise around my thighs to secure his threshold, his drooling mouth clamps onto my tender bud. I clench, gripping his head, gasping for air from his slippery affliction. Teardrops tumble from my eyes and my breath escapes, "That is exquisite, lover."

I feel Callie about to enter the realm of spasms. I unlatch my suction. My eyes narrow at her splendour, inspiring her bouquet. Tracing my tongue around my lips, I take stance. Coaxing my belt undone, my jeans slump to the green felt. I punt them off our sin wagon with a swift kick. Spreading my legs, I tower above her tiny frame. Callie scrutinises my sac of jewels. I turn on the seduction and disengage one button at a time down my shirt. My cock is jabbing at my shorts like a tent pole, spewing pre-cum.

I close down to an inch from Callie's face staring into her eyes. I dribble to her lips, my vulgar talk emitting signals through her convoluted mind, snaking my head from side to side like a deadly cobra.

"I'm going to wank the knob of my cock up and down your tight little cunt, feel your juices squirt and lube the head of my cock, mixing with my pre-cum," I sneer as I tease Callie's mind, "then I'm going to stroke your slit till you cum again. I'm going to impale you so deep inside your pit that you are going to choke. When my throbbing meat parts those pussy lips of yours, I'm going to nail your brains out. I'm here to fuck your cunt long and hard."

Curling my lips, my hand wraps around my pulsing cock, stroking it roughly through Callie's trembling folds.

His knob ripples along my slit, my fingernails tearing into his arse cheeks, I'm desperate to feel him inside me. I arch up to push his knob in deeper. He holds me still. We are locked in a trance. My seal grips his cock knob.

"Now, I'm going to roll on my back," I hiss, boring into Callie's dark almond eyes. "And you are going to drop your twat onto my face while you suck my cock."

Callie's nectar hole almost suffocates me; my hands tame her flexing arse muscles as she brutally roots my

face. My chin grinds her clit, my tongue flicks whipping at her snatch, greedily slurping her nectar. I slink my finger under her lacy knickers seeking out her wetness, cowering it into her black slit. I delve in, feeling her taut little ring clamp on like a vice.

"Give me your jism. I want your cock juice," I demand, gasping and growling like a vixen. Tom disengages, as I descend on his knob, my mouth opens wide to accommodate. I salivate spilling drool along the entire length of his pulsing cock. My clenched hand moves briskly, my tongue tormenting his knob, his salty pre-cum lining my mouth. My hand grips his balls and my finger pierces into his arse hole in tease as his cock blows violently. I suckle wad after wad of ejaculating sperm, it smears all over my face as I lick up his hot sticky goo. My head spins, he whips me around to clamp his mouth on my bud. I ejaculate in a rebound spasm as he viciously sucks me off.

"If you thought you were finished, you came to the wrong whore house," I threaten as I devour the sight of Callie's sexy curves in that negligee.

Tom grabs me, plucking me from the table, my legs clamping around his waist. A surge of hormonal adrenaline wallops my consciousness. My dishevelled lace negligee is barely clinging to my body as he propels me into Jess' plush bed.

"This is bad," I say. He glares in return. Yes, in his marital bed. It has always been an off limit aphrodisiac. The image of him nailing Jess in here gets me off. I cum with a savage spurt, my trail of scent left across the bed linen.

Tom's lips are locked on mine; I arch my back, sex oozing out of every pore of my body, I allow him access to whatever he wants. He can take me however he wants to, I don't care. I'm crazy with lust.

I beckon for Eugene's monster cock with a twisted snigger. I want to feel two cocks play havoc on my body, in every entry hole. Tom descends between my legs, his tongue dancing like a wicked serpent on his prey. I'm in tortuous ecstasy. Taking his head in my hands I drive him in fiercely, grinding my lascivious hips into his face. I tremble as he corrupts and devours me. His physical extraction of lusty, sinful sex has me salivating in haste.

Tom unplugs his gluttonous lips, his face covered in lubricious juice, my pulse races in my veins. I toss my knickers aside and straddle Eugene. My head punches back, I hold his cock in my hand and drop my pussy to let him spear into me.

"Oh. My. God," I screech, cumming as I screw into place. My head thrashes back again, I gasp and sputter, tears stream down my cheeks, my head whipping from side to side. My fingernails tear at Eugene's rubbery contours, grinding into his flesh-like base, parting my lips further as I sink down and luxuriate transfixed.

Tom's strong hands initiate an erotic massage all over my back. Warm oil trickles over my shoulders and down my spine. His palm thrusts me forward in horizontal array. His chest slides along my back and his bolt of steel inserts into the tip of my vagina.

"Fuck," I shriek. Tom's cock begins sliding along Eugene's massive stiffy, both thrashing at my boundaries.

Spurting oil onto Callie's back, the slickness leaves a trail along the black lace and I thrust her down further. Spilling more oil along her bare flesh, it trickles along her body like ribbons dancing. I scrutinise Callie's greedy lips devouring Eugene's cock, her arse cheeks motion in and out with each zealous thrust.

Callie's pussy is a gaping mess. I feel her chute expand to welcome me into the fray. I begin to stalk her with evil trespass. My knob slithers back and forth along Eugene's imposing cock. I'm using every ounce of skill not to knock the top off as spasms cascade through my loins. Sweat drips from my body and I clench my eyes shut, gulping for breath. Callie screams as I plough into her, deeper.

My opening begins to loosen to the shock of two cocks impaled inside me. I'm in a vice-like grip, my muscles begin to pulse, ejaculating in multiple spurts, and I just can't stop it. The hot flushes are continuous.

"Tom, I want you to arse fuck me, now," I plead. I'm so high. "Right now."

I grit my teeth as my anal passage is invaded, my arse cheeks relaxing in acceptance. Tom's cock nearly splits me in two. I choke a massive cough and a head exploding orgasm hits me between the eyes like a banging hammer.

Pulling my pussy-juiced tool out of Callie's slot, I take aim at her plughole. Penetration is immediate; she gobbles my cock like a bitch on heat. She pushes back and I push forward and drill her completely as I begin to carve out my track. I muster the focus I need. Callie, your piece of hot arse is all... Mine. I wrap my arm around Callie's throat and pull her up harder.

Pushing down on Eugene... I hold still. Tom is slamming into me. I'm totally sandwiched and my entire being is spasming as I drift into a state of one long, divine orgasmic flow.

Callie's body is limp. I turn my mind off self-control. I want to empty my load into her dark hole. Her tight little arse hole gulps at me. Sucking, it draws me in deeper. I body surf harder, sweat pours out of me and my back arches for one final inward drive. My cock explodes like a fire hydrant. Cock juice pours in as I root up hard. A pulse of cream escapes, I hump again, another pulse releases with wad after wad I inseminate her in wicked relief. My eyes roll, my body is exhausted, my balls are spent, and my being is totally dusted. I lie on Callie's crucified body. We are utterly annihilated.

Dwelling in the spa, I crawl up Tom's chest, the warmth of the water relieves the thrashing my body has endured.

"That was one hell of a session." I smile at Tom.

"I told you, you were going to be annihilated," I say, swirling the water.

"I think you nearly killed me. A 69'er out of the blocks and then a threesome with Eugene. I loved it when you spouted in my mouth," I admit. I have just been totally and utterly hammered.

"Welcome to my zone."

I lean forward to gently kiss Callie.

"I love you, Bear."

My head sinks to my chin.

"I love you too, Yogs," I say. I wrap my arms around Callie in a tight squeeze.

"I can't believe we have three whole days together," I say. My eyes close, my arms slipping around his cuddly frame. I have died and gone to heaven.

I'm falling for him so deeply, but I'm not sure if he wants this to be more than sexual interludes, more than a discreet engagement or more than an intensely erotic rendezvous. My love for him is growing deeper with each word we share, each touch we impart, and each glance we exchange.

"This is going to make you laugh, Jess," I crow, perched on the bench-top, the ale going down nicely.

"And, what's that, dear?"

She finishes peeling the vegetables then places a tray of sausages under my nose to be barbecued.

"One of the guys at work came out with some interesting facts." I lean back taking another pull, my mouth dry from being out in the hot sun. "He reckons that he's got to stick

it into Margo at least once a week. She doesn't care if all he's done is work all week, 'cause if I don't, someone else will be doing it for me, he said."

"That's gross," Jess frowns. "He's just a deadhead and she could do a lot better."

Firing up the barbie, I watch the night sky reflecting on his comments. Just like a plumber, another job to be ticked off for the week. Ticking off a job is a process, we all like processes and structure, and it ensures that things get done. We also like feedback. My brain is ticking with these thoughts and I ponder how I'm going to progress Callie from my Student to my Protégée.

The flashlight comes on; it's amazing there are no glowworms shining in my ears. My lips turn a wicked smile, the can of worms twist with my answer. I need to give Callie feedback. I will do a report on her activities, something that is a little bit of fun, but with a twist. All through dinner I ponder these thoughts and can't wait to tackle the beast to put my thoughts down for further perusal.

∞

So Yogi, did you enjoy your time in the classroom? I hope so, because I'm going to do your appraisal, yes, that's right, you've been watched and marked.

Sleep wet in anticipation, I've almost finalised it.

I love you, Luscious.

xxx

Have you been scrutinising my arse?

It has been amazing; do I need to repeat a year?

Good night lover, you sleep well too.

XXX

∞

It's Saturday and I'm sitting back with a few girlfriends sharing cocktails. Mine's easy, a wicked purple Pornstar.

"What's that?" Asher picks up my drink and takes a sniff.

"A Pornstar…Take a sip."

"I like it," she says and takes another taste.

"Where did you stumble onto this one?"

"That's a long story, needless to say I ended up a bit broken by the time I'd finished that evening," I say. If she only knew what that initiation was like.

"I'll bet, the taste is addictive, mind if I make one as my next one?"

"Go for it."

"Can I try it too?" Ruth takes a quaff.

"Callie, there is just something about that drink that would get me very drunk and I'd be anyone's," she giggles handing it across to Bev to sample.

It never ceases to amaze me how often the flow of discussion moves towards sex and the male species when females get together. A few cocktails absorbed; and the mind settles into convivial mode and the secrets are divulged one by one. Women need to know what other women are thinking along with all the sophisticated, juicy and intimate details involved. Sharing experiences and trusting in this confided circle of alliance, the barriers retract and the confabulation sizzles. It's definitely a girl thing, but makes a female feel accepted and understood. I've certainly changed, no longer Miss Innocent,

I've been seduced and taken to somewhere I didn't even know existed.

"Well, girls, we all just have to find ourselves a lover." The purple beast is taking hold of my tongue.

"I've been there and it's all too complicated," Bev concedes. "You know what the problem is? The penis is attached to a body that you have to deal with."

"I don't know if I could, like, it'd be fun, but I'm so busy trying to make enough to pay for my new house," Asher sighs, "it has taken me ages to get used to the one I've got, I don't know if I could be bothered breaking in a new one."

"That's a worry, I'm hornier than I ever was," I admit, the purple tipple loosening my lips.

"Yeah, I'd like to be done as good as I can do myself with my vibrator for starters," Ruth adds. "I've had more than a couple of tries and each time it's over in less than thirty minutes and I'm yet to even get into a rhythm."

She raises her glass with a warped smile.

"Well, you might have to change that," I boldly tempt, my own sphere of conduct was once upon-a-time in line with their thoughts until my world was obliterated and my presupposition took a one hundred and eighty degree turnaround. My secret lover is still a secret, it is a delicate subject to tackle without giving away my 'secret life' too much, but I have to let these girlfriends know there's more out there than they are presently receiving and they need to experience being done well.

"Thank heavens for the invention of the vibrator," Asher blurts out. "What would we do without them?"

Nods of agreement follow around the table and the laughter is contagious. Infectious giggles mix well with the cocktails being consumed and the conversation takes on a whole new level.

"Vibrators come in all shapes and sizes and a girl can never have too many toys to play with," Ruth admits with a chuckle.

“The sites that sell this type of paraphernalia are a booming business as we pursue a quest for bigger, better and more mind blowing orgasms to stoke up our erotic desires,” Asher pipes in, “the more intense the delivery the better, as long as it feels good, go for it. Nothing wrong with experimenting in all manner of ways to find that pleasant buzzing sensation, then that sudden release of all that tension followed by an overall rush of fire throughout your whole body, it is so exhilarating.”

She is blushing.

“You got to get that new toy for two, girls,” I slur under my cocktail breath. “It stimulates both man and woman simultaneously and the effects can be explosive.”

Fits of laughter explode.

"I love my iridescent wand," Bev says. ‘That does things to me and gets me there every time.”

More raucous laughter fills the air, any barriers completely absolved now.

“It’s great to be wined and dined, but a subtle kiss or a stray loving touch is high up there on my wish list,” Asher admits.

The girls all agree in loud unison.

Sneaking off to retrieve my phone, I have to see if I have any hot, horny emails in my inbox. It’s so addictive that I can’t even go anywhere without checking to see if (1) is there. I’m totally hooked.

There are six sexy emails awaiting perusal, I quickly scan through the contents. Hot and flustered, I return to the job at hand, entertaining my girlfriends.

“Thanks for having us, Cal,” Asher’s voice is a little slurry.

“I’m glad you’re not driving, Ash,” I admit. “Thank heavens for cabs.”

∞

The girls just left, had a great day with heaps of sexy girly talk, hilarity and way too many cocktails.

I would have liked to be a fly on the wall.

My thoughts exactly. A bit reserved to start, but all was let loose when the alcohol started flowing. Bottom line, men are selfish bastards in bed.

Plastic to the rescue?

'Hell yeah' was the consensus. The moral of today, men don't realise they only lose by the selfish thing and it turns girls off, and they wonder why they are not interested.

It is because they are useless and the woman gets no pleasure.

Yep, always said a man will be replaced by plastic if they don't get good at it.

So the woman thinks, why go there, what is in it for me?

Most men have no idea about a woman's body at all and how it works and what feels good for them. I have been lucky I was well trained.

You are not afraid to ask the woman what feels good and what doesn't. That is the key: communication.

I'd like to hear about your training one day? Intrigued.

You will know sooner than you think. I told you I want to come back as a woman so I can experience

multiple orgasms, the best I can do is dish them out and watch and feel the energy.

You were meant to be a man in this life as you enjoy giving more than receiving. Gives you a buzz and that is soooo unselfish of you.

K, sleep tight my love xxx

Sleep like an angel

xxx

∞

21

I close my eyes sinking into a semi trance, my own body shivering at how I'm going to take Callie. My nerve endings are pulsing, my back tingles and legs quiver at the site I'm visualising. My spasms twist my gut inside out. My hands clench into tight balls of sinew and my lips prickle. My eyes are soaked with tears of ecstasy as I leave this mortal world. I almost stop breathing as my chest heaves to gather oxygen. I'm going to levitate Callie.

As the morning sunlight filters in a soft glow, I take a sip of my lukewarm coffee. A sarcastic grin unfolds on my face as I reflect back to my school days as a 'good little boy' where I was taught all the wonders of mathematics, English and most importantly, science. Sex and the mating game was a no-no, and if a thought entered my head about the 'sins of flesh,' I was in deep trouble. I'd be off to the black box and a man on the other side cloaked in darkness would absolve me. Power and manipulation frightened the daylights out of me and it was to be avoided at all costs.

After my Teacher gave me a taste of the euphoric highs of dopamine and serotonin that lie naturally inside my brain, I impatiently wait for my next high, constantly. I need to extract my fix from Callie. Today I will be taking

Callie to a whole new level. I'm going to take her on a magic carpet ride.

"Where are you off to today?" Jess asks, her tone casual, slotting some bread into the toaster.

"Me? I have a small report to finish off, then I'll need to run through it with the guys at the workshop," I fib, using my work as an excuse as usual.

"How long are you going to be out today?" she asks.

"You know what it's like, once you get there it's hard to escape and they want to show you through everything and download on you," I say, trying to appear half interested. I have become accustomed to telling half-truths now.

"Oh, okay, well I'm going in to see mum and my aunty," she says. Why do I suspect a possible drive-by? There are too many questions. My hunting instincts sniff.

"After that I'll probably go over to the farm and see what they are up to," I say, trying to extend the vagary for additional coverage. "I need to check on them all the time, they're hopeless."

The toast smells good as the machine pops a batch.

Thinking I'm through the danger zone.

"I need to finish a few pieces on the report and I'm due over there around ten this morning," I finish, heading toward the office a little nervous. Peering over my shoulder, I print Callie's assessment out, editing services I don't need.

∞

Good morning, Luscious,

Ten still suit you?

XXX

Good morning, gorgeous,

Will text when clear, but all good at this end.

XXX

Remember that bearskin rug I gave you? You will need it today.

It will be ready and waiting.

The bearskin will smell of you, saturated in perspiration that will come from every pore of your skin and there will be a stain, un-washable and un-removable.

What the hell do you have planned? I'm getting nervous now. Do I need backup on standby?

Place the black bearskin on your kitchen bench-top, please. And you will need a pillow for your head. Once I'm finished with you, you will never be able to look at your kitchen bench in the same way ever again.

∞

Kitchen bench? My mind swings into another gear, my imagination takes me there picturing what might occur in my kitchen. He has no idea how sexy he sounds online, or does he? He is always hunting and searching for new ways to change tactics. It keeps me on a constant edge. He has such a wicked way of temptation.

∞

I have a surprise for you, a G stroke swerve. Plus a little nibble, then I'm going to levitate you.

Ready and waiting… Enter at your own risk.

∞

"Are you still going to the club meeting today?" I ask needing to move this along. I know Tom will be here soon to flatten the living daylights out of me. I'm nervous Rob is loitering, nothing new I guess. I must find patience.

"Yeah, I have to be there at nine this morning and won't finish till after six tonight," he confirms.

"I'll have dinner ready for you when you get home. Just text me when you are leaving so I can be organised." I want to make sure I know where he is at all times.

"That'd be great, Cal." Rob smiles, planting me with a kiss goodbye.

Now, what to wear? It's always a dilemma. I need to treat Tom's eyes to a little slice of heaven. A sliver of red lace and a dollop of bulging tits should be a welcoming snack to sample. A smidgeon of lip-gloss and careless hair, and I'm ready.

I don't bother knocking, I know my way in. The kitchen bench-top is set up as instructed; it'll be my workbench for today. I want to deliver this session on Callie's bench-top, hence her home soil invasion. Our conclave needs to be in her environment, just like I did her initiation at my shag pit.

I place the sealed envelope on the counter.

Tom's confidence embeds a trust in me. He shines a devilish smile my way as he enters my kitchen. Today, I'm told, knows no boundaries. He wants to explore my sexual capabilities, unsuppressed, unreserved and unrestricted. I'm so caught in his plan of inveiglement of being his best student, how could I even begin to resist?

"Do you know why I wanted you to set the bearskin up on the bench-top? Because the bench-top is the perfect height for me to do what I need to, are you ready to be levitated?" I say. My lips and tongue begin the onslaught not waiting for Callie's answer. I lean in toward her earlobe, sticking my tongue in her ear while running my hand along her inner thigh.

"I can lean into you from this height, the angle is just right for me to do all the things I have planned. It allows me to do it with ease, to kiss every part of you as I feel and desire. I'm going to nibble your bud while my finger strokes your G spot. I'm going to take you beyond anywhere you've ever been. Today, you will experience something out of this world," I whisper, my voice husky as I toss Callie's knickers to the floor. I peel her lacy negligee off and throw it to the far reaches of the room.

"They are not needed anymore," I confess, fingering her slit while sucking her nipple.

My mind darts. Tom's seriousness shakes me. I know I'm in for a wild ride. The lead up to this interlude has been nothing short of a constant string of raunchy emails since we last screwed each other's brains out. Something big is about to happen I can sense it.

Putting my hands under Callie's arse, I lift her up onto the edge of the bench-top and lay her out flat. Today, I will need my total concentration to make this happen.

I stare up to an unfamiliar setting. The high-pitched ceiling looks miles away, the skylight sifts a hazy glow. Aligned under my torso I feel the luxurious lambs wool. My head immersed in a plump cushion. The butterflies in my stomach taunt as Tom's caressing tongue dances over my erogenous zones.

Callie is at my mercy. Her knees are bent, her legs spread wide and her nipples are erect. Her swollen lips are engorged and her bud is throbbing with excitement. I absorb my feast of naked woman flesh, salivating as if I'm about to make a spiritual sacrifice.

I lower my face inches from her, inhaling her sweetness. I dip in to taste her honey. She smells pristine and raw. I wrap my hands around her outer thighs digesting her full cleft with my tongue, stirring her mound excruciatingly slowly.

My head jerks from side to side as Tom's tongue explores my wet slit. Each stroke of his walloping tongue submerges deeper into my pussy. I am wet and ready for the thrill of his invasion. Delightful goose bumps grace my flesh, perspiration dripping a clamminess of dew like sweat beads.

My tongue slides higher up to her bud as moans of pleasure filter through the room. Opening my eyes, I stare along the body before me. A rhythm of ecstasy is building. I digest the first decanting of Callie's secretions into my mouth and my lips surround her fleshy female cock. I clamp on like a suction pump, lowering my teeth, encasing her erection, working my tongue for a triple attack.

Indulging my nibble on the eight thousand nerve endings of her pulsing bud, my tongue movement slowly traces around her erectness, creating a groove. A spasm of muscle contracts, an orgasm erupts as Callie's hips and thighs grind into my face. Her hands clench around my head pulling my hair, her body is beginning to enter the

sphere. I adjust my massage. I need to do this as if there is only a touch of connection. The tip of my tongue presses into her bud and I move it ever so slightly, only when I sense the need for movement. Tiny movement. I am glued to her for over an hour in this single position.

I begin to drift, one orgasm after another begins to pierce me, I am convulsing and the string that holds the sensations together is getting shorter. Whatever Tom is doing, I want more. The backs of my eyelids take me to a place I have never been before. A velvety darkness at my eyebrow centre draws my mind to a central focus. My body seems to appear beneath me. A kaleidoscope of colour flashes before my eyes in a mesmerising fashion. I'm oblivious to my surroundings.

Insertion of my finger creates a flood of wetness, her sweet smelling amber flows freely, her pussy beckoning for more. The weld to her flesh is unbroken like tendrils creeping into the ground. My fingertips begin feeling the inner workings of her G spot as I torment her with my G stroke swerve. Gently I toy in a snakelike configuration, Callie erupts with steamy vocalisation. Her moans spark my vigour as I become relentless, I'm on a mission, and it's takedown time. Without breaking contact, my hypnotic drug is infusing and a final overflow of endorphins triggers a high as mortal life is temporarily extracted as she moves to a new threshold. Callie's body lies limp and ragged. A sacrifice to the god's has been made. She is levitating.

I'm in a trance-induced state and unable to relinquish my shaking body tissue, unable to breathe. My body is sensing levitation beyond my control. I flourish through the waves of contentment coursing through my soul, pursuing every nerve ending in its path. Tears stream down my face. My head feels heavy, my mind still oscillating. Pirouetting on the clouds, let me dance in the sky…

Circling my prey, I scan Callie's body with intrigue. Her spasming flesh convulses and contracts in overwhelm. Her lustrous eyes overflow with tears, her body heat crystallize minerals that encrust her skin. Her facial expressions contort her beauty, she is incoherent, her mouth incapable of voicing sound. Her inner workings are barely functioning and her heart beats hard striving to pump oxygen to her lungs. Entranced, I sense Callie's mind is elsewhere. I am in awe. I cautiously leave her in her blissful state, undisturbed. This is not about me getting my rocks off today. This is about taking Callie to a whole new sphere as I deliver and not receive this levitating fuck.

The spa is filling nicely, I poke my head into Callie's refrigerator finding everything prepared. I anticipated no less, I admire that about her. Glancing up at the clock, it's eleven thirty; it has been an hour and a half takedown. Her body is totally decimated. My annihilation has been executed, one passed out Student. Welcome to Protégée status. I drink in her exquisite body.

"Bear, please hold my hand," I say, mumbling my words, "I need to feel grounded."

I sigh.

"How long have I been here for?" I ask, "I left this world, I can hardly explain what just happened to me."

I'm whispering, confused.

"Well, you've been on the workbench for two hours now. And you've been out of it for about twenty minutes," I whisper, squeezing Callie's hand to reassure her.

"That was the best experience I have ever felt in my life," I whisper, "I am in awe."

"I'm glad you liked it," I whisper in return, placing a gentle kiss on her forehead.

"I feel like I have been totally levelled," I utter. My eyes are just starting to focus. "How did you do that?"

I am intrigued, twisting my facial muscles to regain some feeling.

I glance down but don't answer, that's my bait for where I'm taking her next. I inhale Callie's glowing aura. I'm spellbound at how high a woman can go.

"You didn't even use your cock on me. Well, I don't think you did. Did you?" I ask. I was so out of it I couldn't tell.

"No, I didn't," I confess and smile, still holding her hand.

"I know there were no artificial drugs or substances involved, you just walked straight through my door and entranced me. That was something else."

"I've been working away at your bud for a long time now. I had to condition you for this level. If I tried to do this day one, it wouldn't have worked. Your bud had to be conditioned and your mind had to let you pass the over-stimulation to accept my deliverance, otherwise you would have been pushing me away. The nibble technique is what does it, if you want to know the truth," I explain.

"So that's why you pull off me to change things around?" I probe, recalling how Tom manoeuvres his technique.

"Yep, you've got it in one. Now, the spa's full and lunch is ready, let me help you off here."

I pluck the envelope from the bench.

I wrap my arms tightly around Tom and snuggle in close, god, I feel like I have just been taken across the threshold day one.

"It's your lucky day," I boast, reaching over to grab a towel to dry my hands, handing the envelope to Callie.

"Before you open it, pass me your glass, please, we have some celebrating to do," I request, leaving her guessing for a bit longer while I fill both glasses. I relax back, admiring the view.

I laugh till I cry, realising how much we have done in such a short time. It's almost embarrassing. I'm fascinated by the work Tom has put into formulating my assessment, no wonder he gets into my knickers and into my head. I am impressed no end.

"I take it I passed," I smirk, taking a sip of bubbles to celebrate. "Cheers."

"Cheers, you passed with flying colours. You are my best Student ever. I didn't expect anything less from you, lover," I cheer, placing my foot on Callie's soapy covered chest, I slither my big toe between her breasts.

"I see the Sex Savant was very generous with his score sheet." I peek again at my impressive tally. "You will be rewarded with the pleasure of my horny body."

I'm gloating. I continue reading.

"A Sex Savant, ha, well, I want to be your Protégée," I demand. I am definitely in. If what Tom just did to me was the start of Protégée status, I want more. I'm delirious with anticipation.

"You think I'm kidding you? I *am* a Sex Savant. You already worked out that you were in some sort of training, but you didn't know you had entered a secret society. Firstly, you are observed to see if you graduate to the next level. Watch this space now. What do you think?" I laugh.

"I thought you undertook some secret training or something like that. I've never heard of it, but it doesn't surprise me," I joke and he winks at me.

"So, tell me more about this tradition," I prod, tilting my glass, "bring on the Sex Savant, I want your horny arse as mine."

I pant with enthusiasm.

I finally divulge my story of the Teacher. Callie listens without uttering a word.

∞

Hey you gorgeous hunk of flesh,

Thank you for an incredible day.

Is my Sex Savant ready to take his freshly graduated Protégée further into bountiful bliss?

Thank you so much for an amazing day.

Your Sex Savant is ready.

You are the best student I have ever had and the pleasure of taking you to Protégée I can't wait for. I want to take you all the way to be a Savant.

You have challenged me and been the most creative by far, I've loved every minute of it, It has been nothing short of incredible, lover.

I love you xxx

My bud convulsed with that thought. I'm eager to take on the next stage of my training.

Thank you lover, I love you too.

xxx

Thank my Teacher.

Did your Teacher teach you everything you have laid before me?

That's my secret; you will discover that in your next learning phase.

I'm devilishly intrigued now.

∞

22

Tom is destined to traipse the Canadian mountains where eagles soar and grizzly bears roam the rugged wilderness landscape. I have an ache in my gut and the aircraft hasn't even left the tarmac. I would dearly love to go with him but circumstances won't allow. Contemplating such a move would bring down the convoluted house of cards we have fabricated into an imploding heap. My free spirit will be champing at the bit while Tom is away for three whole weeks. I love the mountains and being deeply immersed amongst nature and all its intricacies, it is food for the soul, hiking in the wilderness and exploring the outdoors. I can only dream of my past experiences, this time visualising it through Tom's eyes.

Tom's itinerary has him inbound early morning. The scoundrel in my head is creating mayhem as I scheme to get my hands on him when he steps foot back on our dusty soils. I have devised a proposal to pick him up from the airport, have my wicked way with him for the entire day and send him home completely shagged. Well, isn't that what lovers do? I'll book in to our favourite hangout for a massacre of their bed linen. I will have the advantage, he'll be jet lagged and I'll want to nail his horny arse. I'm so excited. I shoot off an email for additional information to hatch my plan.

∞

Hey lover,

Just wondering, how are you getting home from the airport? Have you booked a hire-car or is your B picking you up?

Howdy Luscious,

Why, are you planning something?

xxx

I'm always planning, that's my job. How about I pick you up from the airport so we can play and I can have my wicked way with you before you go home? I'll drain, feed and water you and then do you again.

Are you serious?

Yes, I'll organise the day off work so we can play.
Are you in or what?

Always. It takes two to party and make things happen. Of course I'm in.

Okay, cancel the hire-car or change the pick up location, whatever works for you. Please send through arrival flight details. Leave the rest to me.

I will log on now and cancel.

Awesome. I'm so excited.

How are you going with the packing?

I'm on a mission today and now on the home run.

Everything ticked off?

Nearly.

You must be so excited.

I'm excited for you.

Can I be your underwear so you can sneak me in?

You can be my knickers any day.

It was just a bit tough to get this one across the line, next time you'll have to come with me for sure. That would be amazing. There's a challenge for you, pull that one off and I'll be really impressed.

Anyway, at least we have our New Zealand trip to look forward to together.

Can't wait. That will be an awesome challenge.

Great we have our trip to look forward to. That will keep us going.

You work so hard, it's good that you are taking time out to follow your passion.

I look forward to sparring with you each week. All the planning and anticipation makes the coming week so exciting, week after week. I'm an adrenaline junkie and you push all my buttons like no other, lover. I just have to have you.

Keeps us hot and horny for each other.

That it does.

∞

The plan is simple. Callie is the clever one. It must be in the female gene pool, they seem to have a greater imagination. I struggle in comparison and it frustrates me. I'm a mere male and a basic model when it comes to creativity.

Slouched in my chair, I close my eyes pondering for a moment. My flight heads east across the pacific to Vancouver where the Rocky Mountains spill out in all directions revealing their magnificence. I stare out of the window in reverence as my excitement inflates and an adrenaline hit surges through my veins.

The mountainous peaks and hidden valleys capture my very soul. There's a peaceful silence out there, yet it is alive with the sound of birds, wild winds, heavy rain and the bugle of a distant elk. Steep valley walls have been carved out by millions of tons of ancient ice over thousands of years, revealing the spectacular native beech forests. It is the most magnificent place on earth in my books.

I'm lost in these thoughts; glancing back down at my screen, there's (3) in my inbox. I chuckle to myself, I'm a one finger typist, auto correct drives me mad and it beats me every time and now Callie is three in front and will be thinking I am offline.

∞

Hire-car cancelled, Luscious Legs. It's a goer.

My flight arrives in at ten thirty in the morning. I'll be out of customs at say eleven and we'll be on our way.

It would be fabulous if you could pick me up.

I'll book the hire-car from the local airport, if you could drop me there after playtime that would be great. It would look a bit suspicious me walking up the driveway, considering I am an ugly looking hitchhiker.

Consider it done. I'd pick you up, any day.

∞

Rearranging my hire-car booking, the light on the printer glows as it spits out the updated confirmation to file with my travel documents. I have deleted any incriminating email threads, 'Inspector Hercule Poirot, take that one,' I gloat with smugness.

∞

I'll do you like a bachelor when I return. I'll be ravenous to taste you.

No shooting off while you are away. Think you can handle that?

Yes, that's a deal; I'll keep three weeks worth to explode into you. It'll be cumming out of your ears.

That'll feed me for a week. Delicious intake of your juice, I want it all.

I'll let you polish my knob for a while and then I'll lift you off as my sprouting seed projectiles up my torso. You can sample three weeks worth and sponge it up like a mop.

I'll sponge it up with my lips and let your seed soak into my flesh.

I have you thinking now. Three week's worth in one hit, then another two shots before we leave, three pulses will drain me. Be very ready.

Looking forward to the extraction.

Okay, Luscious one,

I'd better get some zzzzzzz. It's a big day tomorrow.

Sleep wet.

Love you lots.

xxx

Sleep well,

Love you so much.

XXX

∞

"Who are you calling?" Jess questions, sipping a glass of wine.

"Chris," I reply, placing the phone on the bench-top as it dials.

"Hello," he booms on the other end just as loud.

"How are you, mate?" I bellow down the receiver, beer in hand, "I'm just about to go and chase some elk."

"Awesome, Bro."

"I just wanted to check with you about our arrangements for the next hunt with these guys," I say, ticking the list in my head.

"Hit me with it, aren't we going the same time next year?"

"Yes, I asked them last time to book us in for this time next year. I know it sounds like a long time in advance, but the system is such that we need to be that organised, otherwise they'll sell out," I speak from experience.

"Yes, I'm one hundred percent in," he confirms.

"Okay, I'll get it squared away while I'm over there. You'll love it."

"I see you had our last hunting story in New Zealand published? I received my copy of the magazine. It looks great. You should have seen my boys' eyes light up seeing their dad in the pictures."

"That was a classic trip, I hope we can pull the same next time, that isn't such a long way off you know? Make sure your personal trainer is still whipping your arse," I snigger as the last drop of beer disappears down the hatch.

"Yeah. I will."

"Okay, I got to go. Talk when I get back."

Last job, I have to nail Jess before I leave. Three weeks is a marathon without sex.

I'm up ten minutes before the alarm springs to life, showered, freshly shaven and a coffee in hand. My pupils are bug-eyed, too excited to sleep a wink. My pack is stowed in the hire-car all ready to go. I lean over giving Jess a departing kiss.

"See you in a few weeks' time," I say, stroking her on the cheek and another peck on the forehead for brownie points.

"Be safe, won't you?" she utters in a sleepy tone.

"I always am. Okay, I'm out of here. Watch Mr. SPOT." I flick the bedside light off as I depart.

I'm not expecting a reply at three o'clock in the morning. Why do I think like that? I should know better, of course there's an instant reply. Callie is online, I chuckle.

∞

Morning, Luscious Legs,

I'm all packed and ready to hit the road.

xxx

Good morning, Sexy arse,

All packed? How exciting. It's going to be awesome.

Can I fit in your pack?

I can curl up in a tiny ball. Please?

XXX

Yes, I would love you as my travel companion any day.

What are you doing up? I thought you would be sleeping.

Promise, I don't eat much, only your hard-on six times a day.

How could I sleep? I'm way too excited for you. I wanted to make sure that I received your goodbye kiss. It was worth the wait.

Okay, Luscious,

I'm out of here.

You have a good one today at work and look after yourself.

Blowing you kisses.

Love you so much.

XXX

Blowing you kisses back.

Travel safe and drop me a line when you arrive so I know you are okay.

Love you too.

XXX

∞

Armed with a notepad and pens, the fourteen-hour flight is an excellent opportunity for me to put some uninterrupted hours into our project. With unoccupied seats on either side of me, I'm captured in the ideal environment.

We have laid out the framework for our project, now is the time to put some meat on the bones. The takeoff goes unregistered; my mind is elsewhere, reminiscing. The words flow without hesitation, after several hours I extract my goggled eyes from my notepad. Glancing down, I see there are four thousand words etched across the pages. My head flops back in exhaustion. I push the flight attendant's button to place an order.

"Whiskey on the rocks, thank you," I decree, the stewardess nods and quickly disappears down the aisle.

The liquid amber infuses the ice into meltdown, swirling as the whiskey blends. The aroma excites my palate. Like a ravenous tongue whirling around a swollen bud, my muzzle wafts the teasing fumes in anticipation of tasting the sweet liquid honey. The taste is simply divine. Holding my tumbler aloft, I whisper,

"Thank you, Teacher. I don't know if you are still alive, but your spirit lives imprinted in my soul."

I have fortified my Teacher's guidance reveling in the blissful joy of sexual intimacy. The journey with Callie has unveiled many hidden pleasures for me as I strive to delve deeper, keeping the tradition alive. Callie has all the synergies to attain Savant and more. I have tinkered at the edges of her ability to absorb, sculpting her into higher levels of erotic pleasures as we enter the quiver sensation. I have pushed her to the edge, taken her beyond, and held her at the rim in torment. Callie is displaying tremendous

capabilities as she reaches out for orgasms without rushing over the edge towards one off body blows. She has mastered the techniques of attaining the natural high of continuous orgasms, testing the edges of quiver. It will be my pleasure to guide my Protégée through the quiver passage in preparation for her final induction. This stage of the program excites me as it is not often ever reached.

I'm impatient as I wait. My eagerness soon disintegrates into thin air, but somehow I find tolerance to progress through the more mundane tasks at hand. While Tom is away I take every work shift I can manage to break up my day. It makes the day pass by quicker and gives me something to focus on. It's so hard to stay motivated without him. Where is my Sex Savant and all his hot and horny emails when you need him?

I need to tap into my reserve tanks. Our project is in its infancy and with Tom away, it's a great opportunity to make a start. My mind still wonders. I'd love to be in the mountains with him. My earthy desires are basic and I adore nature in its simplest forms, the scent of fresh pine, the silent stillness of the forest and the majesty of the trees where nature heals, nourishes and gives strength to the body and soul.

Quickly becoming absorbed in the process, I construct my contribution without haste. Every line brings a reminiscing grin to my face as I relive our adventures. I am optimistic the end recipient will adopt a devil-may-care attitude and grab the dragon by the tail and dare to flirt and be more impassioned in the bedroom.

"Cal, where are you?" Rob says. I hear a voice from upstairs.

"I'm down in the office, Rob," I yell as his footsteps near, I'd better get out of this program quick smart.

"Ha, there you are," he says, stating the obvious.

"I yelled out to you," I respond, closing down any obvious screens.

"What are you doing?" Rob enquires raising his eyebrows. "I thought you normally worked on Tuesday's?"

"Not for the next three weeks, the lady who works Thursday's wanted to swap, so I'll be working later in the week instead," I advise, logging out.

He's unaware that I normally use this as one of my Tom play days.

Swiveling around on my chair to face him with a smile, butter wouldn't melt in my mouth.

"I was just doing some research on a course I think I'd like to do," I gesture to the yoga books lying all over the floor.

"I thought you had finished that course?" Rob probes, a little edgy. He doesn't like me studying. It takes my attention away from our time together. I accepted his passions taking him away from me in the infancy of our relationship and was forced into cutting my own niche to fill my idle beginnings. I don't intend to give them up now, folding my arms, he gets the hint.

"Okay, would you like a wine?" he offers turning to go upstairs.

"That would be lovely, thank you, I'm going to run a bath."

Floating in the warm water my body feels listless, free and heavenly, soaking up the aromas. Closing my eyes, fully letting go of the tension in my body, I feel weightless for a few precious minutes. I would love Tom's big toe on my bud right now, feeling a twinge run through me. Oh, lover, I miss you.

Towelling dry, I climb into bed. I love the feel of fresh, clean linen on my skin. Sinking into the pillow, it surrounds my head snuggly as I open up my new novel. Opening the first page it reads:

Admitted infidelity in women is much lower in percentage, compared to men, interestingly the gap is closing rapidly.

I bet it is.

Closing my eyes, my imagination fills the gap between the erotica in my hand and my object of desire. I visualise Tom sitting across from me, a shot of intoxication overrides my rational thinking. He fascinates the root of my thinking, I'm unable to help but get drawn into his magnificent sapphire stare. His full lips are so edible. His casual sense of self draws me in, hanging on every word he expels. Wicked cravings weave mischievous thoughts through the hub of my mind with secret indulgences. It is potent.

Back into civilisation, a real bed and I don't have to wear gloves this morning to keep my fingers from falling off. A couple of days at Ed's place with his wife Di will be just what I need. Di is a pint-sized package with short cropped greying hair and a warm smile. We have become good friends over time. Tonight I've promised to cook and relieve Di of her chef's duties. She pokes Ed in the ribs.

"Where do I find one of these Australians?"

"So Ed, how is Haley going with her new job? Just before I came over I had a snippet from her saying she scored a better paying job over in Alberta." I wink at Di.

"She loves it apparently, she was telling me her savings are going well and that you are taking her hunting," Ed says looking at me as if all I do all day is go out of my way to impress the female gender.

"Excellent. Yeah, next season she is talking about heading down-under."

∞

Good morning, Luscious,

I trust this email finds you safe and well.

It's minus nine degrees outside and it's almost lunchtime.

Good day for staying in bed.

How have you been?

I love you to bits and miss you like crazy.

xxx

Good morning to you too, lover,

Was it amazing out there?

I can't wait to hear your stories.

Glad you are out safely.

I love you too and miss you terribly.

xxx

I'm looking forward to telling you all about it. I just wrote a snippet for the article I'm going to submit for the magazine.

"Sapphire Basin," old Bill proclaimed, "that's where you and Ed should head today. No hunters have been

in that country for several years. It's just the place for you guys to find a big old bull." His historical knowledge is a wealth of information dating back to my birth. Reminiscing, he shares his tales with us on how he guided a hunter to the legendary Sapphire Basin monster elk.

And, yes, we did get a bull.

Awesome, your article sounds great.

Pictures to show and tell, too?

I took heaps of pictures.

Brilliant.

Looking forward to a viewing, after I view your sexy arse.

Nice weather over there?

It's a beautiful day. I'd like to be staying in bed and rolling between the sheets for hours making love to you. Ready for a sucking and a licking that will send you over the edge?

I've been dreaming of that.

Missing you like you wouldn't believe.

Missing you like crazy, Luscious Legs.

Is it Saturday morning where you come from?

Yep.

What are you doing today?

I'm cooking shanks and cleaning up my gear. Having a Canadian beer, it's beer o' clock somewhere. Well, it is for me.

Okay, it's work time for me.

Send me emails when you can, just love to hear from you.

Love you.

XXX

Okay, have a good one.

Love you too.

XXX

∞

I'm reawakened; my excitement escalates to a new high. Tumultuous butterflies wreak havoc with my insides. I'm overwrought with hysterical eagerness. There's only one sleep to go.

A sleepless night at that, piqued with restlessness as my jumpy nerves cause internal commotion. Tiptoeing out of my home in the early hours of the morning, I'm on my way through the hive of traffic, it's peak hour and frustration sets in.

Anticipation blurs my sensory overload as I make my way into the all-consuming bubble of air travel. I'm swallowed up by the flurry of travellers darting every which way. Locating Tom's arrival gate, I'm an hour early. Anticipation builds as I pace up and down the hallways observing the sea of faces and colourful luggage. It's all too hectic for me. I reflect on Tom's communiqué.

'When you arrive at the airport, have a good look around. I don't think we will have any unwanted visitors or prying eyes. Just be vigilant.'

He had mentioned that he'd received an email from home asking if he needed to be picked up. Hire-car booked was his response.

Back at the arrival gate, I scour the crowds of people. Wracking my brain to visualise Jess' face from the framed photos I'd glanced at on the mantelpiece last time I was at Tom's house. Our escape plan is in place. If I am suspicious in any way, to disappear and communicate when we are able. Gazing around the hall, I see no leery characters of note, my mind skeptical and unbelieving that anyone else would show to pick up my lover today. I'm oblivious to my surrounding and nervous as hell anticipating his arrival.

Landed.

Impossible excitement gathers inside my soul. Several aircraft arrive at one time and confusion reigns supreme. I glance from side to side as streams of passengers disembark through two different adjoining gates. Walking away, I compose my breath surveying the onlookers. All looks clear to me and a space clears in the front row. I skulk in to secure my position.

The sliding doors open, I'm back on home soil, and yes, my gut spasms with anticipation, I can't wait to see Callie. My eyes scan the crowd of people, focusing, she appears from the throng with her beautiful beaming smile.

I inhale and consume her like my long lost lover. My tongue devours her in divine indulgence, my hand muscles the pit of her back dragging her in tight. I lovingly drink in the sparkle in her eyes. In each other's arms, we briskly escape the maddening horde.

Rugged, raw and hunky as all get out, my mind replays him strutting down the ramp, beaming a delicious smile straight into the pit of my heart. Racing towards him, he sweeps me into his arms latching on for a bear hug that swallows my body. Our mouths latch tight, the seal can't be broken. Greed consumes our frantic kiss, my body reducing into his possession.

His large hand envelopes mine, holding on tight, I feel a squeeze of love as he leads me to the outside world. Backpack in the car boot, we slide into the front seats. He ravishes me with hungry kisses. A finger discards my knickers to one side and pierces my fissure revealing oozing wetness. Finding my swollen button of joy, he strokes me and I disgrace myself, gushing upon impact. Releasing his finger, he parts the seam of my lips and smothers my tongue with my own juice.

Welcome back, lover…

I've been in grizzly bear country, a sixth sense is always with you when you are in the wilderness and sometimes the hunter becomes the hunted. My gut instincts tell me, all is not well, that instinctive raised hair on the back of the neck stuff haunts me as we journey back. I try to kick that nagging feeling into the far reaches of my mind as we steal a few hours of pure passion.

I am not disappointed by my sixth sense.

When a woman does something different, men just think they are weird, when a man does something different, a woman suspects he is up to something weird. Unknowingly, I have been weird and my double life of delusional insanity has been a mirror that has been easily seen through.

Unbeknown to us, a CSI expert was watching from the airport coffee lounge, we were being observed...

∞

Good morning, Luscious one,

Don't freak out when you read this, PLEASE.

Guess who was at the airport yesterday? Mrs C. S. Fucking I. herself.

FUCK is an understatement.

FUCK—The word for every occasion, but in this instance, it is still a BIG FUCKING understatement.

Fuck.

I feel thoroughly sick. I am so incredibly sorry.

∞

Oh. My. Fucking... God. Months and months of secrecy and we have been discovered. My heart feels like it has been squeezed, twisted and entirely wrenched out of my chest cavity and strewn across the floor, to be left bleeding. I am utterly gutted. My head sinks into my hands, shocked tears stream down my face. I gasp for breath struggling to comprehend the events of yesterday. This is not happening, I beg... Please... NO.

Communication grinds to a standstill. Tom is completely surrounded. My body slumps onto the desk like a muscle-less bag of bones, heaped in heart piercing pain. I check and recheck my emails, and check them again. No replies. What now? I am devastated. My desolate mind struggles to focus on anything. What if she calls Rob to get even? I'm petrified; my worst nightmare might be just about to unfold.

My iPhone alerts me to a new message. It's from an unknown number. The number is only one digit different to Tom's. I slide the message bar across to reveal my foreign correspondent. Two words:

I Know.

Acknowledgements

We are especially thankful to our editor for her expertise, enthusiasm and endless support throughout the process of helping to make this book a reality. Thank you for providing feedback to help polish our efforts.

A huge thanks to all those who have offered critiques and poured over our manuscript tirelessly. Your time and effort has been all important to our final version.

We wish to acknowledge the support extended by the professional young university students who assisted us with the design of our website. We greatly appreciate your motivation and understanding towards our vision.

We would like to express our appreciation to the team at *Australian eBook Publisher* for helping to finalise our product.

Without this team effort, your contributions and support, this book would not be. We are indebted to you all and graciously offer our gratitude.

Printed in Australia
AUOC02n1142190515
267697AU00003B/3/P

9 781925 271300